Between

ANGIE ABDOU

ARSENAL PULP PRESS  VANCOUVER

BETWEEN
Copyright © 2014 by Angie Abdou

US edition published 2015

ARSENAL PULP PRESS
Suite 202–211 East Georgia St.
Vancouver, BC V6A 1Z6
Canada
arsenalpulp.com

The publisher gratefully acknowledges the support of the Canada Council for the Arts and the British Columbia Arts Council for its publishing program, and the Government of Canada (through the Canada Book Fund) and the Government of British Columbia (through the Book Publishing Tax Credit Program) for its publishing activities.

This is a work of fiction. Any resemblance of characters to persons either living or deceased is purely coincidental.

Cover photograph: Getty Images © PM Images
Design by Gerilee McBride
Edited by Susan Safyan

Printed and bound in Canada

Library and Archives Canada Cataloguing in Publication:

Abdou, Angie, 1969–, author
Between / Angie Abdou.

Issued in print and electronic formats.
ISBN 978-1-55152-568-6 (pbk.).—ISBN 978-1-55152-569-3 (epub)

I. Title.

PS8601.B36B48 2014   C813'.6   C2014-903544-6

C2014-903545-4

MIX
Paper from
responsible sources
FSC® C107923
www.fsc.org

With gratitude, I dedicate this book to Andy Sinclair, who has read it nearly as many times as I have.

Thanks for the friendship and support.

ONE

Hangga't makitid ang kumot, matutong mamaluktot.
When the blanket is short, learn how to bend.
—Filipino proverb

CHAPTER ONE

Vero Nanton's life has been hijacked, and she hates herself for being surprised. Every woman she knows told her this would happen—motherhood would change everything—but either she didn't hear them (because her fevered response to the biological imperative to procreate had drawn all power away from her ears and redeployed it to more biologically useful parts of her body), or she paid these naysayers no heed because, simply, she believed that she and Shane would be different (because they had before, on so many counts, been exactly that—different). For whatever reason, Vero did not process the warnings that female friends and family members, generously or otherwise, fired her way the moment she stepped over the threshold of thirty-five and displayed the usual symptoms of baby fever, intensified (as they so often are) by delayed onset.

"You want a career," Cheryl, Vero's mother, said when she saw Vero turning doe-eyed over new babies. "Women of your generation don't have to do all that nose wiping and gah-gah-ing. Thanks to us. Be whatever you want." Cheryl had stepped out of parenting somewhere around Vero's thirteenth year, choosing instead to focus her energy on what she called her womyn's group. The closest Cheryl got to mothering was to ask Vero to join her and a circle of friends in some asanas or a heated discussion of *The Golden Notebook*. Vero, of course, did not.

At twenty-two, after completing a Masters in English Literature, Vero had softened to Cheryl for a time. She went as far as to participate in one of Cheryl's yoga sessions, as a gesture of good will. "Puff up your chests," Cheryl chanted. "You're proud pigeons. Carry that pride into the rest of your day." But there was no pride for Vero; there was only pain, intense and sharp, stabbing deep into the core of her hip socket. Vero vowed to rebel. She would lead a picket line around Cheryl's living room, waving her placard: "I am not a fucking pigeon." She wondered if hell has a ring where sinners spend eternity in pigeon pose. If so, Vero could be inspired to live a pure life.

"I want to be a mom," Vero said in the flat, steady voice she reserved for Cheryl, "*and* I want to be a publishing academic. I can be both. I will be."

"There is no both." Cheryl's eyes drifted to the window. Her own daughter bored her.

Now the sheer magnitude of the change in Vero's life flattens her.

"I'm the robot Wall-E." Eliot bends his arms in jerky robot movements. "JJ-Bean is my best friend Eve. Mommy, you can be the Robot-Who-Cleans-Up-So-Much."

They're crawling up and down a makeshift slide in the basement. It's Wall-E's spaceship. He lives in a garbage dump in space, and he's trying to get back to Earth. Or something like that. Vero can never quite follow. She sits in front of a daunting pile of warm clothes, hands in her lap. Stacks of colour-coded paper circle her. She works as an editor for a manufacturer of light armoured vehicles—LAVs, they call them. Because it's slow season—no government inspections this month—she can work from home some days and save on childcare costs.

"Peace-making machines," she calls the light armoured vehicles.

Never "*army tanks.*" "Peace-making machines" jibes better with her pacifist sensibilities.

The Engineers write the operational manuals. Vero adjusts The Engineers' punctuation. "Just sign on the line and off she goes, Vero Baby!" So Vero moves the commas around, and she signs. Shifting a few punctuation marks from here to there, or changing an effect to an affect, hardly makes her a war-monger, she rationalizes.

"I can be the Robot-Who-Cleans-Up-So-Much?" Vero asks Eliot, her hands still clenched in her lap. "That's about perfect." She aims her words straight for the heap from the dryer. Her own shirt is splattered with coffee, mushed carrots, and—perhaps—a spot of poo. This laundry needs doing. If she looked closely at herself, she would be forced to admit that a lot of things need doing. She, for example, needs to get one of those mommy-cuts, so close to the scalp it never needs combing. Her shapeless mass of black hair falls to her shoulders in tangled dreads. She ties some of it in a knot on top of her head to stop the itching at the back of her neck. She wears a faded T-shirt with the logo of Shane's favourite football team, a wet circle of breast milk staining the football. "I can also be the Robot-Who-Does-Laundry-So-Much," she tells Eliot. "And the Robot-Who-Fixes-Grammar-So-Much." She makes a conscious choice to laugh instead of cry. Laundry and apostrophes—not the life she dreamed of as a child. She piles literary journals by the side of her bed, hoping she'll occasionally squeeze in an essay, a story, or even a poem before she's bludgeoned by the hammer of fatigue. One day last month, she miraculously got through an entire essay. Before she fell asleep, she grabbed a notebook from under her bed, stashed there with a pen in case she should have any late-night profundities that need capturing. She opened the first page (still blank) and copied out the essay's conclusion: "If you're not pushing against the boundaries, if you're not making at least one librarian mad, what's the point?"

That's the kind of person she used to think she would grow up to be. That's the daughter Cheryl wanted.

"Well, actually, Mommy, robots don't usually do laundry." Eliot holds his hands in front of him, palms toward the ceiling, and speaks slowly, professorially. He rolls his eyes upward as if addressing his lecture to his own brain. This particular demeanour is new, and potentially annoying.

"What?" Vero rubs her eyes. "I mean pardon. Pardon me, Eliot?"

"You said you'd be the robot who does laundry so much, but actually, Mommy, robots live in garbage dumps, usually. They clean garbage. You're the Robot-Who-Cleans-Up-So-Much. Your name is Mop."

Jamal, whom they call JJ-Bean—though Vero can't remember why—has fallen face-first into the carpet at the bottom of the slide, legs splayed above him, and he screams, "uck! uck! uck!" His heavy diaper reeks of asparagus pee. That's the smell of Vero's new life: pee and peanut butter. Always.

Vero's best friend Joss was raised by Buddhists and her husband Ian is a Quaker. "Silence is what Ian and I have in common," Joss once told Vero. "It's a better base than you'd think." This seemed odd, back before Vero had kids, back when she only dealt with Joss's boys in brief intervals involving wine, but at this exact moment, Vero recognizes the value of silence.

"That's okay, Mommy, Jamal's just crying. Babies always cry. Because that's what babies do."

Vero gets Jamal unstuck, righting his little body with one tug on his heavy diaper, and returns to her stack of laundry. She wants to stick her whole head deep into the warm, fresh pile and leave it there. She'll breathe in the organic lemongrass scent until it fills her, cleaning her from the inside out. *Ding!* goes the timer. Fresh new Vero.

"What if I don't want to clean up anymore? How about if I be the captain?" Vero forces herself to list the things she loves about Eliot: his thick tussle of coarse hair the colour of sand, his sturdy little linebacker's chest, his sticky-outie ears. She loves the warm curve where his neck meets his shoulders, his moss-coloured eyes that slant slightly downward like Shane's, and his respect for order, which was just like hers, until she traded it in for kids.

Although it's too early to know for sure, Jamal looks like he's more of a replica of Vero: slight and dark.

"You can't be the captain, silly!" Eliot's so shocked by her suggestion that he forgets his professorial tone and is a three-year-old boy again. "You're a girl. Daddy can be the captain. When he gets home from work. He has very important work. He helps sick people. He needs to rest when he gets home from work."

Eliot's reverence for work should surprise Vero more than it does, but she's already checked out of this conversation. Eliot lost her on: *You can't be a captain because you're a girl.*

From the child of a feminist. Grandchild of a feminist. In the twenty-first century.

Vero knows who to blame: The Engineers. *Vero Baby!* That's what they call her. On her days at the plant, in their e-mail exchanges, it's always "*Vero Baby!*"

"Didja get those proofs, Vero Baby?"

"You need a deadline on that, Vero Baby?"

"Just pop that bastard right back in my box when you're done shuffling the commas, Vero Baby!"

Vero knows The Engineers don't like being corrected by a younger woman, and "baby" is their sharped-tipped dissection pin, sticking her hard and fast to her rightful place. But she feels sorry for the old, paunchy guys—so easily threatened—and she lets it slide. A "baby" here and there never killed anyone, she rationalizes. (Vero is an excellent rationalizer.) But then Shane picks up on it: "What's for dinner, Vero Baby?"

"Got a welcome-home-hug for your old man, Vero Baby?"

"Save some of that mama's milk for Daddy, Vero Baby!"

Shane goes as far as buying her a personalized license plate for her birthday: VRO BBY in hot-pink block caps. His VRO BBY, of course, oozes irony, but Eliot's too young for irony. So now, Eliot thinks girls can't be captains, and Vero feels certain it's The Engineers' fault.

"How about if I be the captain, and when Daddy gets home from working at the pharmacy, he can fold the laundry?" She pulls Jamal away from Shane's new Italian racing bike. *Cervella*, he calls her. She is now propped up on a wind-trainer so that, in the dead of winter, on the snowiest days, Shane can avoid the icy roads, spinning around and around, pouring sweat and getting nowhere. Vero's job is to keep the boys from spinning the sleek bike's overpriced wheels and amputating their little fingers in its overpriced spokes.

"That's okay, Mommy." Eliot pulls at Vero's hand, pushing her forehead until he can see her face. "Don't cry. Mommies don't cry, silly. You like doing laundry. Because that's what mommies do."

Vero envies Eliot. He can be whomever he wants. Only, very infrequently, he'll announce, "I'm Eliot now." Mostly, though, he's someone else.

"Excuse me, can I pretend I'm a robot?"

"Excuse me, can I pretend I'm a football player?"

"Excuse me, can I pretend I'm an astronaut?"

"No," Shane answers, every now and then. "No you can't. We've had quite enough pretending for one day." He looks at Vero, the pain of exhaustion in his eyes a mirror of her own. Parenting has aged them, made their skin looser, less shiny. "That's funny, isn't it?" He seems truly uncertain, like he's working with a foreign language. He runs his hands through his coarse white-blond hair. Usually, it springs out from under a ball cap, and he looks almost exactly like the second-year chemistry student Vero fell for at twenty, back when everyone called him the Candy Man and vied for invitations to the psychedelic parties in his sweet suite above his parents' garage. Only a subtle bagginess in the skin around his eyes and at the corners of his mouth hint that he's entered his forties. "Enough pretending? I love pretending. I'd never say 'enough pretending.' Not for real." He nods, one quick pulse of his chin, as he always does when his mind's made up. "It's hilarious."

They're both delirious from lack of sleep. His words come to Vero as if spoken underwater, wavy and weak, parts of them floating away. She can't tell whether the problem is his voice or her ears.

Last week, when Vero went to the dentist to fill the holes that the acid reflux of pregnancy had gnawed in her teeth, a hygienist asked her name. Vero, with her jaw ajar, stared at herself reflected in the woman's protective glasses until they both blushed. "It's not exactly a skill-testing question, is it?" Vero finally said. "I should know that one." Another unfilled pause. "Is it Mommy?"

Some evenings, when Shane gets home from the pharmacy, Vero pushes both boys in his direction, snarling, "It's your turn." Without looking back at her family, she marches out the door and up the hill into the woods. No goodbye hugs. No goodbye kisses. No *Mommy loves you so much, be good for Daddy*. Just gone.

Deep into the woods, she crouches on the ground, leaning into a spruce tree, curling tight into herself. If she keeps still long enough, animals come. Sometimes ground squirrels. Sometimes rabbits. One time, a fox came close enough that Vero could've touched her—a mother with two kits. Vero didn't care about the babies. She held her breath to keep still, her rear-end damp and cold, devoting her attention entirely to the mama, sniffing the dirt, licking her paws, oblivious to the little ones at her tail, trusting they would take care of themselves. When the fox saw Vero—or maybe just felt her eventual gasp for breath—she bolted fast into the thick brush. The kits disappeared with her.

Other times—when Vero doesn't get her solitude in the woods—she erupts after the kids have gone to bed, her anger and frustration splattering everything. She runs into dark wet nights, barefoot in the thorny grass and up into the forest, its floor strewn with twigs and sharp rocks. She races away from Shane and the house, revelling in each sharp pain to her tender soles. *See! See what you all make me do to myself? Your laundry! Your demands! Your dirty dishes! What happened to my life? MY life!* She pulls her hair and shrieks, beyond caring what neighbours think. But always she remains very aware of Shane, his white skin and blond hair shining from the porch steps against the darkness of the night.

"What, Vero?! *What?*" He holds his arms out to her, all supplication. "Geez, Vero, come back here!"

Vero does come back, later, soaked from the rain, clothes torn, feet bleeding. She sits with her feet in his lap while he dabs and bandages.

"You can't keep doing this, Vee. You're acting crazy. Like a wild animal."

But Vero has watched the wild animals. None of them act this way.

"Don't yell at me," she yells.

"I'm not yelling," he says, so quietly it's loud. His eyebrows, a high arch of nearly invisible blond, give him a look of perpetual surprise.

Vero counts each of the stubby hairs instead of responding.

"We need some help, Vee. Live-in help. Just because you can sometimes work at home doesn't mean you can do it all. Work is work. Parenting is work. That's two works." He tries to meet her eyes, winks. "I'm excellent at math."

They have this conversation often, and she's given him all the excuses: She doesn't want a stranger taking care of her kids; full-time support is too expensive; she couldn't stand someone they don't know living in their house. The real reason, though, is that she's observed the live-in nannies—in the playground, in the school programs, at the mall. They're ghosts hovering at the periphery of real life, animated and alive only until she gets close, and then they freeze, their features slack, their eyes empty, their faces so blank she can see right through them. Vero doesn't want a ghost living in her home.

"No," she says, this time with no explanation. She speaks to her lap and shakes her head, water from her long bangs trailing down her nose and dripping onto her clasped hands. "Just. No."

The next morning, Eliot holds his jacket in one hand and a glass of milk in the other, high above his head away from his baby brother. Jamal lunges at it—"mik! mik! mik! mik!" Milk slops into Eliot's hair as Vero kicks his Lightning McQueen runners toward him, scooping Jamal away from the dripping milk.

"You have to help me, Mommy!" As he reaches for his sneakers, Eliot's cup drops, splattering white liquid on the floor, on the bannister, on the wall, on his jacket. His whimper turns to a wail. *"I can't do everyfing at the same time!"*

"I know, Eliot." Vero hears her own voice as a whimper now. She pulls his stiff rain jacket around his shoulders with one arm while she bounces Jamal gently with the other. Her briefcase, full of light armoured vehicle specifications, falls to the floor. "That's just it, Eliot.

Neither can I." She listens to make sure Shane isn't around the corner in the kitchen, then says it again, relieved to finally hear it aloud. "Neither can I."

◊◊◊

Vero curls on the couch after dinner, tight to Jamal, his warm, wet mouth tugging at her breast. Eliot straddles her hips, hands tangled in the wild otherworld of her hair. The three of them wind around and latch onto each other, so connected they feel like a single being. A three-headed wildebeest.

She repeats Eliot's favourite story softly in his ear. "You were so beautiful when you were born, I couldn't sleep for three days." The words hardly carry meaning for her anymore. They come forth from her mouth, one sliding into the next, like a well-loved song. "I just sat and stared at you for three days. Your hot little cheek pressed to my arm. My face hurt from smiling. You were the first time I saw a miracle."

"No sleep at all! For three days! And did you let the nurses take me?" He knows the answer, but wants to hear it again.

"No, Eliot, I wouldn't let anyone take you away from me. Not for a minute. I loved you too much."

"So much you couldn't put your eyes anywhere else. You couldn't even close them to sleep." Eliot's voice quivers with excitement but stays low. He won't disturb Jamal. He wants this time to be his. "Like a super mom! No sleep is your super power."

"No sleep at all, Eliot." She strokes the back of his neck, soft as a seal pelt. "Like a super mom." *But everybody needs to sleep, Eliot. I need to sleep.* She doesn't say that.

"See you in sixty," Shane's voice pulls her from Eliot and Jamal.

His face peeks through the crack of the door for only a flash before it snaps shut between them, and his spandex-clad ass disappears. He too speaks in a stage whisper, scared to disrupt whatever spell has been cast on the placid Jamal.

Fine. We don't need you. That's what Vero thinks—the words that swim through the thick sludge of her mind. But it's not what she feels. The extent of her need weakens her.

She imagines Shane on his fat-tire winter bike. She sees him mashing up the big hill five miles out of Sprucedale, the slick whir of his tires scrubbing the crust of the work day from his brain, a soft mist hanging in the mountain air, cooling his skin and sharpening the sweet scent of the pine air just off the highway. Alive. Not a hint of pee or peanut butter aroma on anything.

Before kids, they rode together.

"I need this," he'd say, his face flushed and eyes bright. "I've got half this town on pills. *'Here you go, Sprucedalians: one big one and two little ones for everybody!'* The big one so they don't kill themselves and the little ones so they don't kill anybody else." He knows too many of Sprucedale's secrets, he says, and pounding up a hill, tasting his own heartbeat, wiping his sweat on his neoprene sleeve, helps him to forget.

She remembers that cleansing, cathartic quality of a good, hard ride. At the crest of a hill, her whole body buzzed, a physical sensation so concentrated and powerful that it was nearly sexual.

Shane would be feeling that soon.

"You begrudge me every second on my bike," he complains, "as if Cervella is my mistress instead of a piece of inanimate equipment." He points at his quads, flexes until his pant leg stretches tight across the muscle. "See that? Shane Schoeman was made to cycle. I already wasted my youth banging heads with my brother on the football field." He pets his thighs, as if they're the family poodle. "Now I bike."

Jamal has fallen asleep at Vero's breast, his new teeth resting against her nipple. She worries that Eliot will squirm and wake him, but Eliot too seems content, his weight warm on top of her as he sucks at a piece of her hair, a habit he's acquired since Jamal's arrival.

Today, Shane took Vero to the Sprucedale office of the International Nanny Agency on Broad Street to meet Bernadette. Bernie, she said to call her. She looked like a Bernie: lean, with a pixie haircut and low-slung faded jeans hugging her hips. Her T-shirt read "Well-behaved Women Rarely Make History." A hint of skin, golden from this year's Indian summer, peeked out between the T-shirt and her jeans. Shane tightly shackled Vero's wrist in the grip of his index finger and thumb and pulled her in the door. "Let's just see. It doesn't hurt to see."

"My wife thinks she doesn't want a nanny. But I know she does," he said, leaning his elbows onto the counter between them and Bernie, just the way he leaned into Cervella's aerobars. "She's got some weird North American hang-ups. Liberal guilt, let's call it. Tell her: Nobody else in the world has trouble hiring servants, if they can afford them."

Vero cringed on the word "servant" and watched for Bernie's reaction. This little woman gave Shane nothing. No nod of understanding, no smile of approval, no glint of camaraderie in her eyes. Vero's shoulders loosened a little. She'd assumed that someone working in the office of an international nanny agency might be on Shane's side; Bernie, after all, was the one in the nanny business.

"The life we've got is not the one we signed up for, that's for sure." Shane put his hand on the back of Vero's neck, fingers creeping up into her hair. "Before Vero and I got married, we talked about trekking in Nepal, doing opium in Thailand, surfing in Bali. Now, date night's a trip to the grocery store with two screaming, dirty kids clinging to our pant legs." Vero noticed that Shane rambled like this more frequently as he coasted into middle age. The Shane-Overshare, she called it, but she just now connected it to young, attractive women. She checked the pit of her stomach to gauge her jealousy, but felt nothing.

Shane watched himself in the mirror behind Bernie as he talked, his eyes rimmed red. His unforgiving fair skin showed everything, especially fatigue. He looked like he was wearing pink eyeliner. "I suppose that's life, isn't it?" he continued, unable, it seemed, to stop himself. "You're presented with decisions. You make them. You're presented with decisions. You make them. Again and again. You think this smorgasbord of options will always be there. Then suddenly you realize that you've decided yourself into a tight little box." Vero saw that the metaphorical turn this Shane-Overshare had taken pleased Shane, that he expected it would appeal to young Bernie, with her trendy haircut, feather earrings, and studded nose. "So we decided on kids. That's our box. We can't change the box, but a nanny would sure help us fluff up the pillows in there, make it a little more comfortable. You know?"

Vero wanted to tell Bernie and Shane about Lito, a round Filipino man whose face was usually all sunshine and happiness. He served her coffee en route to the LAV plant. Vero wanted to tell them about last week, when she asked Lito how he was and his big sunface cracked open.

He'd looked up at the ceiling as if saying a quick prayer and then spoke into her still empty mug. "I have a new son," he whispered, "a new son I have never held. Never held. Back home. My boy." Lito's voice cracked on the word "boy" so that it came out in two syllables. She wanted Shane to feel the pain of that break. Lito's mouth bunched up and twitched and his eyelids fluttered. He lost control of the muscles of his own face, for just a second. But then he licked his lips, shook his head, and spoke more loudly. "I'm sorry. ma'am. So sorry. This, not your problem."

No. Vero's problem was deciding what she wanted in her coffee. She ordered a double.

"Yes, ma'am, most certainly." Lito's face lifted into a smile Vero knew well, one so sparkling and sincere that she'd never before thought to question it.

She wanted to tell Shane and Bernie all of that, to tell them about the grip of humiliation that held her, toes to head, when he handed her a mug of coffee and wished her a good day. She nodded and said nothing.

"Think of the nanny as a present, from me to you," Shane said, his forearms pressed into the countertop, fingertips stretched toward Bernie, even while he looked at Vero. "You don't have to make any decisions now. I make the decisions. You just say 'thank you.'"

Bernie pressed her lips together until she had none and dropped her head back to sigh at the ceiling, as if it were the only other rational presence in the room. "Have you heard what they say about getting a puppy as a present?" asked Bernie. Vero expected her to waggle her finger at Shane. "A nanny? For a present? Even worse." She tapped her fingers on the counter. "Not cool at all." Her gaze fell on Vero, and she very nearly rolled her eyes.

Shane back-pedalled then. Of course, he wouldn't think of giving someone a nanny as a present. Of course, the hiring of a nanny would be a Serious Family Decision. Of course, Vero needed to have the biggest share of the input. Clearly. "That being said," he smiled in a way he knew accentuated the deep dimple in his left cheek, "it wouldn't hurt to set things in motion, get the wheels spinning, while *Vero Baby* makes up her mind."

Vero waited for him to launch into his spiel about growing up in South Africa, where everyone had servants. His family had four: a driver, a nanny, a maid, and a gardener. When he was eight, a black man came to the house, and Shane famously yelled over his shoulder to his family, "A boy is at the door to see you." It was Bishop Desmond Tutu coming to discuss church policy with Shane's grandfather, an Anglican minister. A "boy"—that's what they called all their black servants. How would young Shane know this black man was different from the rest of their black men? He didn't.

The incident turned into one of those embarrassing moments that he couldn't stop re-telling, as if reliving it through story was his self-inflicted penance. Vero could see Shane biting down hard on the story this time, though.

Good thing, too. Bernie softened to him by the end, walked them through the application process, and gave them a stack of nanny profiles to browse. Afterward, Shane pulled Vero into his back office at the pharmacy and spread all of the pictures out on his desk like a pack of tarot cards, each one pointing to a different, less difficult future, a future in which his wife had more time for backrubs and blow jobs, and less cause to list his (seemingly infinite) shortcomings.

"Life is short," he said, lifting Vero's small body onto his desk and drawing her legs around his waist, lowering his mouth into the crook of her neck. "We *can* have everything. Let's take it."

Chapter Two

The small apartment is quiet and dark. No feet pound above Ligaya, no bossy women yell orders next door, no newlyweds squawk like strangled roosters in the apartment below. Finally, the world is still, and Ligaya can unfold her mattress in the closet and get some rest. If she falls asleep quickly, she will get five hours before she must wake to prepare Madam Poon's breakfast.

Madam likes her congee on the table by the time she comes out of her room at seven. When she eats, Ligaya must not look at her, even though there is nowhere else in the small apartment to look. Ligaya has become skilled at looking nowhere. When Madam Poon finishes her breakfast congee, the dishes must disappear at once, and still Ligaya must not look at her. When Ligaya has washed every dish and bathed and fed baby Hui, she will take him on the bus to the market. They will buy white fish and fresh vegetables to steam for dinner. Maybe Mister Poon will be home from his business trip by then, and Ligaya will spread a little extra butter on the fish and use one pinch of salt, just the way he likes.

Madam never says when to expect the Mister. Ligaya hopes he comes today. Madam always treats Ligaya with more kindness when he is home. Jiao is Mister Poon's first name. Ligaya has heard Madam Poon call him that in their bedroom; the apartment is so small that Ligaya hears everything. She can tell from the volume of the rustling sheets through the thin walls which of them fidgets in the night.

Hui does not call his father anything. Sadly, the boy's mind is not right. "There is delayed development," Mister Poon told Ligaya just after she arrived in Hong Kong, and that is all the explanation Ligaya ever gets. For this delay in development, Ligaya has grown to be grateful. It makes Hui pliant, one blessing in a job far more demanding than Ligaya imagined when she flew out of Manila.

Even though Ligaya looks forward to Mister Poon's time at home, she knows she must be careful not to encourage his interest in her. If he speaks to Ligaya often, Ligaya pays for it when he leaves. Last week, the night after he left, Ligaya had only a small, cold piece of leftover milkfish to eat, and only after Madam Poon had finished her dinner, after Ligaya had washed every dish and scrubbed every pan, after she had teased every crumb out of every corner.

"You eat what I tell you to eat," Madam Poon screamed, waving her scrawny arms in the air like a scarecrow in a tornado. "We cannot afford you filling your face on every luxury. We bring you here to work, not to eat!"

Ligaya nodded. "Yes, Madam. Sorry, Madam." She shaped her face to express docility and subservience, but her thoughts were her own: *Panget ka. Mukha bruha.* You, Madam Poon, are an ugly little witch with no bum. Who could ever love you? *Nobody.*

But Ligaya tries not to think of last week or next week or even of tomorrow. Ligaya tries not to think at all. Now is the time for sleeping, not thinking. She digs for her phone, hidden far under the shelves in her sleeping closet. Madam has forbidden Ligaya to have a phone. But Ligaya cannot use the Poon phone either.

Madam says no to many things: no phones, no Tagalog, no days off. But the fish-brained woman has less control than she thinks. Ligaya tries to silence the weak *but* rising in her mind. *But Madam Poon's husband is always away, and she too is lonely. She too is unhappy. Even as lonely and as unhappy as me.*

A home does not have space for two adult women. How could this sad, lonely woman care for Ligaya? Ligaya, who cooks Mister Poon's favourite dishes. Ligaya, who sleeps with Hui cradled close to her breast.

Ligaya does the job of a wife.

She is younger than Madam Poon.

She is prettier than Madam Poon. Nobody would say otherwise.

These things matter. Ligaya knows they do.

And then Mister Poon goes away, and Madam Poon sleeps alone. She is meanest when she sleeps alone.

Yes, Ligaya could pity Madam Poon, if she allowed that single "*but*" to take hold. That kind of pity will not help anyone here. *When the blanket is short, we must learn to bend.* Ligaya's mother said that, just before Ligaya left. Mother cupped her hands around the back of Ligaya's head and pulled her close, until their foreheads touched. "My daughter." She stroked her hair with one hand. "When the blanket is short, we learn to bend. We must."

Hating Madam Poon, making her a fish-brained, scrawny witch, is only one of the many ways Ligaya tries to make this shrunken blanket fit.

Ligaya taps the calendar application on her forbidden phone and checks off one more day in Hong Kong. Already she has checked seven months and twenty-three days since she arrived from Manila. Even then, eighteen hours had passed since she said goodbye to her family in her hillside village before walking into Taal. Ligaya did not cry then, and she did not cry during the four-hour bus trip to the airport. She rested her forehead against the dusty glass of the window and counted the reasons she must go. There were many.

Ligaya packed no photographs when she left. She wishes now for one of Nene. She brings an image to mind. Just before Ligaya left, she cut Nene's hair, inadvertently leaving the girl's short bangs slanted and the hair at her shoulders jagged. In Ligaya's mind, Nene runs through long grass, her too-short bangs crooked and her six-year-old arms outstretched as she chases chickens around the yard. Ligaya always let Nene "help" with the chase, but then shooed her inside when it came time to butcher.

Ligaya wishes for a picture of Pedro too. Her whole body wishes for that. But she blocks his image. She will see him again, when the right time comes. For that, she must trust in God.

Ligaya did not cry on the bus, she did not cry on the plane, and she will not cry here. She sets her face hard against the possibility of tears and powers off her phone. She slides it back into a dark corner where Madam will never have occasion to look. Ligaya smiles into the dark at the thought of Madam down on her knees in this dusty corner, her cheek next to the floor, and her bony rump in the air.

Ligaya first heard about the work available in Hong Kong during a summer heat wave, while up to her elbows in cold washing water. She'd known about Hong Kong always, it seemed, but not with any awareness that it could mean something to her, could impact—absolutely alter—her life. But there, out in the yard, bent over a barrel of washing, forearms cold and chafed in water straight from the well, the message penetrated. She dipped her mother's dress, stained with a spot of menstrual blood, and scrubbed hard, barely registering the noise blaring from the radio propped in the dust by the back door. Instead, she listened to Totoy and Nene playing. She couldn't see them, but she imagined them engaged in a match of *luksong tinik*, Nene raising her hands for Totoy to jump over, up and up until he missed, tripping into the dust and running back to Ligaya with a bloody nose, a skinned knee. If more kids came, they would play *luksong baboy*, all bent over in a line taking turns leaping over each other's backs. As she scrubbed, the radio volume seemed to increase by itself.

"HONG KONG! STEPPING STONE TO CANADA!"

Ligaya, we mean you! That's what she heard.

Her mother and her father were in the house, hiding from the hot sun. It was still dry then, but monsoon season was fast approaching. "Fish for dinner again," her father would joke when the rains came, flooding their house, the riverbanks overflowing with fish that swam right in the front door of their little home. "The Lord provides." In monsoon season, the slippery tilapia were plentiful and easy to catch, swimming through the living room, their silver scales shimmering gold as the evening sun caught them at the right angle through the open windows.

From this high rise towering above Hong Kong, such a thing seems impossible, as if Ligaya is remembering a dream. But they were real, those fish in her house. Disoriented by furniture and splashing feet, the tilapia darted into corners, quivering but otherwise still, as if waiting to be caught.

Ligaya and her family never went hungry in monsoon season.

"Hong Kong! Follow your dream—"

Ligaya looked quickly toward the house and turned off the radio. But after that, she saw the ads everywhere, no longer irrelevant background noise. On the radio, in the newspapers, popping up online: "Hong Kong, the gateway to happy life in Canada!"

Well, she is here now, in the gateway, but memories of the Philippines come to her at night in her closet, not so much floating across her mind as bashing down the door. Lying under the stars with Pedro, warm earth beneath them, her head rested in the firm crook of his arm. He smelled of fish oil and Marlboro cigarettes. A plane flew overhead, and her eyes followed the thin trail of white in its wake until it disappeared.

"I don't want to go."

Pedro rolled toward her, rested a calloused hand against the skin of her belly.

Because he didn't tense at her objection, she continued. "I understand the reasons. I will be paid in dollars. I will bring the family later. But why do I have to be the one forced to go?" Ligaya had heard other women ask these same questions, raking leaves behind the houses in the morning, complaining of the sacrifice.

"Ligaya." Pedro whispered the word, as if it were a song, a wish. "Women shouldn't talk politics." He put his mouth to hers and held it there, stopping her words.

No tears, Ligaya reminds herself now as she hugs her knees into her chest on her bed, a cushion so thin she feels the floorboards. The mattress smells of dying people's urine. Of course, Madam would not have wasted money on a brand-new mattress for Ligaya.

Ligaya knows exactly what she's worth here, but she will tolerate this place and these people for the good of her family, to create a life of opportunity. Her beautiful Philippines has become the land of no opportunity. She pulls her only sweater over her shoulders, rests her face against this old mattress that is temporarily hers, and closes her eyes.

CHAPTER THREE

Shane's brother Vince sports a pineapple across his crotch, Shane a Mexican flag. A bushy line of hair runs up toward Shane's belly button, and hair grows down the inside of his legs to mid-thigh. Vince appears to have shaven for the occasion, smooth as river rock. Even his tree trunk legs shine, lit golden as the evening sun slides into the Pacific.

The angle of the sun suggests that the whole family should be leaving the beach to prepare Christmas dinner, but Vince has christened Christmas Day "Speedo Navidad." He has declared, in the way that Vince does, that he and his brother will spend the day wearing bikini briefs and downing girly drinks at the swim-up bar. "Feel free to call it Bikini Christmas, if you're more comfy with *Inglés,*" he assures them. "It's a multi-lingual celebration."

Mexico Christmas with the Schoemans is an annual tradition. While Shane clicked away on Expedia booking this year's flights, Vero envisioned her father-in-law, Gregory, waving his fat privileged fingers at the harried waiters who ran from one beach umbrella to the next, balancing trays of coconut shells filled with rum. "*Una mas! Por favor! Una mas!*" Before Vero had even stepped off the plane, she felt the weight of Heather Schoeman's perpetual judgment.

"You're giving Jamal Advil? *Again?*"

"Television can be very detrimental to the developing brain."

"Never sleep with your babies. Adults have to have…some…privacy. The husband needs his wife too. Sharing a bedroom with your kids is—I'm not the first to say it—a recipe for a doomed marriage."

Listen here, Heather Schoeman, Vero wanted to scream, *get the fuck out of my bedroom!*

As Vero and Shane prepared and packed the mountain of equipment required to leave home with two young children, Vero avoided thinking about her brother-in-law, his biceps the size and shape of softballs, a knife tattoo running from his elbow to his wrist, the bloody tip pointed at his pulse point, where he'd tattooed his college football number, 72, in thick black lines. Vince, she knew, would bellow his beer-sodden way into the condo in the middle of Jamal's nap. If she dared to ask him to turn it down a notch, he'd tiptoe around like a cartoon character, raising his knees to his chest, and delivering a stage-whisper soliloquy about King Jamal's royal sleep. Vero also knew that Vince would monopolize Shane's time in Mexico, acting like the two of them still wore the same high-school football jersey. When the three of them were together, Shane belonged to Vince.

But that's what Shane's family did: they spent Christmases in Mexico. In-law time wasn't supposed to be fun, Vero reminded herself. At least her in-law time had a beach. So Vero braced herself and came to Mexico prepared for the worst.

But it's worse than the worst. With her nerves rubbed so raw she feels like one big, gaping cavity, even the thing she looked forward to—the sun—becomes a curse. It's too bright, too hot, too loud. It makes her too faint, too nauseous, too tired, too sad.

Vero has spent the last two hours waiting on the beach for Shane and Vince to return from the tequila volleyball match up at the pool. Heather and Gregory arrive first, telling Vero that "the boys" have gone to get some beer so they can watch the sunset and then go back to the condo for a late dinner.

"Perfect, there's nothing a one- and three-year-old like better than a late dinner." A shudder of nausea runs the full length of Vero's body. This is not the Christmas she wants.

Both Heather and Gregory slur their words slightly as if they've made an attempt to keep up with their sons drink-for-drink. Vero turns away from them and watches a group of young adults at the shoreline, the girls wearing only bikinis and Santa hats, posing with their coconut drinks as the boys take their pictures. Their limbs hang loose, and they fall into each other in clumsy hugs, as if they too are on Vince's Speedo Navidad program.

By the time Shane returns, Jamal has eaten one cigarette butt, exploded his diaper, bitten Eliot's leg, and toppled over the neighbour's table, bathing himself in a sticky mess of lime juice and tequila.

"Hey, Shane, how about we go back to the condo and make some Christmas dinner for the boys? They're getting hungry." Vero holds a hand before her eyes, squinting up at him and trying to focus on his face instead of his lumpy, tubal Mexican flag.

Shane ignores her question and looks at neither of his sons as he pushes out his pelvis and shimmies his hips. "How about this look, Vero Baby," he slurs. "You feel like you've got a European for a day?"

Vince sways even harder. Everything about their Bikini Christmas walk says, *Look right here. Check out this package.* Shane leans his full weight onto Vero's shoulders, his breath hot in her face. She has been too absent and preoccupied with the boys to count his drinks today, but based on the weight of the lean, she guesses he's well into the double digits.

"Hey, babe, time to ramp up this Christmas party!"

She turns her face away from the smell of tequila and sweat.

"That's right, this party's just getting herself started," Vince agrees. "BIK-EEEN-EEEE CHRISH-MAS! Jush like I tole you. Nobody rocks shpeedos like me and my bro."

Vero watches as Eliot digs his fingers into the cooler and sticks a cube of E. coli-infested ice into his mouth. Almost instantly he starts choking. She smacks him between the shoulder blades, just a touch rougher than she intended. He coughs up the cube of ice, but glares at his mother, betrayed, as if there's nothing he wants more than a case of Montezuma's Revenge. An extra-fun guest for the Speedo Navidad celebration.

"Vince. Okay, we get it. You're awesome," she says, lifting Eliot onto the side of her lawn chair away from the cooler and close to his grandma Heather, then grabbing hold of Jamal's ankle as he makes a spirited dash for the E. coli cubes. "Awesomely awesome! But just keep it down. Everyone's looking."

Shane falls back into Vero, and she pushes him upright, urging his stinking weight away from her.

Vince holds his fingers up to his lips in an exaggerated shushing motion, imitating Vero at her most aggravated. "Shh! Shh! Everybody *shhhh!* Nobody can make any noise now. Jamal's sleeping. Shhhh! Quiet for King Jamal, whose sleep reigns above all."

This catches Jamal's attention enough that he stands still for a moment, and Vero can release her hold on his ankle. He smiles up at Vince, trying to decide if his uncle has made a joke that he should laugh at. Vero studies her baby's puzzled little face in the golden light, the uncertain slant of his mouth—he'd make a perfect picture, tottering here at the brink between innocence and cynicism. A perfect picture, Vero thinks, if he were some other woman's son. The sight of her own toddler on that innocence/cynicism teeter-totter is too much for Vero.

"No, he's not sleeping, Drunkle Vince. He's right here, and he doesn't know what you're talking about. You're confusing him." Vince stiffens on the word Drunkle, and a nasty glint forms in his eyes. Vero should take that as a warning, but she's not done. "Make fun of me all you want, but you don't have to act like a raging alcoholic in front of your nephews."

Vince's fist clenches, then gradually his whole body clenches until his face too is a fist. But Vero can clench too. Vince has awakened the sleeping grizzly-bear mama that took up residence inside Vero's skin when she bore her first son. She senses the hair on the back of her neck rising and her fangs baring as she positions herself between Vince and her boys. Her body tells her: keep angry male away from little cubs.

"Who pissed in Professor Nanton's carbonated water?"

Vince calls her Professor to remind her of her failures. She wanted to be a writer, but she's an editor. She wanted to be a professor, but she's a mother. He doesn't point his question at her, though; he directs it straight to Shane and his parents, drawing the line—there's *us*, Vero, and then there's *you*—on your own. "Are we not following your rules, Professor? Maybe nobody should be allowed to have fun because *you* can't have fun. Maybe we should all act like we're nursing mothers." He slumps and holds his hands to his forehead, "Oh lord, life is such a drag. Mexico is such a drag." He throws his arms to the sky. "Poor, poor me with my free Mexican vacation courtesy of Shane's horrible family. Life is so awful."

Vero steps away from him and starts piling Jamal's clothes and

Eliot's beach toys into her shoulder bag. Red pail. Blue shovel. Yellow truck. Fucking sand stuck to all of it. "You don't have to get aggressive, Vince. All I'm saying is you're loud when you're drunk. You know you're loud when you're drunk. Just tone it down." She hurls the last of the dirty toys into her dirty beach bag and turns to face her brother-in-law.

Vince's clenched face turns red, droplets of sweat rising on his wide brow. His face is much like Shane's, but everything is bigger, like someone has taken the balloon of Shane's head and blown until it's ready to burst. Vince places his giant head so close to Vero's face that she can smell the tequila on his slow, fat tongue. She scoops Jamal onto her hip, squeezes Eliot's hand, and repositions herself to create as much distance as possible between the boys and Vince.

"Right." Spit pops off Vince's tongue on the click of the t. "I'm loud when I'm drunk, and you're a bitch ever since you had kids."

A hatred rolls over Vero then, a physical feeling so intense that she knows, even in this moment, that her rage is not just about this moment. Vince might as well be Shane. Shane and Vince: one and the same.

Shince.

"God forbid Shane should have some fun on his holiday. What does he need to do for you, Vero? Cut off his dick and put it in a drawer? He's done everything else!"

Vero hates Shince. And Shince's parents. And Shince's stupid holiday. And Shince's Speedo Navidad. Blood charges into her arms, and before it crosses her mind to control her body, her own fists turn to tight little balls.

"Clench your fist at me?" she yells inches from Vince's nose. She doesn't remember exactly what she says after that, but it's something ugly. Something predictable. Something like: "You want to clench your fist at me? I could punch you in the face right now. You're such an insult! Such a pig!" Something festive like, "I hate you!"

"You gonna punch me in the face?" Vince shows his teeth in a way that might be mistaken for a smile in another circumstance, but the rest of his face freezes, his eyes hard. "Do it then. Go ahead! Do it." He pushes his chin toward Vero, his face almost comic in its grotesque display of anger.

Later, she will wonder what Eliot and Jamal did during this time, and Shane, and Shane's parents. She will imagine Heather and Gregory looking blankly at each other, mirror images with their noses and lips coated in white sun block. *This? These are our adult children? This is the reward we reap from dedicating our lives to parenting?* But now, everything is Vince's face—everything Vero hates, everything wrong with her life. Right there in the flesh. She wants more than anything to punch her fist right through it. She wants to feel teeth loosen, to smell blood spilling.

She bounces Jamal's weight onto her hip to let loose one of her hands. She tightens her fist hard, her fingernails carving four crescent moons into her palm, and raises it to shoulder level. "I'd love to!"

"Do it!" Chin out.

"I'd love to!" Fist raised.

"Do it!" Chin higher.

"I'd love to!" Fist closer.

While Vince and Vero hurl threats back and forth, some violent magnetism drawing them so close that their chests nearly touch, she runs through scenarios. She imagines taking every bit of her force and pushing the heel of her hand hard into Vince's nose, watching it explode, blood smearing across his face.

And then what?

"C'mon, Eliot and Jamal." She lets her fists fall loose. "We're going. Let's get away from this crazy family."

Let them have each other, she thinks, *I have my boys.*

"You shouldn't have to see this, babies," Vero speaks so evenly and with such calm that you'd think she hasn't been involved, that she hadn't raised her knuckles to Vince's sweaty face and spoken so viciously that spit balls splattered his cheeks.

She lops her beach bag over her shoulder and grabs the boys, lumbering off under her load with as much dignity as she can rally. But she does nothing to stop her tears or to control her face, contorted with sobs. As she winds her way through beach chairs, eager to put distance between herself and Shane's crazy family, she grows aware of tourists all around her. Families on bright blankets share Christmas feasts of seafood and salsa, the festive holiday aroma of coconut oil, rum, and dead fish heavy in the air. *Look at me,* she wants to say, *pity me. I deserve your pity. Do you see what I endure?*

Nearly off the beach, she can still hear Vince shouting: *"Your wife's a fucking bitch! Your wife's a fucking bitch! Your wife's a fucking bitch!!"* The refrain grows fainter as she nears the beach-side showers, not making eye-contact with anyone.

As she steps off the beach and onto the stairs up to the first pool, a Mexican waitress squeezes her elbow and whispers, *"Feliz Navidad."* Vero lets go of Eliot's hand and wipes her eyes on the back of Jamal's blue shirt that's decorated with big piranhas eating little piranhas. She doesn't know this waitress. She doesn't know if this exact waitress has been serving her all week. The help here, all the carefully pressed servers in their white ball caps and orange golf shirts, they blend together. Vero knows then that she's no better than Gregory Schoeman with his fat-fingered *Una mas!*

She can't smile at the kind waitress, but she nods and takes a moment to really look at her. She sees a clover-shaped mole near her right ear, a deep brown line circling her pupil, a thin space between her two front teeth. She reads the woman's nametag. *Maria*. She can't speak, but she thinks, *Hello, Maria*. Tries to put it in her eyes. *Hola. Gracias.*

◊◊◊

When Heather and Gregory come back to the room, Vero pretends to be deeply absorbed in *Dora the Explorer* with the kids. Dora and her monkey friend remind Vero of Vince and Shane, the big-headed leader and the unflagging follower. Vero hates that bossy little Dora bitch. "Say map! Say map! Say map!" And then, just in case one little kid in one little country in one little town hasn't yet said *fucking "map" already*, Dora insists once more, "Say map!" Dora is just like Vince— *Say what I tell you to say, and then follow me.* And Shane—he's the monkey.

The blaring TV gives Heather and Gregory the space to have the whispered dispute they would usually avoid in front of Vero.

"He's forty-three years old. It's not funny anymore," Gregory says. Vero can't see the level of distress on his face, but she watches his back in her peripheral vision. He still wears nothing but swim shorts. Little grey hairs curl up his spine. Two rolls of flesh hang at his waist, beads of sweat speckled across them.

"It's never been funny, Gregory, but you always encouraged it. Your football-star Vince, exempt from everyone else's rules." Heather's bathing suit has ridden so high that Vero can see the white of her dimpled buttocks that glow against the angry red burn on her upper thighs. "You set the rules, and we followed. I let Vince do anything. We raised Shane to do whatever his brother Vince said. You encouraged

Vince to think he existed in a space apart from the ordinary. You led him to expect too much from life."

"I encouraged it? *I* did?! I didn't want to mention it, Heather. But." That single word carries a lifetime of meaning. *But.* He opens the fridge door, ice clinking. "Whose family has the history of alcoholism, Heather? Whose? It's not my family."

"Oh." A not-for-long empty glass slams on the countertop. "So now it's *my* fault?"

"I'm just saying. Alcoholism, it's hereditary." He throws his beach towel over the bar chair and steps toward the six-headed shower, carrying a cocktail glass, ice clinking with each step. At the base of his spine a dark globe of sweat stains his shorts. *They have got their faces in the trough*—that's what Vero's mother, Cheryl, says of Mr and Mrs Schoeman. *That's the problem with our society. Everyone's face is in the trough.*

"And all *I'm* saying is you should do *something*. And Shane too. He gets dragged into Vince's debauchery every time. Talk to them."

"I should talk to them? For god's sake, Heather, I'm sixty-six years old. I'm nobody's daddy anymore. You talk to them if you think it's so important. You're their mother."

But the Schoemans stick to their plan for dinner. It is, after all, Christmas. There will be a Christmas feast. The condo units all come equipped with full kitchens, complete with convection ovens and full-sized fridges, but Gregory calls down to one of the five-star restaurants. Before there's any sign of Drunkle Vince and his monkey friend Shane, Gregory orders heaps of pozole, guacamole, menudo, burritos, tamales, and chimichangas. "What do you eat for Christmas?" he bellows into the phone, as if volume alone can break the language barrier. "Give us it all!"

Jamal and Eliot have long fallen asleep by the time Vince barges through the door with his pineapple crotch and Shane stumbles after him, his entire body a crisp pink. Shane has tucked a small towel into his Speedo. The towel almost meets in the middle at the treasure trail running from his bellybutton into the ever-so-small bottoms below.

He's too white for the Mexican sun. When Vero first said she wanted to name their second son Jamal, he'd balked, "Look at me: I'm practically an albino. And we're going to have a kid called Jamal?" But she waited until the birth, knowing that after Shane watched her push out a baby, she could call him whatever she wanted.

"A skirt," Vero mumbles, pointing at Shane's towel, not letting herself pity him and his sun-beaten sensitive skin. "How civilized of you to dress for Christmas dinner."

Heather smiles at this, though her eyes water. She *has* dressed for dinner, pure silver teardrops hanging from her ears and a silk scarf the colour of merlot pinned at her neck. *She sure thinks she's something*, Vero's own mother would say. In Vero's family, there's no worse insult.

"I'm fine. I'm *fine*," Vince insists, as Heather holds his elbow to steer him into his chair for the extravagant feast of cold Mexican goop.

"Shis dins shanks its," says Shane, looking down to his plate. He closes his eyes. Vero wonders if he might fall face-first into his five-star food. She craves the drama of that splat. But then he opens his eyes. "Ish versh pand Imssh." He closes his mouth, holds two fingers to his lips and looks at Vero, so lost that she nearly pities him.

Lecker like a crecker. That's what Gregory usually says, rubbing his hands over his full plate, just before they start a feast. *Lecker like a crecker.* It's something people said back in South Africa. Another family joke that Vero is not in on. But now? Vero craves that joke. She almost says it herself, rubbing her own hands above her plate.

"This dinner is very good, Mr and Mrs Schoeman. Thank you."

Vero hasn't called them Mr and Mrs since Shane first took her out of his bed, down from his sweet suite, through the garage, and into their house nearly two decades ago, but the extent to which they've become a satire of family Christmas dinner calls for such formality. Vero nods her head at them and raises her purified water in a toast. She tries to enjoy the dinner Gregory has paid for, but lumps of melted cheese and mashed avocado stick in her throat.

"You're welcome, Vero." Gregory holds his glass of Argentinian Malbec up to her. "Merry Christmas." He takes a polite sip.

Heather reaches for her glass. "Yes, Merry Christmas, everyone." Her sip shows equal restraint. She wipes her lips on a linen napkin.

"Delishish," Vince says. But he hasn't taken a bite. Even sitting across from his bare chest now, so close she could touch him, Vero can't work up any of the rage she had on the beach. He's nothing but a puddle of booze. Who could rage at that? Vince has recently declared himself a stand-up comic, performing at nightclubs to create a muted sort of post-football limelight for himself. His routine relies on pushing that boundary between offensive and funny. Vero keeps her own checklist; if Vince hasn't said all four of these words within the first seven minutes of his show, she knows he's off his game: rape, faggot, child-fucker, cunt. She's waiting for him to use all four in the same sentence. He gets away with it because he's big enough to discourage anyone from marching out of the audience and punching him smack in the face.

Looking at him now, a drunken middle-aged man at the dinner table in Lycra bikini bottoms, Vero wonders how long it will be before he performs his alchemist's sleight of hand and transforms this day of dross into on-stage gold.

Shane dips his fork into a sticky pile of refried beans and lifts it, with effort, to his mouth, hand shaking. He takes two bites before clanking his fork across his plate. "Ifsh you exchushe…I'm…Goonight." He stands up and falls through the door into their bedroom.

Vero sets her fork down and stares at her plate, not knowing where else to look. The next morning she will open the balcony curtains to discover that he's barfed off the edge and into the blooming bougainvillea, bright purple below. The efficient Mexican gardeners will have it cleaned up before lunch.

"Maybe you should call it a night too, son." Vero has never heard Gregory call Vince "son." The forced formality is catching.

Heather pushes Vince's plate away from him. "Be careful. You're going to get sick." The silver teardrops dangling from her ears swing hard, once, with the force of her movement.

"I'm *fine*." Vince pulls the plate back and shovels some squished avocados into his mouth. "The thing about Bikini Chrishmash iz, you never say die. Ish not over til therz a winner." He swallows one forkful of sour-cream coated mush, then another, then another, competitively. "A winner finishizz the day. The *whole* day." He takes five more quick bites until the plate's nearly empty and then rips a piece of tortilla, sloshes it around his plate to slop up the remnants of his meal, and tears it with his teeth. "I'm a finisher," he says with his mouth so wide that everyone can see his tortilla and refried dinner. "We gotta show Shpeedo Navidad who'z boss." He grabs the edge of the table with both hands, bracing himself in his chair. His muscles flex as if he's doing push-ups. "Ishn't that right, baby?" He wobbles as he wipes his greasy hands on his bare chest, seeming to direct the "baby" at Vero. "Now. Who iz ready to go dancing?" He answers his own question with a burp so loud and wet that Heather winces, and her chin wobbles twice. She will cry. But then burp number two turns into a hiccough, a gag, and then a full-body spasm. The rest of them watch, immobilized, as Vince's convulsing, sweaty body races for the bathroom. He leans spread-eagled over the bathroom sink for one violent heave before he falls to his knees, bent over the toilet where they can all see his Speedo-clad ass. Vero tries not to look at the line where his careful shave ends. Her body softens with gratitude when he finally kicks the door shut.

Nobody leaves the dining room table until Vince finishes his gagging and retching and belching and horking in the bathroom and then staggers, a slouched and deflated beast, into his bedroom. They sit and stare at their plates. Not looking at the bathroom. Not looking at each other. Afterward, Heather spends a good hour at the bathroom sink fishing chunks of Vince's five-star vomit out of the five-star drain with a five-star butter knife, apologizing so repeatedly to Vero and Gregory that anyone new to the scene would think she made the mess herself.

Vero can't go into the bedroom where Shane snores obliviously. She sits out on the patio, a towel wrapped around her shoulders against the chill of the night, and watches brightly lit cruise ships haul their drunken passengers out of the harbour for the night journey.

She thinks of her mother, living so far across the continent from Sprucedale that they see her only once a year. Cheryl Nanton isn't big on giving advice. She isn't big on a lot of things associated with motherhood. Vero can't remember the last time she called Cheryl "Mom." Cheryl goes by Cheryl. "Don't saddle all that 'mom' shit on me," she says. "You're a big girl now, honey. Consider me retired."

When Vero first told Cheryl about her engagement to Shane, Cheryl held Vero's face hard between her hands and stared straight in Vero's eyes as they sat in her beaten-up, economy-sized Ford. She tugged at Vero's chin until their eyes met over the worn gearshift. "Listen carefully, and don't for a second think I'm exaggerating about this. Ask yourself—*Am I ready to say, 'until death do us part' to that mother? How about to that father? The brother?* They are all part of the package." Cheryl gave Vero's cheeks one firm squeeze, then dropped her hands, looking away as if she knew her words were futile even as she spoke them. "And let me tell you one more thing: when things go bad, and they will, you don't talk shit about your spouse's family. Ever. A husband knows his mom's a glutton or his dad's a big loud mouth. He knows if his brother's a letch or a free-loader or a sexist, or if his sister's a slut or a bigot. He can see it without his wife telling him. *Blood defends blood.* Always. You talk shit about someone's family, and things are gonna turn nasty. Fast." She put both her hands on the steering wheel, at ten and two (some things Cheryl insisted on doing right). "And now, you do what you want, but never claim that I didn't warn you. Nobody ever warned me. I warned you." Just when Vero expected Cheryl to squeal out of the driveway in her usual rally-racer style, she turned the engine off and fumbled in her purse. She quickly lit a cigarette, but then held it away from lips. Cheryl didn't smoke anymore.

◊◊◊

Vero crawls into bed around midnight after watching a couple of impotent firecrackers fizzle up from the beach and the last of the holiday-in-a-can vessels push into the open sea. She lies awake in the bedroom all night, a palm spread flat on Eliot's warm back. As her hand moves with the rhythmic rise and fall of Eliot's breath, she listens to Jamal's soft snore and watches Shane drool on his pillow. She feels their weight on her, as if she's at the bottom of a pig-pile, their presence squeezing the air right out of her. She struggles for just one complete and satisfying breath, and thinks a single, lonely thought over and over again: *I could not be more stuck with this guy.*

That single sentence—as much as the rush of breast milk, as much as the screams of labour, as much as the omnipresent fear for a child's well-being—unites Vero with mothers across the generations and world over.

I could not be more stuck with this guy.

She will tell Shane, "I stayed up all night just waiting for you to wake up so I could divorce you." But that's a lie. If she had decided upon such a clear course of action, she might have slept.

Shane hasn't even opened his eyes in the morning when Vero attacks him. As soon as he stirs, she lunges to his side of the bed, puts her face inches from his, and hisses, "You go out there right now. You apologize to your mother. And then you apologize to your father. You tell them you're sorry for acting like a delinquent teenager. You tell them you're sorry for ruining their holiday. You tell them you're sorry for wrecking everybody's Christmas." Even as she issues this demand she wonders why she should worry about them. They made Shane what he is. But nobody will ever accuse Vero Nanton of thinking she's something: she will not make it all about her. At least not at first. "And then you come right back in here and you give me one reason I should stay married to you."

Two reasons—the only two—still sleep soundly, but Vero, like the mother fox, ignores them. She also ignores the voice of Cheryl who insists, *Leave him.* Cheryl never needed anyone. As soon as a man thought it time to move his socks from his suitcase into her chest of drawers, he was on his way out. Vero grew up a spectator to a parade of leaving men.

"You didn't even follow me. You didn't come to find me. You didn't care to make sure I was okay," Vero hisses. "You left me. You let your brother yell at me and then you left me. On Christmas."

"I had to talk Vince down, Vero. You know him. I needed to explain you to him, let him see where you were coming from. I smoothed things over for you." Shane's voice rasps through phlegm in the back of his throat. He scrunches his face like he can't stand the taste of his own mouth.

"You do not need to explain me to him. You do not need to go after him. You need to come to me. Your wife." She bites off the words *because it's Christmas*. She doesn't want to use that, again. "*I* am your family. *I* am." She shushes Cheryl, who has appeared again. *Blood defends blood.*

"Of course you are." Shane holds his hand out toward her arm. He still hasn't opened his eyes.

"We're a family. And you didn't even come back to me. For dinner. On—" She pounds her fist twice, hard, on the mattress next to his head. "CHRIST-MAS."

He rubs his head, licks his lips. "C'mon, baby. Nobody even told me we were having dinner. How was I supposed to know?"

How was he supposed to know?

Vero holds him coldly in her gaze, willing him to say more. Eventually, he breaks. "It's my family vacation. Just one week a year," he says so softly she barely hears him. "It's Vince. My brother." Shane sits on the edge of the bed now, and his head hangs so low that his chin nearly touches his chest. The head looks heavy—whether weighted from fatigue or shame, Vero cannot tell. When she still says nothing, Shane adds, "I'm sorry." He holds his forehead in both hands and does not look at her. She can think of nothing to say, not even when he brushes by her, careful not to let his skin touch hers, and mumbles, "I was drunk, Vero. Very, very drunk."

Vero stands in the doorway to their bedroom while Shane mumbles a sheepish apology to his mother. Heather doesn't even look up from the game of solitaire she plays on her laptop. Without a word, she nods her acceptance of his apology.

Or maybe her nod simply means, *Go away—I don't want to think about you right now. Leave me alone to spend my winters somewhere warm and peaceful while I wait to die.*

Shane's apology to his dad goes more smoothly. Gregory takes a deep breath and smiles, "Ah, that's okay, son." He clasps a heavy hand on Shane's shoulder. "Been there, done that. Believe me. Back in my day. Who hasn't? It won't be the last time. Save your apologies for the wife." Vero tries to reconcile this been-there-done-that version of Gregory with the grey curly hairs on the spine, the sweaty rolls at the waist, the charges of hereditary alcoholism, the slammed glass, and the blame hurled at Heather.

She can't.

Vero knows they won't see Vince until noon, and then they will all act like nothing's happened. "Morning, buddy. How goes it?" *Vince is Vince,* that's what they all say.

Vero would like to think that, in the wake of Speedo Navidad, Shane might realize that "Vince is Vince" doesn't have a particularly satisfactory heft to it. Those three words are cotton candy next to the emotional T-bone of this family Christmas gone wrong. But Shane grew up with those three words, a family truth as real as *"Brothers Look Out for Brothers"* or *"Second Place is the First Loser"* or *"Sunday Afternoon is for Football."*

Vince is Vince.

Vero knows all the stories. When Vince was thirteen, even before he had a learner's license, he smashed Heather's car into a telephone pole; Gregory responded with, *Vince is Vince.* When Vince got suspended for pissing on the gymnasium floor at a high-school dance, Heather said, *Vince is Vince.* When Vince played college football for four years but failed to get a degree, Heather and Gregory shook their heads, but still insisted, *Vince is Vince.*

Shane tries, again and again, to explain *Vince is Vince* to Vero, but he fails. Regular codes of conduct and standards of behaviour don't apply to Vince because…well, fuck, he's Vince.

Vero watches Gregory Schoeman slap a meaty palm to Shane's shoulder, "Boys will be boys," he says to his forty-two-year old son, and points at the line-up of bottles on the side table, "Hair of the dog?"

Vero leans against the doorframe, holding her breath against the smell of stale tequila emanating from their unmade bed, and commands herself not to cry.

CHAPTER FOUR

Ligaya rises early on Christmas. Madam Poon has given her most of the day off, but still Ligaya must prepare the congee and finish the cleaning before she leaves the apartment. Because she hopes to be gone by the time the family wakes, she set her phone alarm for two hours before sunrise and placed it right under her mattress where only she will hear its beep.

She slides on heavy socks and walks through the small apartment on her tiptoes, inching cupboard doors open to avoid the creak. She lays two towels out on the counter—one on top of the other—and places pots and cooking dishes on that cushion so they don't clank and disturb the Poons. She commands her body to be light. She will be a spirit, airy enough to walk through walls. More than on any other day, Ligaya makes no noise. She has no desire to be present, even on the outskirts, for the Poon family Christmas.

Especially not on the outskirts.

Mister Poon came home last night. Ligaya has become so accustomed to looking at the floor that he had to bow his head to meet her eyes. She felt childish, as if she'd deliberately hidden them from him, a little girl curling into her mother's skirts. For him, she lifted her eyes and nodded, ever so slightly.

"Hello, Ligaya. You've had a good week, I trust."

Just that, the three fat syllables of her name in his mouth, warmed her to him, but as soon as she felt the unfamiliar stretch of a smile, she stepped away and dropped her gaze, studying her brown house slippers.

Mister Poon brought Ligaya a small wrapped present. He held it out for her to see, a square of tissue paper the colour of mango, and then placed it under the small tree with the other gifts. He will want her to open that present this morning.

And Madam Poon? She will want Ligaya gone. Ligaya cannot pretend, even to herself, that she does not understand that desire.

She fingers the mango paper before turning away from the small package. Nobody has given Ligaya a present since she left home. The morning of her departure, Pedro sent Totoy toddling over with a pile of sliced coconut in the tiny cup of his palms. Pedro had climbed the coconut tree himself. Ligaya watched from the porch steps, the muscles of his bare brown back glistening in the sun. But Ligaya will not think of them—not of Pedro, not of Nene, not of Totoy—not on this day of all days. She turns to her work.

As she moves the pot of congee off the hotplate, she eyes the small plastic Christmas tree on the window sill. Even in the near dark, she can pick out her little square of mango, but she will leave for Christmas mass without Mister Poon's present. If she accidentally wakes Madam, Ligaya fears she will find herself gutting fish and scrubbing floors for Christmas day.

She has other plans. She will wear her one dress with formal shoes and go to the church on Caine Road for the Tagalog mass, where she will meet Corazon, her cousin from Batangas. Afterward, Centre

Street will be thick with Filipina nannies, Tagalog words bubbling up and rising to the skies. On this day, the streets of Hong Kong belong to them.

Ligaya must be back to the Poons by dinner, to clean the dishes, bathe Hui, and then lie with him, holding his chubby body close to her chest until he falls asleep. But now, dinner feels so far away—first she will spend an entire afternoon deep in the alternate reality of Tagalog.

Corazon will gamble, getting playing cards from the *ate* at Kabayan. *Ate*, they call her, "big sister," the same name they use for all the old Filipina women. They don't know her real name. Corazon will lift each tab, hoping for a straight flush or a full house to buy her way home. Ligaya doesn't dare purchase playing cards. Madam Poon has warned her: "Gambling is illegal in Hong Kong!" But Madam Poon herself bets on everything. She bets on mahjong games, on whether a certain street cat will survive the birth of her kittens, on how long it will take a fly to walk up a wall. Madam Poon bets on her own life: if a hearse passes, she bets she will soon die. If she sees a car full of nuns, she bets the nuns will save her. The skinny witch fills her days with bets. But Madam Poon says Ligaya must not gamble, and Ligaya does not wish to discover what will happen if she disobeys. Ligaya will sit with Corazon, who hides her poker cards under a blanket in her lap, her body falling into a fuller slouch of disappointment with each newly opened tab.

Afterward, they will go back into the Filipino store. *Ate* will think they want more cards and reach for the hidden box under her till as she always does. But Ligaya and Corazon will wave her off and smile toward the food—for Christmas, they will treat themselves to pancit and chicken adobo, eating from the heaping containers in the streets, huddled together against the damp December air. *Ate*, so small that only her head and shoulders are visible above the counter and so old that she curls in on herself like a bloated earthworm, will pile a few extra noodles into their boxes today.

Ligaya imagines herself later today, her belly full and her head leaning into Corazon's shoulder, their hands on each other's knees, wrapped in the comfort of their own language. Eager to see faces from home, Ligaya gives one last sweep of the floor, sets the broom in the closet next to her mattress, and grabs an umbrella. She lets out her breath as she slips into the hallway of the high rise, gently closing the door on the smell of sticky rice.

CHAPTER FIVE

Sometimes Vero sneaks one of Shane's Percocet pills to add a pleasant fuzziness to her morning. Other days, she takes two and, now that she's no longer nursing, pours just a few drops of Baileys into her morning coffee.

Today, she meets Joss for a morning jog instead. There's no snow this January; the ground is frozen hard but it's bone dry, perfect for running. Vero needs to be home in time for Shane to be at the pharmacy by nine, so she and Joss often run in deep darkness through the worst of the winter. Their planned route ends with a torturous climb up Cardiac Hill to Joss's house, where Ian meets them with water and espresso and then drives Vero home on his way to work. Usually, Joss starts running right after they say their quick hellos, leaving Vero straining to keep up. Today, though, Joss hesitates, puts a mittened hand on Vero's arm.

Although Joss was raised by Buddhists, she never calls herself one. "I'm interested in many religions," she says. "I take a bite from each." Vero imagines Joss penning a book one day: *World Religion: The All-You-Can-Eat Smorgasbord.* Joss insists she doesn't "self-identify" as Buddhist, but when people describe her, they never fail to mention the Buddhist parents. Looking into Joss's eyes is a hit of Valium for Vero. This morning, Joss's golden curls are pushed up under a big wool toque and a balaclava covers her full lips, protecting her face from the cold. But still: the eyes. Anyone who knows Joss would recognize her instantly, even with the rest of her face under cover.

At first, Joss says nothing with her mitten on Vero's sleeve. She has a habit of pausing before she speaks. This time, Joss is slower than usual with her words, standing there on the cold corner, a mitten on Vero's arm, and only her eyes showing.

"You okay?" That's all she finally says.

Vero nods.

"Let's take the easy route this morning." Joss runs her mitten to Vero's elbow and then to her wrist, gives her hand a squeeze before letting go. "Let's be kind to ourselves."

Maybe even Joss can't find wisdom before sun-up.

◊◊◊

By late afternoon, the air is still cold enough to sting Vero's throat, but the sun warms her face and casts a beautiful glow across the treed hills to the west of Sprucedale. She wishes Joss were here now with her and Jamal and Eliot, but Joss's boys are too old for the playground.

"Look at the forest! E, come see! JJ-Bean, look!" Vero's enthusiasm isn't her usual plastic-mother charade (*Oooooh! Tree! Look!*). This time, that hint of awe is real. After Mexico, Vero sunk into a slump so deep that she rarely looked up to take in the scene around her. Now the grand beauty of the thickly forested hills assaults her, as it does when Sprucedale's been socked in for days and the sun finally appears, the clouds lifting. This time, the clouds are inside her. Depression isn't heavy, as she'd imagined it. Rather, she's light, a hot-air balloon floating high above her own life, all of it miniscule and irrelevant. *How could any of it possibly matter?* "Aren't the trees so beautiful, Eliot? Jamal? Just like a postcard." Vero forces herself to focus on the beauty, suck it in as though her eyeballs are hungry, feel it inside her full and solid.

But Eliot and Jamal don't care about postcards. They know no other view. They expect no less. Eliot runs for the slides, JJ-Bean toddling full speed after him.

The chill air must be enough to dissuade most parents from an evening outdoors; the playground is nearly empty. Normally, kids coat the park equipment like ants swarming a puddle of Coke, and Filipina nannies circle the perimeter, giggling and texting while daredevil children perform death-defying stunts on the monkey bars.

"Someone's going to die," Vero once charged, dragging a particularly wild boy by the wrist and intruding on the Filipina cluster. "Can one of you watch him before he breaks his neck?!" One nanny—Vero couldn't distinguish one from the other—reached for the boy, as all of the women's faces went blank. *You get close, we're not real.*

"You overreact," Shane told her when she complained that the kids ran wild with no supervision. "What's the worst that could happen?" So Vero told him what could happen—kids torn in two by the semis blazing down the nearby highway, brains smeared on windshields, organs ripped open; toddlers floating face-down in the adjacent duck pond, stomachs distended; hide-and-seekers hiding so well that nobody finds them until they start to smell. "And that's not even the worst," she said. "You don't want to think about the worst."

This afternoon, though, only one other kid plays on the park equipment. Two parents sit on the far park bench, their attention deep in the iPhones on their laps. Eliot runs traffic control on the jungle gym. "No going up the slide," he announces, "just going down." He swings his arms in serious, grand gestures, the lift at the corners of his mouth betraying his enthusiasm for a well-enforced rule, as long as he gets to be the enforcer. "Up this way." He points. "Down that way. I'm the one who makes up the rules." Shane must've said that to him as a joke once: *Who declared you the person to make up all the rules? You think you're the boss?* Pragmatic little Eliot would take that as an invitation. *"Why, yes. Yes, that's exactly who I am. The boss who makes up all the rules."*

Life flows most smoothly when Jamal accepts Eliot's role as enforcer, which he's doing today, trudging along behind his big brother, as they crawl across the sliver-ridden bridge, climb over the rusty train that Vero calls "the Tetanus Express," swing up the climbing wall meant for much bigger kids, and end right back at Vero's feet. "We flew to the North Pole, Mommy! Hunting for polar bears." So much of the adventure takes place in their minds. Vero wonders if the same could said about the lives of adults.

The sun dips into the trees covering the big-bellied hills, and Vero pulls her sweater tight around her shoulders. It's barely past four, and already the sun is falling. Traffic roars by on the highway, a tall wire fence between them and it. Vero wonders where they're all in such a hurry to get to. She can't think of anywhere she'd like to go, anything she'd like to do. She wonders what used to give her pleasure.

Shane says she's just tired. She's shuffled through his deck of nanny profiles, wondering if these mug shots really might, as Shane claims, offer the portal to a blissful, easy future. She tries to imagine each one of these women on a collision course with the Schoeman family. Their dark, smooth complexions speak of youth and their big round eyes of innocence. She can't be responsible for exposing even one of them to the likes of Drunkle Vince.

Vero hasn't even told Joss she's been looking at nanny profiles. She's afraid Joss will think she's hiring someone else to raise her children. Or exploiting vulnerable foreign workers. Or maybe Vero simply thinks that saying it aloud will make it happen, and she's not ready.

The dad across the park on the bench looks up from his iPhone, glancing at Vero and the boys. She smiles his way, but he drops his head back to his lap. The woman beside him wears a familiar vacant expression. Vero spends enough time with new mothers that she barely notices. They've all left their brains at home in the dryers. They're bumping around in there like old shoes fluffing up the down duvets.

The sunset turns the sky a brilliant pumpkin orange, especially stunning this evening. The colour always shows best when the weather is dry, the light refracting through airborne dust of the local coal mine. The couple on the bench shows no interest in the sky. They must be the parents of the bigger boy, an eight- or nine-year-old, giant next to Vero's kids. He wears a black ball cap with the Sprucedale city motto—*Where the Living Is Good*—embroidered in red. He climbs up the slide, his long legs conquering the slope in just two steps.

"Don't," Vero says, the command loud and deep. Dog-training manuals claim that's the surest way of encouraging obedience.

The boy stops to look at her, but says nothing.

"It's against the rules, sweetie, to climb up the slide." She lifts her voice up out of her chest, loses the growl. "We don't want you to get hurt, do we?" This boy is a son just like her boys. She fills her voice with sugar.

But again, he just looks at Vero. He doesn't roll his eyes. He doesn't smirk. He says nothing, betrays no response at all. It's as if he can't hear Vero, as if an impenetrable shield has grown up between them. He takes another step up the slide.

Eliot and Jamal both watch Vero. She expects Eliot to get hysterical, the way he does when people don't follow his rules, closing his eyes and waving his hands, pounding his fists into his own thighs, but he looks at Vero, and his face breaks into an impish grin she doesn't recognize. He takes a big step after the other boy. One step, two steps—a look over his shoulder—three steps, four steps, right to the top of the slide. He towers over Vero, glancing up at the big boy close to his shoulder.

"Eliot!" Vero hears her own shrill voice. "No!" Someone has to enforce the rules. The boy has to listen to Vero. It's the natural order: young people obey old people. "No walking up the slide," she says again, without the sugar. *They could get hurt.* "It's the rule." At the bottom of the slide, Jamal scampers like a crab rolled on its back, making a futile effort to catch his older brother.

By then, the boy in the ball cap is sliding down, banging into Jamal at the bottom. Jamal laughs. Things have turned rough, just the way Jamal likes. Vero ignores the laughter. "See!" She yells. "See! This is why there's no climbing up the slides." Her heart beats fast, rattling her ribcage. "That's why they're called slides. You *slide* down them." She tries to reason with the boy. His face shows no expression of insolence. It shows no expression at all, not even the slightest awareness of Vero's presence flickering in his pupils. He takes another big step back up the slide, with Eliot following fast at his heels, his face alight with the glow of mischief.

Vero lunges for the strange boy, locking her strong grip around his ankle. "No. Climbing. Up. The. Slide." The boy tries to pull his foot from her grasp, a flicker of awareness in his eyes now, but Vero holds on tight. Eliot races by the boy to the top of the slide. "See!" Vero shrieks now. "See! The little ones will copy you. You *must* follow the rules." Her hand aches with the force of her grip. She imagines yanking hard and pulling the boy to the dirt, holding him firmly by the shoulders, fingernails digging into his chest, as she marches him around and then watches him climb up the ladder. Why has nobody taught him the basic rules? Why can't he see that someone will get hurt?

"Tyler!" Vero feels his father's deep voice close behind her.

Good, she thinks, *his father will tell him. Finally there will be discipline. Respect.* She feels saved. From the moment. From herself. She breathes.

"Tyler! Let's go. Come on." The man holds out his hands, lifting his son off the slide.

Here's where he'll make the boy apologize, Vero thinks. *Here's where order will be restored.* She tries smiling at the man, staring at the auburn stubble of his chin, but he has a matching ball cap pulled low over his eyes and refuses to look at her. Vero watches and waits as he and his boy march away in their matching leather hiking boots.

"It's okay," the man says to Tyler, both of their backs turned to Vero. "Let's just leave the grumpy lady alone."

Vero's eyes bug. Her kids gasp. "Grumpy," she lobs the word toward them, a weak repetition. "Grumpy? I was just...I had to...I was trying..." She drops her eyes to Eliot and Jamal, both stalled open-mouthed at the bottom of the slide, legs wrapped around each other. They look as small and cold as she feels. "There are rules. We need to have rules," Vero shouts at the man's back. "They could have been hurt!"

She sits down on the slide next to her boys and drops her forehead into her hands, listening to the long-haul trucks roar by on the other side of the fence. "Mommy," Eliot finally says, looping his small hand through her arm and holding her elbow. "Is this what Daddy means when he says you're going a little bit crazy?" Jamal puts his lips to Vero's cheek and opens his wet mouth, the best he can do for a kiss so far. Eliot gets her on the other side. "We love you, Mommy." Vero's heart does that thing that only her kids can make it do. Her chest turns so soft that Eliot and Jamal could reach out and put their little hands right through it.

She remembers seeing her obstetrician just a few weeks after Jamal's birth. "Have you bonded with the baby?" His pen marked the spot on a list of post-partum questions, and his eyes stayed there rather than reaching for Vero's.

"Of course I have bonded with my baby." Jamal slept, his head warm and heavy in the crook of her elbow, his tiny mouth resting against the bulge of her breast. "Of course."

"Good. Perfect. Some women don't." The doctor tucked his pen behind his ear and pushed the clipboard away from him on his desk. His eyes followed it before darting to Vero. They rested on her for a moment, and then he rose to signal the appointment had come to its end.

"Well, I most definitely have." Vero focused on Jamal's long slow breaths, rising and falling in synch with hers, and knew she would never tell this doctor that he had asked the wrong question. This thing that had her in its grasp—it could just as easily take a hold of a man. It didn't have to be about motherhood. Not exactly. Vero suspected that if she touched this doctor's arm and really explained— *it's too full, it's too fast, it's too busy, it's too much*—his shoulders would sag, he would meet her eyes, and he would say, "I know. I feel it too. Yes."

◊◊◊

"Don't use the word 'power.'" Edward, her boss at the LAV plant, sits behind his giant oak desk, fondling a golf trophy shaped like a driving wedge. "The Arabs don't like it." He pronounces it "eeee-rabs," pounding out the syllables on a stack of manuals Vero must edit for the Saudi Arabian National Guard. "Only Allah has power or some such shit. *Power* off. *Power* on. *Power* switch. No good. Fix 'em all."

Vero leans against the wall next to Edward's desk and keeps an eye on the clock: she's on babysitter time. She forces herself to hold onto each of his words, line them up into a row like a sentence, decipher their meaning. She's too tired for this process to come naturally. Jamal kept her awake through most of the night with a rear-end explosion, liquefied apricot acid drenching his sheets and smearing the walls. She knows she looks at least as rough as she feels, her hair gathered into a paisley scrunchy on top of her head, a throwback to '80s fashion. She sported this look often, circa-1985, after she'd snuck off to have sex in her boyfriend's car between English and algebra (instead of attending physics). She fingers the worn scrunchy as Edward talks, wondering if it could be the very same one she wore to post-coital algebra more than twenty years ago.

"So Ed*ward*—" she stresses the last syllables. He hates being called Ed. His ex-wife called him Ed. "What word do you suggest I use, if not power?" Vero tries to concentrate, but can't stop thinking of last night's little finger smear of shit on Jamal's music box, evidence of his attempt to self-soothe before giving into his urge to release a scream that would wake even Drunkle Vince from a coma.

Edward's office always smells of red licorice, and Vero breathes the synthetic candied smell deeply to block the memory of shit-soaked Jamal.

"Hell, fuck. That's what we pay you for, isn't it?" Edward pounds his trophy on the desk, the clunk reminding Vero of the heavy thud Jamal's pyjamas made when she dropped them in the trashcan. "Use *voltage*, fuck."

He is a healthy dose of military crossed with head-of-the-class at engineering school, lightly sprinkled with the niggling fear of death that comes when a man can just about touch his retirement. So far, his primary response to a long-range forecast of mortality has been to buy a motorcycle and a good camera. Vero avoids his eyes by studying the wall behind him, plastered with pictures of Edward straddling his machine—on the Vegas strip, at the Mexican border, in front of a sign for Route 66—a photo-journalistic rendering of his bucket list.

"Okay, sure, *voltage*." Vero scribbles it in her notebook, doing a quick calculation of how much each minute of this meeting is costing her. She's left the kids home with Chantal, the boys' favourite babysitter. Little Chantal probably has them both performing back aerials off the top bunk by now. Or, worse, Shane's home, sitting with her in the kitchen; she's probably wearing a short skirt, knees open, a bright triangle of candy-apple red showing at her crotch.

"And the Arabs also don't like talk about male and female parts." Edward's black bushy eyebrows grow right together in the middle. He jiggles that fuzzy worm of an eyebrow on the word "female." His wife left him more than two years ago. He spent one long year in puffy-eyed grief and another in dogged pursuit of the only female engineer on staff, a provincial squash champion in the over-forty age category. Danilla, three years divorced herself, was all in at first. ("He lets *me* call him whatever I want," she winked at Vero.) Within less than a month, Danilla and Edward quit eating their egg-salad lunches together on the front lawn at the plant. No more holding hands across the picnic table. Eventually, Danilla confided to Vero that the bushy black eyebrow was only a small hint of the dense fur covering Edward's chest, back, and arms. "It's like going to bed with a grizzly bear," she said. "The mind is willing, but the body is out."

"The Arabs find the sexual innuendo of female parts offensive," Edward continues, pulling two pieces of red licorice from his top drawer and handing one to Vero. "*Screw, socket*, whatever, find something else to call them. Not *male*. Not *female*. They don't want to think about dicks and cunts when they're operating heavy machinery. Here it is, Vero Baby, a chance to earn your keep."

With the new, unedited Saudi Arabian National Guard manuals stuffed in her briefcase and a piece of licorice dangling from her mouth, she follows Edward through the plant. He wants to show her the anti-tanks. "Can't write about 'em, if you've never seen 'em."

But Vero doesn't want to see them. She wants to believe in her own etymology:

anti-tank = the opposite of tank

Whatever the opposite of tank might be—she doesn't care—a bouncy castle, a skateboard, a bar on wheels. Her capacity for denial is astonishing, matched only by her capacity for rationalization. She knows this. Again, she doesn't care.

Vero has no interest in learning how fast a real anti-tank will blow an oncoming enemy to smithereens. She simply wants to move the commas around. *That*, and that alone, is her job. But Edward drags her right up to the anti-tank, makes her touch its cannon. "Here," he points at the pipes running just underneath the benches in the back, "we have a design flaw. Where are the soldiers sitting? Right here." He pounds his flat palm on the bench. "Where are their calves? Right here." He raps the hairy backs of his knuckles hard against the pipe. "The poor fuckers are burning their calves to shit. Put something about that in the manual. Tell the Arab saps to straighten their goddamn legs." For a moment, Vero thinks that Edward, on the verge of tearing up, is sad for the soldiers, but then she realizes he's caught sight of Danilla across the plant. "Next month, you're on-site full-time, Vero Baby. Government inspection season. Enough staying home and playing happy housewife."

By the time Vero gets home, her Subaru packed to the roof with Edward's binders, the family's groceries, and her own guilt, she feels squished right out of the car, squished right out of her own life. As she moves from the driver's seat onto the driveway, loaded down with bags of food that will need replacing within the week, she accidentally bangs the voice-dialing button on her Blackberry.

"Say a command," the cheerful voice prompts.

"Fuck off!" Vero clenches the demonic device in her palm, poking savagely at its buttons, kneeling in the driveway as apples and canned soup roll into the neighbour's yard.

"Say a command," the mechanical but happy voice insists.

"Fuck off!" Vero smashes the Blackberry against the car door.

"Say a command." This lady doesn't give up.

"Fuck off *is* a command!" Vero throws the phone at the garage door.

She can feel the rise in her blood pressure, a dull pounding at her temples, an ache in the veins at her wrists.

In the house, she storms by Shane, who squats in front of Jamal. Her son screams on a potty in the middle of the living room. Shane pounds his fists in the air in time to an enthusiastic cheer: "Poo it out! Crunch it out! Waaa-aaay out!"

Neither of them looks at Vero, but Eliot grabs her pant leg, "JJ's poo's stuck, Mommy! It's stuck in his bum!"

Jamal yells and tries to squirm out of Shane's grip and away from the potty. He cries so hard a long worm of saliva falls from his mouth and sticks to his chin. Shane holds his shoulders, pushing him down, and sings to the tune of "Baa, Baa Black Sheep": "Baa, baa brown poo / When you gonna come ..."

Vero shakes her leg trying to loosen Eliot's grip on her pants, but he clings hard.

"…coiling, stinking/out of JJ's bum?" Shane drags out the "mmmmm" on bum, and Vero hopes that signifies an end. JJ's scream has lowered an octave, which could be promising. But then Shane starts in again: "Baa, baa brown poo…"

"You should sell your songs, Daddy!" Eliot still tugs at his mother's pants. "You could make money, and we could buy more cars." He smiles up at Vero, proud of his grasp of the North American economic system. She shakes her leg with greater force and drops the bag of groceries on the cluttered counter. Her phone falls with it—"Say a command! Say a command! Say a command!"

"Good idea, E!" Shane still squats before the potty, and Vero notices he wears spandex pants and a fleece jacket. Now she remembers seeing his fat-tire winter bike propped in the driveway, and she knows he's planned his escape. "We could sell our songs with a potty shaped like a train. We could call it the Potty Train. Get it? The Potty Train."

"Put your flushing song in the book we sell too, Daddy!" Now Eliot sings: "Bye-bye brown poo/So sad to see you go/swirling, twirling/down the toilet bowl."

"Shane, this room smells like shit! Can't you put the potty in the bathroom?" Vero swings her whole body, trying to loosen Eliot's grip on her pants. Her elbow hits the grocery bag. One by one, beautiful ripe tomatoes roll to the floor, each splat tightening the vice-grip around her scalp. "*For god's sake!*" Vero holds her hands to her head, covers her eyes. "Eliot! Let go of my leg. *Now!*"

Suddenly, Shane stands at Vero's side, his hand moving up and down her arm. "God, Vero, breathe. You're so stressed, you're brittle."

He clicks on the TV, and the boys fall silent, the bright moving images rendering them stupidly good. Vero keeps her eyes covered. Shane's words expose her, leave her standing naked in the kitchen, cold under his stare. He's nailed it: she feels brittle. If he touches her, she will fracture, dissolve into a thousand particles of dust. Or explode, dangerous shards of her flying everywhere. Destroying oncoming enemies, just like her anti-tank.

But she won't give him the satisfaction of being right.

"I'm fine. I could use some help around here." Vero turns her rage on him. "You could pick up a dish once in a while. You could get up with the kids in the middle of the night. You could act like some of this mess had something to do with you." She swipes her hand across the kitchen counter, sending dishes flying into the sink.

"You know what this is?" Shane uses the voice he usually saves for his patients. "A bumpy landing. You always have a rough time with work-to-home transitions. Maybe go upstairs, take a few minutes. Can I fix you a drink?"

"Oh yes, that's the answer, isn't it, Mr Candy Man? Drown the problem." He looks at her like she's pulled out his brain, plopped it on the kitchen table, and labelled it for him. She stomps across the room and turns off the TV. Jamal and Eliot scream.

Shane holds up a hand to them, but keeps his eyes on Vero. "You need a break. You're tired. I can see that." He puts his hand tentatively on her shoulders, applies pressure. She doesn't know why he keeps doing this lately, palming her shoulders like they're basketballs and pushing down as if he might push her right into the ground. "Do something for yourself, Vero. What do you need? Tell me—we can do it."

"Right." She smacks his hands away. "Shane will fix it. It's always about Shane. About what you did to me, what you did for me, about what you can change. Always back to you." She can hear her hysteria as if it comes from someone else, her head a balloon floating high above, watching the performance.

"Geez, Vero. It's like you want to fight. I said, 'whatever you want.' Just tell me."

Vero wants be alone. She turns her back to him, shoulders heaving. Tears will get rid of him. "You're prettier when you smile," he always says. He likes her happy.

"C'mon, boys. Mama needs a little rest." Shane packs up Eliot and Jamal, hurries suits and towels into a grocery bag, and heads for the swimming pool, leaving her sprawled at the kitchen counter.

When he leaves, Vero can't just be sobbing into the granite countertops. But with him gone, she doesn't know what else to do. Neurotic energy buzzes through her body, and she paces small, fast circles around the kitchen. She could call Joss, but the idea of this spectacle of herself reflected in those calm eyes shames her. She could go for a bike ride like Shane always does, or she could run deep into the woods like she usually does, but she doesn't have the energy for either. Not that kind of energy.

Vero opens the cutlery drawer and pulls out a steak knife. She holds the blade against her wrist, pushes until it hurts. A trace of blood rises from her skin in a thin flat line, a number 1. Or a small "l" for love. She laughs aloud.

She doesn't want to kill herself. And if she did, she certainly wouldn't do it with a steak knife. She imagines the fun Drunkle Vince would have with that in his stand-up show.

My dead sister-in-law is soooo stupid...

How stupid is she?

Vero drops the steak knife to the floor and grabs a bottle of white wine from Shane's beer fridge, its long neck cool in her grip. She fumbles through the medicine cabinet above the stove, safe out of the reach of the boys: children's Advil (four bottles, all coated in sticky blue); Metamucil (supersized); generic anti-inflammatories (three bottles); antibiotic eye cream; Robaxacet; Tylenol 3 (nearly empty). Someone has taken all the fucking Percocets.

What, she wonders, *is the point of being married to a pharmacist?* She laments, not for the first time, her failure to marry a massage therapist or a chef, or at least a bartender, and grabs the mostly harmless pills, spills them onto the counter, as if setting a stage. She wants Shane to be alarmed when he returns home.

She grabs eight of the geriatric back meds and rolls them around her palm before dropping four back onto the counter and popping the remaining four in her mouth, bitter against her dry tongue. She screws off the wine top. A Pinot Grigio. She prefers reds, but gave them up because of the terrible headaches. *Good thing,* she thinks, *I wouldn't want my allergies acting up during my staged suicide attempt.* She swallows three long hauls of the wine and then crawls into the pantry with the rest of the bottle.

With the door shut, Vero feels better. A closet of one's own. That's all she needed. She takes another long swig from the bottle, puts her legs up against the shelves of canned food. She likes Pinot Grigio, she decides; it's refreshing and fruity but not too sweet. She takes another couple glugs. Her trapezoid muscles fall open, flowers blooming from her relaxed shoulders. It's quite lovely in here. She wonders why she hasn't thought of it before.

As she nears the halfway mark of the bottle, she feels her anger squirm and die, an ant under a hot magnifying glass. Shane's not her problem. A slideshow of Shane runs through her mind: him posing like Jesus with arms outstretched to her from the back porch; his spandex-clad ass sneaking off to one of his bikes strategically stashed in the driveway; his Mexican-flagged crotch following Vince around the beaches of Puerto Vallarta. As the Schoeman family would say: *Shane is Shane.* He's awakened into middle age to find himself with two kids, a full-time job, an aging body that requires full-time maintenance, and now, a wife who looks less like herself every day, his life distorted and warped as if he's looking at it in a fun house mirror. He's doing his best. Vero wets her lips with wine and wonders, from the comfortable distance that alcohol provides, if the same is true of her.

◊◊◊

Crouched on the floor, head resting on a dustpan, Vero wonders whom she should call first. She wants to talk to someone. If she could, she'd call the BlackBerry Lady, Ms Say-a-command. She'd been especially rude to her. But how can Vero call her if she doesn't know her name? She laughs, swirling the last bits of wine in the bottle, grateful there are more bottles in Shane's beer fridge just outside the pantry. She fingers the dirty broom bristles at her cheek. The room has grown so dark that it feels good to touch something so familiar, to ground herself.

Her neck has developed a sharp kink where it meets her shoulders, so she pulls down a bulk bag of rice to use as a pillow. Finishes the bottle.

She pinches her cheeks. Numb. She imagines Jamal and Eliot splashing at the pool, Eliot ramming things with his head and telling everyone what to do, Jamal quacking like a duck. If she was a good mom, she'd be there with them. She moves to stand, tries to remember where her car keys might be, imagines the boys' delighted surprise when she joins them. But the floor tilts, first this way and then that. She holds the walls to steady herself.

Instead, she will call Joss. Joss can come for wine! It will be a party!

That's what she needs, what they all need—a party! She leaves the pantry long enough to grab her phone and a new bottle of wine.

After just two rings, Joss and Ian's voicemail clicks on. God, doesn't anyone answer their phones anymore? On the recording, Ian sings, strumming his guitar loudly in the background. "We're not going to ... *strum* ... answer our telephone ... *strum* ... so leave a message ... *strum* ... at the ... (pregnant pause) *beep!*" Ian's voice radiates optimism, so bright and hopeful on that last word that Vero feels a moment of embarrassment for them, pictures Joss holding up the iPhone while Ian sings enthusiastically in her direction, their pre-teen boys rolling their eyes in the background.

"Hi. Joss. It's me. You're right. I'm run ragged, just like you said. I guess I just wanted to say, hey, thanks for seeing that." This isn't at all what Vero meant to say—she wanted a party—but she lies back on the floor and listens to the unexpected words flow from her mouth. "Not everyone takes time to look, really look, at each other in this crazy-ass world." Vero's words run together, each indistinguishable from the next. She makes a concentrated effort to pause after each.

She thinks of saying, *I'm drunk on the pantry floor.* "Parenting's hard," she says instead, her tongue slow and heavy. "Whatever made us do it? I mean, really, imagine trying to sell this experience to some-one, if we hadn't all bought it already. Here's the pitch: You'll get preg-nant. Your body will warp in ways you hadn't thought possible. It'll never be the same again. You'll pee your pants for months afterward, maybe forever. Delivering a baby will hurt until you think you'll die. You'll wish for death. You won't recognize your own screams. *What's that awful noise?* you'll ask the doctor. As a reward, you'll have years of shit and barf and endless sleepless nights of screams and whines. You don't even know what that noise will do to your nervous system." Vero stretches her legs, resting her feet on a shelf, and kicks a can.

It falls down and dings her square on the shin. She lets out a curse, grabs her leg and holds it before continuing. "But then, the baby will grow up into a teenager...who hates you. *I don't have to listen to you*, he'll scream. *You don't know anything!* He'll disrespect you and spend all your money and tell you he hates you. That's it: the pitch for kids. Who would buy that? How could you sell it?" She rubs her shin and lets her leg fall to the floor, drinks some more wine. It feels good to let all these words out. From now on, she decides, she will be this honest all the time. "Oh, there are good moments," she adds, to be fair. "Sure. Build that into your marketing plan—there are good moments."

God, Ian and Joss have a long voicemail recording. Vero can't beat it. Maybe they never answer their phone, just leaving people like her to conduct these one-sided conversations that they'll get around to when they they're in the mood. Maybe, with their shared reverence for silence, they'll never get around to it.

Vero thinks about what else she wanted to say, rubbing her shin where the mushroom soup has dented it. "Oh, yeah. It's Vero. Call me."

◊◊◊

By the time Shane and the boys get home from the pool, Vero is loose and warm on the pantry floor. She feels like that pile of clothes fresh from the dryer. *Ding! Brand-new Vero!* She giggles and cradles the second empty wine bottle to her chest. She listens as Shane prepares the boys for bed: teeth, jammies, stories. The standard protests at each stage: *But we're not tired!*

Vero wonders how long it will take Shane to look for her, to notice the pills on the counter, the steak knife on the floor, the open-mouthed beer fridge, the missing bottles of wine.

Her eyes are nearly closed, her cheek heavy against the floor when

Shane finally does come into the kitchen and stops abruptly in the middle of the room, stone still. She imagines him adding up the pieces: the pills, the knife, the booze, the quiet. *I'm good at math,* he often tells Vero. He won't like this equation.

When his body starts moving again, she hears it kick into overdrive. His feet pound up the stairs into each bathroom, his gait clumsy and panicked. She listens, unmoving, as he races to the garage, imagines his face pressed against windows as he checks the car, while she hugs her wine bottle. He's talking aloud to himself by the time he comes back into the house, a one-word prayer: *no, no, no, no, no.* He throws himself down the stairs to the basement, banging against the wall the whole way down. She imagines him panting like the pursued protagonist in a horror flick, his heart beating so forcefully it shows through his heavy sweatshirt. She know he's thinking the worst, praying *please, please, please* to a God he doesn't have time to believe in.

Please, please, please, no, no, no, no—in room after room, looking under furniture, looking up to rafters—*please, please, no, no,* racing through the house in a rush of air that smells like chlorine and kiddy-pool pee.

Let him worry.

When he finally slides the pantry door open and finds her curled into a small ball on the floor, resting her head on a bag of rice and clutching a wad of papers at her chest, she smiles up at him as if they've been playing an innocent game of hide-and-seek.

She watches as he takes in the empty bottle rolling at her feet, the other one cradled in her arms. She doesn't budge when he opens the door, and when he pries the paper from her hands, she lets him have it. She watches as he reads. Across the top, she's scribbled: *A is for Asylum: A Mommy's Alphabet.* Most of the verses are illegible or incomplete, but the ones he can make out, he reads aloud:

A is for asylum,
The place mommy would go to stay
If she didn't have her happy juice
To keep insanity at bay.

C is for the condoms
Your mommy shoulda thought to use,
They woulda saved her lotsa money
On her monthly bill for booze.

M is for martinis
Mixed while running at full throttle,
But smart mommies know it's easier
To drink straight from the bottle.

B is for the breakdowns
Mommies sometimes have to fake.
Sadly, it's the only way
They'll ever get a break.

"Not bad, hey, Shince?" she slurs, closing her eyes like a sick child on a wild rollercoaster. "Maybe I'll write that book one day after all. Just needed a closet of my own." She hugs her bag of rice. "When you left, I didn't hold such high expectations for this night. Poetry. Wine. Laughs. It's been a while since life has exceeded my expectations." Vero speaks into the bag of rice, the words so muffled that even she can barely make them out.

"Vee. C'mon. Pull it together. You're a mom." Mom: as if that one word were a suit of armour she could step right into.

Shane's words are steady and sure, but his eyes don't land on her.

They dart from one side of the pantry to the other, two panicked minnows in a clear plastic bag.

"I like it in here," she slurs, semiconscious, taking the crumpled papers dangling from his hand. "Smells like cinnamon." She clutches her poems to her chest and curls her knees until she's one tight period. "Close the door, please. *Vero Baby!* is tired."

CHAPTER SIX

Ligaya is moving out of her closet. She's endured her twelve months of servitude to Madam Poon and now has the one year of experience she needs to apply to the North American nanny agency. Of course, the agency fee is dear, well out of Ligaya's reach. But the same was true of the Hong Kong agency's fee. Or, even before the fee, the compulsory three-week schooling in the Philippines. To earn the privilege of paying to apply to Hong Kong to care for Chinese babies, the agency told her, she would have to learn the history of China, the language of China, the culture of China. Her Chinese employers, of course, have learned nothing about her language, her history, her culture.

Fine by her. Madam Poon did not deserve to know. *When the blanket is short, we must learn to bend.* Ligaya feels the skin of her mother's forehead against her own, her mother's fingers in her hair.

There are costs piled on costs piled on costs. And then there are the hidden costs. But Ligaya will get the money, again and however, because she must. It's a "necessary investment in her family's future." She's said this phrase so often in the last year that the individual words no longer hold meaning: the phrase is just one lump of energy pushing her ceaselessly forward into an increasingly unknown future.

It's her Sunday afternoon off, and she stands against the damp wall of *ate*'s Kabayan, sheltered from the heavy rain by a narrow eaves trough. She phones her Uncle Andres, named after the patron saint of fishermen, though he's never been to sea.

Uncle Andres most closely resembles Ligaya's mother, his full lips out of proportion on a skeletally thin face, with a neck so short that his head seems to sit right on his shoulders. But his thickly lashed eyes, the rich brown of coffee beans, detract attention from his less attractive features. Ligaya's mother is blessed with the same arresting eyes, and though Ligaya is too modest to say so aloud, hers are identical. Unlike Ligaya and her mother, Uncle Andres has tufts of hair growing from his ears. Ligaya will think of these when she asks him for the money.

As she engages Uncle Andres in small talk of home, she fingers the gold cross at her throat, her gift from Mister Poon. Pure gold, she thinks. After she put Hui to sleep on Christmas night, she retreated to her closet and discovered the small square of mango-coloured paper next to her mattress, this golden necklace inside. At the Poons' apartment, Ligaya wears the cross tucked deep into her maid's smock where Madam Poon will never see it. Ligaya has learned that she enjoys keeping secrets from Madam Poon. She focuses on the small pendant warm against her skin as she scrubs the scrawny witch's dirty clothes. "Yes, ma'am. Sorry, ma'am. Right away, ma'am." *You know nothing about my present, ma'am. It's from your husband and rests flat against my naked skin. Ma'am.*

Ligaya thinks this secret of the pendant feels almost like love, but it's not that. The pendant—its touch of something that wasn't hers and now is, even if it shouldn't be—gives Ligaya a rush of energy that reminds her of love. Something given for free: such acts of kindness are rare in Ligaya's Hong Kong life. But Ligaya has nearly finished with Hong Kong. Uncle Andres will give her the money. It's his business. He owns a money-lending company in Manila. He will give money to anybody who asks. The ease with which he parts with money is matched only by the steepness of his interest rates.

"Business is business," he says to Ligaya through the crackling phone line, "and family is family. Money, that's business. Always."

She pictures the nuggets of wax clinging to his ear hairs, the miscellaneous free-floating particles that have attached themselves to those dense bushes. Each hair contains a galaxy of life. "Yes, I know, Uncle. I will pay the interest. You needn't worry." People of her village say that a man with low morals has a horizontal intestine. Uncle Andres' intestine is maybe only a little diagonal.

Ligaya watches Corazon across the street with the other girls, bright blankets across their laps. They look demure and innocent from this distance, but Ligaya knows the blankets are props to hide their gambling cards.

Ligaya conducts her business with Uncle Andres quickly. If she lingers, she will think of the interest building on the money she already borrowed to get to Hong Kong. If she lets her thoughts go there, her legs weaken and her intestines turn to cold water. Corazon will have to pick Ligaya off the pavement and drag her back to the Poons' high rise. She owes Uncle Andres far more money than she's made in her entire life. More money than all of her family added together has earned, ever. But, she tells herself for the tenth time today, she just has to make it to North America—there she will find opportunity. That's where it is, everybody knows. Instead of thinking of money, she imagines telling Madam Poon she is soon leaving. Ligaya will spend her final weeks in Hong Kong sleeping late and eating whatever leftovers catch her fancy. Let the wild-limbed witch yell.

Before Ligaya ends the call, Uncle Andres tells her that he has visited Taal for business and climbed up to her hillside village to see the family. "Those American do-gooders have been over with their help again," he laughs, two sheets of sandpaper rubbing together at the bottom of his throat. "Thousands of dollars of toilets, carted across the ocean to a town that has no plumbing." The sandpaper rubs again. Ligaya feels obliged to offer a titter from her end of the line. *Those silly aid workers*, her tinny laugh says. Uncle Andres continues. "The Kapitan and Konsehal declared: 'Turn the toilets into planters! They will decorate the town square!' Ingenious. A big circle of shitters filled with red and yellow santans right in the middle of the village: an ode to North American generosity." The sandpaper has moved to the top of his throat, just behind his tongue, and Ligaya holds the phone away from her ear.

She's in the deep toilet planters with those flowers, dirt up to her neck, her face in full bloom. She knows the grating sound of Uncle Andres' laugh will haunt her for a week.

The rain falls harder and the wind blows icy sheets of it into her face. She presses her body firmly into the wall and puts her nose down the neck of her jacket. "But, you have to credit the crazy Americans this time: it's the first time their aid has not done actual harm," Uncle Andres concludes. "Just imagine! A whole garden full of shitters!"

CHAPTER SEVEN

"*We're* *getting a new nanny!*" Vero hears the way she and Shane say it, as if they're getting a new station wagon or a new fridge. A new pair of designer jeans. The sentence sends a shiver of displeasure down her spine. Her whole body clenches, the way it does late at night, moments before her babies cry, or after a crystal glass falls from the counter but before it smashes on the floor.

"I know, I know," she says to Joss. "It's...I know."

Joss holds Vero in her gaze. Joss's brow doesn't furrow. Her eyes don't squint. She chews her bottom lip and looks. Finally, she says simply, "It's whatever you make it, Vero. Be good to her."

"But who's my old nanny?" Eliot asks. "You said this is my new nanny, but then who is my *old* nanny?" His eyebrows squish together as he puzzles over this language trick.

"Nobody, Eliot honey, this will be your first nanny. First real nanny. Before this, we just had babysitters. Part-time nannies." All the fight has gone out of Vero. The Pantry Incident, as she and Shane call it, has forced Vero to admit she needs help. The degree of that need is, so to speak, completely out of the closet. In the evenings, after the boys go to bed, Vero works her way through nanny profiles. She reads out details to Shane as he grunts his way through his nightly floor exercises and avoids looking at him while he crunches and lifts. She cannot bear the desperation with which he fights this particular battle, imagining a darkly cloaked figure wielding a dangerous farming implement, looming above him and chortling, "Do as many abdominal crunches as you like, my sweaty friend, you're still on the one-way highway that leads straight to my house."

Within a week, she and Shane narrow the nanny field: no women with kids back home (that they couldn't handle); no women over thirty-five (how could a middle-aged woman keep up with these two "active" boys all day?); no women without excellent English (Vero and Shane want help, not a pet project). Their nanny will need as much of a foot up as she can get. Once Vero narrows the pile to six, she arranges an interview day with Bernie at the agency.

Bernie urges Vero to narrow her selections to three. "No sense wasting your time with so many phone interviews. Go with your gut instinct. You'll know." Vero looks at the pictures again and narrows the choices once more, picking the three women who look nicest. But what does "nice" look like? Maybe she just picks the three prettiest.

After dinner on the chosen Sunday, she passes the kids off to Shane. He stands over the kitchen sink with a beer mug full of orange Metamucil and water—the cure for some digestive issues, the details of which he hasn't, thankfully, shared with Vero. He looks at that mug of solidifying liquid the way he used to look at a smouldering joint just before he took his first toke, the anticipation nearly as pleasurable as the effect. *Shane Schoeman knows how to party.*

As she heads upstairs with the phone, he gives her a thumbs-up of encouragement and puts his mouth to the lip of the mug.

While Vero waits for the phone call from the Hong Kong agency, nerves rumble her stomach, a field mouse running laps deep in her gut, as if she's the one being interviewed. Vero uses the office above the garage because it's quietest. She sits on the floor in the window nook. She's rarely been in the office since having kids. She forgot about the view—one of the features that inspired them to buy this house—of rolling hills thick with trees and, in the far distance, just a glimmer of lake. "Waterfront property," they'd exaggerated when they first moved in, cuddled in this nook, sharing a bottle of Vero's favourite Malbec.

Mayumi calls first. Twenty-eight years old. She has three girls of her own in the Philippines and currently cares for an eighteen-month-old boy in Hong Kong. Shane and Vero agreed, in the end, to interview one woman with kids. Who were they to judge? What did they know of these people's hardships? Besides, Mayumi already lives in Hong Kong away from her children. Wouldn't it be better to allow her to live in North America where she could create a real future for her family? Vero looks at Mayumi's card as she talks to her and imagines that the weight of her life shows in the few thin lines at the corners of her eyes.

"Why do you want to come to Canada?" Vero asks, her mouth so close to the receiver she feels her own breath.

"Yes, I come, ma'am!" Mayumi sounds nervous, her words too shaky, too emphatic. Her thick accent makes it difficult to understand her, even this short sentence.

Vero feels uneasy about asking the same question again, but she and Shane had insisted upon this one point: they *need* someone with good English. They're bringing the woman here because they want help. It's not an act of charity. "Thank you. Yes. But, um, *why*, Mayumi, *why* is it that you would like to come to Canada?" Vero yells the one syllable into the phone: *why?!* She thinks of Gregory Schoeman's loud *What do you people eat for Christmas? Give us it all!* Again, she feels that sickening rush of energy up her spine and pictures a glass just before it smashes.

"I come now, ma'am. I come whenever you ask. You say come, I come. I do everything. I be what you want. I do laundry. I do bath. Food. Bathroom. Kids. I do all. I come. I make you life easy! I do all!" The words come fast, as if Mayumi has committed them to memory and practiced until she simply opens the crater of her mouth and they gush out.

The tentacles of Mayumi's desperation reach for Vero through the phone line as she runs her fingers across the office floor's berber carpet which, according to the designer magazines, is a shade of espresso— never merely brown. Shane recently hired someone to shampoo the carpet, and the soapy aroma wafts up at her. She studies Shane's bookshelves: manuals of golf tips at the bottom, bottles of scotch at the top, biking magazines spread out at its base, with articles such as:

The Highs and Lows of the Home Mechanic
Don't Be a Hard Ass: Finding the Best Brands of Bike Shorts
Descend with Confidence: Learning How to Go Down
Days of Suffering: Training Tips from the Pros

Vero's eyes water. She doesn't know why.

Vero does not know this woman, she tells herself, taking a deep breath. She does not owe this woman anything. But because she wants to be kind, wants to help, because she is generous, Vero gives her one more chance. She looks out of the window, framing her next question. Spring has arrived early this year, and the trees are already turning green. But she's been in Sprucedale too long to be fooled into optimism. It will snow again.

"Is there any particular *reason* you've chosen Canada, Mayumi?"

"I do whatever you want, ma'am. Anything."

Vero doesn't ask any of the agency questions, though Mayumi has likely memorized answers to many of them. She doesn't ask what Mayumi will do if Jamal refuses to eat his broccoli. She doesn't ask how Mayumi will respond when Eliot kicks his little brother. Vero knows she must be firm on this one point, about the English.

"Thank you, Mayumi. It's been nice talking to you. Goodbye."

The poor overseas connection makes it impossible to know for sure, but Vero thinks Mayumi's voice breaks when she repeats Vero's final word: *goodbye*.

Vero rifles through her small deck of nanny cards fighting off tears for this woman who apparently doesn't understand the simple question "Why?" yet wants to come to North America to make a better life for her children. *I know why she wants to come,* thinks Vero. *Why did I keep asking when I already know?* Suddenly, she's angry. Angry at Shane, at Bernie, at the Schoemans, at Mayumi.

She pulls Iska's card from the deck and places it on top of the small pile. Iska, the card says, is twenty-four years old with no kids and currently cares for two school-aged girls in Hong Kong. The card claims she has six years' experience. Iska looks younger than twenty-four in her picture; two long braids hanging to her shoulders, yellow bows tied at the bottom of both. When the phone rings, Vero already feels less optimistic; her *hello* is wary. Mayumi's desperation has blown a cavernous hole in the stage-set of this whole nanny operation. Vero can see the wires.

"Hello, ma'am. My name is Iska. I apply for your position. In Canada."

"Thank you, Iska. Thank you for calling. And why is it that you would like to come to Canada?" The field mouse increases the pace of its laps in Vero's stomach as she asks her question, again.

"I love to come there and help your family. I see pictures on the Internet. Very beautiful country. I hope to make home for me and, one day, for my family." Iska's accent is heavy, but not like Mayumi's. Vero has no trouble understanding Iska.

"You're working with girls now, I see." Bernie told Vero to always ask questions. Otherwise, the Filipina women won't know they're expected to respond. This sentence escapes Vero's mouth before she realizes it isn't a question. She tries again, "Do you especially like working with girls?"

"I love girls. I love to do their hair. I make braids and bows! So pretty! Girls always so cute." Iska giggles. Vero sees that she has set Iska up, posed a trick question. There's an awkward pause during which Iska remembers that Vero has only boys. "I sing them songs too. I love all children." She giggles again. "I do nice things with boys and girls."

"So," Vero reads from the question sheet provided by the agency. "Let's imagine you've taken my boys to a program at the library. Jamal wants to stay upstairs at the books, but Eliot wants to go downstairs and do crafts. What do you do?" Vero nearly adds that they're both screaming, Eliot's pounding his fists into his thighs and turning purple, and Jamal's biting her in the arm. But she decides to save that information for another time.

"I talk to them both. I use reason, ma'am. I be calm. I convince them it better to go downstairs now, ma'am, and then after, we look at the books." Vero imagines this girl in braids using reason with Jamal while his teeth dig deeply into her wrist.

The agency website admits to the challenge posed by gauging a stranger's compatibility and competency based on one overseas phone call, but also assures potential clients that asking the right questions (the ones provided by the agency) will result in "the good personality and philosophical match that are imperative to selecting the best nanny for your family." Vero hopes Iska isn't being as selective with the truth as she is. It might get in the way of the agency's promised "good personality and philosophical match."

Vero and Iska work through half a dozen of these questions—Vero reading the stock scenarios and Iska responding with the predictable answers. Mostly, they understand each other, though Vero knows Iska can't really imagine life with the Sprucedale Nanton-Schoemans (the "Baa Baa Brown Poo," song, Speedo Navidad, the closet of one's own) any more than Vero can really imagine Iska living in their basement. Vero writes a dark "maybe" at the top of Iska's card.

"You don't have children, Iska?" Vero holds her breath waiting for Iska's answer. Her card says no, but Bernie told her to ask. "Their situation may have changed."

Or maybe they lied? That thought blows into Vero's mind in one hot puff. *Then I will make them lie again.* Vero runs her finger along the pane of glass in the window, draws a flower in the condensation. It's too dark to see the lake in the distance, but she imagines it.

"No, ma'am. I will care for your children like they're my own."

Vero's field mouse turns into a twenty-pound rat and starts slam dancing. It would seem, according to Vero's stomach, she does not want another woman caring for her children as if they are her own. Not exactly.

"Thank you, Iska. It's been nice talking to you," Vero closes the conversation just as she had with Mayumi, but then adds: "We might be in touch. The agency will let you know. Thanks for your time."

"Oh, I hope so, ma'am, I hope so." Again, Vero feels the tentacles of desperation and backs away, grateful when the line goes dead.

After Vero hangs up, she lays on her back, propping her feet up on the window ledge. She holds up the last card. Ligaya. The card says she is twenty-six and single, working with a special needs child in Hong Kong. Her card doesn't have the same mug-shot quality to it as the other nannies' cards. Ligaya looks less like a trapped criminal and more like someone Vero might want in her house, cooking her family's dinner. Ligaya's full lips edge up toward a smile. She has soft laugh lines around her eyes.

When the phone rings, Vero nearly doesn't answer it. But she begins the interview by making small talk.

"Your name is very pretty, Ligaya."

"Thank you, ma'am. It means happiness."

"Okay, let's imagine Eliot and Jamal are in the bath. Jamal jumps out and runs down the hall. What do you do?"

Ligaya's been coached for this one, and answers instantly. "I never leave a child in the bathtub alone. I take Eliot out of the bath, and only then we go and get Jamal. Before the bath, I make sure to close all troublesome zones so I know Jamal cannot find any trouble."

Only someone who's never met Vero's children could speak with such confidence. She imagines Ligaya hauling Eliot—a hulking three year old who probably weighs over half as much as Ligaya does already—out of the bath. And Jamal will invent "troublesome zones" that will have this woman hitch-hiking home to the Philippines within a week. Vero tells Ligaya none of this.

But she feels a palpable sense of relief when Ligaya answers all the standard questions easily, with none of the frantic emphatic quality of Mayumi's replies, no giggles like Iska.

"Do you like to travel? My husband's family has resort property in Mexico. Perhaps you would like to visit there with us?" Vero likes the look of Ligaya, the calmness of her voice, the clarity of her English. She offers this hypothetical travel as a reward. She blocks the unbidden image of Drunkle Vince's bikinied ass high in the air, his face against the porcelain toilet seat.

"Oh, yes," Ligaya's voice has gone up an octave. "I would love to travel and see Mexico! I see pictures on the Internet. Mexico is warm with beaches, like my Philippines. Such a beautiful country."

It's unclear whether the beautiful country is meant for Mexico or the Philippines. Either way, Ligaya's high-pitched enthusiasm for heat and beaches worries Vero. She doubts Ligaya will find Canada so beautiful in the dead of winter. At the thought of the brown-skinned Ligaya who loves beaches stranded in Sprucedale during icy February, Vero is overwhelmed by a need to offer her more.

"Do you like hiking, Ligaya? I go every day on beautiful trails through the woods. You could come with me." Vero wonders if the neighbours would approve of this word she uses to describe her sporadic and loud barefooted bolts into the woods.

"Hiking?" Ligaya's voice wavers, uncertain. Vero has veered from the script. She imagines Ligaya looking at the administrator in the Hong Kong agency, a question in her eyes.

"It's a great workout. The hills—I sweat buckets." Vero realizes this description doesn't match the enthusiasm in her voice. "I just love it! Invigorating! Cleansing! You feel great after!" She leaps off the shampooed carpet with the force of each of her exclamation marks. She's an infomercial selling herself.

"Oh, ma'am, that sounds very funny. In my country, we sweat when we work. I have never sweat for the fun." There's an echoing pause on the line, and then she adds, "But if you like, I come with you, ma'am."

"We should talk about the weather. It's very cold here from November to April. How do you feel about winter?" Vero poses the question out of a sense of obligation, but then prompts her. "Are you excited to see snow?"

Ligaya picks up the answer that Vero hands her. "I love to see snow!" Ligaya's voice rings. "I love it very much!"

Vero's grip tightens on the phone as she imagines Ligaya staring out their living room windows late in February, stunned by the mountains of snow, opening and closing her mouth without making a sound. Just a mute oh-oh-oh. A cartoon goldfish. What could Ligaya possibly know about winter weather, coming from the tropical Philippines and having been nowhere else but Hong Kong? Vero might as well have asked her how she would like living in a moon crater.

"Do you have family?"

"In the Philippines, I have little sister and brother, Nene and Totoy. We live with my parents." Something in Ligaya's voice—a full-bodied grief so present and solid that it might be contagious—stops Vero from asking more.

"How do you like working in Hong Kong, Ligaya? Tell me about your employment there."

There's an extended silence. Just when Vero thinks Ligaya has hung-up, she says, "My employer is called Poons." She pauses again. "Hong Kong is very hard, ma'am. But I come here so I get to Canada. I nearly done Hong Kong now. I don't speak bad of my employer."

"We want you to be part of our family, Ligaya. Not a servant. Never that. I would like if you just call me by my first name. Just Vero. That's all."

"Yes, I will be like your sister. Your little sister helping you with your babies, Vero. I can be like their auntie."

Yes, an auntie. Vero smiles into the receiver. *It's her. The one.* Ligaya will be Shane's promised portal into an easy, blissful future.

"I have no more questions for you, Ligaya. I guess I'll talk to the agency, now. I'm not allowed to make an offer to you directly, but you will hear from us very soon. We will talk again, Ligaya. I promise."

"Oh I hope so, ma'am. Vero. I hope I talk to you again, Vero. I will love your family."

As Vero emerges from Shane's office, she feels heavy and jet-lagged as if she's just flown in from Hong Kong itself. She fans Ligaya's nanny card at Shane and extends her hand for a high-five. "She's perfect. She'll be here in six months. By the fall for sure."

Every muscle in his face relaxes. "This is a huge step in the right direction. You'll see, Vero Baby! Things are looking up for the Sprucedale Nanton-Schoemans. We'll think back to this night as the moment when things really turned around for us." He holds his arms out, and she steps into him, pressing close to his sticky warm chest. She notices the glow on his face and realizes he's just come up from the basement, from a workout with Cervella, propped on the wind-trainer. She holds her nose against the evidence of his workout. "You'll see," he says again, planting a firm kiss on the crown of Vero's head. She lets herself nod ever so slightly, but can't help picturing Edward's hairy knuckles rapping the hot water pipes of the anti-tank. She closes her eyes, shaking off her nagging questions.

Yes, but at whose expense? What gives us the right?

Chapter Eight

Trees and rocks.

Trees and rocks.

And then:

> more
>
> trees
>
> and
>
> rocks.

That's all Ligaya sees as her plane lowers toward Sprucedale. Nothing but forests and mountains, green and grey as far as her vision can stretch. Is this what opportunity looks like, then? Ligaya had expected something different. High sparkling buildings, maybe. Smooth paved roads. Golden statues. Something that looks like money.

In the terminal, the world swirls and dips around her, bobs and sinks. Her senses gulp, trying to take in this new place. Perhaps this spinning and whirling is what people mean by "jet lag," her inner senses lagging a step behind the external world. Or culture shock, it could be that. The nanny agency manual warned her of both.

The woman who meets Ligaya at the luggage carousel speaks no more of wealth than the trees and rocks. She grabs at Ligaya's hand, squeezes her fingers hard, and pulls Ligaya so close to her body that Ligaya hears herself squeak.

Wealth does not pull, Ligaya thinks. *Money never needs.*

"Ligaya! Hello! I'm Vero!" The words jump from the woman's mouth, the force of each practically lifting her from the ground. The woman looks a bit like Ligaya herself—her little body, her dark hair—but she vibrates. She seems to bounce on the spot, nervous as a hunted street cat. Ligaya expected this North American woman to look different—more like someone in the movies. Taller. Blonder. Redder lips. More serene. This woman, this Vero, looks small and dark and tired.

Ligaya knows she must say something by way of greeting. She opens her mouth, but nothing comes out. Her eyes feel dry as day-old chicken, her throat tight. It's been too many hours since her feet touched the ground. And she's dizzy too; her head thick with the transitions in altitude. She tries to shake off this cloak of disorientation, but instead she finds herself picturing Pedro catching a street cat, tying a noose around its neck, and slamming it hard into a cement wall. "Cats don't die easily," he had said, "and people have to eat."

Vero is trying again, less emphatically. "Welcome, Ligaya. You must be tired. You've had such a long trip. Did you sleep? Have you eaten? You had long layovers. Oh! You must be so jet lagged!" Her words pick up speed as if they run down a hill. She reaches for Ligaya's carry-on bag. Their hands brush, but Ligaya pulls hers quickly away. "Let me help you with that, Ligaya." Vero stresses the last three syllables as if saying Ligaya's name will pull her into this place.

"Yes, ma'am," Ligaya makes herself say. "Trip very long."

"God, this bag's heavy!" Vero slumps under the weight as she swings Ligaya's travel bag over her shoulder. "What's in here?!"

"My laptop."

Vero looks surprised, as if Ligaya should have arrived from the uncivilized wilds, trekked out of the jungle wearing nothing but bamboo sandals and a palm-leaf skirt.

"I bought it during my year in Hong Kong. There is many electronics there. I use it to talk with my family. If that okay."

"Of course! Of course! Excellent! Shane and I planned to buy you one ourselves!" Vero's eyeballs bulge with each exclamation and Ligaya feels herself flinch at the force of the words.

"Indian summer," Vero explains in the car, rolling down her window. "Hot, hot autumn. Roll down yours, too. If you want. Let's get some air in here." The vehicle smells of new leather. Ligaya knows the scent from the airport store, a bin full of brand-new Ralph Lauren wallets. Ligaya wanted to put her face right up against them. She held one in her hands, looked at the price, pretended she might buy it.

Ligaya cracks her window open. The air is heavy and humid. She expected her new country to be cold and has dressed too warmly. She unzips her heavy coat, a present from Corazon, peels it off her shoulders, feeling foolish.

"I didn't mean that to sound like an order. About rolling down your window. I mean, you don't have to roll anything down if you don't want to. It's up to you. I hope you know that. I mean, I'll never order you around. You should know that, right? Ordering's not my style. All that 'ma'am' stuff, too—not my style. We're all equals here. Being equals, *that* is our style." Vero nods quickly, keeping time with the words and looking at Ligaya sideways as she drives. Ligaya wishes the woman would just watch the road and feels her fingertips digging hard into her thighs as she stares at the oncoming vehicles.

The radio plays loudly, an upbeat song about suffering and loneliness, but Vero rattles along over top of it:

life will be so different here
you need something just ask
    democratic   *rules of course*   *but*
        must never, especially, let the boys boss you around
your home too.

She has two mouths. That's what Filipinas say of Corazon with her non-stop chatter. This Vero, then, she has twelve mouths.

Ligaya says nothing, just sits and sweats, moisture springing up on her chest and back until her bra is damp. She wipes the sweat above her upper lip on to her sleeve. Drops slide down her spine, pool in the roll at her waist. The world outside the windows passes, simultaneously too fast and too slow.

"These are evergreen trees," Vero says of the blur. "Ever green: they won't change colours. You can see the larch, though, they're starting to go. This hillside will be entirely golden within the week."

Gold. Like money. Ligaya smiles. She doesn't even know why.

Vero points out the other window. "And here's the amusement park, where we take the boys. Do you like roller coasting?" Vero swings her head around to look at Ligaya again, and Ligaya wants to take the woman's chin in her hands and twist it until she faces the road. "Up there's the ski hill. I know you won't have skied. We'll get you out there. Over here's the golf course. An old-people sport, Shane says. We're not taking it up seriously until we hit sixty. He has to golf for work sometimes, of course, like everyone. But we certainly don't call ourselves golfers. But you're welcome to golf. Then there's the strip mine." She points up the mountain. "Ugly. We try not to look there."

The road, the road. Please look at the road, prays Ligaya. The trickle at her waist has turned to a waterfall.

"And now here are the malls. You know Manila, so I know you know malls. This is where we'll find you, isn't it?" Vero winks.

Ligaya pictures her small home in the Philippines, with *ibong bahay* flying in and out of the kitchen as they pleased. The closest shopping mall was a four-hour walk followed by a thirteen-hour bus ride.

Ligaya shapes her brief answers to give no encouragement. She just wants this woman to watch the road, but still Vero's mouth moves. Eventually, Ligaya's brain will no longer compute the English. She knows she must look terribly blank, a simpleton. Her body has arrived in Sprucedale, but her mind is elsewhere; it's fallen off the luggage trolley in some foreign airport. She gives up and tries to relax into the warm leather seat. This Vero, in her tight blue jeans and her dangling earrings, will take Ligaya for an imbecile and send her and her single suitcase of possessions packing, straight back to Madam Poon.

Who will not take her.

Ligaya forces herself to nod at Vero's mouth, opening and closing. She picks up what words she can.

Boys, winter, lake, room.

Phone, family, Skype, food.

Ski, bike, boat, swim.

Ligaya smiles at the words she recognizes. Otherwise, she wonders if Vero speaks English at all.

In the driveway, Ligaya's jet-lagged swirl and dip turns into a full-fledged sea storm. She grabs the passenger door to steady herself, her nails digging into the leather. This house is as big as a hotel. The front staircase alone is bigger than Ligaya's home in the Philippines.

But children. Children she knows. Children are the same everywhere. "Eliot and Jamal," she says. Inside the front door, she reaches a hand around each boy, smiles until she feels her face stretch, knowing this moment is important. The older boy has cheeks plump as guava fruit and hair the colour of santan flowers basking in the sun. *"Ang guwapo,"* Ligaya's mother would say. Ligaya's mother watches too many Filipino telenovelas. She will bike for an hour to her sister's house for only thirty minutes of television and then bike another hour home. Her legs will ache for days after, but she will do it again the next week. She says any male who is not ugly is *guwapo*. Ligaya suspects she just likes the roll and pop of the words in her old mouth.

The smaller child is dark and slight. Indistinct about his features. Babyish, she supposes, as if he hasn't quite found his looks yet. He could be Ligaya's own son. People might mistake him for such.

"I am your nanny. Ligaya. I have gift for you. *Pasalubong.*"

"No!" Eliot screams. "Lee-lee! Lee-lee! Lee-lee!"

Ligaya does not know what this lee-lee means. She steps away, looks toward the parents. *Quick*, she wants to say, *he is turning blue. Get him this lee-lee. Lee-lee, someone, fast!*

"Sorry, sorry, sorry." Mister Shane steps between them, pulls on the boy's arm. "Sorry. Eliot is very … particular. He likes things a certain way. We told the boys that your name is LiLi. He's been expecting a LiLi." Mister Shane twists his mouth, cringes, as if his own words embarrass him. "We figured it'd be easier for the boys to pronounce. LiLi." He looks to Vero for help.

"LiLi fine," Ligaya says, to help them all.

"First we change your name," he blushes. "Next, we'll arrange you a marriage. We'll write you a whole new life before you know it. Just check in with us for updates. We'll tell you who you are." Ligaya does not know what to say. This is not in the manual. She looks to Vero.

"Don't mind him. He's joking. He's always joking." She swats him across the behind.

Behind him, red and white balloons are scattered across the floor. Eliot jumps around, gallops from one side of the room to another, throwing balloons over his head. "It's a party! It's a big party! It's a new nanny party! A welcome LiLi to Sprucedale party!" Each "party!" gets louder until Ligaya feels herself backing away from the wild boy.

She squats down and digs in her bag for the presents she has made on the plane—origami. She learned in Hong Kong. A swan for each child. She made them both the same so the children would not quarrel. She hands each an aqua blue piece of tissue with a delicate neck and tiny, fragile beak. She shaped each perfectly, distracted by the detailed work, as her plane roared over the Pacific Ocean.

"From me. I made these for you. The beautiful swan."

"Oh. We don't play with this kind of thing here in Sprucedale," Eliot explains as if he is the adult and she the child. "But that's okay." He kneels down to put his hands on her knees where she squats, and smiles into her eyes. "I know you're new. Mommy says it might take you some time to get used to it here." He puts the piece of folded paper down on the floor. For a second, he looks puzzled, as if he's forgotten something. Then his features clear. "Thank you, anyways!" He sings the words, smiles up at his mother and father, pleased with his own manners. "Thank you, anyways!"

Ligaya wonders if he knows what the words mean, and then feels a nauseous rush of shame. She should not let herself be stung by a child's words. But before she can dwell on it, Eliot grabs her hands and pulls her around the room, showing off each of his toys. "That's Yellow Horse. This is Green Cup, JJ's favourite. He also likes this toy—Little Baby—but I'm too big for babies." Eliot tilts the baby violently back and forth, showing how its eyes open and close, then throws it over his shoulder. "Some things you need to make up names for, and some things come with names already." He leaps across the room to a bin by an empty fireplace, reaches in and pulls out a handful of toy cars. "This car is called Lightning. It came with that name. This car came with no name. We call it Very Fast Black Car. We gave it that name. You can use my cars. You can borrow them, I mean. I'm very good at sharing. But not these cars. These cars are my favourites. You can use those cars, though." He points at a different full bin. There must be a hundred tiny cars inside. "You can use some of those. Whenever you want." He puts one in Ligaya's hand. It is jet-black and has no roof. The doors slide open. She holds it to her chest and smiles her thanks. "I used to live in mommy's tummy. I slept in there, way up high near her heart. JJ lived there too. For longer. He was more down by her bum. He only came out one year ago—he isn't two yet—that's why he still seems like a baby. He can't even hardly talk yet. But I can tell you what he wants to say."

Even the children in this family have twelve mouths. Ligaya will need twenty-four ears to keep up.

"He says hi. That's what he wants to say now. Hi, hi, hi." Eliot grabs his little brother's hand and waves it. "Hi, LiLi, Hi!" Eliot laughs. The little brother starts to cry. Ligaya reaches for him, thinking her work has begun. She will find herself in the work. But Vero scoops the boy easily onto her hip.

"Tour?" Vero throws the word to Ligaya like it's a life-preserver, hands the boy to Shane, and pulls Ligaya by the elbow out the side door. Then they are in what seems to be another house, though not as pretty as the first. The walls are plain, bare wood and plaster, nails showing in shiny neat rows. Ligaya wonders if this might be where she will live. Her head swims at the thought, *so much room*, and then she shakes it off. She should not be so presumptuous; her whole family could live in here. Her whole village would fit if it weren't for all the equipment, which lines the walls, clutters the floor, and even hangs from the ceiling.

Without the equipment, this could be a party hall. She imagines a village dance. Girls and children with their bright dresses dance in the space below. The men lean up here, sipping beer or gin and peering over the railing at the pretty girls below. Ligaya will dance until she glows, pretending the whole while that she's unaware of Pedro watching her from above.

"So this is the garage," Vero says. "Nothing fancy."

"Garage?" Ligaya repeats. In her home, a garage is an open-sided shelter under which one parks a car. She does not know what this building can have to do with that.

"Where we keep the car." Vero moves her hands as if they grip a steering wheel, lifts one hand and honks the pretend horn with force. *I speak English*, Ligaya wanted to say, *just give me the words*. "When Shane manages to keep his junk out of the way, that is, and leaves enough room for the damn car. All the bike stuff is supposed to be up here in the mezzanine, so the car fits down there." Vero points over the railing and rolls her eyes. Ligaya knows that look. Annoyed wife is universal.

Ligaya looks from the ceiling to the floor down the stairs far below them, lets her eyes bounce off all four of the walls. *A house for a car?* But she does not say that aloud. Bernie from the agency has advised her. "Watch and learn first. There will be much that is new. Nobody will expect you to understand it all at once. Give it time." Bernie has a funny way of saying things. *Give it time*. As if Ligaya's understanding is a wild beast, and she must feed it little bits of her life, in five-minute chunks, to tame it.

But even kind-hearted Bernie has not warned Ligaya of car-houses with mezzanines. Ligaya feels faint. Black pushes in at the edges of her vision, and she looks for windows or a door—somewhere for air. Maybe there's no oxygen in a car-house. Ligaya holds the mezzanine railing, closes her eyes. A car does not need air.

Only when she feels Vero's hand in the middle of her back does she realize there's no oxygen because she has forgotten to breathe. Ligaya opens her eyes, but Vero's face blurs until she has no eyes, no mouth, just a smudge of skin. Ligaya fills her lungs, and Vero's hand moves with her rising breath. "We call it the Gah-Raj-Mahal," Vero says, "Our little joke."

"*Mahal* in my language mean love. Or expensive. I will need to learn so much new in this country," Ligaya says as her vision clears. She's relieved to see Vero nod as if she understands.

Ligaya breathes deeply, soaking in the smell of rubber, and follows Vero down the stairs of the garage. Vero points at a rack with five bikes in a neat row, her nose wrinkled like someone has waved durian fruit in her face.

"How many bikes does one guy need? It's embarrassing."

Ligaya has not even recognized the scattered equipment as bicycles, hung sideways on walls and upside-down from the ceiling. There's a pile of bike seats in one corner and a mess of bike tubes in the other. A partially dismantled bike sits propped in the middle of the downstairs space, where Ligaya guesses the car is meant to live.

"Oh, so many bikes," she hears herself say, but then swallows the words as she learned to do in Hong Kong.

"Seriously, you're not kidding. He's got a winter bike, a summer bike, a townie bike, a country bike, a hills bike, a flats bike, a racing bike, a cruising bike." Vero's hands fly off in all directions, pointing out each of the culprits. For a moment, she reminds Ligaya of angry Madam Poon, a skinny scarecrow, arms flapping in the wind. But Ligaya forces her mind back to this place, one she does not yet understand.

It would be so much more pleasant to leave her mind to drift.

"That's Cervella." Vero's hand picks at something in her hair, as she glares down at a disassembled bike. "This one's his favourite. Do you bike?"

Ligaya nods as she remembers the fat-tire red bike. Pedro's. He let her borrow it to visit family in the next village. She touches her thighs as she remembers the feeling of freedom, covering such distance by the strength of her own legs, not minding at all when she had to ride home in the pouring rain, her sweat and the rainwater indistinguishable on her cheeks.

Again, she feels the uncomfortable vertigo of her body being in one place and her mind in another, the two so far apart.

But Vero does not wait for an answer. She pulls Ligaya—not roughly—her fingertips soft on the exposed skin of Ligaya's wrist. But Ligaya is unaccustomed to touch. Nobody touched her at the Poons. She breathes deeply and counts the bikes. She must not flinch, wills herself not to pull away; she cannot afford to give offense.

Vero twirls her around and points at a poster above the workbench. "That! Read it!" But Ligaya does not have to read it. Vero reads it for her.

> Since the bike makes little demand on material or energy resources, contributes little to pollution, makes a positive contribution to health and causes little death, or injury, it can be regarded as the most benevolent of machines. —Stuart S. Wilson

She pauses as if she might expect a response this time. She gestures at the room stuffed with bikes until it seems the very walls and ceiling are made of bikes, the scent of rubber tires replacing oxygen. "Ridiculous, right? *The bike will save the world*, he says. *Yes, but you just need one*, I say. One bike. That I can see. That I can even admire. I'm sure Stuart buddy here couldn't even imagine this … this … biketrocity. And that *he* should be to blame?!"

Biketrocity? The look on Vero's face tells Ligaya the word could be nothing but an insult. Ligaya says nothing. She will not smile. She will not even let her eyes meet Vero's, lest the gesture be mistaken for empathy. The nanny manuals are especially strict on this point—do not get involved in domestic disputes.

"Never take sides," advised the nanny manual. "*You must live with these people and share their home but know when to disengage, for the healthy functioning of a long relationship.*" Ligaya did not expect to have occasion to apply these rules so soon.

"May I see where I sleep, please, ma'am?" It is the first question Ligaya has asked and it requires a physical effort, as if she must push the question up and out of her body. "Please," she says again with less push. Her breath catches, and she hears her own voice, high and squeaky, the sound of a mere girl child. But Bernie told her—it is different here, not like Hong Kong, you never have to be afraid. So she meets Vero's gaze and waits to be taken to the place where she will sleep.

Down in her bedroom, giant posters cover the walls—children's pictures of snowy mountains and evergreen trees in bright sloppy paint. Adult's words in steady black underneath:

WELCOME TO OUR NEW NANNY!!!
WELCOME, LILI!!!

"I hope you don't mind," Vero says. "The LiLi." Her voice is soft. It is the first thing she has said slowly.

It's only my name. Why would I mind? Ligaya's eyes water, hot and fast. She blinks, wishing the tears away, hoping Vero does not notice.

She will not be one of those weak women who wear their tears on the surface.

Under the posters, she sees: a single bed with a rainbow comforter, worn but not ragged; a night stand; and a tall dresser with six drawers. Vero pulls each out: "A place for all of your stuff." Then she waves at a closet that stretches the full length of the wall, its hungry hangers waiting.

All of Ligaya's "stuff" could fit in a single drawer.

Across from the closet, the room has a window which looks out at ground level onto the front lawn. "Sorry," Vero says following Ligaya's gaze, "it's brown. Shane's given up on watering it for the season."

Ligaya nods. "Thank you." *Thank you for the airplane ticket,* she means, *for the tour, for the room, for the bed, for the drawers, for the hangers.* That's what she means. But she cannot make herself say it, cannot make herself put down her bag or step out of the doorway and into the room. "Thank you."

She gives her eyes a second run around, tries to think of it all as her own. A clock radio blinks unset on the bedside table.

11: 11   11:11   11:11

Next to it, there's a framed picture. Ligaya's swoop and bob accelerates as she tries to focus on the picture, unable to believe what she sees inside the frame. There, behind glass are Ligaya's mother, her father, arms around each other, leaning against the hood of a car.

Why? From where? These questions come at her with an angry force that she doesn't understand. Peering between her parents' shoulders, there on top of the car, sit Nene and Totoy. Nene's bangs still hang crookedly across her forehead, but the rest is combed into tidy pigtails that hang to her shoulders, bare in her sundress.

But what? What are they doing here? The questions rise in a fizz of panic, up from somewhere deep in Ligaya's guts. They sit hot and wet at the bottom of her throat.

Slightly apart from the others, Pedro leans against the car door. He's wearing his white tank top. His arms cross in front of his chest, his muscles glistening as if he's just shimmied down a palm tree. A cigarette dangles from his mouth.

Again, the oxygen is gone. Ligaya puts a hand to her chest, pushes, reminds her lungs to breathe. Now her eye catches framed pictures scattered around the room. All variations of the first. Her family is everywhere—on the tall dresser, along the window ledge, taped to the wall above her rainbow bed. She turns to Vero, tries to put the question in her eyes, cannot find the words, does not trust her voice.

"From your mother!" Vero beams. "She friended me on Facebook. After you signed our contract. I was so surprised, but she says she can connect from her sister's village sometimes." Vero pulls on Ligaya's arm and leads her to the nearby bathroom. More pictures hang from the walls. Pedro climbing a tree. Nene and Totoy playing *luksong baboy*. The whole family sitting down to a table filled with rice and chicken. "I emailed and asked her for photos. We want this whole level of the house to feel like home. *Your* home." Maybe Vero sees that Ligaya cannot speak because she keeps going. "I was surprised by the Facebook request. I didn't imagine your family having computers. In the Philippines." She gestures at Ligaya's laptop in the bag on the floor. "Not in a village." She picks at a loose thread on her sleeve, looks almost embarrassed. "I guess that was naïve. I know very little about your country. You should teach us."

Ligaya walks back to her room. Vero follows. Ligaya tries the phrase in her mind. *My room.*

I wish to be alone in my room.

Vero picks up a framed photo from the dresser, and Ligaya must fight the urge to grab it from her hands. She swallows so loudly that Vero must hear the grind of her tonsils.

"Who is the boy? The young man?" Vero smiles. Ligaya recognizes this smile. It is one she and the other Filipina women wore in the streets of Hong Kong, when they traded their secrets.

Ligaya's eyes run across the picture, but a door slams shut in her mind. She yearns for the warm breeze of home. "His name is Pedro. He is, how do you say, a neighbourhood friend? Of the family."

He is the other half of my heart. That she does not say.

"Ah." Vero still wears that smile. "Not a boyfriend, then?" She tilts her head one way, twists the corners of her mouth the other way, lifts her eyebrows.

"Oh, no," Ligaya meets her eyes, "not at all," but then lowers her gaze. "He has holes in his pockets, we say. Very poor. Like all in my village. He does not make a good boyfriend." She holds her breath for three seconds and says a private apology to Pedro.

"I'm sorry about the single bed," Vero says, bending to run her hand along the comforter, smoothing imaginary wrinkles, "and I'm sorry about the basement room. I hope it's okay."

Ligaya is too tired for apologies. She sits on the bed, wishes she could put her head on the pillow.

My pillow, she tries.

"And I'm sorry—there's no lock on the door." Vero leans into the wall as if she has no intention of ever leaving. "I know the manuals insist upon it, the lock. And it's in your…contract." Vero says "contract" like it's a curse. "But we didn't get around to it, and you won't need it here. This whole level is yours. Nobody else will be down here. A lock? We didn't want it to feel like a prison."

Ligaya fingers the small gold cross hanging below her throat. Nods.

"And I'm sorry about the grass being brown."

These people apologize a lot, Ligaya thinks, but she nods again. "Yes, ma'am, you said. It's almost…winter. No more watering."

"Come, let me you show you the rest of the house."

Ligaya says a sad goodbye to her pillow and follows Vero. The number of bathrooms alone leaves Ligaya reeling. She counts five toilets. As many toilets as there are people. And she will be the one to scrub them all.

Back in the living room, Eliot again begins chanting, "party, party, party!" Jamal squeals in his wake. But Ligaya turns toward the basement. When she finally says that she is tired and will go to her room to rest, she swears she hears her new bosses sigh their relief.

◊◊◊

Ligaya's mother's face flickers onto the small computer screen. Madam Poon forbade Ligaya from speaking to her mother. Ligaya has travelled farther from home to be closer. Her mother plans to stay all week at her sister's house to celebrate the renewed contact with her daughter. Ligaya reaches out to touch her mother's tiny face on the screen.

"*Kumusta*," her mother says. *Hello*. "*Anak*." *My child*. "You have arrived in your new home."

Ligaya nods but cannot speak.

"Now life will get better and better. You will see."

Still Ligaya says nothing, but she holds her mother's look in the computer, her eyes just like Uncle Andres' eyes, just like her own.

"Show me your new home, daughter. Show me with the camera. Take me on a walk-around." Her mother's sentences push Ligaya up and off the couch, propel her forward. Her mother will not allow her to stay in this motionless slump.

Ligaya lifts the computer and spins it around so her mother can see the whole room. "This is the sitting room," Ligaya hears herself say, finally, her voice her own. "A room just for sitting. These people have a room for everything." She's surprised to hear laughter in her words.

"Be happy then, *anak*. In Hong Kong, you had no time to sit, let alone a whole room dedicated to it."

One half of the room is filled with couches circled around a television, the other half with Mister Shane's exercise equipment. Ligaya walks her computer-screened mother through the basement, showing her the weight-lifting equipment, the laundry room, her own bedroom, her own dressers, her own bathroom.

"All your own?" Her mother's voice bounces.

"Mostly. The man will come down to do his exercises. And the children, Eliot and Jamal, can play down here when I'm working, Madam Vero says, but the rest of the time, yes," Ligaya nods. "All my own, Nanay." Mother. She smiles the word.

"Now! Isn't that better than a closet? Life gets better. See? You are a lucky girl. Don't forget to thank God when you pray tonight. I pray for you always."

Ligaya traces her fingers along Nanay's smile. "Yes, Nanay. I am. A very lucky girl." But Ligaya does not feel this luck. Not yet.

"Bye-bye, Nanay." She waves and blows a kiss and then pushes the red "end" button. Instantly, Nanay disappears back into Ligaya's old life.

Ligaya didn't ask after Pedro, Nene, or Totoy. As if knowing just how much Ligaya could bear tonight, her mother did not mention them.

Ligaya digs in her bag for a postcard from the airport. She bought one just for them with a picture of a moose. The big ugly animal drinks from a lake, its spindly legs barely managing to hold up its barrel of a body, its giant mug of a head. This animal will make the children laugh.

Sprucedale is my new home, Ligaya writes, *soon it will be home for all of us. I think of you every day and send my hugs, kisses, and prayers. Soon I will send real gifts.*

Love,

She lifts her pencil and thinks of how to sign the card. She remembers Nene's habit of crawling into her lap when tired. She'd tuck her fingers up Ligaya's shirt, fall asleep with her warm hands against Ligaya's belly, breathing little piglet snores into her chest. Ligaya also thinks of Totoy, his *tagak* cry for weeks after his birth, his mouth pointed her direction, opening and closing.

Ligaya puts her pencil back to the card and writes *LiLi*. Here, LiLi is her name. For now, she will be LiLi for everyone. She pictures her other name, the one from the Philippines, written in water, and then gone.

LiLi places the card on her nightstand. She will post it as soon as she receives her first pay and can buy postage. Her head has stopped spinning, but it is heavy. She rests her chin on the window sill. Vero is right. Shane has left the grass to die.

Tomorrow Ligaya will find the watering hose and see if it's not too late.

TWO

Ang taong walang kibo, nasa loob ang kulo.
She who does not speak has something boiling up inside.
— Filipino proverb

CHAPTER NINE

The change to Vero's life after LiLi's arrival is instantaneous. Vero has heard of depressed people coming out of it, surviving. They talk of a fog lifting, something wet and dense just rising off them, steaming right out of their skin.

It's not that. Rather, it's as if someone has changed the channel. There was static, then there is no static. The volume lowers. The sound clears. The main characters of her life come into focus. Just like that, the plot is discernible. She *gets* the jokes. She can follow.

Look, Ma! It's easy. She's a kid on her bicycle, coasting down a hill, feet lifted off her pedals, legs stretched out at her sides, an upside down V, a party hat. She's proud and relieved at the same time—as big and little as that. Sure, she's only doing what all the other kids in the neighbourhood do every day, but until now she was afraid everyone would discover that she was the only one who couldn't. For the first time since the birth of the boys, Vero wishes Cheryl would visit. Vero wants her mother to see her in this new, sane, grown-up life. They could drink chamomile tea, practice hatha yoga, discuss the latest Naomi Klein. Maybe Vero *can* be everything—with help.

LiLi has come in and taken over—the kids, laundry, groceries, cleaning, cooking—LiLi's got it all covered. At eight every morning, Vero and Shane sit down to a table set with sliced oranges, steaming scrambled eggs, buttered toast, a thermal *carafe* filled with fresh coffee. They asked for none of this, but LiLi does it. *A carafe, for God's sakes!* thinks Vero. Where did LiLi even find such a thing in this house? It must be an unused wedding present, dug from the dark corner of some cupboard, scrubbed clean of years' worth of dust.

"A carafe? Cool." Shane nods at the set table, impressed. "We just drank it right from the coffee pot before you came, LiLi. Sometimes we ate the coffee beans straight from the bag."

LiLi looks uncertainly from Shane to Vero and then back again before she lets the corners of her mouth rise in the imitation of a smile.

"He's joking, LiLi. Remember, Shane is always joking."

At the first of these breakfasts, Vero and Shane smile at each other stupidly across the sliced fruit and the steaming coffee, as the boys play with LiLi in the basement.

"Hi, you."

"Well. Hello there, yourself."

But.

LiLi does not look happy. This is the problem, the kernel of truth that nags at Vero during the early months. LiLi scurries about Vero's house with buckets of laundry that must weigh more than she does. She does three jobs at once, cleaning supplies in one hand, squirming kid in the other, and a load of wash on the go. She hardly speaks a word, and when she does, she ends every sentence with "ma'am." Vero tries to engage her in conversation about her transition to North American life, but LiLi simply drops her eyes and tells the ground, "Yes, ma'am, it okay. I like it. Thank you very much, ma'am."

Vero complains about Ligaya's unhappiness to Joss during their morning runs, Vero's breath fast and short, her words laboured. "Ligaya means happiness, for God's sakes." The words hang, a white frost in the winter air. Vero and Joss cover two full blocks before Joss responds. In her peripheral vision, Vero sees a white puff of breath with each of Joss's words. "You can't control other people's happiness, Vee. Be kind. Be empathetic. That's what you can do." Joss hardly sounds winded, so Vero forces her legs to pick up the pace.

After breakfast, Vero visits the nanny agency where she and Bernie drink espresso from doll-sized cups, stirring with sticks made of brown sugar. Bernie shares many of her Filipino quick-facts with Vero, all in the same nose-held tone—*I can't say it stinks, but let me make one thing clear: it stinks.* "When the Live-In Caregiver Program started in 1991, we expected workers from all over the world, but now we deal almost solely with women from the Philippines," Bernie tells Vero. "It's all about the right skills having passed from the conquerors to the conquered. Filipinos know how to serve. We like their English. We like their manners. Of course we do. They're ours. Our forefathers have done the training for us. They lessened our load. That's why people like Filipinos as workers. It's been bred into them through generations of subservience." Bernie's words carry a thick, sticky layer of irony. She makes it clear that while she has no doubt her statements are true, she does not condone them. Her tone holds the words apart from her, a soiled diaper stretched to full arm's length while she announces, *Yep, it's shitty.* Bernie speaks in a nasal drawl and twists her mouth when she's done as if there is something in there she can't swallow. She'll just hold it in her cheek until Vero's not looking and she can spit it on the ground.

"I just don't know if LiLi even understands me," says Vero. "*Yes, ma'am. Okay, ma'am*—it's always yes and okay. But then she does...things." Vero moves her hand through the air once quickly, as if waving away second-hand smoke. She waits for Bernie to ask what kinds of "things."

Bernie sets down her espresso cup but says nothing, so Vero continues. "She put my wool toque in the dryer. It won't even fit Jamal now. I had just left it sitting on a counter, not even put it in the laundry. We tell her, 'Keep the thermostat low; heating the house is expensive. Put on a sweater.' Then we go to the basement, and it's tropical down there, the dial cranked as far as it'll go. We say, 'Don't cook in the basement,' next thing you know the whole house smells like fish sauce. From the basement. She says everything is okay, but in the morning her eyes are all dewy like she's spent the whole night crying. If she would just tell me when she doesn't understand, just say *not okay* when it's not okay. Be honest. We can explain things more. We can help her. But she needs to tell us." Vero has finished her miniature cup of coffee and holds it out for more. She's no doll. Bernie fills it before speaking.

"Think of it, Vero. Communication is going to be tricky. Communication can be a challenge between two people who speak the same language, between two people who were raised in the same family." Bernie's eyes flit to the front entrance of the agency. She locked the door for their meeting, hanging up a "back in fifteen" sign. She now uses her eyes to tell Vero that her time is nearly up. "Maybe you need to lower your expectations."

Vero sighs and carries her empty cup to the sink in the backroom. She wishes LiLi would just tell her what's on her mind.

But when LiLi does finally say what's on her mind, it surprises Vero—not like a cake with candles, but like an unexpected gust of wind that nearly blows her vehicle off the highway.

LiLi sweeps the kitchen floor as Vero and Shane eat a beef and wild mushroom curry LiLi prepared for them. She has given the boys ice cream in front of the television, and the house is deliciously quiet.

"You can stop, LiLi. We're done work for the day now. Time for you to be done too." Vero smiles. "You work too hard."

LiLi moves the toddlers' chairs to sweep under the little table where Jamal and Eliot ate earlier. "It okay, ma'am. I just cleaning the boys' dinner table, and then I go to my room."

"Your dressing room, LiLi?" Eliot is going through a football phase and understands everything in its terms. In his world, LiLi plays for the opposite team.

"Yes, Eliot, my dressing room. I rest for tomorrow's game."

"Thank you, LiLi. I appreciate your hard work." Vero hates the constant gratitude in her voice, as if she can't think of anything more real to say and must hide behind the veneer of etiquette. She takes a healthy sip of her Pinot Grigio. "But I guess it is easy for you here, I mean, if the only other time you've taken care of kids was in Hong Kong. Here—better pay, better working hours, better treatment." She smiles at Shane as he tops up her glass. "Here, you have such a good relationship with these kids. Almost like having your own."

The look that crosses LiLi's face is one Vero has never seen before. It starts at the crease of her hairline and rolls over her face, pulling everything down with it. Vero hopes LiLi does not have the stomach flu. That's the last thing they need in the house.

"In the Philippines, we love children," LiLi says as if holding her breath against an onslaught of nausea. "There is no adults' table and kids' table." She pushes the little chair into the little table and gives the surface a harsh swipe. "In Philippines, there is only family table."

As if the words and their tone surprise LiLi as much as they surprise Vero, she scoops Jamal up under her arm and runs for the potty as if in response to some emergency.

Vero listens to Jamal screaming while LiLi sings the Baa Baa Brown Poo song and wonders if LiLi will ever be able to call this frozen land *my country*.

◊◊◊

The snow doesn't let up at all that winter. Skiers smile. Business owners smile even harder as tourists pour in from all over the continent. From the writing desk in the window nook of Shane's home office, Vero works—a new insert for the Piranha III—and watches LiLi push the boys away from the house, her face bent down away from the cold as she sludges through the snow, all her weight forcing the stroller forward.

"I never know cold," LiLi says when Vero asks. "Here the cold is until my bones."

It takes Vero longer than she imagined to get to know LiLi. She's embarrassed by her own naïveté, as if she believed LiLi would just move in from across the world and be an instant confidante, a help-mate, a friend—a sister. She pictures Bernie sneering at this. Vero knows now that she will have to work at this relationship. Sometimes, while Jamal sleeps and LiLi plays quietly with Eliot, Vero brings her stacks of LAV specifications and spreads them out on the dining room table. Checking last year's manual against this year's, she highlights suspicious differences. She makes sure the soldiers know to bend their knees and duck their heads. She does this work in the kitchen so she can ask questions of LiLi, can engage her. She will put in time and make LiLi a friend. Even in the privacy of her own mind, she no longer uses the word "sister."

"How are you finding the Sprucedale Catholic Church?" Vero taps her highlighting pen against the cannon of a diagrammed LAV-IV as she talks.

"It's okay, ma'am."

"You must be happy that you've found the other Filipina nannies and have made friends so quickly?"

"Yes, it's okay." LiLi pulls food from the fridge, piling it on the counter, but she pauses and makes eye contact with Vero at each answer. The effort is concentrated.

"You're bonding nicely with the boys. Your work is going well?"

"Yes, it's okay, ma'am." She spreads peeled carrots in a neat line on the cutting board. Eliot is watching *Cars: The Movie*. He is allowed only one hour of TV time per day. Shane and Vero have been firm on this rule. As they've become more comfortable with their employer role, they've admitted to themselves that rules are necessary.

"Really, LiLi, you don't have to call me ma'am. I'd prefer you didn't. Please."

"Yes, okay."

"Vero."

"Vero."

LiLi chops the carrots, moving the sharp CUTCO knife. Another unused wedding present. Shane pulled it from deep in the drawer when LiLi arrived, demonstrating its impressive sharpness by cutting a penny in half. Shane loves tricks like this, but LiLi looked mystified. "Why would anyone want to cut pennies in half? In Tagalog, we say *Sayang naman. Pera din yan.* It translate maybe like 'What a waste, this is also money.'"

Now LiLi moves it so quickly that Vero fears for her tiny, almost childlike fingers. LiLi races through carrots, garlic, onion, ginger, the rapid *click, click, click* of the knife's blade tap dancing on the board. *Be careful*, Vero wants to tell her, but the set of LiLi's face does not invite advice.

When Eliot's hour of TV time expires, LiLi lures him over to her with a strategically placed miniature football field of building blocks. Vero envies how easily Eliot comes to her and plays Lego at her feet. She sings to him while she chops. *Building, building, everybody's building*. All of LiLi's English songs are this one song, always to the same tune that Vero does not recognize.

Clean up, clean up, everybody clean up.

Eating, eating, everybody's eating.

Sleep time, sleep time, everybody's sleeping.

Vero gives up on conversation and focuses on the engineers' commas and apostrophes. "Just get these ones done pronto, Vero Baby." That was Edward's instruction. "We need 'em now. Nobody ever died from a misplaced punctuation point." The government requires an editor's signature. Vero is paid to give that signature. But she will read everything first—the instructions for the air conditioning, the high-capacity generator, the Caterpillar diesel engine, the MK 19 40-mm grenade launcher. That is her job.

She's happy to leave it when she hears Jamal call from upstairs.

"LiLi! LiLi!"

"It's so good to hear a new word in his vocabulary," Vero says to LiLi. "He has so few I recognize." Vero holds up a hand as LiLi makes a move for the stairs. "I'll get him. I'm sick of work anyway." Vero drops her highlighter on the dining room table and scrapes the chair across the floor as she pushes away from her manuals. "No fair, is it?" She winks. "You're never allowed to say that to me. *Sick of work.*"

When Vero returns, she bounces Jamal on her hip and watches over LiLi's shoulder.

"Mmmm, carrots, JJ. Can you say car-rots?" Vero holds the orange nub before him. He reaches for it but says nothing.

"Mommy, JJ doesn't say carrots. He's a duck," says Eliot.

"Looks delicious, LiLi. So much healthy food." Vero gives the carrot to Jamal. "Thank you." She mouths the words, slow and deliberate, to Jamal. "Thank. You."

"It's no problem, ma'am. I love to cook."

"Did you cook a lot at home? Seafood?" Vero strives for some image, however fuzzy, of where LiLi comes from, what home might feel like.

"We not go fish at sea. I live far from coast. In land. But yes, we eat fish sometimes."

"Inland? I didn't know that!" Vero's voice rises, and she cringes at her performance of enthusiasm, as if she's speaking to a child who needs to be lured into the adult world of conversation. "Are there mountains?"

"There are much rice farms. Very hot. We are near a river, where it is a bit steep, but very flat just below."

"What kind of food do you cook there?"

LiLi smiles into her piles of neatly chopped vegetables, "We eat rice and rice and rice."

"Would you like to go back?" Vero has asked this question in so many ways since LiLi's arrival and always gets the same answer: *It's okay, ma'am.* LiLi is a poem written in a different language, and Vero cannot translate her.

This time, though, LiLi pauses, her knife hovering as she tilts her head to one side. "I like to see my family. My mother is a teacher. My father a mechanic." Vero knows this much already, but LiLi says it as if to herself, summoning them. "But there is no work. There, it's so …" She brings her knife down hard across a carrot's tip. "So, I send my money. The government there, it's very …" She turns on the tap, scrubs hard at a pile of mushrooms. "But I work here and I help my family. So …" She turns off the tap, sops the remaining moisture off the mushrooms with a paper towel, and wipes her hand on the front of her apron, letting the silence hang between them. "I stay."

Everything Vero wants to know lives in the ellipses.

"You must be homesick," Vero says.

LiLi uses the dull end of her knife to sweep the mounds of vegetables into an oversized crockpot, another of her domestic discoveries. "Oh … I … it's … I like Sprucedale." She nods quickly, her face bobbling. "Very nice. I lucky. *Sa awa ng Diyos*, we say. Through God's mercy."

"Do you have a boyfriend back home?" Vero has hinted at this question before, but has never been so direct. She's seizing on LiLi's opening today, wants to force a story out of her.

"Before I left the Philippines, we were … There was a boy." LiLi bites her lip in an expression that reminds Vero of a different time. High-school dances. Dorm-room secrets. LiLi looks almost mischievous, for a second. "Then …" LiLi focusses her attention on an unopened can of tomatoes, and Vero feels the story slide out of her grasp. "Things change. I here now." LiLi looks like herself again. Closed. All the meaning is in the silences.

One Sunday afternoon, Vero sees LiLi in the Walmart with her gaggle of nanny friends, and she looks like a different person, wearing eyeliner and lipstick, laughing as she hides her smile behind her hand, an elbow looped through the arm of a Filipina woman. They load their cart with shampoo and cooking pots and running shoes—sending it all home for family—glowing with the thrill of each purchase. But when Vero steps close, their faces go blank.

"Hello, ma'am. Vero."

"Enjoying your day off?"

"Yes, it's okay. We like to shop." LiLi is polite but her face is distant and cold. She wishes Vero was not there, that is clear. Vero longs for that little crack of warmth LiLi showed to her in the kitchen. The biting of the lip, the near smile, the boyfriend confession.

The two women she's with look younger than LiLi. Their long hair shines and they wear too much makeup, reminding Vero of teenagers who put their faces on in a gas-station restroom only after passing the inspection of their parents.

Vero knows she looks a wreck. Shane has the boys, and she has just come from a run with Joss. She's wearing a Petro Canada toque she got for free at her last fill-up. No makeup. Grey, torn sweat pants. She knows she does not match the image these women have of a well-off North American lady. She disappoints them.

"Who are your friends?" Vero smiles. Her insides hurt, like they're being pulled in two directions. These women don't want her in their Sunday. She should leave.

But Vero doesn't leave, so LiLi introduces her to the others. *She must*, Vero sees Bernie smirking, *she has the social skills of the conquerors passed onto the conquered.*

"This is Lualhati. We call her Lu. She works with family on the west side. This is Jennalynn. She works for a doctor. They both nanny." Vero shakes the hands of both women.

"This," LiLi turns to her friends and gestures toward Vero, "is my boss." Vero is surprised at how much this hurts, this way of naming her. She turns away before they can see the sting.

◊◊◊

LiLi seems least closed when Shane is out and she and Vero have the house to themselves. At those times, Vero can imagine they might one day be friends. Vero can at least imagine that LiLi remembers their phone conversation, the promise from Hong Kong: *I will be like your sister, an auntie taking care of your boys.*

They sit on the double bed in Jamal's room watching him play in his crib. He doesn't cry or talk, not in any words that make sense, but he does not sleep either. When the rise to leave, Jamal cries, a whiny string of nonsense. "Wag ka alis! Wag ka alis!" They don't know what he means, but his distress is real enough. So Vero and

LiLi sit on the bed and look at him. "He's two now," Vero says. "We should move him into a bed. Soon."

You're done for the day, LiLi, Vero thinks to say. *You do not have to stay with me.* But she keeps her silence. She likes that LiLi hasn't scurried down in the basement the moment her work day ended.

LiLi smiles at Jamal. "You have good boys, Vero."

Not beautiful. Not brilliant. LiLi does not exaggerate. But from her "good" means more. "Thank you, LiLi," Vero reaches toward LiLi's arm, almost touches it. "I can see their goodness, feel it, more with you here to help me." She looks away from LiLi, sensing she's making her uncomfortable with so much attention. "It's true: they are good." Vero begins to explain what she means, but from the corner of her eye she sees LiLi nod.

What LiLi asks next surprises Vero.

"Do you find giving birth hard? Vero?"

Nobody has asked Vero that before. Shane was there so he doesn't have to ask, and Vero has no little sister. Cheryl had said all she would ever say to Vero about motherhood before the babies were even born. "My generation worked for a world in which women *could* do *anything*. Your generation misinterpreted that to mean that you *must* do *everything*." Vero remembers Cheryl wearing a turtleneck and corduroy pants that flared at the ankle, a joint smouldering in a Mason-jar lid on the coffee table at her elbow as she made this statement. But Vero does not trust this memory. It feels invented.

"Eliot was an emergency C-section," Vero tells LiLi, crossing her legs and leaning into the headboard. "That was like getting a package in the mail. There was no baby and then, suddenly, there was a baby. I felt like the arrival of that little baby had nothing to do with me. Even after … everything else." She has adopted LiLi's ellipses. All that is important lives there. "With Jamal, I had him the old-fashioned way.

I wanted to run through the hospital corridors screaming, 'Did you see what I just did?' I have never felt stronger. I told Shane, 'Let's have ten!'" Vero laughs with LiLi, who gets the joke: Vero cannot handle even two. "Shane was so worried that I really meant it, but the doctor told him to take me home, lock me up for a few days, and let it pass. 'They get it a bit crazy,' he said. 'She'll snap out of it.'"

Jamal burrows his face into his pillow while Vero tells the story of his birth, as if its retelling bores him.

LiLi watches these thoughts pass across Vero's face, waits. "It hurt very much, Vero?"

"Yes, it hurt. With Jamal. Of course, it hurts. Everyone tells you that. What they don't tell you is the feeling of accomplishment. I felt like Superman. Wonder Woman."

She stops to explain the North American cultural reference, but LiLi waves her off. "Oh yes. I know."

Vero forgets how small the world has gotten in some ways. "You like to have kids one day, LiLi?" Vero finds herself doing this sometimes when she speaks to LiLi, mirroring her syntax, sometimes even her accent—as if that will solve their communication problems. The more she talks to LiLi, the less she sounds like herself. It is stupid, she knows.

The stomach-flu look Vero remembers from the kitchen rolls down LiLi's face, and Vero doesn't know why, but she feels the cold lump of apology rising in her throat, almost opens her mouth to let it out. Then LiLi smiles, and her features lift back into place.

"I have a boyfriend in my village when I go to Hong Kong. Yes," she says as if telling the story to herself, checking off the key plot points. "I tell you about him—he is poor. When I go away, he gets close to my best friend. They get caught in the bed. Together. In my country, when young people get caught like that, they married."

Vero senses LiLi needs room to tell this story. There is something too private about her face. Vero cannot watch. She turns toward Jamal, whose lids look heavy.

"They have baby now. My friend and my boyfriend. Her husband. I—" LiLi's face breaks into laughter as if in anticipation at a coming punch line. "I the godmother. They ask. I say nothing. Nothing to either of them. But my nanay, my mother, say *you must*. She go to baptism. Substitute for me." LiLi shrugs. "Now I godmother. Life goes on at home. With no me." She performs a dramatic sweep with her hand. The flourish reminds Vero of a magician making a rabbit appear from a hat, but LiLi has made something disappear.

"I'm sorry, LiLi." The rightness of the words surprises Vero. She feels that rare click—the appropriate words spoken at the right time—and she says them again. "I'm sorry."

"Yes." LiLi pulls a baby blanket from the floor and folds it, pressing hard into each crease. "But now I in new country. You my family. You, Jamal, Eliot, Shane." LiLi places the folded blanket into Vero's lap. "Goodnight, Vero." Jamal has finally fallen asleep, and LiLi closes the door softly behind her.

Chapter Ten

"*Maybe* it's time we start our own family traditions." Vero hates her hypotheticals. Why not just say, *It is time*. Not *maybe*. She stands in the *en suite* bathroom wearing plaid pyjama pants and one of Shane's old football T-shirts. "We've never been on a vacation with just *our* family. Just me, you, and the kids. It's always your family's Mexico place. How about *we* have a holiday? Us?" She wishes she had saved this discussion for bed, where she could stroke her thumb over Shane's hip on each of the dual pronouns—*our, we, us*—her chin jutting out above the covers, the rest of her body pulled tight into his side, her head cradled in the warm nook of his arm.

Instead, Shane lies on the carpeted bedroom floor, sweating. He's recently bought the 100-push-ups app for his iPhone. It counts down his rest, and then he's back on his hands and toes, belly down, grunting. Toothpaste foams at the corners of Vero's mouth. "We could even go without the kids. Leave them with LiLi. Your family could help out. For one week. Have a second honeymoon." She wipes her sleeve across her lips, striving to look honeymoon ready. He continues to grunt through his push-ups, so she puts the brush back in her mouth. "Think piña coladas, think suntan oil, think quiet." Her tongue wrestles with her toothbrush to get these words out.

"Geez, Vee, take it easy on the toothbrush." Shane comes to a panting stop, rolls flat on his back. "You don't have to wage war on it every time you brush."

She looks at the bristles, worn flat, shrugs, and presses the tired toothbrush hard into her back molars. Cars splash by in the early spring melt of the dark street below their window. "Or maybe, you'd prefer LiLi came with us? I bet she's hot in a bikini." Vero doesn't know why she says this. She's never before mentioned LiLi's body. She has, though, thought of it. LiLi is twenty-seven and Shane is forty-two, the same age as Vero herself. How could Vero never think of that? *One house is not big enough for two adult women.* She won't say it aloud.

Shane runs his fingers up and down the newly solid lines of his abs, while his iPhone beeps out his rest time. His torso glows white. "You're cute when you're jealous," he says, but he's not looking at her.

If they were in bed, she would forget about LiLi. She would circle her index finger around his bellybutton, kiss the fleshy lobe of his ear. She would show him what this holiday could be. Instead, she spits toothpaste into the sink, noticing the beginnings of a ring of mould around the drain. She will have to give LiLi some time to do the bathrooms tomorrow. "Please." she puts all the force she can into this plea. "Let's *go* somewhere."

In bed, Shane smells like pine pit stick. Cheryl had kicked men out of her bed for less. Vero doesn't mind, though. She rolls into Shane's warm side and takes her turn running her fingers up and down his torso. He slides his hand into the waistband of her pyjama pants. "Missy Frisky. First you talk about a second honeymoon. Now you want to make more babies."

She laughs. It comes without effort. They have more of this softness, this ease, since LiLi joined them. "My will to procreate has died, but my will to fornicate—never." She swings her thigh across him, pinning him to the mattress.

Shane used to say there should be a horny bonus in any hotness rating. "Take a girl who's a seven. She's horny? An instant nine. For sure." He'd set his hands low on Vero's hips. "You're an easy twelve."

"Twelve out of ten," he says now, close to Vero's ear, rolling on top of her.

"What if this desire never leaves me alone? What if I'm destined to be one of those horny old women in the long-term care facility, strapped to my bed so I don't chase down the bewildered old men, trap them in a corner, and dry hump their legs?"

"You can dry hump my leg." Shane pushes his hands into the mattress on either side of her head, sitting up across her torso, his knees pressing down into her shoulders. "In fact, you can strap me to the bed *and* dry hump my leg." He grins. "But I get to go first." He pulls her shirt up over her head, and lowers himself into her, skin on skin. She lets go, her body melding into his.

A groan escapes her. She hears it as if it has come from somewhere else, as if someone in the street has stepped on a kitten. "Wait." She struggles to rise.

"Wait?" He pushes his heft off her. Her body expands in response. "What wait?"

"Baby monitor."

"Baby monitor?" He says the words like they are in a different language.

"Is it on? Downstairs? In LiLi's sitting room." Vero smacks herself in the forehead. "It is. I know it."

"I guess we'd better perform well then...If we have an audience."

Shane's mouth is so close to her ear canal that she feels his words.

She pushes against his chest. "Shh. I'm serious, Shane. She'll hear us." Vero's body is rigid again, her boundaries clear.

"We can be quiet," he whispers, lowering himself back into her against the pressure of her hand. "So, so, so quiet," the words move down her ear, toward her neck. "So…so…so…qui…et."

"Shane, stop." Vero is up, pulling on her sweatpants, her hoodie, her heavy wool socks in short angry motions, though she doesn't know where this anger has come from. "No."

"Okay. I got it. I'll run downstairs. I'll get the baby monitor." He's out of bed and into action. "I will destroy the baby monitor. I will smash the baby monitor into a thousand pieces. There will be—" he strikes a heroic naked pose, standing on one foot, the other stretched behind him. She turns her eyes away from the clear evidence that retrieving the baby monitor is the last thing he wants to be doing. "—no more baby monitor!" He jerks on his T-shirt. "Just hold that thought."

But Vero has already lost the thought. "Put some pants on there, Super Shane. Your magic wand's showing."

He tugs his shirt below his hips, holding it stretched down his sides as he races out of the room to the stairs.

"God, Shane, put on some pants," she shouts after him, but he's gone.

Vero slithers her head under her pillow. It's just too easy to forget that LiLi is in the house, until she remembers, and then it's impossible to forget. This afternoon, Vero set a globe on the counter and spun it once. "Okay, Eliot, show me where your nanny comes from."

He twirled the world again with his two middle fingers, Australia and North America flying past in quick succession, then he palmed the ball in his left hand, a miniature God. His pointer landed firmly on the Philippine Islands.

"LiLi." He stared as if he could see her there, if only he tried hard enough.

"LiLi," Jamal repeated and reached for the globe. Vero expected him to knock it off the table with his clumsy toddler limbs. She already heard the crashing, saw the broken pieces of land and ocean scattering across the floor. Instead, he leaned in, slowly traced a circle around the island and petted it. "LiLi," he smiled. Even for Eliot and Jamal, the biggest part of LiLi remained in the Philippines.

By the time Shane returns, baby monitor in hand, Vero is curled on her side in the hazy limbo between sleep and wake. "Mmm, Shane, sleeping," she murmurs from that other world.

He slides his hand under her heavy sweat shirt, his fingers tracing swirling circles just above her hip bone, the spot he knows she's most ticklish. "What about we start that second honeymoon now?" He touches his nose to hers, and she imagines Eliot giggling, *Eskimo kisses!*

"I can't, Shane. It's hard to concentrate. With someone else in the house. I can't focus."

"You just lie there then. I'll focus for both of us." He pushes her shirt up with both hands and his mouth is on her ribs tracing a swirling path down. With her body rigid, her desire gone, this suddenly seems like a ridiculous thing to do.

"Shane. Don't. I'm serious." She palms his forehead, pushes.

He falls heavily onto his back, staring at the ceiling like he did between his set of push-ups, only now there's no panting. Guilty, she sets her hand on his arm.

"I love you," Shane says into this new kind of silence. His sentence lifts up at the end. A question reaching toward her.

"Sorry, Shane. I know. Doesn't it just seem weird sometimes? Someone else living in our house? Taking care of our children? Here. All the time."

"Vero, don't." A distance opens between them without him moving. Neither of them speaks again until morning.

◊◊◊

Both Vero and Shane turn forty-three in April. Vero opens a card from Cheryl showing a haggard woman with a two swimming-pool sized glasses of wine. Inside it reads: "As we get older, we should limit ourselves to just a couple of glasses of wine on our birthdays." Cheryl has scrawled: "I hope you feel real good on your birthday. Take some time for yourself. Love, C." A crisp fifty-dollar bill falls to the floor when Vero opens the card.

"Well," Vero says, closing the card. "It should be: I hope you feel well. Not good."

"Cheryl means no harm, Vee," Joss says in her Joss way when Vero complains over the phone. "Imagine her as a child. Picture her that way. Be as gentle and generous with her as you would be with Eliot."

But there's no energy in Joss's words this time. She has her own worries. The cost of living in Sprucedale has climbed dramatically in the last few years since it has become a popular destination for tourists. *Sprucedale: Where the Living Is Good.* Now that the whole world knows how good that living is, it comes with a price tag as steep as the skiing terrain. Joss and Ian have finally had to admit they can't afford their lifestyle—can't even afford their boys' hockey fees—and Joss has taken a job at the mine. "My parents disapprove. In their own quiet way. *An environmentalist at the mine? Oh, Joss, is this what you want?* I tell them unless we're all done using coal, we're hypocrites to blame the mines."

These days, Joss has enough trouble finding compassion for her own parents—or for herself. Her efforts on behalf of Vero are weak.

And with an early-morning start at her job, their sunrise runs have come to an end. Vero misses them.

To celebrate Shane's forty-third birthday, Vince brings his new girlfriend Adele over for a dinner party. Vince met Adele at a local comedy club where he performs every Wednesday. Adele tends bar there on the three nights a week that her ex takes the kids. Over dinner, Adele runs her finger up and down the knife tattooed on Vince's forum, and they lock eyes in a way that makes Vero think of the fantasy pail that Shane and she started when they first moved in together, a glass Mason jar filled with little squares of paper, secret wishes scribbled on each. On a slow night, they would pull out the fantasy pail. *Voilà!* Anything could happen. Now the jar sits buried deep in the sock drawer, the little squares curling and brown around the edges.

S is for the sex toys
Disintegrating to dust.
The filthy house and nonstop whines
Have cured your mom of lust.

When Adele moves into Vince's lap at the conclusion of the main course, Vero excuses herself and goes to help LiLi with the dishes. *We have enough chairs for everyone*, Vero wants to say. *We're real adults. This is not a Cialis commercial.*

Vero tries to imagine Adele tearing her hair and storming into the woods, barefoot and shrieking, back in her first marriage when her kids were young and her relationship was old. Vero feels sure that Vince and Adele don't have fights like that now.

In the kitchen, Vero picks up a tea towel and stands next to LiLi. She thinks of herself as taller than LiLi, but shoulder-to-shoulder, she remembers they are nearly the same height. "I'm sorry things are loud in there, LiLi, and it's getting late. Shane thought it would work well—to pay you overtime and have you serve for the celebration. But it's weird. I know it is." Vero takes a plate from LiLi and wipes in slow steady circles. "You're not a servant. You care for our children. That is your job."

"That's okay," LiLi doesn't look up from her soapy suds. "I know it's not Canadian way. But I was called *servant* in Hong Kong all time. My job not that different here. It's okay."

They work next to each other without speaking for several minutes before LiLi raises her face to Vero's. "You no need to help me, Vero. You like maybe to visit with your friends."

Those are not my friends, she wants to say. Shane's party. Shane's brother.

Adele and Vince took up CrossFit as a New Year's resolution. Her body is tight and hard. And beautiful. Well aware of her own beauty, Adele wears as little clothing as possible, her muscled arms and shoulders and back on display for all. Vero is tired of Adele's beauty.

"I like to visit with you right now." Vero hears herself falling into her annoying habit of adopting LiLi's syntax. She tries again. "When's your birthday, LiLi? Remind me. We'll have a family celebration." Vero reaches for another dish, dripping in LiLi's hands. There's a cake on the side table. LiLi made it this afternoon, carrot cake with cream cheese icing, Shane's favourite. A wax 4 and a wax 3 are speared into the top, waiting to be lit on fire.

Adele calls from the dining room—"The party's in here, Professor Nanton!"—but Vero doesn't answer.

"I'm not a professor," she says to LiLi. "She's copying Vince. He says that. To be mean." She expects LiLi to ask why "professor" is a mean thing to call her, but LiLi asks nothing.

"My day of birth is in August. But we don't do birthday like this."

"No cake and candles? No celebration and wine?" A rhythmic splashing fills the pauses between their questions, soothing compared to clanking cutlery in other room.

"Oh, no," LiLi laughs, and then covers her mouth. "No. Not like this."

Vero waits for LiLi to explain how they celebrate in the Philippines, but she says nothing. She focuses on her task as if she's forgotten Vero is even there.

"How does your family mark a birthday then, LiLi?"

"Oh, we take whatever we having for dinner. Maybe, you know, chicken," LiLi searches for the words. "And when we kill it—" Her brow furrows. "When we butcher it." She holds up her hands and snaps like she's breaking a twig. "We spill some blood on the ground. Like that." She sprinkles imaginary blood on the kitchen floor. "Then we say some words for the birthday person. For special birthday, the family and friends—sometimes the whole village—have a party. Maybe cake and games for children. Maybe singing for adults. That's how."

In the other room, they've broken into a rowdy chorus of Happy Birthday to Shane. They'll want the cake now, but still Vero lingers. LiLi scrubs hard at a big pot, rice brown and burned to the bottom.

Vero's shirt cuffs are wet, and she pushes her sleeves up to her elbow. She holds the counter with both hands. She needs either to drink more or to go to bed.

Adele's voice bursts into the kitchen again. "You sure you want to be leaving me alone in here with these two gorgeous men, Vero?" The words are so loud that it seems Adele has entered the room and yelled the question in Vero's ear.

Vero folds her tea towel neatly, hangs it over the oven door handle.

"You should join us for cake, LiLi. I'll get the candles. It looks delicious. Thank you. For it."

LiLi scrubs hard, her gaze directed at the water. "I hear your conversation. A while ago now. On the baby monitor."

Vero feels a hard twitch deep in her wrist, imagines the pulse breaking through her thin skin. She says nothing. LiLi must interpret silence as lack of comprehension because she clarifies. "What you said about...me...in bikini...jealous." LiLi lets the pot sink into the suds and meets Vero's eyes. "Madam Poon in Hong Kong is like that. She yells at me all day. They are jealous. The employer there think their husbands look at us. We are younger. Some think Filipina women very pretty." LiLi drops her eyes back to the water, tucks a loose piece of dark hair behind her ear.

She *is* pretty.

"But different in Canada. You don't think that. I hope not."

"I'm sorry, LiLi." Vero holds two fingers against the inside of her own wrist, pushing the rogue pulse back into its place. "I didn't mean for you to hear that conversation. I barely remember it. I was...I'd been drinking. Too much." Vero doesn't know why she says that. It's not true.

"Yes, I thought maybe that. I never wear a bikini."

"It's an ugly habit. Drinking. Do you drink, LiLi?"

"No. In the Philippines women don't drink so much like here." Again, LiLi speaks in the present tense, as if she still lives there. "Maybe just my father drink. Men like the beer in my home."

Adele calls again. "If I have to come in there and get you myself, Professor Vee, it's not going to be pretty. This wine is not going to drink itself." *Professor*. It is Vince's insult. Adele uses it with no understanding of the complexity of its meaning, the layers of the insult, its assessment of Vero's failed life. *Adele*, thinks Vero, *is the conquered using the language of the conqueror.*

"I'm coming! Give me a minute!" Vero's voice sounds breathy, frazzled, like she's been caught in her bedroom with a lover. *Just a second, honey, I'll be right down*—zip, zip, button, button.

"There's so much I don't know about the Philippines. About your life. Maybe you can tell me more." Vero touches LiLi's shoulder lightly, and steps away, toward the party. "Some other time, when Ma'am Adele is not waiting." Vero winks on the "Ma'am" and has her best moment of the evening when she sees LiLi press her lips together to stop herself from laughing.

CHAPTER ELEVEN

Vero's life now fills up in the way that only obsession can fill it. Bikram yoga, that's her new thing. In the wake of losing her morning runs with Joss, she spends her time in a 105-degree Fahrenheit room with forty-percent humidity, pushing her perspiration-stung eyeballs toward her slippery wet shins, her nose nearly lowered to the greying carpet soaked with years' worth of human sweat. This is not the yoga of Vero's youth—Cheryl and her circle of women meeting somber-faced every morning before sun-up as if they could save the world through deep breathing and hydration, wearing gauchos and bandanas and chanting in the living room, drinking an ocean's worth of chamomile tea after each practice. No, Bikram is something else entirely, and it belongs to Vero.

"Oh, Vee, you don't want to do Bikram. Really. You have too much heat. You carry it in your abdomen, your chest." The earnest tone of Cheryl's entreaty grated against Vero's eardrum, and she held the phone away from her head until she could barely make out Cheryl's next sentence. "You have high metabolism. Like me. You need something cool and slow. Too much heat will just make you aggressive and bitchy."

"Actually, *Mom*, I like it. The Bikram yoga. Quite a lot."

With the increased time and energy to focus on work that LiLi provides, Vero has come to realize that the engineers don't care if she fixes their punctuation. They don't even care if she fixes any of their other errors. They have no idea what the manuals look like once they're translated to Arabic: why should they care if they're perfect in English?

"We need you here full-time for the next while," says Edward. "A whole slew of government inspections coming up." He suggests that Vero bring *National Geographic* magazines to read during the downtimes. It's what the last editor did. "We need you around. For the regulations. The signing-off. But our guys know the machines. Make yourself look busy. Be there when we need your autograph." He even shows her how to slide a *National Geographic* under manual pages so nobody will notice if they walk by her cubicle. "I've done it now and then myself, Vero Baby!"

Vero's work does not matter one bit. What the engineers are after is her signature. So she gives it to them.

No changes required
—V.N.

She swirls the vowels so they're barely legible, the way Cheryl taught her when she got her first chequebook at sixteen. "If you have a signature that can be copied, you're just asking for forgery and fraud." According to Cheryl, Vero "just asked" for a lot of things. As an adult, Vero understands this as the primary message of her upbringing: *Don't trust anyone.*

If Edward wants to tour her around the floor, pointing out the newest features on the latest tanks, she lets him. In a booming voice, he instructs her on the minute but significant differences between feature models. She lets the words pass through her. *Swiss Mowag, US Stryker, Canadian Leopard 2A4, Vero Baby.* She's numb to his curses, his sexist exclamations, his commentary on the "Eee-rabs" and their aversion to "cunts." She pretends she's watching a television show, the volume low, while she directs her thoughts to inner, invisible concerns. She wonders, for example, how long it has been since LiLi has had sex.

Shane has told her to stay out of LiLi's private life. "We meddle in LiLi's life enough. Let's leave sex out of it."

"But sex is a metaphor," Vero argues. "LiLi's sex life—or lack thereof—is a way to think about her personal sacrifice, desire, agency, bodily identity."

Shane finds it laughable when Vero talks like this. "A metaphor," he smiles. He and Joss—the scientists—have this in common. "Quit talking like an English major," they like to say in unison. Ian joins in too when he is there. They all gang up on her. The scientists.

"Vero," Shane says this time, with only the slightest trace of patience, "sex is *not* a metaphor."

That's what Vero thinks about as Edward explains the design flaws on the new anti-tank. "Soldiers have to be quick when they release this bugger or the fucker here will swing right back and cut off their goddamn heads." Sex and metaphor.

Yoga has taught her this detachment.

She's getting quite good at it.

After her meetings with Edward, she rewards herself with an organic rooibos low-fat soy latte, but always drinks two cups of water for every one cup of diuretic. "The major cause of depression is a lack of water attacking the liver and disabling the body," the head instructor, a man named Roger, told them before the last Bikram class, his face so stony that Vero was able to take him seriously despite his pink Lycra shorts. "Dehydration is deadly. Drink water." He jumped with both feet up onto the instructor's block, his knees nearly pounding into his face. "Before class and after class, drink. But not during class. During class, you drink only when I say."

In early May, the snow melts for the fourth time that spring, and the ground finally dries. Vero drinks water in long, deliberate swallows, sitting on the grassy hill in the backyard. She and LiLi watch the kids play in the new warmth. In the spring sun, LiLi's face opens like a blooming flower. In the winter, her skin was sallow with a faint line of acne just under her cheekbones. Now her full cheeks blush pink, her coffee-brown skin complementing her white smile. She holds her bare arms out in front of her, open to the sun's caress. "Ah," she smiles. "Yes."

She's not built for this harsh climate, Vero thinks. *She will be happier now, with winter done.* "Last week, I met a man I know from the Philippines," Vero tells her.

Vero doesn't know what makes her tell LiLi about her encounter with the man at the coffee shop or why she lies and says it only happened last week. Maybe it is the new openness in LiLi's face, maybe the warmth on her own arms. "Lito," she continues, "who came here to work in a restaurant. He told me he had to leave his wife and children at home." She doesn't tell Ligaya about the crack in his voice or how quickly he regained his composure and took her order with a smile. "I asked him if he missed his country," Vero says putting a hand on LiLi's knee. She means it at as a gesture of kindness, of understanding, but LiLi stiffens under her touch, and Vero pulls her hand away. The neighbour revs up his lawnmower. He wears an oversized yellow ball cap propped high on his head and aviator sunglasses. He pulls off his shirt, tucks it into the back of his shorts, and starts pushing. He's young, maybe twenty-three, and cute. Vero wonders if LiLi will turn to watch him. The scents of fresh grass and gasoline fill the air, but LiLi does not turn to it. "He said, 'Every day. I miss my Philippines every single day.'" He'd sighed when he said it, as if he released actual physical pain with the admission. There was a hint of gratitude in his eyes, as if he believed that Vero, a stranger, could carry some of that pain for a while. She'd heard similar sounds come from her own body in the Bikram classes.

Vero says no more to LiLi about her exchange with Lito. She waits, applying the pressure of silence to force a response from LiLi, some confession that might release the pain Vero imagines beneath each of LiLi's movements. *I too miss my home.* Vero wants to hear it aloud. Maybe she thinks the admission will be an invitation to help, to comfort. Vero tries to imagine what LiLi was like in Hong Kong, pictures her in the streets chattering away to her Filipina friends. Vero's stomach does a familiar clumsy flip when she thinks that perhaps it is the "land of opportunity" that has silenced LiLi. The possibility that a multidimensional LiLi, who Vero searches for, has not yet found her way here—that possibility frightens Vero.

Eliot bounds toward them like a St. Bernard puppy, his oversized feet getting in his own way. "JJ-Bean and I used to live in Mommy's tummy. We told stories in there." He flops himself across LiLi's outstretched legs and pulls her arm across his face to shade his eyes. Vero clasps her hands in her own empty lap as LiLi giggles and throws a handful of grass in Eliot's moppy hair. "Jah, jah, jah," she says, imitating Eliot's odd German inflection, "You tell me this story so many times before, my Eliot." There's a dimple deep in LiLi's right cheek, one Vero rarely sees when they are alone. The boys touch something in LiLi that Vero cannot.

"The doctor cut Mommy open," Eliot continues, brushing the grass out of his hair and scrunching his nose against the tickle of it on his face, "and took me out of her belly in a surbery."

"Surgery," Vero says, grabbing his sneakered toe and squeezing.

"Jah. Right. A *sur-jer-y*. I didn't want to come out by myself. I even tried, but I couldn't. The doctor had to come get me. But Jamal, he came flying out of Mommy's penis so fast he almost hit the wall, so fast he forgot to breathe." Eliot stops, wide-eyed in the wake of his offering. He looks like he expects applause. "He probably came out so fast because he missed me in there."

"Eliot," Vero says with an embarrassed smile at LiLi. "I don't have a penis."

"Oh, yeah!" Eliot lets out a hot huff of laughter. "Your vagina. Sorry, I forgot."

Oblivious to his big brother's story, Jamal lays stomach down pulling petals off daisies. Vero thinks to stop him. The spring flowers are so pretty, his movements quick and cruel. But Vero remembers Cheryl's hatred of daisies. *An invasive species*. She's passionate about gardening now, and Vero wonders if she turned to plants to fill the space created when the final man packed up his suitcase and left her bedroom. Cheryl's front yard is thickly overgrown with local vegetation bearing Latin names—*Sempervivum, Sedum, Stachys*—and with violets, pansies, and petunias thrown in to provide colour. "A lovely hobby, I suppose," Heather Schoeman had said when she saw Vero send gardening books to Cheryl for Christmas. "I wouldn't have minded taking it up myself. I never did, mind you. People did that work for us in South Africa, you see."

Cheryl spends her days in the garden on her knees, weeding, planting, and pruning. In her dirty overalls and oversized Tilley hat strapped under her chin, she's androgynous, nearly impossible to reconcile with the Cheryl of Vero's teen years, the Cheryl who played

Vero's big sister on "family holidays" where the resort staff encouraged this delusion. "Mother—no! Sister, yes, I believe that. Same beautiful eyes. But mother and daughter? Too impossible!" The young men would sit skin-to-skin with Cheryl for the rest of the night, while she paid for their Cuba Libres. This is the Cheryl who still dominates Vero's recollections, but if she squints hard enough to hold her memories at bay, she can see what she otherwise misses: Cheryl is an old woman now. A relic. A curious remnant of a time that has come and gone.

The sun has roasted Eliot's nose and cheeks. They're the colour of steak, medium-well. But he runs off before Vero can accost him with sunscreen. Without his rambling sentences, the silence between LiLi and Vero grows. Vero should be working. She's supposed to be working. This is the sole justification for LiLi's presence in their life: Vero's work. But Vero stretches her legs out on the grass and decides she deserves more time in the sun. Five more minutes.

"I put some sunscreen on Eliot, Vero. I be right back."

Vero lies back in the grass, raising her arm against the sun, listening to JJ's nonsensical rhymes above her. "Bah hay koo boh ... munti ... sari" and other gibberish. Vero focuses so intently on making sense out of Jamal's sounds that she doesn't realize LiLi has returned until she hears her voice.

"Maybe I say that too," LiLi says, quietly.

Vero rolls her head to see LiLi sitting on the grass next to her and looking up the hill, where Jamal still pulls at the flower petals while Eliot recites, "I-love-mommy, I-love-her-not."

"If you ask me that question in the winter, if I miss my home, I say same. Every single day." She glances at Vero then, and Vero rolls toward her, nearly slides an arm around her waist, pulling her close, warm in the sun. She imagines whispering near LiLi's ear, *I know,*

LiLi, I know. They could talk about loneliness, not like sisters, maybe, but like friends. Even good friends. LiLi would admit, *Yes, yes, I am lonely.* Vero imagines them having this conversation cross-legged on LiLi's single bed, under the posters that LiLi has never taken down (though she has removed the photos of her family). *I understand, LiLi,* Vero will say with her hands cupped around a pottery mug warmed by tea, *I really do.*

But LiLi's face lifts. They are there, on the damp lawn with the lawn-mower roaring next door, and Eliot and Jamal squabbling over deflowered daisies. "Now summer comes," LiLi pushes her small hands into the ground, bounces to her size-five feet. "Things get better." Playfully she throws herself into the middle of the boys' feud, distracting Eliot and Jamal easily. Rolling on the grass with the two of them, LiLi looks like a teenager.

Why does Vero want to share a portion of LiLi's pain?

She does not know.

◊◊◊

Shane has introduced weekly childcare meetings. *Left to chance, too many things go wrong, and there are too many miscommunications. That's the concern.* Vero can't even think these words without feeling that Shane is the ventriloquist, she the sock puppet. These are his words.

But, it's true, there have been "issues." One spring day, LiLi opened all the windows, forgetting how quickly it cooled in the evening. Shane and Vero got home after dinner to find the windows open and the thermostats cranked. *A disregard for energy use, a certain oblivious-ness to household finances, a lack of restraint.*

More of Shane's words.

On Fridays, Shane comes home from the pharmacy early and he

and LiLi sit up in his office. For the first meeting, he invited Vero. She argued, though, that her relationship with LiLi worked better when it stayed less professional and more friendly. "I work at home sometimes. We share a space throughout the day. I don't want to be the big boss lady and have her cowering around me. I'm trying to make friends with her."

But when the office door closes, LiLi and Shane on the other side, Vero's exclusion feels wrong to her too. She imagines Shane sitting tall in the big leather chair behind his desk and LiLi like a kid in the wooden chair on the other side. "Just a few things to talk about," he'll say, "some logistics to keep things flowing smoothly."

LiLi will not like it. Men intimidate her. Plus, she wants so badly to be very good at her job. She does not take criticism well, does not understand the fine distinction between constructive criticism and unconstructive criticism. She will get teary. She will shake. Vero stands on the wrong side of the door picturing LiLi's caved, submissive posture. She vows to tell LiLi not to take the meeting too seriously. *Shane is Shane,* she'll say. *This is just Shane playing at grown-up.* But LiLi won't get "playing at grown-up." Language gets in the way.

◊◊◊

Later that night, Shane plays at patient. He has hurt his back. Vero warned him to ease his way into the new biking season. "You have all spring and summer to bike," she says. "No need to kill yourself at the first snow melt."

Now he lies face down on their mattress, and Vero digs her thumbs into the base of his spine, just above his buttocks. The doctor says it's a simple lower-back strain. There's nothing for it but time. Time and Percocet.

Vero has taken two Percocet as well, to keep him company, she says. Now neither of them will be able to sleep, not fully, but they'll have the most tranquil and dreamy of non-sleeps. Percocet blocks pain receptors to the brain, Shane has explained, creating a feeling of euphoria. Vero wonders if physical pain and emotional pain register as the same thing in the brain.

Shane has already fallen into Percocet's downy embrace, his muscles loose, eyes closed. She rarely has him like this, vulnerable. It puts her in mind of their early years, when they swapped secret stories in a kind of willful exposure of weakness, a way of showing, *I know you won't hurt me, I trust you.* Shane told her a story about when he was nine, and the Schoemans spent spring break at the timeshare in Mexico. His dad played catch with Vince all afternoon while Shane ran toy cars around a sand racetrack. Near the end of their stay, Vince missed an easy lob, and his dad reprimanded him for closing his eyes like a girl. Irked—and careening toward his teen years—Vince snarled, "Whatever you say, fat man."

Gregory turned, without a word, from Vince and reached out his hand to Shane. "Let's go for a walk, son."

He'd never asked Shane to go for a walk—or to do anything really—without Vince. But "fat" is the cruellest insult to any ex-athlete. Shane followed his father into the single track trail along the rocky shore. They must have walked for over an hour. Shane talked about his teacher who had a smiling owl statue that he and his classmates could turn to face the back wall on days they were sad and the basketball coach who promised Shane that he'd grow into his looks and girls would be crazy about him when he hit high school and the girl with long braids and freckles across her nose who could run faster than any of the boys and how Shane hoped that girl was still in his class when he got to high school and grew into his looks, and if she was maybe they could get married or at least go to the prom together but he should be sure to get his braces early in high school so they'd be off his teeth before the prom but if not, you know, maybe he could just smile with his lips closed, for the pictures at least, and he heard you could kiss with braces as long as the girl kept her tongue out of your mouth, and he thought the idea of someone else's tongue in his mouth was kind of gross anyway, wasn't it?

Decades later, telling the story to Vero, Shane smiled as he remembered the giddy rush. He'd skipped over to his mother, feeling, *See that? I'm worthy! He knows now too, just like you.* Shane expected his mother to share his excitement, but instead, her face twisted in rage. "How could you do that to your brother? You know your father only invited you with him to get back at Vince! You hurt your brother. How could you be so selfish?"

In adulthood, Shane reminded his father of this incident, hoping for a sign of remorse, an apology. *You should have paid more attention to me.* "I wasn't even forty then," Gregory Schoeman responded. "I wouldn't have been fat. Not then."

When Vero first heard this story, she held Shane and stroked his hair as if that nine-year-old boy still lived in his skin.

But on less sympathetic days, Vero grabs him by the shoulders, faces him square to her. "We've all got an excuse to be broken, Shane. I had no daddy at all." She hates the way she presents him with this assertion as if it's a contest: *Who has suffered more?* But once started, she can't stop. "You have to make yourself strong, Shane. Nobody can do that for you."

As she massages, she leans forward, brushing her breasts across his mid-back, pushing her hands hard down into the solid cycling muscles of his ass.

"That holiday you wanted?" He grunts the words into his pillow.

Vero is wary of this opening, recognizes a trace of the strategic in his inflection.

"Mmm-hmm." She's found a string of pea-sized knots along his sacrum and thumbs it in small even circles.

"I've been looking on the 'net," he says. She picks the biggest of his knots and places the point of her elbow right into its heart, repositioning herself until all her weight drives into his spine. He groans loudly but not without pleasure. "How about you and I take a real *adult* holiday?" The particular way he emphasizes adult worries her. "A little spice. Ramp things up a bit." She wishes he emphasized *little* and *bit*, but Shane's force falls clearly on *spice* and *ramp*. He wiggles as if he might roll on his back to face her, but she holds him tight with her thighs, grown strong from the Bikram yoga. She's not done with him yet.

Bikram has turned out to be Vero's answer to Cheryl's flake-fest yoga. Bikram instructors never chant. "Lift your foot! Lift your foot!" Roger bellows instructions out like a deranged drill sergeant. "Make your legs an upside-down L. Lock knee! Leg on the floor must be straight. The pose hasn't started yet until you lock your knee. That's your two-word mantra: Lock knee! Lock knee! Lock knee!"

But Vero has her own two-word mantra: *fucking hurts, fucking hurts, fucking hurts*. The grounded leg aches deep in her kneecap, which seems ill-equipped to hold her full body weight and unwilling to do so without loud protest. Her leg in the air refuses to straighten, her hamstrings inflexible as dried concrete. After a class, her sweat-soaked clothes fall with a heavy wet slap at the bottom of the laundry chute. When she sees them again, LiLi has cleaned them and folded them neatly, ready for the next class.

Vero is admiring the sharp rise of her new quad muscles clenched against Shane's torso when she hears Jamal cry out from his room.

A single shrill complaint and then nothing. Vero's skin still prickles when her babies cry at night. That pins-and-needles sensation alerts her one fraction of a second before the sound waves register with her eardrum, but she no longer goes to them. Most often, they can work it out on their own. That is better, she knows, in the long run. Last night, she'd made a rare exception because Jamal cried just as she passed his door. "It's okay, sweetie," she murmured, smoothing the sweaty hair at his temples. "Just a dream."

"Mahal kita, nanay," he cooed back.

Gibberish. Still.

"He's only two," Shane said, annoyed by the quick furrowing of Vero's brow. "Kids develop at their own pace." It was the same empty platitude she herself would offer any other mother. She probably gave Shane the words in the first place. "You love to worry, Vee. If you had nothing at all to worry about, you'd worry about that."

Maybe he's right. It's his X-rated holiday scheme that has her worried now. She tries to guess what he might mean by 'adult' holiday. Las Vegas? That's something they've never done. Sin City. Gambling. Strippers. Hookers. She's never even been tempted.

"This line of muscle is nothing but knots." Vero pulls herself onto his buttocks, crouching like a cat, presses a kneecap hard into each side of his spine. "It runs straight up the left side of your spine. Hard as a pipe."

After a month of Bikram, Vero's muscles are pipes too. She watches them flex in her forearms as she kneads Shane's back. The tyranny has paid off.

"I found this place," Shane's voice is tight, as if she's gripping his testicles rather than massaging his back. "Sort of like Fantasy Island. X-rated version. In Jamaica. One week." The phrases come out pained in short, shallow breaths. "What happens there. Stays there. A break.

From real life. A little. Trip. To the. Wild side." Vero forces as much pressure as she can through her legs and knees into the muscle spasms in his back. Shane's hand grips the side of the mattress, arm rigid, face contorted. "Totally safe. Respectable clientele. All controlled." He talks fast now, as if he's afraid that if he leaves any space she'll jump into it and pour cold water all over his plan. "Pretty affordable. If we go in summer. No pressure to do anything you don't want to do. People do. Only what they're comfortable with."

Vero picks through her memories of their life together for clues to what exactly he might be suggesting, and what she has done that would lead him to believe she might be open to such a suggestion. They once watched a movie set in the 1970s in which married couples at a party dropped their keys in a pail at the door. Wives picked a key and got the corresponding husband. Then something bad happened—somebody's child died, something like that—all the fault of the swinging. "Weird," had been Shane's lone pronouncement on those antics.

Parties in the old sweet suite were wild in their own way. Once, on Ecstasy, Vero got a little flirty with Vince's date. She and Vince both kissed her midriff, competitively, Vince raising her shirt, daring Vero to go higher.

"Which of us does it better? Tell us!"

"Keep going," the date giggled, squirming under their lips. "I can't decide yet." When Vince wasn't looking, his date put her mouth close to Vero's ear. "Girls always know what feels best. You're the winner," she said, a flick of her tongue at Vero's earlobe.

Shane watched quietly the whole time, but he only mentioned the incident once. "Not with Vince's girls." That's all he said. Those parties were tame compared to what went on today. Just last month, Shane clamped down at the pharmacy in response to rumoured "rainbow parities." Any dosage or frequency that hinted at suspicious behaviour, and he called the prescribing physician. Kids were allegedly robbing their parents' medicine cabinets, mixing together the most colourful tablets, and popping handfuls of them just to see what would happen.

"That's not a rainbow party," Adele had said.

"It's not?"

"No, a rainbow party is when each girl puts on a different colour lipstick, and they all give the same boy a blowjob."

"How would you know that? Your daughter is nine."

"But my son is eleven."

"Eleven?"

"Yep."

Shane dismissed these rainbow parties with one word too: "Sick."

Now it sounds as if he has his own "sick" ideas. "What exactly do you have in mind?" Vero rolls off him, spreading herself thin at his side. She wants to see his face when he answers this question.

"I don't know," Shane says with a smile that tells her he *does* know. "An adventure. Something sexy. Fun. A little daring. You know, hot-ttt." The phrases pile onto each other, teetering like one of Jamal's block towers. Shane runs his index finger up her torso on the "t" and then puts his hands on her face, palms flat against her cheeks. Vero doesn't recognize this gesture. He's never done it before. It turns him into a stranger. "I worry about us getting bored. That maybe you're bored. This trip would fix that."

"Is this about LiLi?" Vero doesn't know where her question has come from, but suddenly it's between them, breaking some hovering possibility. Maybe that was her intent.

"What?! No." Vero expects him to pull his hands away, but he holds her cheeks tight. "No." His fingertips press hard against her back molars. "Why would you say that?"

"Just—" She yanks his hands from her face, but then holds them gently between hers, pulled into her chest. "Well, having a young pretty woman in the house ... maybe it's made you all—" Partway through a Bikram class, a moon glows in the mirror where Vero's face should be. The whole room fuzzes around her. She has the same sensation now. She looks out of the window to steady herself. When the blinds are up, they have a view down into the valley to the lights of town, but she and Shane never leave the blinds up anymore. Instead, the streetlamp sends tiny beams of light through the shutters, spreading lines across the comforter over their feet. "What's that word Vince uses?" Vero has her own words, but Shane wouldn't like them. "Randy." *Maybe LiLi makes you randy.* What a thing to suggest.

"It's only you who makes me randy." Shane pushes her hands down his flat, taut stomach to the proof. "You always have."

She lets her hand be led.

"The resort," he says, "it's called Hedonism. That name made me think of us, *hedonism.* Remember when we used to call ourselves hedonists? 'If it feels good, we're in.' That was our motto. I mean, I was the *Candy Man.* We didn't hurt anyone. We didn't care if anyone judged us. *Prudes. Bores.* Let them judge."

She does remember, but only as if she's recalling an old movie she saw just once. She remembers the mornings after more vividly, sex-sore and hung over, a toxic sweat that clung to her even after her shower. She remembers an inability to meet and hold Shane's eyes, a twisting echo in her abdomen that she could only describe as shame.

"We could go in August. You used to talk about girls," he says. "About *you* and girls. I'd like to see that just once."

She tries to remember talking about her and girls. Maybe once when they were drunk or high or both. There's something in her memory, just a hint—Shane's face floating in front of her, his lips moving not quite in time with his words. *The kisses felt good, didn't they? Do you think you'd like more? I wouldn't be jealous. Not with a girl. I'd just watch.* His eyes so sharp and serious, his hand so heavy and warm against her waist, she couldn't laugh. She might have nodded, might have bit her lip, rolled on top of him, might have done a variety of things that could have been interpreted as encouragement. *Not with Vince's girls, but with another girl?* Yes, she might have nodded. But that Vero was twenty-one. Not even the same person.

Shane is as hard as he gets, the tip of his penis jutting out through the fly of his boxers. Vero circles her thumb and forefinger around its smooth head, wants to crawl under the covers and put her lips to it, only the way she'd kiss a crying child. *There. All better.*

She senses fear. Shane is scared. That's what this is about. *One crazy week at a sex resort won't make you young again.* That's what she wants to say.

"How much does it cost?" That's what she hears herself ask.

"Not too much. Not in August."

"Who'll take care of the kids?"

"LiLi. My parents. We'll piece it together."

That night, Vero dreams of Jamal at her right breast. He meets her eyes, sucking with a ferocity that borders on cruelty. His face shifts from desperate to fierce to angry, but it's an adult's expression of anger, radiating right from his pupils' cores. When she turns her head away from the meanness in his eyes, she finds Vince, suckling on the left side, with matched ferocity.

Vero tells Shane of the dream, but she substitutes his name for Vince's.

"It's the Percocet," he tells her. "Don't worry."

◊◊◊

"Don't beat yourself up. Many couples believe they are doing the nannies a favour. Go with that. Think of how much your nanny makes here. One month's salary is more than most women earn in an entire year back in their impoverished home countries." Bernie often sounds like she's quoting someone, but never more so than when she's reassuring Vero about her discomfort around LiLi's seeming unhappiness. There's a distance in Bernie's voice as if she's standing a solid metre back from her words. "You're following all labour laws. LiLi chose to come here. She has a contract. She makes a legal wage. There's nothing exploitive about it. So says the book." Bernie pours Vero a cup of jasmine tea from her Teaopia pot and motions for Vero to sit in the black leather chair at the front of the nanny office.

Yesterday, Vero saw Lito's face on the national news. He has charged his employer with exploitation. Dennis, the owner of the coffee shop, has been paying Lito and the other Filipino workers overtime, but then he drives them to the bank, has them cash their cheques, and return the overtime cash to him. Everyone in Sprucedale knows Dennis. He swims laps at the Y every noon hour. He is a Shriner. You can see him on weekends wearing a silly cap and driving a little car to raise money for sick children. He seems like a nice Sprucedale guy. Vero wants assurances that she is not at all like this man. She needs Bernie to convince her that this blatant abuse of vulnerable foreign workers has nothing to do with the Sprucedale Nanton-Schoemans. Nothing to do with LiLi.

Noon sun streams in the large windows. Vero's skin grows sticky, her sundress damp at the back of her legs. She tries to nudge the heavy chair into the shade.

"And do yourself a favour. Quit trying to be her friend. She can't be your equal." Bernie wears shorts. Vero has never seen her legs before. Her hard calf muscles, the shape and size of baseballs, bulge as she stretches onto her toes to reach for another cup. Vero wonders if she rock climbs. They've never discussed how Bernie spends her weekends.

"Here's what you need to accept: You pay her. She's an employee." Three hard lines of muscle flex in Bernie's forearms as she pours herself some tea. "She's not your family. She's not your friend. When you accept the basic employee-employer contract, life will be easy."

Vero wants to tell Bernie that her menstrual cycle has synched with LiLi's. Last week, the boys followed Vero into the bathroom. When Jamal saw blood on the toilet paper, his face crumpled into the exaggerated expression of sorrow tolerated only in toddlers. "Dugo dugo dugo," he mumbled nonsensically, tears rolling down his chubby cheeks.

"That's okay, JJ." Eliot patted the back of his head like a puppy, while Vero tried to deal with her situation without causing further alarm.

"Poor, poor Mommy," Eliot cooed at his little brother's ear. "Just like poor, poor LiLi. When LiLi has blood, poor Mommy has blood too."

"The live-in situation is a bit intimate for that kind of detachment," she says to Bernie. "Not everything falls neatly into the employee-employer categories, not when you're all trying to make a home under the same roof." Vero speaks to Bernie but addresses her comments to a large poster by the entrance. "Making the Right Connections" it reads in big pink letters across the top. In one corner, a blonde mother hugs her blonde daughter. In the opposite corner, a beautiful Filipina woman wears a tank top that shows a hint of cleavage. She reads to the same girl, both of them smiling widely into the open pages. With the mother, the girl is tucked into her armpit, both arms wound tightly around her. With the nanny (and there is no question which is which), the girl sits at a distance, framed by the arms but separated from them.

Lower-case details on services provided fill the rest of the space.

Bernie sells these services, but she's never lived them. Vero decides it's best to change the topic. "What're you doing this weekend?" She turns away from the poster and tries to remember if Bernie has ever mentioned a husband or a boyfriend. Their meetings have all been here in the office over paperwork and tea. There has been drama and even tears, but all of it belonged to Vero. Heat rises up Vero's neck as she thinks of how she's exposed herself but seen nothing, taken but never given. Or is it the reverse? Given but never taken?

Bernie's small hands bear no wedding ring. Her nails, though painted a bright orange, are trimmed short but not bitten. These could be the hands of a climber. "You're closed Saturday and Sunday, right? Any fun plans?" Bernie has the same cute pixie cut that Vero noticed the first time they met, but she has new red highlights, and Vero wants to ask where she gets her hair done.

"I gotta get the hell out of this place, that's all I know." The curse startles Vero. It took just one personal question and suddenly, Bernie's not quoting anybody. Her voice drops an octave, and she's right in it, as if she's been waiting for the invitation to rest there. Vero has never heard Bernie swear before, but it suits her. "This cow employer calls me up today and—" Bernie interrupts herself, smiling apologetically. "You whine a lot, but you're not a cow."

"Should I be embarrassed to admit that I'll take that as a compliment?" Vero asks with her lips touching the warm rim of her teacup.

"Seriously. This woman, she calls me up screaming. Her nanny—that's what she always calls her too, 'my nanny.' Never a name." Vero's drawn to the new gruffness in Bernie's voice, feels she should be at the pub, slugging pints of Guinness with this Bernie. "'My nanny has rubbed raw chicken on our plates. I just know it.

Diarrhea—the whole family! You explain that!' As if I'm a gastrologist. As if this woman's intestines are any of my business. As if I really want to know about their diarrhea." Bernie throws her head back and exhales loudly at the ceiling.

"Do you think she did?"

"Did what?"

"Rub raw chicken on the plates?"

"How the hell do I know?" Bernie aims all her hostility straight at Vero.

Vero holds up both hands, palms facing Bernie as if she can push the anger back at her, or at least send it forking around her.

"Look. It's one of two things. Either the nanny did no such thing, and the woman is paranoid—likely—or maybe the nanny did give the whole family salmonella poisoning, which begs the question: how badly did they have to treat her to inspire that revenge?"

"Right," Vero says quietly into her lap.

"Right?"

Vero admires how much aggression Bernie can pack into the one word. "I just meant, yes, sure, that makes sense." Vero hates the weakness in her voice. She sounds like Shane's mother: 'I wouldn't mind going to the market today, I wouldn't mind having seafood for dinner, I wouldn't mind getting in a round of golf.' As if she can't imagine any greater way to assert herself than not minding.

But Vero's conciliatory tone seems to calm Bernie. She pours Vero another cup of jasmine tea, gesturing for her to relax into her chair and stay. The flex of her forearm matches the tension in her jaw, and Vero doesn't dare object.

"I tell you, by the end of it all, I wanted to rub raw chicken on the woman's plate." She lets out a mirthless laugh, a single huff of air through her nose.

Vero studies the poster, tries to imagine the beautiful woman in the tank top rubbing raw chicken on the blonde mother's plate.

"This same employer—and don't get me wrong, she's not the only head case around here—but when her nanny first got here, this lady calls me up to discuss what she calls 'the personal hygiene issue.' 'Her body odour is not a pleasant one,' she says. 'Well, Mrs Mc—' I mean, I say, 'Well, Mrs So-and-So, she's has been travelling for thirty-six straight hours. I can't think of anyone who would smell too great. Give her a chance to settle in, get some sleep, take a shower.' I hoped 'the hygiene issue' would pass, but no. Mrs So-and-So stayed completely hung up on smell. She left the nanny 'gifts' of deodorant. A douche spray too. The nanny didn't even know what that was. You should've seen the colour she blushed when I had to tell her. I wouldn't be surprised to hear the bag Febreezed the poor nanny. Welcome to North America: You stink."

Bernie leans forward again, putting her elbows on her knees and letting her head fall between her hands. "Argh." She shakes her head. "So this weekend: No nannies, no nanny employers, no nanny smells, no nanny chicken." Bernie collects the cups and saucers. Vero watches her impressive calves strain against her skin as she makes her way to the sink behind the front counter. Maybe she's a body builder.

"This woman, yesterday," Bernie shouts as if one last story has forced its way up and out of her throat, "asks me, 'Do the nannies have sex in our country?' I swear to god." Bernie pushes her sleeves up and dips her arm into the soapy water. She waves her head when Vero pushes up to help. "Sit. Relax." Vero obeys but really she wants out of the heat of the window. The back of her sundress feels drenched, and she knows she'll leave an embarrassing puddle in the chair when she stands. "'I'm sure that's none of my business, ma'am,' I say. You know what she says back? 'Well, I just don't feel comfortable with someone having sex in my house.' So I say—" Bernie's voice rises an octave, and again she sounds like she's quoting someone. "You're welcome to institute house rules, of course. Many employees forbid house guests." Bernie pulls her long-sleeved shirt over her head, her face glowing above the sink of hot water. Underneath the sleeves, she wears a sky-blue tank top with Shred Kelly stencilled across the chest. Likely some band Vero has never heard of, a band for people who still have time for energy and fun. She has biceps to match her calves. "So I think that's the end of it, right? Wrong. She says, 'I'm not really comfortable with her having sex in other places, either. We're responsible for her behaviour in this country.' Every time Vero hears the word 'sex,' she thinks of Shane's plan to go to an adult resort in Jamaica. Hedonism, it's called. She suspects they will go. Shane wants this so badly. She feels weak against the force of that will. She can't think of anything she wants that much. She's suggested alternatives, of course, late at night, under the covers, hands groping each other's bodies, Shane's naked body as familiar as her own—more familiar, even. That's the only place they speak of this adult holiday.

"What the hell am I supposed to say to that? 'We don't want our nanny having sex!' Just be happy if she's not having it with your husband, honey. That's what I'd like to say." Bernie doesn't seem to mind, or even notice, that Vero no longer participates in the conversation. She speaks straight into the sink of dishes. Maybe she hopes her stories will drown there.

Between the sheets, Vero has suggested tamer versions of Shane's holiday—a trip to the big city where they're anonymous, a night at a sex club, even a prostitute, if he really wants to try this girl-on-girl thing, just once. If it's that important. Vero attempts to imagine herself with a woman, tries to decide if the possibility excites her. But even as she does so, she knows a possibility is different than a reality. She wonders if Shane knows.

Her sex-worker suggestion offended Shane, even though she'd been careful to use the term "call girl."

"Vero, we're not the kind of people who *pay* for it," he said, in a tone that left no doubt the discussion had come to its end. *Shane*, she wanted to say, *with the price of your "adult resort," even at the summer rate, we will be paying for it.* That's one thing Vero had begun to understand. There's precious little you don't pay for in this life, one way or another.

She gets what she paid for in Bikram. She gets sinewy. Goodbye lumps. Goodbye rolls. Each time she looks, she sees less and less of herself in the mirror. But she also sees more: more ribs, more hips, more muscles. *If we're all just dying animals, let me be a strong one,* she thinks. Vero was most aware of herself as an animal when she gave birth to Jamal, leaning into the wall and kicking her back leg, a horse making a rut in the dirt. That's how she thought of it too: her *back leg*. As if she had four. She might as well have been in a barn, pawing in the dirt, gnawing on a wooden gate, kicking up clouds of dust. The pain made her animal, wild and frothing, but in the end that birth satisfied her in a way that the C-section with Eliot had not. Bikram Yoga gives her the same satisfaction. It takes her out of her mind and into her body. That's what she means when she tells Shane, "It makes me feel alive."

She has that same feeling of being alive in her body when Bernie hugs her goodbye at the agency door, a sure hand on her waist, her newly defined transverse abdominal muscle. Perhaps, Vero thinks, she *will* follow Shane's lead and take this alive body for a single week of adventure, a mere seven days of recaptured youth, one week that will not be her real life.

CHAPTER TWELVE

Nobody in the lobby of Hedonism looks like a hedonist. The men remind Vero of junior high boys at their first school dance—a little too keen, a little too desperate, but working hard not to look it. The women don't look like themselves either. Vero can tell that much even without knowing them. They all wear expressions they've practiced at home in their bathroom mirrors. Vero knows because she wears her own carefully practiced expression. It says: *I do this all the time, no big deal, sex and fun, that's me.*

And then: *Don't get too close, I never usually do this, it's not who I am.*

It's the waffling that betrays Vero and the other women.

Vero and Shane have decided to use their real first names to avoid any embarrassing slips. They won't offer up last names, though, and if anyone asks they'll use a fake combo: Schanton. Shane and Vero Schanton. From Seattle, they'll say. They'll be dentists.

"We're *both* dentists?" Vero asks.

"Sure. Lots of dentists marry each other. They meet at dentist school doing dentist things, fall in love over their first root canals. Plus, our story doesn't have to be believable. Everyone will know we're lying. It's expected."

"Do dentists even go to swinger resorts?" Vero still can't figure out what she's supposed to call this place. Shane's nostrils quiver slightly as if he's walked into the kitchen to find old fish under the sink. Strike "swinger resort" off the list, then. Perhaps she's meant to call it nothing.

"Oh yeah. Sure, they swing. Dentists—they're sickos. They're into everything."

Are we sickos, then? she wants to ask, but she just sips her welcome-to-Hedonism piña colada, eyeing the lobby, the pale couples arriving, the sun-kissed brown couples leaving. Those leaving wear more relaxed expressions and fewer clothes. Their chests puff out, shoulder blades pulling in toward each other like Roger has taught Vero to do in mountain pose. Vero imitates the posture of the outgoing guests and tries to guess which of the incoming couples have given their real names. There's a Danielle and Henri from Quebec, a Lizette and Georges from Switzerland. There seem to be a lot of dentists. In the lobby filled with nude statues, she and Shane shake hands with half a dozen couples, all of them assessing their options.

"Danielle's cute, no?" Shane whispers as they follow the concierge to their room.

"Her husband looks creepy." Vero has grabbed an extra piña colada from the welcome tray and speaks with the straw cold against her tongue.

"Who cares about the husband?"

"Don't be naïve, Shane. They're a package deal." Her flip-flops slap against the marble floors, echoing their way down the hallway. "Just like we are."

Vero smiles at the concierge as he unloads their luggage. No tipping allowed. She makes her smile suffice.

"Danielle and Henri don't seem to speak much English, though,"

Vero closes the door softly on the concierge's back. "That could be good."

"What do you mean?"

"The less talking in a place like this, the better." She aims her empty cup at the wastebasket in the far corner of the room. She misses. Drops of piña colada sprinkle the bamboo dresser drawers.

Vero and Shane's room is small and plain. "Three-star accommodations for five-star prices," Vero says, hearing the snarl in her own voice. Travel tires her.

"You pay for the atmosphere here, Vero Baby!" Shane is buoyant. Someone has sucked out all Vero's air and pumped it into him. He practically floats.

You mean you pay for the sex, Vero wants to say, but she stops herself. Seattle's Shane and Vero Schanton are not the kind of people who pay for sex. Shane has said so.

Vero flops down on the bed. A deep crack runs the full length of the ceiling. Large germ-bearing insects live there, she knows it. She watches the ceiling fan spin around and around and around, thinking, *Watch your fingers, Eliot, keep an eye on your little brother.* She closes her eyes and works on her ocean breath, tries to match the rhythm of the waves rolling in on the beach below. Holidays always start out rough, she reminds herself. She has trouble with transitions, like Eliot. Again he's there with her. She pictures his red face screaming, "I don't like change!" *Me neither, Eliot, me neither.*

She's been tense since the airport. In the cab, Shane practically vibrated in the seat next to her, pointing out the "hilarious" road signs:

Driving Fast Kills.
Don't be in a hurry to get to eternity.

She faked a laugh, but all she could think was, *If I die in this country, I will kill you.*

Shane knows to leave her alone when they get to the room. He's seen this Vero before. She needs some space. She spreads out on her back like a snow angel, willing the aggravation to rise up and out of her stretched limbs. Cheryl claims she can hear Vero's moods. "It's in your voice," she says. "I know when to steer clear." Vero feels it in her skin, a tightness, a sensitivity. It was there nearly always after the births of Jamal and Eliot, before the arrival of LiLi, so Cheryl stayed away. It's back now.

Shane sends commentary in over his shoulder as he surveys the resort from their balcony—a generous word for the thin space beyond the sliding doors.

"They're all naked down there. Not a stitch. This is going to be wild, Vee. I promise you. A real adventure. Something just for us, you'll see."

The concierge warned them about three o'clock storms, though he phrased it as a promise rather than a threat. "The lovebirds usually like to go in for a nap around then anyway," he winked. Vero can feel a thick warm wind picking up now, carrying the salty air into their room.

She arches her neck to study the painting mounted on the wall above their king-sized bed. It's all breast and butt. A yellow body fills the canvas, the grey shadow of spine dividing the piece in two. A long thin arm runs from the shoulder in the top corner to the knee at the bottom, but the arm is not the only thing out of proportion. "This woman's boob is bigger than her ass," Vero yells out to Shane, still assessing the picture with her head propped upside-down on the mattress. "We'll know it's time to go home when this art starts looking good."

Shane chuckles, clearly enjoying his view. "I might never go home."

Vero slides to the end of the bed, kicks off her shoes, dangles her feet on the cool tiles, and turns on the television. Three channels. "We have porn, porn, or porn," she says loud enough that Shane will hear her above the music, which has just cranked up a notch from the pool below.

He dives in the sliding doors, bouncing onto the bed, thick arms around her waist. He's all charged up, the way he used to be after a college football match, high on adrenaline and testosterone, pushing her onto the bed.

I'm not your tackling dummy, she wants to say, except that she likes it, wants to tackle back, to roughhouse herself out of this mood. *Push me harder, I dare you.*

"I pick porn," he says, tugging at her T-shirt with his teeth, pulling it up toward her breasts. He's on top of her and the comforter is rough against her sweaty skin.

"It's so hot, Shane."

"I like it hot," he says with his mouth full of T-shirt.

"I'm sticky."

"I like it sticky." He licks the skin along the top of her ribcage.

Vero rolls toward the sliding doors. She can see the pool deck below, full of skin. That's what they came here for, what they paid for. They should be down there. Shane rolls in right behind her. Spooning, they called it in the sweet suite. Spooning was what they did after sex. Or before sex. Or in between sex. Back then, even something as mundane and domestic as cutlery could be sexy. *Let's spoon.*

"Should we go exploring?" She tries to loosen his arms, struggles against their embrace. "Check out the resort?" She can't breathe. He's too tight around her.

"I *am* exploring," he says, snaking his fingers down the front of her shorts. She rolls onto her back, watches the ceiling fan go round, listens to the ocean breath rake up and down the back of her throat.

He has her shirt off, then her shorts, but she's still not there. She can't blame LiLi now—that set of ears in the basement. LiLi isn't here.

Vero rolls toward Shane, trying to be a good sport, but pushes away, unable to breathe. She remembers this advance and withdrawal too, from their younger years, but then it was a tease, a strategy.

"I'm a little out of practice here," she apologizes, a hand pressed against his chest like she's straight-arming a linebacker. "This isn't what I do mid-afternoon anymore. I feel like I've still got one ear out for the boys. Another for LiLi. Like I'm supposed to be somewhere, doing something."

"Muscle memory, Vee." He strokes her straight arm, shakes it loose, wraps it around the back of his neck. "The body never forgets. It's like riding a bike." He squeezes hands on her hips, pressure running through each of his fingertips. "Besides, I've got somewhere for you to be, someone for you to do." He pulls her on top of him, his teeth brushing her collarbone.

She closes her eyes and moves into Shane's fingers splayed across her lower back, feels that. Lets herself go into the soft breath on her neck, feels that. His hardness pressing into her, that. Finally, something from her core responds, a loose heat rolling over her, an unclenching that she associates with the end of a Bikram class—or with her third glass of Malbec.

Shane is right. Vero's body does remember. She lets go of her words and follows its lead.

"I think I'm going to like this afternoon nap ritual," she says afterward, yanking the covers over both of their heads. "But let's try that one more time. Just to be sure."

"I'm not fat. I'm affluent." The large man drags out the syllables of aff- FLU- ent in his heavy Texan accent so that even the word sounds fat. He's not nude but may as well be. He wears the tiniest Speedo with an American flag stretched thin across his genitals. "Everyone here calls me Hedonism Hal. You don't need to know any more than that. I'm an institution at Hedonism." He looks toward his wife for approval. She lies flat in a lawn chair, her skin as brown as a potato sack and just as coarse. "I'm the father of the resort, you could say. I've walked more nude brides down the aisle than anyone. You need giving away, I'm your man." He sucks loudly on a soggy-tipped cigar.

Vero studies Hal's ears while he talks, the lobes fat and heavy. The sunburned tips peel in large white flakes that make Vero think of snow. Vero has already learned to avoid eye contact in this place where every glance can be interpreted as an invitation. Shane's gone to fetch her another dirty monkey—1 ounce each of rum, crème de bananas, crème de cacao, and Kahlua, all blended with two scoops of vanilla ice cream and half a banana. It was her breakfast drink the first morning at Hedonism. She hopes he hurries. She's getting thirsty.

Quick, my buzz is wearing off! Do something!

That's Shane's joke of the week. Neither of them has yet been in any danger of their buzz wearing off.

"You should check out my website." Hal fingers a giant gold cross hanging in his grey chest hair. It's gaudy and fake but makes Vero think of the delicate gold cross that always hangs at LiLi's throat. "Just Google my name. You'll find me there, always counting down to my next Hedonism trip. That ticker never stops running. Trip thirty-seven we're at this time." He puts his foot up on the end of his wife's lawn chair, making Vero increasingly grateful for his tiny

Speedo. "Thirty-seven years. That's almost as long as the place has existed."

Vero sucks in her stomach, lifting her pelvic floor just as Roger instructs at Bikram. Even the thought of Roger is incongruous here. "Girls e-mail me there on my site," Hal drawls, the cigar clenched in his back teeth. "All kinds of questions I get from first-timers. How much hair should they shave? Is everyone really totally naked? What's the proper etiquette for spouse-swapping? And everybody wants to know what goes on in the wild tub. Hal's got the answers. After thirty-seven years, I would, wouldn't I, Mother?" He nudges his wife with his toe. She nods up at him with a vague expression—the one that head-phoned teenagers wear when they nod at their parents.

"I stayed off the 'net on this one. Maybe my husband came across your site." Vero is aware of her own nudity, but only tangentially so. After two days, she's almost forgotten how to be self-conscious. The constant supply of alcohol and THC coursing through her blood-stream help. On day one, after the inaugural afternoon nap, she made her first naked promenade down the pool deck, breath held, eyes on the ocean. She headed straight for the water, got in up to her neck, and stayed there until dinner, paddling around in the waves, warm as soup, eyes diverted from the intertwined naked bodies that floated by her on air mattresses shaped like cartoon sea creatures.

But Shane had been even more nervous than her.

"We're going to do this?" He sat on the corner of the bed, a swan towel in his lap, its long white neck pointing to the cracked ceiling. "Really?"

Vero's first walk felt familiar. She'd lived it before in recurring night-mares. At the end of her naked march, she expected to find herself in an exam room and out of time. But after the first few hours, the night-marish quality of Hedonism dissipated, though the dreamy haze of the vacation did not. By day two, clothes seemed odd. In clothes, people pose, draw attention to their bodies. Naked, there's nothing to look at, nothing to call, *Hey, have a look down here!* Without clothes, eyes stay on eyes.

Hal's Speedo flag invites Vero's eyes to his crotch. Vero's nudity extends no such invitation. "I can give you my number-one piece of advice now," he says, "even though you missed my pre-trip tips." He holds his cigar out of his mouth for his announcement. "Stay away from the Japanese restaurant. Where I live, we call sushi *bait*." Hal's laugh rolls over like an old dog, phlegmy and slow at the bottom of his throat.

"No worries: I'm not eating anything raw at this place." Vero lifts her voice at the end of each word, forcing her sentences to turn up in a smile. Hedonism is not the kind of place one wants to make enemies. There's a sign at either end of the beach:

NUDE BEACH ONLY
NO PHOTOGRAPHY

But disobeying a sign would be so easy in a place that builds its reputation on disobedience. Vero promises her Sprucedale self that she will be careful. Even as quickly as this place has become normal to her, she knows she doesn't want remnants of it showing up in her real life. She cringes at the thought of explaining this place to Joss or the Schoemans or Cheryl or Roger or, God forbid, to LiLi.

The resort offers a wide range of activities throughout the day, just as the brochure promised. There's topless volleyball in the tame pool throughout the afternoon, and nude Twister just before dinner on the wilder deck. On the beach, beautiful Jamaican girls offer body painting. For the athletically inclined, there's yoga on the upper deck, but Vero and Shane opted out, knowing they couldn't stomach all those naked downward dogs. The hot tub for the truly daring rages day and night, and Vero and Shane have only got hints of what goes on there. They're working their way up to it.

"You don't have to talk to anyone you don't want to here," Shane whispers as he steers Vero away from Hedonism Hal, who's making a joke about everyone eating raw at Hedonism eventually. "Forget manners. We'll never see these people again. Don't do anything you don't want to do."

Vero takes her breakfast shake from Shane as she plops onto the sand, already hot against her bare ass. "I feel sorry for him, Shane. What would bring someone like that to a place like this? Over and over again. Thirty-seven times. What is he looking for?" They sit leg-to-leg, watching a young Jamaican woman in a bright red bikini painting onto the skin of a pair of naked newlyweds.

"Don't go growing on me now, honey," the Jamaican woman says to the groom. "I only have this little bottle of paint." Her words are flirtatious, according to the script, but their tone is not. She sounds like any worn-out waitress at any greasy spoon back home. A co-worker with cornrows and long sharp red nails joins her to help paint the bride. This painter wears a grass-green sarong and matching bikini top. The workers wear clothes. All of them and always.

"What should we do for you, Missy? Some hearts for breasts? Or do you like flowers? Maybe we should ask your man—you're his now." The worker with cornrows dips her brush in red and starts to work on the bride's naval. "Yep, you're all his now. And he's yours." She looks away from her brush, runs her eyes up and down the groom, once, twice, and then again. "That little bottle of paint gonna be enough for your man, there?" She smiles. "I'm not so sure about that. Not so sure..." she sings the words.

Shane and Vero are content to sit and watch, their legs braided together. The silence between them isn't uncomfortable and angry as it often is at home. It's the silence of the sex-stoned. Shane occasionally puts his fingers in Vero's hair and gives a soft tug. She watches the sun and calculates the hours until their afternoon nap.

As the painters settle into their work, they lower their voices and speak only to each other. They fall into a thick patois, and Vero has difficulty making out their words, but she thinks she hears the one in the red bikini say, "Some people smell, and they don't even know they smell."

When the painting is done, the groom has a black-and-white tuxedo with a bowtie covering his torso and a giant heart around his penis. The bride wears two daisies for breasts and a red tulip growing out of her vagina. They hold hands and smile shyly as Hedonism Hal and the other geriatric nudists admire the art work. Eventually, the painted newlyweds walk hand-in-hand into the ocean and giggle as the water turns red around them.

The average age here surprises Vero. She and Shane are amongst the youngest other than a few college kids whom Vero suspects have been hired. Professional partiers. How could they afford this place? And why would they want to be here? With people as old as their parents—their *grandparents*—parading around nude. But thrill-seekers come to these places expecting beauty, craving sex appeal. Both belong to the young. The resort must provide.

Imena is the most obvious hire.

"Where are you from?" Vero asks her, shouting above the booming bass as they lean into the bar, elbows touching.

"Where are any of us from? It doesn't matter here. I could tell you, but I'd be lying, just like you're lying." She pulls a lipstick from between her breasts and reapplies. There's an imprint of dark red lips on her plastic cup when she holds it out for a refill.

Imena has mastered the perfect mixture of black leather and skin: her dark flesh peeking through slits along her muscled back and torso. A long run of leg shows from ankle to hip bone. The outfit provides a window glance at her firm strong buttock. At six feet, two inches, Imena looks capable of bench-pressing any of the men at the resort, of doing squats with them stretched overhead; her quads and biceps are as big as Vince's. The more Vero watches Imena, the surer she is that she knows her. From TV. Maybe she's an American track star? Vero pictures her powering over hurdles, far out ahead of her opponents, hair swinging wildly behind her. But her name was not Imena then, not when she ran. Vero wants a photograph of Imena, to remember her face when she gets home, needs to see her like that, legs pumping, hair flying loose.

Imena never comes out until after dinner. At the dance club, two skinny men attach themselves to her, humping her legs like dogs in heat. Imena's eyes glaze over, looking far into the distance, but she stays planted on the dance floor, granting them access to her mountain of a body. Done with her legs, the men take on her nipples, each one flicking his tongue at the faux diamonds embedded in leather at the dead centre of each of her breasts, as big as football helmets, cupped in sturdy black. Imena allows the flicking tongue, the thrust of hips, but when the men touch her, she pulls a long whip from its holster, points it at their faces, her expression fierce. They giggle in delight, crossing their legs like schoolboys who have to pee, but they back away.

"Let's just take our time easing into this scene," Shane advises. "Once you pick your group, that's your group. We want to pick carefully."

At dinner, the hedonists wear clothes, but not normal clothes. Togas are most popular. Vero imagines piles of suitcases arriving at the Negril airport, all packed full of nothing but bed sheets.

"You live your fantasy here," a woman tells them at dinner, leaning in close over her jerk chicken. "Save the boring clothes for home." She's dressed in a gold cheerleading costume with a red lion's head painted across her chest. Folds of flab squeeze out over the too-tight underarms. Vero thinks of Eliot pointing at her own underarms—*your skin doesn't fit here, Mommy. It's wiggly.* Bikram has fixed that. Vero's skin fits perfectly now. A poster in the lobby at her yoga studio reads:

> Lose weight to look good in clothes.
> Exercise to look good naked.

It's true. Vero used to hate her short legs, her square box of a torso. Now she sees power. Her quad muscles push against the skin at her thighs, bulge protectively around her kneecaps. Distinct lines of muscles run down her calves. Vero looks good naked. Cheryl once complained, "Why shouldn't these breasts be beautiful? They've survived a pregnancy, they've nourished a baby. They show signs of that: why isn't that beautiful?" Vero couldn't go that far, couldn't bring herself to love the stretch marks and the gnawed nipples, but Bikram has taught her to appreciate the body's work and the signs of that work. She lies back in the sun throwing her own muscled leg over Shane's. Shane spreads his hand across her abdomen. "Almost nap time?"

"I think so," she answers, though they just finished breakfast.

For the first few days, she and Shane spend a lot of time by themselves, which suits Vero fine. Their voyeurism fuels the fun in their room during the late afternoon rainfall. They meet a man with a silver barbell pierced through his tongue. His girlfriend smiles at them. "You know what that's good for?" Vero asks, licking the salt off the rim of her margarita. "It's not just for looks." Later, they see the couple swinging in a hammock, putting the piercing to use.

"How come you never pierced your tongue for me?" Vero teases, back in the room.

"You don't think I'm good enough *au naturel*?" Shane smiles. "I've never noticed any complaints." He grabs her pointer finger between his front teeth, tickles its tip with his tongue.

"I'd need a point of comparison." She traces her fingernail along the outer cartilage of his ear, rounded and firm as a seashell, involuntarily arching her back as he proves his point.

He slips off his wedding ring and slides it around his tongue, nibbling his way down her body.

"Stop! Stop!" she finally begs, laughing as she pushes him away from her. He fights back, but she's strong now too. She curls into fetal position, pulling her knees protectively into her chest. "We can do whatever you want today. Just don't make me come anymore."

"Did Vero Schanton just say *enough*?!" He curls his body over hers, kissing the back of her neck.

"It's a muscle too," she hears herself say as she drifts into sleep. "There *is* such a thing as enough."

In the evening, they phone home. It's Shane's idea. Vero doesn't want to. Eliot will just miss them more, and Jamal only speaks gibberish anyway. But these are things they have agreed not to talk about on their holiday, especially Jamal's speech. So Vero smiles and takes the phone. "It's me! It's Mommy! I miss you!" She shouts her exclamations of love across the ocean. "I'll be home soon! Do you miss Mommy?"

LiLi assures her they are all doing fine but afterward she emails them:

Eliot cry after yr call. He miss mommy so much. But I tak good care. You enjoy fr yourselfs.

That night, Vero goes to bed early, and in the morning they agree not to call again. It's a short holiday. She sends an email asking LiLi to contact them only if there are problems.

Otherwise we'll see you in a week. That's probably easier for everyone. Hugs for you and the boys. —V.N.

All day long, boats float out just past the roped-off swimming area. "Mon! Mon!" old men yell when swimmers get close. "What do you want? I got it. Coke, E, mushrooms, weed. I got it. Good price. Good stuff." Shane swims out and comes back with a stick of weed as big as Vero's Mother's Day bouquets. He holds it high above his head in one hand, stroking the water with the other.

"Are we staying for a year?" she asks as he shakes his hair dry, splattering her with water and then holding his prize up to her nose. The pungent sweet aroma takes her back twenty years. It's true that smell is the sense most closely linked to memory.

"We'll have to make friends. They'll help us polish this off in a week. Some pretty girls, maybe?" He smiles, shaking a finger at her as if it's her idea.

Again with the friends and the girls. Vero wants to make a safe world of just the two of them.

"Women envy what you have in Shane," Joss said once when Vero confided about a late-night fight, one of her barefooted forest fits. "The way he looks at you. He would do anything to make you happy. He would try anything. Hiring LiLi—that was one of his attempts. Maybe he doesn't always know. Maybe he never knows. But he tries." Joss and Ian have been talking again about Ian going off to work in the oil patch: out one week, home one week. Their teenage boys are both still playing hockey. Even with Joss's job at the mine, they can't keep up with costs.

That—the oilfield—is also Ian's attempt to keep everyone in the family happy, to give them all what they think they want. Vero cannot imagine this thin, bearded man, who strums his guitar while he sings his voice-mail greeting, stuck in a trailer in Fort McMurray, a long day's drive from the rest of his family.

Shane rolls ten joints that first night and then stores his bouquet of weed in the safe, its skunky scent spreading to their passports. *Everyone will know we've been to Jamaica*, they laugh.

Stoned, they swim across the boat canal, away from the nudists, to their own deserted sandbar. Boaters shake fists at them, "You will die! Stupid tourists!" But Shane and Vero laugh and laugh. They laugh until it hurts, a muscle ache deep in their abdomens, a scratchy dryness at the back of their throats. Here they could surely die only a cartoon death. They would be cut in two in one scene, and then race off the page in a cloud of smoke in the next. Shane points at a glass-bottomed boat filled with sunburned tourists. "Watch this, Vee," he giggles, diving down, swimming under the boat, close to the glass. He comes up gasping for air. "I rolled over and gave them a view of the North American wild eel. They should charge double for that trip."

When Vero and Shane reach the sandbar, they lie in the warm water, waves lapping at their torsos. *We should've gotten dressed*, Vero thinks, but the words don't make it off her tongue, *we're not at Hedonism anymore*. "Hedonism is a state of mind," she says, pushing Shane's legs apart and rolling between them, leaning back into his chest. She feels him springing to life at her lower back. The sun beats down so hot that water dries between incoming waves, leaving white lines of salt along her stomach.

"Oh, Shane. Let's stay here."

He breathes into the hollow between her neck and her shoulder. Her skin rises to his breath. Goose bumps. From Shane. Her husband of a decade. She couldn't have imagined it. She told LiLi they wanted to spend some time alone on a beach. The way LiLi smiled made Vero blush. "Like a honeymoon? In the movies?" she asked, and Vero nodded, unable to meet her eyes. *Maybe something like that.*

"Let's pretend we're honeymooners." She rolls into Shane. How often do parents kiss? It's like kissing a stranger. "I love salt." Her tongue traces the salty lines down his chest. Waves undulate back and forth over her hips.

"What if someone comes?"

"They won't." She rests her teeth on his hip bone, wants to take a bite. "You taste salty but smell like pineapple," she says into his skin.

"I never knew you could be this much fun." He runs his hands through her sandy hair.

"In a new world with different rules, we change too." She pushes into him with each incoming wave. "Here, I am nobody's mother."

The more sex Vero has, the more she wants. The extent and intensity of this need comes as a tremendous relief. She feared that part of her was dead. Here at Hedonism, sex parks itself right at the front of her brain. She's surprised by how much she likes it there.

"Monogamy," Cheryl said to her just after the birth of Jamal, "is a myth, one with whole industries founded on it."

"Well, it's one I've bought into, Mom." Vero stirred her peppermint tea, letting the spoon clink loudly against the terracotta, enjoying Cheryl's flinch on the word "Mom."

"You're barely forty, and you're never going to have sex with anyone new? Never again?"

"I realize this is your idea of an appropriate conversation, Cheryl, but it's not anyone else's." Vero walked away from the table and dumped her steaming tea down the drain. "And no, for your information, I'm not." She said it with all the confidence she could muster, but the words killed whatever libido she had left. *Nobody. New. Ever.*

"That sure puts you one giant step closer to death, doesn't it?"

But here, here at Hedonism, anything might happen. It turns out that's all Vero needs: the *possibility* of anything happening. Vero is worried, though, about what Shane might think he needs.

"Tell me if you see any girl you like. Anyone who's cute." Shane wants to know who turns her on.

"You," Vero says, taking the joint from his fingers. "You turn me on." She loves how much she really means it.

They play a game of guessing the non-Hedonism identities of the other tourists. A couple around the same age as them keeps trying to make eye contact, positioning themselves strategically at dinner, choosing nearby chairs at the beach. The man is lean and sharp at the corners in a way that suggests meanness. An over-developed muscle always moves at his jaw. Deep lines spread out from the corners of his eyes, but they're not smile lines. His woman—is she a wife? Shane and Vero will never know—has heavy-lidded eyes and long, curly blonde hair that brushes her thin shoulders. At night, he wears a black leather mask, she a studded collar with a leash.

"A vet," Shane guesses. "He obviously loves animals."

"Nope. A banker." Vero can see past the fantasy, knows this man would be more comfortable in a suit. "And she's an elementary school teacher. Kindergarten."

"Uh-huh," Shane moves his head against her lap. They're in a bar, but here at Hedonism, he can lie down in public, can put his cheek against his wife's thighs. Nobody cares. The pierced couple is having sex on the bench next to them. She straddles his hips, legs locked behind his back, like a baby orangutan latched tight around its mother. Shane pulls Vero's head close down to his and whispers that the couple sounds like they're riding bicycles, their grunts and groans matching Vero's at the top of Cardiac Hill. "We should start riding together again when we get home," he says, imitating the breathless groans close to her ear.

Tongue-pierced guy is getting close to the top of the hill now. Vero sneaks sidelong glances. His woman's mouth stretches wide open, but he forces his flat palm against it, keeping her quiet.

Vero strokes Shane's hair. The few days of sun have turned the tips golden.

Shane and Vero agree that they're not into the veterinarian theme, and they steer clear of the banker's probing looks, his throbbing jaw, his dog leash. Shane says he wants someone more relaxed, a couple not trying so hard. For this one week, Vero will play by Shane's rules, the rules of this weird place. They're here now.

Would a couple not trying hard even be here? Vero wonders, but she doesn't say it aloud.

◊◊◊

On day three, Shane panics. The week's nearly half over, and they haven't done anything really wild yet. "We have to put ourselves in the play," he says. "In the centre of the action. We've spent enough time on the sidelines sussing it out."

After sharing a joint in the room, he takes her to happy hour at the swim-up bar, spitting distance from the wild hot tub. A woman with big blonde hair splays herself across a round table in the shallow end. The table's tiled surface supports her torso while her bare legs dangle into the water. Her neck rests against the table's edge, her head tilting back into the pool. Her lips part in a believable imitation of ecstasy. She's a meal of sex: one man at her breasts—all mouth, hand, tongue—while another man goes down. His energy and focus impress Vero. She's stoned and swallows hard to stop the water-rush of giggle forcing its way up from deep inside her.

What's that sex a metaphor for? She giggles, but says nothing aloud. This place works better without words.

Naked tourists gather, plastic cups in hand, watching. There's quite a crowd. The poolside loungers are full. Sunbathers lie on their sides on the cement deck at the edge of the pool. Others sit on stools at the swim-up bar (sometimes two or three to a stool). Some chat, some make out, some just watch quietly and drink their drinks. The woman on the table is ageless in the way of the truly wealthy, her face as plastic and smooth as Barbie's, her breasts as full and round as coconuts. Unaffected by the laws of gravity, her nipples point straight to the sky. She tugs at her own hair with one hand, while the other hand goes back and forth between the two men's heads, pushing, grabbing, clawing.

Vero has to admit that she does not find the woman's performance a turn-off.

"I can't believe she hasn't come yet," she hears herself say to Shane. They stand shoulder to shoulder sipping from their plastic cups. "I couldn't last *fifteen* seconds with the way those two are going at it." Shane nods, his features lit with admiration. She worries he might let out a hearty cheer: *Keep up the good work, boys! Atta way!*

The arch in the woman's back gets higher and higher. A small child could now slither through the space between her and the table. Jamal would fit.

When Shane brings the third round of rum and cokes, the woman's cries finally escalate, pulling attention back to her. Finished, she peels herself off the table, slides into the water, with a shy smile at her audience. Vero half expects her to bow, but then the crowd turns away, facing the bar. The show is over.

◊◊◊

"You're shocked by *that?* Really? That's *so* Monday."

Vero and Shane sit waist deep in the bar pool, Vero sipping on her breakfast Dirty Monkey. It's delicious. The cold sweet cream coats her throat and then her stomach; she feels it moving through her. The rum softens her hangover, dimming the lights just enough to make everything look better. Vero wonders how she has lived without Dirty Monkeys. Every breakfast should be like this one. Shane tips his head toward the action in the far corner of the pool. A pregnant woman squirms in the lap of a redheaded woman's husband. Her beach-ball belly rises and falls below the water line. The woman wears nothing but a straw hat. Her ample breasts overflow the man's hands. Vero tries to be generous and ignore her stretch marks. The man's torso hides underwater. His eyes squeeze tighter with each thrust.

On the next stool over, the pregnant woman's husband has the red-headed woman in his lap, his face as blank as if he's watching late-night TV, his eyes focused on nothing.

"That's what people come here for," Vero says, resting her hand across the back of Shane's warm neck. It's turned a toasty brown. "Don't be a prude."

"But pregnant," he whispers, keeping his face turned away from the busy couples.

"We don't judge. We're hedonists. Remember?" Vero slurps the bottom of her glass clean. Finished, she chews on her straw. This morning she needs another. She tries to imagine what LiLi would make of this place. She pictures LiLi crossing herself, her fingers lingering at the pendant hanging at her collarbone. A gift from her Hong Kong employer, she said. *Inappropriate*, Vero thinks, *so intimate*.

"Enjoying the breakfast show?" she asks the bartender. He doesn't look up, just keeps swiping his dirty dishrag in figure eights across the bar's surface. The skin hangs loose under his eyes.

"I don't even notice anymore. I just do my job." He folds the cloth, picks up a machete, and chops the crown of leaves off a pineapple, narrowly missing his own fingers.

"You look tired," she says, wondering if he's the same guy who was bartending last night. "How long do you work?"

"Long," he answers. This man can wield a knife. Within moments, he's split the whole pineapple into small neat squares. He scrapes them into the blender with the flat edge of his machete.

The longer she looks, the surer she is that he's the same bartender from last night, but something stops her from asking. Her memories fracture and fragment, but she knows Shane took it upon himself, late at night, to introduce Jamaica to a shooter of his own invention, the Teenage Slut, from back in the sweet suite. She's almost certain she remembers him leaping out of the pool and behind the bar, donning a Hedonism bib (wearing nothing but), and making a round of Sluts for everyone.

"Shane," she tried to stop him, "a Teenage Slut is funny when you're twenty-two. Maybe. Not so funny when you're old enough to be the father of one."

Last night's bartender had the same gold cap on his front tooth, the same hooped earring through the top of his left ear, but he wasn't as surly as this guy. Maybe he's not a morning person. The pregnant lady has found her way back to her own husband's lap. That should make Shane happy, but he doesn't look happy this morning. His eyes focus only on the bottom of his glass. Even with all of this, Vero realizes, he is bored. Drinking is the only thing for it.

Sometime after the third round of Teenage Sluts, Imena sidled up next to Vero. She wore a leather swimsuit thong. "Imena means dream," the giantess said to Vero, her voice low and husky, her breath smelling like drugstore lipstick. "I am a dream."

Vero doesn't remember Imena coming or going. Just that. Her giant red lips moving: *I am a dream.*

Vero stretches her neck to see the bartender's nametag. Mike. "Mike: that's not a very exotic name," she says.

"It's my name," he says. Vero hears the drunken slosh of her statement only when it's reflected back to her in his response.

"Who do you think pregnant lady is at home?" Vero rests her bare hip on Shane's underwater barstool, skin pressing into skin. But he quickly shakes his head once. He doesn't want to play their game. She waits for him to meet her eyes. When he doesn't, she goes back to her own stool.

Vero doesn't tell Shane about her own private game, the one where she imagines real Sprucedale people here: Vince and Adele with the dog collar and leash; Heather Schoeman in the cheerleader costume with flab squeezed tightly through her arm holes; LiLi in the role of Imena. *I am a dream.*

It's taken less than a week for her own people to fade, their solid lines smudging in the rum-sodden, THC-addled reality of Hedonism. Vero stretches her arm out over the bar, wiggles her empty cup. "Hey, Mike the Jamaican bartender, can I have another? Please."

THREE

A nanny should respect family rules, keep matters in the home confidential, and communicate any concerns about the children. Open communication is the key to a strong relationship. Engage the nanny in daily discussions about the children's schedule and behaviour. It's also a good idea to schedule regular meetings with your nanny. If you have concerns about your nanny's work, be direct, but don't air conflicts in front of the children. Above all, treat your nanny fairly. A family that treats a nanny with respect will benefit ten times over in her treatment of their children and themselves. She'll bend over backwards for you.
—*Sprucedale Nanny Agency Manual*

CHAPTER THIRTEEN

Ligaya breathes more deeply while Vero and Shane are gone. She pretends that the house belongs to her. But not the boys; they cannot be hers, though that too is tempting. For them, she reminds herself, she is only a caregiver. A *temporary* caregiver. Eliot and Jamal, she reminds herself, will never be her own. They are only a job, and she a minimum-wage worker. A cheap but reliable import.

Ligaya brings Eliot and Jamal down to sleep in her bed during Shane and Vero's absence. She hasn't gotten used to this North American custom of children sleeping alone, especially with Jamal. Surely he is too young. Ligaya cannot let him awaken alone in this giant dark house. Two storeys apart from her. A house this big brims with hiding places, dark corners to hoard monsters, ghosts, and all varieties of imagined evil. The boys would feel safer in her one-room house in the Philippines, a cocoon where they would be always surrounded by adults. Ligaya will, while Vero and Shane are away, keep Jamal close where he knows he is protected. That, she tells herself, is her job.

The boys love the sleepover—the adventure of it—down in LiLi's "house," a space usually off limits after five in the evening. Under the covers, they curl into her, whispering *Ligaya,* as they tumble into the deep dreams known only to children. Jamal weaves his small fingers into her long hair, tickles the nape of her neck. "Ligaya," he says, "Ligaya." The name as natural as breath. The boys love this foreign word that they must never speak around their parents. They love it more, she suspects, for the transgression of it.

"LiLi is my Canada name," she tells them. "Only when we play the Philippines game, only then I am Ligaya. There, in my country, I am always Ligaya." She holds her cheek against Eliot's, saying the name close to his ear. "*Happiness.* Ligaya means happiness." Ligaya always says "happiness" with tickles, and then, when they can take no more tickles, she kisses them where their little necks meet their little shoulders and smooths their wild hair behind their puppy-soft ears.

"Ligaya—" Eliot stretches his lips around the word in an exaggerated stage whisper. "—can we play the Philippines game the whole time Mommy and Daddy are gone?" He cups his hands around his mouth, protecting the secret from his mother and father, as if they can see him from their fancy resort across the time zones.

"Yes," Ligaya grins at him, cupping her own mouth, and dragging out the *ssss* with a hungry serpent's smile. "And in the Philippines, we will all sleep in one bed." She matches his stage whisper, puts the fun of it in her eyes. Children, she knows, are expert eye readers.

"Ligaya!" The word is loud and full in Jamal's mouth. "LIGAYA!" Jamal does not know how to whisper. His enthusiasm reminds her of Totoy. Nothing will ever be small, nothing ever quiet, with these wild boys of hers. Ligaya hugs Eliot and Jamal close to her body and pulls the blankets tight across their chests. "I get the middle," she says, "because I am the adult. I choose. And I choose no wrestling. I choose no giggling. I choose only sleeping. You there, and you there." She keeps an arm around each.

Ligaya's bed is narrow, but she is only a small woman, and the boys like to sleep close. She pulls them even tighter, so nobody will roll out. They all fit. She kisses Eliot near his ear, and then Jamal. They smell of baby shampoo. The exaggerated soapy scent fills her small room. *Happiness.* "No more words for now," she whispers. "Night is the time for sleep in Philippines game. Tomorrow we talk."

"Goodnight, LiLi."

"Gudnayt, Ligaya."

They are good boys, these two. She puts her nose close to Eliot's hair and lets the scent of baby shampoo carry her to sleep. It is a luxury, she knows, an indulgence. But she takes it.

Deserves it?

She will not say.

◊◊◊

There were legal issues to resolve before Ligaya could be left alone with the boys for an extended period. That's how Vero had put it. "LiLi, we must be careful…certain legal issues…we want to be fair…always."

"But as long as you're happy to make the extra money," Shane rubbed his palms hard on his slacks as if trying to scrape off tree sap, "then there shouldn't be a problem."

Ligaya tried to catch all of Vero's words, but even after almost a year with the family, Ligaya found Vero's speech too fast. Ligaya couldn't hold onto the words long enough to string them together and find their meaning. Trying to make sense of Vero's words is like trying to eat soup out of a pillowcase.

There was something in her speech about a labour scandal here in Sprucedale at a coffee shop, something about a national politician breaking laws too, overworking his nanny, something about a government "crackdown"—*what is a crackdown?* Ligaya wanted to ask but Vero left no space for questions, didn't allow for confusion, for the possibility of absolute incomprehension. There was something also about vigilance, Vero kept saying "government vigilance," but Ligaya did not know that word. It sounded strong. Ligaya imagined Popeye the Sailor Man eating a can of vigilance, his muscles bulging with new vigilance.

Vero said "a politician broke the law" with an odd smile, as if it were a joke, a contradiction in terms, something that might need explaining to the slow foreigner. Ligaya nodded and waved off Vero's rambling explanation. Vero must know very little about the Philippines if she thought Ligaya needed lessons on corrupt politicians. In the Philippines, there is no other kind of politician.

"So we're not *supposed* to, *technically* speaking, leave you alone with the kids overnight, if we're going *exactly* by the book." Vero paused here as if waiting for Ligaya to speak, but Ligaya did not know what she was meant to say. She felt relief when Vero continued. "But we will pay you overtime for those extra hours. Overtime to sleep. It's in your best interest." Supposed to's, technicalities, bent rules, and best interests—this is the language of the politicians Ligaya knows. This, she understood. Ligaya nodded at Vero. "Yes, it is no problem. The extra hours. It is fine. It is good."

Fine. Ligaya would take Vero and Shane's money to sleep. She calculated how much she would need to save to send special presents home to Nene and Totoy. Maybe a bright red Frisbee like the one Eliot treasures. Totoy would be old enough now to catch and return a decent throw to his sister. Maybe some nice-smelling shampoo for Nanay too. She has heard nothing from Pedro, so she will send Pedro nothing. Even though Ligaya has agreed to do the extra work, Vero and Shane still arrange for Gregory and Heather Schoeman to help out.

The mention of their names surprises Ligaya. This North American concept of a family made up of people who are never around, of grandparents who may as well live in another country, of grandparents who may as well go back to South Africa, who visit so seldom, they may as well be dead, makes no sense to Ligaya. Less sense than snow. Less sense than an extra house full of bicycles. Less sense than hiring someone to care for your own children.

"They're very busy," Shane said.

"And they're not crazy about kids," Vero added.

But the Schoemans, the absentee grandparents, do respond to obligation. Of a certain kind.

"We can't have you working around the clock for a full week," Shane told Ligaya. "We'll both end up behind bars. You'll be stuck with the boys for good."

Ligaya glanced at Vero to see if these prison bars belonged to one of Shane's peculiar jokes.

"You'll need some breaks while we're away, LiLi. And it wouldn't kill Shane's folks to spend some time with their own grandkids."

This comes to Ligaya's mind when Heather and Gregory appear. They look like the visit with Eliot and Jamal might, in fact, kill them. Gregory hobbles in the door, leaning his full weight on a golden eagle head mounted atop a sturdy black cane. He swings his leg in an odd half circle with every step, as if he has no hip joint. These North American sports, so bad for the body's health. He may have been an athlete in his youth, but Ligaya cannot imagine him running now. How else will he keep up with Eliot and Jamal?

Heather wears a perfectly pressed beige silk blouse. Beige! Who wears beige when caring for children? It will be stained within minutes. Bright green squares of glass hang from her ears. Mr and Mrs Schoeman look like they've never spent a moment with young children in their entire lives. Ligaya suspects a nanny raised Shane through the hardest years, back in South Africa. Jamal would love to get his hands onto those bright squares dangling from Mrs Schoeman's ears and yank. Mr and Mrs Schoeman will never survive the night. Ligaya wonders if she can in good conscience turn the children over to these near strangers, these ill-prepared caregivers. But, Ligaya reminds herself, Jamal and Eliot do not, after all, belong to her. This unlikely couple, these are their blood relatives, their real family.

Ligaya half expects Jamal and Eliot to look at the pair of carefully dressed geriatrics and ask their names, but the boys run to them, hurling their small thick bodies into the bony old legs hidden beneath perfectly pressed pants.

"Granny!"

"Granddad!"

Jamal and Eliot's faces glow, their bodies buzz with energy. They run in tight, fast circles like puppies chasing their tails. They're as excited, as brimming with love, as they might be if this Granny and Granddad showed up every afternoon to take the two of them for ice cream.

The generosity of children, thinks Ligaya, but she cannot finish the sentence. The thought is too big. She hopes Nene and Totoy will be as generous with her when she finally sees them again. She will not let herself think *if*.

"We'll bring them back tomorrow morning," Heather says to Ligaya with a tight smile. She fingers the green glass squares hanging from her ears with one hand and holds Eliot's hand with the other. The way she somehow holds Eliot's hand while simultaneously pushing him away from her, using a stiff arm to keep him slightly apart where he won't soil or crease her beige blouse—that rigid arm gives Ligaya a sad liquid itch in her sinuses.

"You're on emergency standby, though, right?" Gregory's voice belongs to a stronger man, the man he must have once been. He leans clumsily into his cane, and Ligaya hopes he makes it back down the front steps without incident. "We have you on some kind of 911 line?"

Ligaya sees now where Shane gets his odd way of speaking. "Oh no," she smiles. "No 911. But I am right here if you need." She puts a hand on Eliot's head but quickly pulls it away in case Mr and Mrs Schoeman think the gesture too proprietary. And then she instantly regrets the furtive withdrawal. She does not wish to seem nervous, untrustworthy. She is surprised to find herself auditioning for these two. They are not, she reminds herself, her employers. She smiles again in a way she hopes seems more natural. "The boys be good for you. Good for their Granny and Granddad. Okay, boys?"

With Eliot and Jamal gone for the night, Ligaya invites Cheska to the house. She rarely invites friends, even though when she first arrived, Vero said, "Have friends over! This is your home!" Vero made the invitation with her eyes stretched wide open, an expression Ligaya still couldn't decode. Ligaya took her at her word, though, and did treat the basement as her home, at first. She and Cheska sat at the tea table, cross-legged on the carpet, eating bowls of leftover curry, pilfered from the upstairs' fridge. They watched romantic comedies and did each other's hair in complicated braids. They put on makeup that they bought at the Walmart and took photos of their fancy faces, posting dozens on Facebook. *Look! See the fun we're having! In our new country! Life is good!* Still, the house never *felt* like her home. Cheska scurried in the side door and straight down to the basement, scared of being cornered by Vero, harassed by her well-intentioned questions.

"Do you like it here in Sprucedale?"

"Is Mrs Parks treating you well?"

"Do you miss the Philippines?"

Ligaya hated to see Cheska stuck there between the side door and the basement stairs, a look of stupid terror paralyzing her face because Cheska feared misunderstanding Vero's rapid-fire questions, feared that Vero would be unable to interpret her heavy accent, feared that she might answer the questions the wrong way. In Cheska's face, Ligaya saw a mirror of herself and felt humiliation rise in her, filling her like hot water, from her feet up. This liquid heat would drown her. Ligaya suppressed the bubbling rush of humiliation by telling herself that she knew better than Cheska, she understood more than Cheska—she would teach Cheska. She told herself that she only imagined her own face in Cheska's. *It is not so.*

"Don't say okay," Ligaya told Cheska when they were safely in the basement. "North Americans do not like the word okay. Tell them it is 'great!' Everything is wonderful! Don't say 'grand,' though. If you say grand, they think you mock them. It is too much, grand, but *okay,* it is not enough. Say: Good! Good! Good!"

The ridiculousness of these distinctions made Ligaya and Cheska smile and then, in a flood of relief, giggle, and forget their humiliation. How could they be expected to know something is wrong with "okay"? It would take them a lifetime to learn all these silly rules.

Even once they made it past Vero and downstairs—into "Ligaya's house," as Eliot calls it—they were not entirely safe. Shane would come jogging down to his weight room, his shirt off and tucked into his waistband, his chest slick with the sweat of a recent bike ride, his rear end comically exposed in spandex shorts. "Do you girls mind?" he asked, wiping his face with the tail of his shirt. "If I do a few weights?"

They smiled and nodded, Ligaya hating their muteness in the face of this man.

"Just gonna pump some iron here, ladies," he continued, flexing his muscles, pushing an imaginary barbell from his chest. Ligaya wondered if he might be as uncomfortable as they were. "Wanna take a turn? I could give you girls some lessons. We could make a run for the Philippines' Olympic team. The country's first women weightlifters."

"Oh no. No, no, no," they giggled, backing away from Shane's jokes, his naked chest, backing toward Ligaya's only truly private space. Safe inside Ligaya's bedroom, Cheska stuffed a roll of socks down her pants, gyrated her hips, and flexed her muscles. Ligaya clamped her palm flat over Cheska's mouth so Shane couldn't hear their giggles. This country has transformed them into teenaged girls. The place that promised to move them forward into prosperity has taken them backward into adolescence.

Even with Vero and Shane away, Ligaya feels that Cheska's presence in the house is a transgression. Cheska is not Shane's friend, and this is Shane's house. Still, Ligaya puts a mattress on the floor of the sitting room, by Shane's weights, and invites Cheska to stay overnight. "Cheska will be our secret," she says to Eliot and Jamal. "Part of the Philippines game." Cheska looks much like Ligaya, could be a younger sister, but Cheska smiles more than Ligaya does. Cheska eats more too and talks more. Cheska does everything more. "Eliot and Jamal will not tell," Ligaya assures her. "They know this word, *sumbungero*." Tattletale. "My boys are no tattletales." Eliot and Jamal like secrets and they like an extra nanny in the basement, as if their Ligaya has multiplied. Twice the tickles, twice the admiration, twice the treats, twice the applause at their mastery of tricky words like *sumbungero*.

Ligaya and Cheska linger upstairs during their one week reprieve. They eat at the big oak dining room table and watch movies on the giant flat screen television. To torment Ligaya, Cheska threatens to take a bath in the oversized jet tub off the master bedroom and come downstairs wearing Vero's terrycloth bathrobe with its Four Seasons logo.

"I send pictures home to my mama, and she says, 'Cheska, you get fat!' I say, 'Mama, there are no men for me in this country; eating is my only pleasure.' She says, 'With a backside like that, there will be no man for you in any country.' *Hay naku*!"

Cheska stands in the middle of the living room, staring at the leather furniture, the arching windows looking out on a sprawling backyard, the shining black granite countertops. Vero taught Ligaya just how to polish those countertops. "Take special care of these," she requested. "We could feed a family of four for a year on what these cost." Cheska tilts her head back and looks at the high ceiling, the rows and rows of pot lights. She spins a slow circle, eyes wide. The hunger in Cheska's eyes embarrasses Ligaya. Finally Cheska stops spinning, spreads her arms. "One day," she says, "I will have a house like this one." Reverence fills her voice, as if she's speaking in a church. Ligaya wants to slap her, and turns her back so Cheska won't see the violent impulse cross her face. Ligaya instantly recognizes the lack of fairness in her reaction. Cheska only gives words to what Ligaya also thinks, voices a desire that Ligaya feels too intensely for words. Cheska says what Ligaya wouldn't dare.

◊◊◊

Every evening after her shift, Cheska comes over so she and Ligaya can play in the big kitchen. They make piles of flatbread stuffed with garlic peas, deep bowls of pork-blood stew and *puto*, stacks of plantains rolled in egg-roll wrappers. They fill bowls with anchovies fried to a dry crisp. Cheska has brought Zamboanga octopus from a recent visit to

Vancouver. They steam it, and Cheska dangles the raw tentacles from her eye sockets, making Jamal squeal with delight and Eliot shriek in horror. "Cheska, you are a child," Ligaya says, but there is kindness in her voice. Cheska and Ligaya cook as if they will invite an entire village for the feast. The whole house smells of fish sauce. Ligaya has been granted one week free of Shane and his "issues." Let the house smell.

"We're not tattletales," Eliot says, sniffing the fish sauce in the air, knowing his father would disapprove. "I like the smell, LiLi." He wolfs down the fish, fried plain for him. The buttery white flecks fall from his lips when he speaks. "I mean, Ligaya," he says, wiping his bare arm across his food-stained mouth. "It's still the Philippines game, right?"

This is the first time Ligaya has heard her real name full and loud in his mouth, not relegated to basement whispers. A part of regular conversation. No secret. "Yes, Eliot, for a while more we play the Philippines game."

"Well, I like the smell, *Ligaya*. It reminds me of the Philippines."

She does not ask him how a smell can remind him of a place he's never been.

◊◊◊

Cheska lies on her stomach on Ligaya's bed, bare heels in the air, flipping through Vero's running magazines. "Why doesn't she have fashion magazines?" There's a bowl of peanuts at Cheska's elbow, and she eats them one at a time, licking her fingers after each. "Or the celebrity ones?" But Cheska continues to leaf through the pages, the glaze of her eyes matching the gloss of the page.

Eliot digs into Ligaya's secret drawer and passes the well-thumbed pictures to Jamal, naming the subject of each as if they're as familiar as his own family.

"*Nanay*, that means mother."

"*Tatay*, that means father."

"Nene."

"Totoy."

"Pedro."

Ligaya flinches on Pedro. "Nene and Totoy," she repeats, just for the luxury of feeling the syllables in her mouth.

"They're your brother and sister, right, Ligaya?' Her full name has become so familiar on Eliot's tongue that she fears he will use it when his parents return. She should ban it now. For the habit.

"Yes, Eliot. My little brother. My little sister."

"But aren't they too little? Aren't you big enough to be their mommy?" He speaks into the faces of the photograph, his eyebrows pinched in concentration, searching for the answer to some mystery he knows hides there.

"Maybe, Eliot. Maybe I'm big enough." She looks way from the photograph, their bare feet, their dirty shorts. "But they are my brother and sister."

"You *seem* big enough to be a mommy." Eliot scratches his chin, staring hard at the two children frozen in time. "You *seem* too big to be their sister."

"Eliot, *that's how it is*." Ligaya tries to keep the hardness from her voice. It is not his fault. None of it.

Jamal holds the photo of Nanay up to his face; he likes the cool, smooth surface against his cheek. Ligaya pries it from his sweaty boy fingers, places it carefully back in the drawer.

"Knowing Jamal, he will eat the picture as soon as look at it," she says to Cheska to explain the sharpness in her movements. But she will not meet Cheska's eyes or even turn in her direction. She will not try to explain why her voice sounds as if she has forgotten how to breathe. A child's understanding, that is one thing, but Ligaya cannot bear to see the knowledge in Cheska's face too. *Big enough to be a mommy. Yes.*

On Thursday, Mr and Mrs Schoeman take Jamal and Eliot during the afternoon, and Ligaya fills her time by walking to the agency downtown to visit Bernie. She aims for a time she knows the office will be slow so Bernie might offer to make her tea in the special Philippines' way. Bernie keeps a cassava in the fridge for such occasions. Ligaya resists the vanity of thinking it is only for her and assumes Bernie is visited by many nannies who enjoy her company. Bernie understands the Filipina nanny way, and does not leave Ligaya to sit idle while she works, knowing that watching someone else work makes Ligaya uncomfortable and fidgety. She directs Ligaya to slice the cassava into thin pieces while she boils the ginger. Over the steaming water and clack of the sharp knife, they talk. Ligaya tells Bernie things she tells no one else, perhaps because Bernie does not try so hard, does not ask ridiculous questions. Bernie appears to barely listen at all. She makes herself an empty space into which Ligaya can dump her thoughts after the satisfaction of hearing them aloud, just once.

"I'm your advocate," she told Ligaya when she first arrived. "I can also be like a friend, if you want."

It was the "if you want" that won Ligaya.

"How's your *proctalgia fugax* times two?" Bernie dips the tea bag into the steaming ginger water.

"Procta...?" Ligaya is not use to feeling confusion with Bernie. She stops slicing and studies Bernie's face looking for the joke.

"Pain in the ass in Latin," Bernie smiles, drying her fingers on a tea towel. "A pain so bad it sometimes wakes you up in the middle of the night. It's a medical condition. But kids, they sometimes feel like a medical condition, when you're the one doing all the caring for them."

Ligaya bites her lips and thinks of the poster behind their backs. The blonde mother snuggled close with her blonde child, the dark nanny reading to the child held at arm's length. The formality between the nanny and child in this photograph is false. Such formality would be more likely with the parents. The nanny spends all day with the children. Who could maintain such stiff posture day in and day out? Not Ligaya. She doesn't know how to respond to Bernie. Jamal and Eliot can be a challenge, and Ligaya would like a holiday. She would like to curl up in her single bed, pull the covers over her head, and sleep for a week. But she does not call Jamal and Eliot names. Where she comes from, adults do not call children names.

"Oh, I don't say that. Pain in the...! About Eliot and Jamal."

"Right. You can't say it. So I will." Bernie's eyes wrinkle at the corners, and she always seems on the verge of winking. Her expression says, *It's okay to laugh. What else can we do?* Ligaya tries to imitate her lightness.

When they drink the tea, Ligaya opens her mouth wide against the cup and lets the pieces of yam slide past her teeth with the liquid. She sucks on their sweetness during the breaks in their conversation. Bernie picks the yams from her cup and holds them between her fingers, nibbling while Ligaya talks.

It's nice to have this one pair of ears. Ligaya tells Bernie that she wrote a test last week, before Vero and Shane left, for her driving learner's license. "Takes me so long," she says, "Sometimes I am five minutes just to figure out what the question asked." But with an allowance of extra time, Ligaya passed the written test. Bernie says she will take her for driving practice. Ligaya does not know what she hopes to achieve with this license. She has no car and no place to go. But the idea of driving is a kind of freedom. Bernie does not question her motives. She does not ask about Vero, either, doesn't seem to wonder whether Vero knows of Ligaya's plan to learn to drive. Ligaya has not told Vero, who would turn this new goal into her own project. She does not want driving lessons from Vero.

Ligaya watches Bernie drink the tea, expecting her to flinch. With the sweet yam and spoonfuls of extra sugar, the tea is too sweet for North American tastes. Ligaya suspects Bernie drinks it just to be polite, though Bernie claims she makes it at home for her girlfriend, Shauna. "She has a sweet tooth that would put any ten-year-old to shame."

"Maybe she part Filipino," Ligaya jokes, pouring herself another cup of tea, while Bernie has barely begun hers. Shauna drives ambulance for the city of Sprucedale. Ligaya imagines herself doing the same job once she learns to drive, when her family is here and she has graduated from being a nanny.

The August sun shines hot through the agency windows. It's a day to take for granted in the Philippines, but here the sun is worshipped when it finally appears. On Ligaya's walk to Bernie's office, she detoured by the beach, which crawled with athletes jammed into long-sleeved, skin-tight black wet suits. Some even wore hoods. Sea monsters, that's what they looked like to Ligaya. But Shane had previously explained to her that the people in wet suits were training for a triathlon: they swim, they bike, they run. *People in this country are obsessed with making sweat. Humans are curious creatures,* thinks Ligaya. *Those who needn't worry about survival invent ways to punish themselves.* As she walked along the shore watching the triathletes, the sun burned her skin, but its heat didn't remind her of home, except in the not-reminding. In that way, her Philippines home is always with her.

Ligaya would give anything to quit sweating now as she sits in the window, working up the courage to speak. Today, there is something Ligaya wants to tell Bernie, maybe even needs to tell her. She looks into the bottom of her second cup of tea, swirls the sugary liquid. Bernie nibbles, saying nothing, as if she knows Ligaya has something that only silence will pull from her.

"Bernie, I tell you..." Ligaya finally says, eyes still in her tea cup, "about my boyfriend back home? The one who went into the bed with my friend? They forced to marry? I the godmother of new baby?"

When Bernie says nothing, Ligaya lifts her head to see if Bernie is listening. Bernie nods ever so slightly, but says nothing. She has put her cup down and curls a piece of her hair around her finger as she listens.

"I tell this to Vero, like it is me." Ligaya drops her head again. "That is not my story. That happen to my cousin, Corazon. But my true story different."

This time, Ligaya does not look up. Eventually, Bernie prompts her with a single word. "Yes." Ligaya imagines a warning in the word: *Are you sure you want to tell me this?* But she cannot stop now.

"I have my own children. Nene. Totoy. My daughter. My son. Not sister. Not brother. Pedro is their father." As easy as that, it's out. Ligaya turns her attention to her body, checks to see if the confession makes her feel different, lighter, but Bernie's words interrupt her.

"Your application said single. Your application said no children."

Ligaya listens for a note of accusation but finds none. *Tell me*, the tone says. *Explain.* Ligaya thinks (hopes) she hears something else there too, something like, *I will try to understand.*

"What difference does it make? Once I am here, my children are not mine. Once I am here, what kind of mother can I be? I am no mother." Ligaya tucks her hair behind her ears, sets her cup on the table, and meets Bernie's eyes. "I am no mother to them anymore. That is no lie."

"I do *not* know this information, Ligaya. Once you leave my office, it's as if you never told me. Understand?" Bernie's words are firm but her eyes are soft. "Keeping something like this a secret? My ass is on the line. I'd lose my job. Maybe worse."

"Nobody know but you, Bernie. Nobody here will ever know." Ligaya nearly wishes she had kept quiet. What if people in Sprucedale knew? What would they think of her? They would judge. Ligaya's own judgment is enough to bear. "Not even Cheska."

Bernie pinches her lips together until she has none and then holds her flat palm across her mouth, closes her eyes.

"I cannot tell Vero the truth. It will make her too sad." Even if Ligaya wanted to tell Vero, she could not. Her motivation has gone beyond sadness. Now Ligaya cannot tell because of the lie. *There will be legal implications*, she hears Mister Shane. His "issues" would run wild with this detail. And then what? Ligaya cannot go home. She doesn't have the money even for a ticket. "And how will I forget my sadness if I see it in Vero's face every day?" Ligaya thinks she sees Bernie nod, her eyes still closed, but the movement is so slight that it could be Ligaya's imagination, her wishful thinking. "I must forget."

Ligaya makes this confession only to Bernie. She leaves it there. It's the only way.

FOUR

Hedonism is a sandbox for your inner child, nourishment for the mind, body, spirit, and soul. Pleasure comes in many forms. Choose one. Or two. Or more. And with absolutely everything included in one upfront price, you never have to think about money. Not even tips. Just what to do next. And when.

—*Hedonism II brochure*

Chapter Fourteen

The pregnant Swiss woman wears nothing but a broad-brimmed straw hat. It casts a protective shadow over her face and shoulders but leaves an orb of protruding belly exposed to the late-day sun. Her stretched navel, pulled so thin it looks ready to split wide open, is deformed by a lump of foetus head. She digs a toe into the cool damp sand below the scorching hot layer and sips on a Dirty Monkey. Vero would like to think it's just "Monkey"—no trace of the rum that makes it "Dirty"—but Hedonism is not the kind of place where one judges another's parenting choices.

Check your judgment at the door here, Vero Baby!

A thick pink *lina nigra* runs from the woman's breast bone to her pubic bone. Vero imagines tracing a sharp scalpel down the line and pulling the baby free of the pollution.

To the pregnant woman, Vero says only, "Dirty Monkey, that's more of a breakfast drink, isn't it?" And then to Shane, "I guess I'll have something with tequila. It is Happy fucking Hour. After all."

Shane's right: once he and Vero find their group, things move quickly. He's wrong about the choosing, though, deluded to think they might have had some kind of control. As with so much of life, "their group" just happens as a matter of timing and coincidence.

Jamaica blurs. Hazy on the horizon, hazy in the foreground, hazy in Vero's mind. Just when the vacation should be coming to a quick close, time rolls over and stretches out in the sun, puts its head down for a rest in the warm sand. The rules in this booze-sodden place twist and bend and morph until Vero forgets there was ever such a thing as rules.

That surprises you? That's so Sprucedale.

That surprises you? That's so Tuesday.

That surprises you? That's so nine p.m.

"Their group" is made up of non-English speakers—a Swiss couple and a French one—and they work their trades in broken phrases and awkward hand gestures, keeping small talk to a minimum.

Shane and Vero agree: no names. They don't want to turn the Hedonists into real people who might exist beyond this holiday. They refer only to FrenchMan, FrenchWoman, SwissMan, and SwissWoman. Vero started by calling SwissWoman "PregnantLady." Shane glared. He's chosen to ignore what he does not like.

Vero wishes she could mix and match the couples. She likes FrenchWoman—the splash of freckles across her slightly flattened nose, her pink-tinged, fleshy shoulders in her evening sundresses at dinner, the way she smells of coconut even after she's left the beach and washed off the tanning oil. FrenchWoman wears no makeup around her eyes, which are nearly black and remind Vero of LiLi's, but her plump lips are always painted the colour of Merlot. Perhaps it's the power of Shane's suggestion, but Vero finds herself wondering what it would be like to kiss those lips. She imagines them pressed against the curve where neck meets shoulder, and imagines running her tongue along FrenchWoman's small, sharp teeth.

Although Vero calls her FrenchWoman when she and Shane speak, she thinks of her by her real name. *Danielle.* She puts a French spin on it, as best as she can with her English tongue.

Vero's mouth stretches into an involuntarily smile when Danielle calls her *Veronique*, the syllables acrobatic, rolling, sliding, leaping on Danielle's foreign tongue. "For this week," Vero says to Shane, "I am *Veronique.*"

But FrenchMan—with his sunken chest and squinty eyes that never rise to meet Vero's face—he creeps her out. He speaks no English and lurks behind Danielle, eager for her translations, leaning forward, his long muscles tensed with desperation for Danielle to close a deal, complete some transaction he has directed her to conduct on his behalf.

SwissMan, on the other hand, seems likeable. He laughs at the end of each of his limping sentences. *It's okay*, his tone says. *This place is merely a joke. We are only joking here.* "I am," he tells them in a slow thick accent, "an orthopedic surgeon." He punctuates the sentence with a deep laugh rumbling up from his chest, as if nothing could be funnier than any of them, even for one second, pretending that his statement might be true, pretending that anything here might be true.

He has hints of grey in his dark curls. "It is silver highlights," he tells them. And laughs. Vero enjoys spending time with him; his flippancy suits the place, but his wife, one cannot help but notice, is very, very pregnant. SwissMan's laughter allows Vero to sink comfortably into the alternate reality of Hedonism, but his wife's pregnancy is enough to pull her out of it.

"What is it you want?" FrenchWoman puts the question to Vero bluntly. "Why are you here for?" The bluntness doesn't bother Vero. Vero would tell Danielle: *This is not my idea,* she would say, *I want only to survive.* She would hold up her hand, peeling it off her chilled plastic cup of booze, spread her fingers wide. *I'm too old for this*, she would say. *Look. See these wrinkles? Dishpan hands! I have old-people skin.*

"My husband, he want the mouth of another woman. On him. You do that?" FrenchWoman sucks on the arm of her sunglasses, twirls it between her eye teeth. "If yes, I will do for your husband." She makes the proposition with her freckled nose wrinkled in a laugh, a deep dimple cratering her right cheek. Her face grants this discussion no significance, no seriousness. They could be deciding what afternoon matinee to see. *What's better for you, Thursday or Wednesday?* Or: *Your boys, they like scary movies or only funny?* "Maybe the husbands, they like that. Two women. You understand men: they love the mouth. When the week over, we leave for home. To a normal. Yes?"

One day hazes into the next. Vero and Shane hover at the periphery of the poolside debauchery, spectators only, and then take that energy back to their room. Vero grows accustomed to the soreness.

"Does it hurt?" Shane asks. "Are you too sore?"

"Of course," Vero says, pulling him deeper.

As they run out of days, they edge their way closer to the action. First, Shane takes Vero from behind, her body pushed up against the sliding doors. Anyone at the pool below could look up and see her breasts pressed flat into the glass. Next, they have sex on the beach, Shane curled behind her in a shady hammock. Vero can't quite manage an orgasm, too distracted by the DogCouple floating on a mattress just off shore, casting furtive glances back to her and Shane. But she breathes quick and fast as the hammock swings, and Shane doesn't seem to miss her climax. He kisses her neck afterward, pushing his foot against the palm tree so the hammock sways gently. "God, that was good."

That night, she takes him in her mouth behind a plant pot near the wild tub, both of them pretending to be unaware of the bathers watching them from the steam.

"Well," she says, wiping her lips and smiling up at him. "This is what we're here for." But she knows that if they were here only for exhibitionist acts, they could've stayed home in bed with the baby monitor on in LiLi's basement.

At first, Shane and Vero keep a comfortable distance from the other Hedonists. Their need for each other is constant, insistent. They drink, fuck, and smoke, drink, fuck, and smoke until there's no distinction: drinkfucksmokedrinkfucksmokedrinkfuck.

As the week limps on, they're never far from the resort bar. "Don't let the hangover catch up with you," Shane says, passing Vero a Dirty Monkey with a slice of breakfast pineapple. "Drink fast before you sober up."

By Thursday, the wild hot tub no longer seems wild. It's just games and more games. The bodies only bodies.

You can touch here, if I can do that.

I'll put my mouth there, if you'll put yours here.

The hot tub antics would be more comfortable in a bed, but the couples stay at the hot tub, bare bottoms pressing into rough concrete, rather than retreating to private rooms where they might be in danger of real intimacy. The impossibility of these acts happening in public makes the nights seem unreal. They don't count. Shane and Vero will get home and remember the exchanges only faintly, an erotic dream that steps beyond their grasp just before they wake, leaving nothing but a warm tingle, a desire to fall back into that sleep, and stay there. And then they'll forget.

This blindfold's chafing me, Vero thinks on more than one occasion but never says it aloud. Like so much else that comes to mind, the statement deviates too far from the script of Hedonism, the place that sells pure pleasure. Pleasure doesn't chafe. Vero sucks hard on her tequila and melted ice cubes, smiles drunkenly. That the script allows.

The conversations she and Shane have in their room, surrounded by the towel swans with their long twisted necks, are more real, but only slightly. They negotiate details, plan for what they hope to achieve down in the marketplace, what they're willing to barter.

"We have to be on the same team," Shane says, so high that his eyes are nearly swollen shut. Vero tries to picture him with his eyes clear and bright and open, tries to remember the eyes of Sprucedale's favourite pharmacist. She can't. "We need to agree on where we draw our lines," he says. "Present a united front. Agree on where we won't go."

Vero flops across the mattress, studying the painting of the yellow-breasted woman above the bed. *This art's not so bad*, she decides, *once you ignore proportion.* "We should get one of these for our room at home, mount it above our bed." She imagines LiLi averting her gaze from the naked woman during her weekly changing of the sheets. "The yellow skin is perfect: suntan meets liver poisoning. Very Hedonism."

"Vero. Focus. Lines." Shane's looking at himself in the mirror, studying a mole under his armpit for melanoma's deformation.

"Sure," she slurs until the word has three lazy syllables. "Definitely, let's agree on our lines." She can't imagine why it could possibly matter, these lines of Shane's. "Sure," she says, "whatever." She's surprised, in a stoned and hollow way, by Shane's naiveté. He doesn't understand the barter system.

"No men," he says, lifting his eyes to meet hers in the mirror. "I couldn't stomach seeing you with another man."

When she says nothing, he adds, "Because I love you."

A swan towel perches on Vero's belly, its beak pointed toward her chin. She has tried to make one herself, but can't get it to stay stiff and upright. Theanna, the cleaning lady, turns a towel into a swan in ninety seconds flat. It's the only thing she does fast. She's often still in the room when Vero and Shane return for their siesta, moving as if each step is a favour to them, one she grants grudgingly. Vero chatters, playing the enthusiastic tourist, filling the heavy silences. One day, she points down the beach at loose rubble along the shoreline. "What happened there?"

"Oh, that's the tornado, done that. Tornado dohn give a dodo 'ow much money you 'ave. It go everywhere just the same." Theanna bends over the bed, smoothing imaginary wrinkles in the comforter, making no move to hurry her work for Shane and Vero's sake. *I'll leave when I leave. An' you? You can just sidung your pretty white batty an' wait.*

LiLi has never claimed a space like Theanna does. Not at the home of the Sprucedale Nanton-Schoemans. In watching Theanna, Vero sees LiLi's submissiveness. Vero tries to pull LiLi's image clearly to mind. Fails. Even Jamal and Eliot have faded. She could dig her wallet out of the closet safe, look at their pictures, refresh her memory. But she chooses not to.

"So no men," she says to Shane, hearing a floating quality to her words. She deepens her voice to bring them down, pull them into her body. "But you'd like to be with one of the women, maybe?" She lobs the question at Shane gently, wondering if he'll recognize his own hypocrisy. "Maybe with me and another woman?"

His mouth smears into a slow grin. "Well, if one offered ..." He lies beside her on the bed and puts his head on her chest, avoiding whatever it is he sees in her face. "If your FrenchWoman offered."

"Shane. An offer? Nothing is free here. An offer is a request. Accepting an offer—that's a commitment."

"Baby," he twirls his finger in slow circles around the perimeter of her bellybutton. "Relax. We're not signing any contracts. Nobody can make us do anything. Somebody wants to give something, I'll take it."

"Shane." The extent of Shane's naïveté takes all the wind out of Vero. That one word is an effort. "Don't let Danielle do anything to you that you don't want me doing with another man." Vero can't believe she has to explain this to Shane. Hearing herself say it aloud, she's embarrassed, as if she's just had to point to the stove element, as she would caution Jamal, and warn Shane: *Hot! Hot!*

"She likes you," Shane says, "I can tell."

Once, Vero thinks, *we are here only once.* She puts a nervous twitter in her voice, a tease, and says, "I don't know what to do with a girl." She says these words only to hear them aloud. She wonders if they will sound true.

The truth is that she would like to get Danielle alone in their room, with no Shane and no FrenchMan. She is curious about that. But she knows that when she and Danielle meet, it will be a public performance. It will be more about Shane watching than it is about Danielle and Vero responding.

"Just do what you like," Shane says, breathing the words into Vero's stomach. "If you like it, she'll like it too." He rolls over to face Vero, his chin tracing a line up the centre of her body, and pulls the sheet over their heads. "Let me remind you what you like," he says with his mouth open at her neck, ready to take a bite.

◊◊◊

In the mornings, there's much to ignore—the grey ring of scum around the hot tub, the joint butts floating in the pool, the vomit in the ceramic plant pots. Vero thinks of Roger in his hot-pink Bikram shorts. "Paradise is a state of mind." Crotch bulging under Lycra. Waistband stained with sweat. "Nobody controls your happiness but you. Only you create happiness, from within."

It's something Joss would say. Her Bikram instructor she can dismiss. *Roger knows nothing. There's no such thing as paradise.* But Joss. Joss she wants to believe.

"Well, it ain't Beaches!" The Hedonists laugh from behind their oversized sunglasses. "I might have told my babysitter I'd be at Breezes Luxury Resort, but I'm here, getting just what I signed up for. Anyone want a toke?"

Vero nods at her own reflection in the strangers' sunglasses and takes a toke. Hedonism is not at its best before breakfast.

She and Shane speak less and less of Eliot, of Jamal, of LiLi, unable to reconcile their roles as mother and father with the Hedonist version of Vero and Shane. They'll leave the real Vero and Shane back in the airport until this week ends. Nothing from home fits. For dinner, Vero picks a dress that was sexy in Sprucedale. Here, it looks like one of Cheryl's gardening smocks. She does not want to look like, or think of, her mother here. Hedonism makes her nobody's mother, nobody's child. She buys a dress from the resort boutique—thin, transparent fabric, all slits and holes. "This costs more than my nanny makes in a week," she says to the clerk. "And where would I ever wear this outfit again? Nowhere."

The teller rings in her purchase without meeting her eyes. "Nanny?" She rolls the dress in tissue paper, careful not to tear it with her sharp red nails. "No nannies here. A child-free zone, this." Even when she hands Vero the package, she does not meet her eyes. "And thank heaven for that."

Over dinner, in her new dress, Vero tells The Group that it's her birthday. As soon as she says it, she already doesn't even remember why. Perhaps she's grown addicted to the flutter that buzzes behind her pelvic bone with each new lie.

Shane's a dentist!

We're from Seattle!

It's my birthday!

They pile one lie on top of the last—another and another and (can they do it?!) still one more—like Jamal with his wooden building blocks. How high can they go before the tower of lies comes toppling down?

Shane takes the blindfold first. "A birthday game for Vero's birthday!" SwissMan and SwissWoman fill their voices with joy as if they're leading a group of five-year-olds in Pin the Tail on the Donkey. SwissMan guides Shane over to the row of naked women: SwissWoman, FrenchWoman, VeroWoman. They stand on a bridge between the wild tub and the main pool. Suspecting a show, bathers reposition themselves so they can watch from the hot tub. They're lazy about it, though, their movements slow. If they're going to make the effort to adjust their view, this show had better be good.

Shane can touch the naked women wherever he wants—that's the game. His goal is to guess which one is Vero. Vero knows he'll keep his hands away from midriffs. He won't want to think about SwissWoman's belly.

Shane pinches Vero's ass on the first run-through—almost at first touch—a quick tweak followed by a playful swat. The gesture lets her know he could pick her out of any line, instantly, but then he plays dumb and goes through the line three more times petting and stroking and squeezing. "Just to make sure," he whispers in her ear afterward, the blindfold looped around his neck. Vero keeps an eye over Shane's shoulder on the crowd of spectators in hot tub. DogCouple stretches out on the far edge in bathing suits made of leather and chains. DogWoman lies with her curly hair fanned across DogMan's crotch. He loops his hand around a collar at her neck. They watch intently. He meets Vero's gaze and holds it with his icy blue eyes. Danielle giggles, swinging an arm around Vero's waist. "Be careful of them," she whispers. "For them it is not for only pleasure. They are not like us."

When Vero dons the blindfold and starts stroking her way through the men's line, she has a moment of panic. She had been sure that Shane would stand out from the others in many ways. But the three men all feel the same. Skin and hair. Legs and arms. Torsos. The asses rising up in round humps off the thighs, the hip bones jutting out sharp and angling down to the pelvis. She can't tell one from the other. On the first go-through, she jogs the line, hand at navel level. Shane's taller than the other men—she'll get him immediately. Isn't blindness supposed to improve the senses? Instead she closes in on herself, her senses shut down. On her fourth try, she bends at an awkward angle and strokes their thighs. The women giggle. They know. SwissWoman whispers, "Ah, she look for her man's strong legs." She hopes Danielle's laugh is not aimed at her. She knows how ridiculous she must look—nude but for a blindfold, crouched and pawing her way through a line of men's legs.

But there in the middle—there is no mistaking them—are Shane's cyclist's quads, bulging and hard. The relief punches a hole in her sensory deprivation. Hedonism is back. The smell of sunscreen, stale sex, and cheap rum. And under that, the hint of skunky pot and sunbaked sweat. Vero pictures hungry tourist faces all around her and wishes she could leave the blindfold on. She puts her hands on Shane's cheeks and kisses him hard on the mouth before pulling the cover off her eyes.

"I could tell you right away," she lies to Shane, her own blindfold hanging at her chest like a string of pearls. "I just wanted to take a turn at my fun too."

FrenchMan winks. He does not believe her. That's what his wink says.

Vero thinks about following Joss's advice: picture the man as a child, see his vulnerability, show him that kind of compassion. But Vero cannot. Vero very much dislikes the particular tone of this man's disbelief.

◊◊◊

Danielle and Vero slide through the pool toward each other in the moonlight as "If You Asked Me To" by Celine Dion plays on the stereo. *This is it,* Vero thinks, *show time!* She bends her knees, scrapes them along the pool bottom, so that only a hint of cleavage and occasional peek of nipple show above the waterline. Danielle mimics her pose and stride. Vero could be walking into a mirror.

When they reach each other, Danielle's smile verges on a laugh. "It's fine," Danielle whispers in Vero's ear, palming Vero's shoulders. "They think it's for them. These men. We will let them think that. But in truth it is for us. Women always know what feels best." She glances Vero's earlobe with her teeth, slides her hands down to sit at her hips, her thumbs circling at Vero's waist.

Vero squeezes a plump breast below the waterline. She wonders if she can tell if they're fake, as Shane claims. "Gravity," Shane says, "Does not allow for that." He's the scientist. Vero does not argue. But she's curious. Danielle squeaks in response. Vero squeezes. Danielle squeaks. Like Jamal's old teething ring:

Squeeze.

  Squeak.

Squeeze.

  Squeak.

But when Vero lowers her head to suck at a hard brown nipple, Danielle pushes her away and she tugs on Vero's hair, bringing

Vero's lips up to meet her own. Vero wonders if the pulling sensation on Danielle's nipple reminds her of nursing, if Danielle too has versions of herself she's trying to forget.

Kissing hasn't felt this new since elementary school. The thrill of the forbidden, that's what excites. Vero pokes her tongue past Danielle's lips, feels those sharp little teeth, and puts her attention into the woman's small fingers at the base of her spine.

Everything about Danielle is softer than Shane.

"Your lips are so soft," she whispers to Danielle because she feels she should say something.

Other thoughts spin in Vero's head, breaking off and crashing into each other, circling like flotsam in a current. Danielle's fingers are now in the hair at the back of Vero's neck and Vero wants to say, *I loved nursing Eliot and Jamal—it's the only time they rested, the only time I could look on them with pure honest feelings. With nothing but love. Is that what my mouth reminded you of? Nursing?* Danielle breathes into her ear and spins her around so the men can see their profiles, their breasts pressing into each other.

I don't know, Vero wants to say, *if my nanny LiLi will ever have her own children to nurse.* Danielle's teeth clench Vero's bottom lip, drawing her back to the moment, back to the flesh.

"So soft," Vero says again. Hedonism is about flesh. Flesh alone. "We should get *them* to kiss. We could watch. Is that sexy?" Vero throws her head back as Danielle nibbles on her collar bone. Her words don't match her actions and she doesn't know why she says them. Danielle only laughs. To Danielle, everything is funny.

"Do not speak," Danielle giggles, pulling Vero to the side of the pool, pushing her up onto the rough cement ledge. Danielle's mouth works its way down Vero's body without hesitation, as if she's been doing this all her life, a steady and systematic march toward her goal.

Danielle's hands are small, half the size of Shane's. On Vero's hips. On Vero's torso. Fingers pressing hard into Vero's shoulders. The illicitness is in their smallness, as if a man with small hands would give Vero the same transgressive thrill. It's an absurd thought. But it belongs to Vero.

The pool edge presses roughly against the dip where Vero's ass meets her legs. To keep her balance, she stretches her legs and toes, reaching for the underwater bench against the pool wall. Danielle interprets Vero's arched back as encouragement, and her tongue works faster, her small fingers squeeze tighter into Vero's hip bones. Danielle knows the spot. All the spots. Shane was right about that: a woman knows what a woman likes.

Vero pushes her awareness away from the gritty cement deck under her ass and into the hot hold of Danielle's mouth. Hedonism Hal lurks in a far corner of the hot tub. His browned chest hovers above the steamy water, the giant gold cross nearly buried in grey curly hair. His eyes could be open or closed under his steamed-up glasses.

Vero thinks of Imena at the dance bar, little men pointing their tongues at her diamond-studded nipples. Imena is never at the wild tub. The wild tub doesn't need her.

Shane and FrenchMan sit apart from each other. An onlooker would assume they'd never met and were only at the same pool by an uninteresting coincidence. Vero will not study FrenchMan's face. She fears even a glance could be interpreted as acknowledgment of something she has no wish to acknowledge, agreement to some act to which she has no wish to agree.

Shane smiles, encouraging, as if he might shout: *Go, Vero Baby! You're doing great!*

Vero must smile back. She tries for seductive and seduced. Puts it all into her smile: *It's okay. It's great. This is good fun.*

She thinks of LiLi's okay. *Yes, ma'am, it okay.* This is okay.

The Swiss couple has disappeared, angry that they were not invited to participate in this game. Shane, put off by SwissWoman's pregnancy, insisted that she be left out. Vero wonders what it would be like to have her here. Could Vero have resisted letting her hand linger on the midriff, feeling for the kick?

"I guess we don't make the cut," SwissMan said, his laugh not fooling anyone. "We're not on the A-list." He laughed again, steering his pregnant wife away from the group. She did not even pretend to laugh.

When Vero comes, her whole body quivering in clenching spasms, circling and sinking and sucking into that one spot marked by Danielle's soft and fleshy mouth, she forgets everyone. Even, for a moment, Danielle. She wants to curl into fetal position afterward, as she does with Shane at home, him stroking her back while she rides the final waves—but she's too aware of her audience, knows she's not done.

When her body stops waving and spinning, she slides into the water, wanting to go right under, to sit at the bottom with her nose plugged and her eyes clenched tight. Looking at anyone now would be to own what has just happened. She would rather disappear.

But then she remembers: Danielle gets a turn too. She must. *Nothing,* as Vero keeps telling Shane, *is free.* Here or anywhere.

Woozy, she gives Danielle a hand up onto the pool's ledge. *Your turn.* Vero tries her best to smile before she puts her tongue to work, imitating the confident march of Danielle's mouth.

◊◊◊

For each fantasy Shane ticks off his list, he adds another. He gets what he desires; he wants more. Vero wishes she could draw a deep black X through the remaining days, like she does on the family calendar at home. She wants to see herself and Shane, recognizable, on the other side of those X's.

"It's our last night," he says, clasping her fingers too tight across the bar table, whirlpools of desperation where his eyes used to be. "There's something I never thought could happen...two women to...you know...at the same time." Vero wishes it weren't so easy to fill in his blanks. His laughter punctuates the sentence, tinny and nervous. Vero thinks of Danielle's Merlot lips forming the words *All men love the mouth.* Vero can't even pretend to feign ignorance. *What, Shane? What could you possibly want from two women?* She thinks of the mystery in LiLi's ellipses and holds tight to Shane's fingers, saying nothing.

"We'll never do anything like this again. It's our last night." He pauses and waits for her to speak before continuing. "Danielle has more or less offered."

Vero wonders if Danielle has children. Chances are good. Most people their age do. Are hers at home with a nanny too, one who thinks her employers are on a second honeymoon? Or are the children with a mother-in-law who imagines the couple relaxing in luxury at Beaches Resort? Or maybe Danielle has a sister, one who said "Go! Hedonism did wonders for our marriage! Live your fantasy."

Vero wiggles her empty glass at Mike, or someone who looks just like him, over behind the bar. He drops his head, focusses his attention on the task of chopping pineapple. No table service here. Vero chews on the plastic rim of her cup. Sighs. "It's a barter system, Shane." This warning sounds old to Vero, but again he doesn't hear her.

Hedonism pulls them forward, into the promise of all desired fulfilled. As if such a thing might be possible. As if such a thing might not turn sordid.

You're shocked by that? That's so midnight.

"You taste like Danielle's lipstick," Vero says afterward, when it's her turn, her chin propped on Shane's knee. "Mmm, Merlot," she giggles at Danielle whose forehead still rests against Shane's hip. "Your lips taste like Merlot."

They're so high that this observation strikes them as hilarious. They say it over and over all night—"*just like Danielle's lipstick*"—Danielle and Vero kissing to celebrate the hilarity of it all. "Shane tastes like Danielle's lipstick." Mike the bartender fills Vero's glass but won't meet her gaze.

"You have a mark of my lipstick on your tooth," Danielle says, holding Vero's chin firm for a moment before she leans forward to lick it off.

In the midst of it all, Vero thinks of Roger, his leg stretched out before him, his short shorts pulled so high that Vero could see a hint of groin. "Precision! Precision! Precision!" He bellowed the words from his stage at the front of the Bikram studio. "Don't let the body get sloppy!"

◊◊◊

FrenchMan looks. He lurks and looks. Whispers angrily to Danielle. Looks again. Vero tries to ignore him, but feels his eyes on her when she turns away. His mouth is set at an odd angle, an angry snarl crossed with a sullen pout. Danielle whispers back to him, strokes his arm. She tries to smile over to Vero reassuringly, but her eyes are fast and restless, her smile pasted on.

"I told you," Vero says to Shane.

"What?" Shane slumps happily in the water, arms spread out on the ledge above him. He's the King of Hedonism tonight. Vero slides into his side, sitting close to him on the underwater bench. She picks up his arm and wraps it around her. It's not about intimacy. It's about blocking herself off from FrenchMan. *I'm with him. Quit staring.*

"He wants his turn, Shane."

Shane makes a half-hearted effort to turn in FrenchMan's direction but changes his mind before he gets very far. He pulls his arm tighter around Vero. "We never promised him anything. It's not happening."

"We took and therefore we'll give. It's implied."

She watches Danielle as she speaks. Danielle nods quickly at her husband, stroking his arm again. She kisses him on the lips, resting a flat palm across his concave chest, and then makes her way to Shane and Vero on the other side of the pool. She bends her knees as she walks so she's mostly covered in water. All the women at Hedonism walk like this. What's hidden is more alluring.

When Danielle gets close she smiles, but it is the smile of a door-to-door salesperson, with no happiness in it. Vero wonders how Danielle has managed to reapply her lipstick. Where do you carry lipstick when you're naked? Her hair is wet but artfully tussled, framing her face, highlighting her sharp cheekbones dusted with freckles.

She's cute.

"You're cute." Vero says it aloud almost as soon as she thinks it. Bass booms from the speakers above the pool and the water ripples with each note. When Vero's high, she feels everything.

Danielle pulls her aside, nodding at Shane, pretending to be unable to find the words. Danielle's hands are soft but insistent against Vero's arms. Vero feels each of Danielle's fingernails against her skin—long and shaped, unlike Vero's cut quick to the skin.

"My husband, he want to take his turn. He want the mouths of two women, too." Anxiety shows itself in the wrinkles around her eyes when she speaks. She's no longer a tourist on a fun holiday. She's a tired mother arguing with a bank teller who has given her the wrong exchange rate. "He says to me, he has the right. I told you this, when we did first meet." She wraps her hand around the back of her own neck, and pulls until Vero can see a line of definition in her arm. It's the only accusatory thing Danielle says. She doesn't reach out to touch Vero now.

Vero feels the itch of tears. "I can't, Danielle. I can't." Vero works on her excuses, feels them pool inside her, intends to release them in a long fast stream, leaving no room for objection. But Danielle drops her arm to her side and nods. She bites her lip and then rubs her hand hard against her chin. Nods again. "Don't worry. You did never promise. I told him that. He says because I did it to your husband, you must do it with mine. I tell him there was no promise. He says—are they stupid?" Danielle holds the back of her fingers to Vero's cheek for a second, drops them, and smiles her sad smile again. "I will say to him, yes, they are stupid." Danielle laughs now.

Vero notices the bathers watching them from every corner of the pool, from the patio chairs. People walking by on deck look. Everyone will recognize Vero and Danielle from their performance near the wild pool. They watch for more of the same. "You and your husband did not promise. But me, I promised. Before we were here. To my husband, I promise." She shrugs. "I find someone else." She points at the cup in Vero's hand. "What is this drink?" Without waiting for an answer, she takes the cup from Vero and downs all the liquid in four long gulps. She wipes her mouth on the back of her hand—the same fingers she'd held up to Vero's cheek—and hands the empty cup back to Vero as if it's filled with something precious. Then she breaststrokes off toward the wild hot tub.

◊◊◊

"It's our last night. We can sleep when we get back to sleepy old Sprucedale. We can sleep when I'm Shane the pharmacist, Jamal and Eliot's daddy." Shane pulls Vero into his lap and orders another round of drinks. Vero is saturated—with alcohol, with water, with sex. Her whole body is wrinkled like a raisin and she can't bear to think about what germs live in these tubs. But it's almost over, and she has survived this much, so she stays.

It's somewhere on the fulcrum between night and morning when Vero sees Danielle. She's heading toward the rooms with FrenchMan and DogCouple. DogMan's jaw muscle is flexed and he pulls his woman along with him, the leash strained tight. The muscle in his face is rigid and his eyes are cruel when he smiles at Vero. *He wants me to come with them*, she thinks. *Not Shane, just me.* He must've seen Vero and Danielle together. Everyone saw that. Vero is cold and tired and longs for home. Danielle smiles at Vero as they pass. *I'd rather be with you*, the smile says. *Sorry*, the smile says. Vero looks for blame in her expression—*You forced me to stoop to this, to these DogPeople*—but finds none.

FrenchMan refuses to look their way. He has a hand on Danielle's lower back and another on DogWoman's. He looks almost happy, the closest to it since Vero has met him. The tension in his face has released, his scrawny shoulders sit lower. He will finally get what he has come for. What he has paid for.

Vero says nothing to any of them as they pass, just lifts her hand above the water and wiggles her fingers in a wave at Danielle. How could she save a person like that? In a place like this? Shane rests his hand on the back of her neck. "We decided on our lines, Vero. We're doing the right thing."

Let's go to bed, she wants to say, but now she can't leave. She holds watch for Danielle, her eyes on the walkway where they've disappeared into the rooms. Shane lights another joint. "We're closing this party down tonight, Vero Baby. No sense taking it back with us." So Vero sits and watches and helps Shane smoke it all.

The sun is threatening to rise when she finally spots Danielle. This time, there's no graceful movement as Danielle slinks through the pool half covered by water. This time, she thrashes through the water, big boobs swinging, arms waving. FrenchMan watches from the edge as Danielle throws herself into Vero's arms, and then he disappears back toward the rooms. Vero tries to calm Danielle, stroking her arms. She's no longer soft. Her muscles are rigid, and her body jerks violently. Vero squeezes her tight, trying to hold her in one piece, until the loudest sobs subside.

When Danielle has calmed, Vero holds her like a baby, one arm cradling her neck and head, the other looped beneath her knees, waving her gently so water sloshes around their bodies. Danielle tucks her face into Vero's shoulder. "I did not want to," Danielle cries, her whole body shaking. "I did not want to. He said we would not do it," she cries. "Not that."

"Shh, honey, shh." Vero rocks her body in time with the waves of the pool and kisses the top of her hair. It smells of coconut.

Vero waves her head at Shane—*go away*, the wave says—and he sidles up to the bar to order a breakfast drink from Mike. Vero ignores everyone else—the gawking breakfast crowd. She waves an angry arm at Hal when he comes close to them.

"She's drunk too much," he says, jowls jiggling. "Get her somewhere private. This is not that kind of place."

Vero won't look at him. She just pushes her hand toward his fat, hairy chest. *Go.* She's ready to punch him right in his fat red nose if he doesn't. But she knows her anger is not about him. For some reason she cannot understand, Hedonism is Hal's home and Vero and her group have broken some house rules. Maybe it's something about making spectacles at breakfast or something about forgetting to leave emotions at home or pushing the line into fantasy too far. Maybe there is some honour in Hal and his insistence about what kind of place Hedonism should be.

But Vero does not care to understand him right now. She does not want to understand what he needs from a place like this. What Vero needs is for everyone to leave her and Danielle alone. She strokes Danielle's hair. *Shh. Shh. Shh.* Up close, in the light of day, Danielle is covered with freckles, her upper lip, her eyelids, her earlobes.

Eventually, Danielle tells her. She and her husband had drawn their lines too. No intercourse with strangers. Not that far. But as soon as they were in the room, DogWoman took the bed with Danielle's husband, and DogMan pulled Danielle onto the other. Danielle looked to her husband for help, to reinforce their lines, but he had DogWoman straddling his face while he pulled on her leash. He was busy. DogMan pushed Danielle to her knees, forcing himself behind her, wrapping a bathrobe belt around her neck. "It didn't hurt," she tells Vero, "he just pulled it lightly. But still."

Still.

Between sobs, Danielle gives her story to Vero. "'It's fun,' he kept saying. That's what we're here for. 'It's fun.' But this word, it sounded ugly on his tongue." He wrapped both arms around Danielle's waist, roughly pushing himself into her from behind. "'Your husband's doing it. He's fucking my wife. Right there. Look. Look!' He said we wouldn't. Not that."

Vero lets Danielle talk and cry. She rests her face against Danielle's hair. "It's okay, It's okay. It's okay," she whispers.

What is okay? What could possibly be okay about this?

When Danielle has cried herself dry, she tells Vero that she and her husband came on the trip to save their marriage. "He does not want me as much since we have the children," she shrugs. Even the movement of her shoulders is sad. "I get these ridiculous things," she points at her breasts. "I come on this…this…this…'oliday? I do everything." Danielle tries to smile, but her lips just bunch together and quiver as if she might start crying again. "Maybe he does not love me anymore. What I do makes no difference."

Vero wants to comfort her, to tell her she deserves better. But she knows the words carry no weight coming from her. She too is here.

Danielle is out of words and out of tears, nearly asleep, when Vero walks her back to her room. Other tourists fill the path, walking lazily toward the pool and beach, but Danielle and Vero push in the other direction against the traffic, smiling and nodding their apology the whole way.

There are palm trees in a straight line along the path. They don't give Vero the sense that she's travelling through a foreign landscape— one she has flown far to experience. Each is so artfully arranged that it could just as easily be planted in a mall in Edmonton. The place is plastic. She could be in Cuba, in Mexico, in Whistler, at any resort. *Hedonism*, Vero realizes, *is not Jamaica*. It's nowhere. And everywhere at the same time.

After Vero gets some sleep, she pulls a Sprucedale sundress over her head, its cotton sensible and solid against her skin. She slowly untwists a swan, swings it loose until it's just a bath towel, and spreads it out over her legs, pressing it flat.

"Let's go home," she says to Shane. In her mouth, the pronouncement feels existential. *Home.*

FIVE

Habang may bahay, may pag-asa.
Where there is home, there is hope.
—Filipino proverb

CHAPTER FIFTEEN

At home, Vero sees her world as if refracted through water—the fridge, the stove, the dishwasher—none of it looks quite right, quite real. None of it belongs to her. She cups her palms around the solid swell of a teapot. It waves in her vision as if she could push her hands right through it. "It's a teapot," she says aloud to nobody, "for making tea." Even the clunk of the pot when it meets the counter sounds hollow and far off. It's a clunk in somebody else's life.

A clunk in the life of some woman who doesn't go down on a man's wife in a public swimming pool.

"You all right, Vero? I make you tea." LiLi loosens the teapot from Vero's grip. Vero squints at her, makes no effort to hide her confusion. She's nearly forgotten LiLi's face, the plump lips that rarely smile, the dark hair that lifts toward a curl at her shoulders, the nearly black eyes, sinkholes into a soul that Vero will never know. The resemblance between LiLi's eyes and Danielle's eyes is more striking than Vero had thought.

"Yes, tea, please," Vero says in her new strangled voice. Her fingers brush LiLi's palm as the teapot changes hands. "No. I mean, no, thank you. No tea, Ligaya." Something like fear crosses LiLi's face. It embarrasses Vero. "I meant to say LiLi. No tea, LiLi. I think I'll just go lie down. For a bit." Vero has been lying down a lot since she and Shane returned from their holiday last week. She can't face people. She wants to tell the clerk at the grocery store, the engineers at the plant, the investment salesman at the bank—this is all a lie. Such a lie. Vero guessed as much before their visit to Hedonism, but now she knows.

"Maybe you catch sickness, Vero. You rest. I bring the tea to your room." LiLi sets a hand, tentatively, on Vero's shoulder and steers her toward her bedroom as if she thinks Vero has forgotten the way. The boys sit, impossibly quiet, on the couch, holding hands, their four legs braided. They're scared of their own mother.

Vero would say they look like twins, their expressions and postures of discomfort so precisely alike, but they're too different in every other way—Jamal dark and slight and wiry, Eliot fair and hulking and soft. Vero and LiLi look more like twins, both small and dark and unhappy.

◊◊◊

Vero would like to fall into deep, dreamless sleeps, but she does not. She dreams and dreams and dreams until nothing seems real but her dreams. She dreams of a dozen hands roaming her body, of champagne falling like rain from Jamaican skies, of disembodied tongues licking the champagne rain from her belly. She dreams that her body is a table covered in sliced fruit, sticky against her sunbaked skin. Henri and Danielle face each other over her ribcage, forks poised. Somber-faced, they pick at the strawberries. Vero tries to whisper. *Run, Danielle, run!* Then she tries to scream. *The strawberries: they're poison!* But her dry mouth sticks. She has no tongue. She dreams of Shane with her in a hammock shaded from the Jamaican sun, their bodies swinging wildly with each thrust, but this time Vero is the one with the penis. In the middle of all the skin and friction and thrusting and licking, she dreams of Edward. His belt buckle fills her field of vision, his voice booming from its golden centre. "You, Vero Baby, can consider yourself canned," the belt buckle says. Big knuckled hands clench the worn leather belt on either side of the shiny buckle. "That's the way she rolls, Vero Baby!" Vero's line of vision pans out until she sees that Edward is straddling a light armoured vehicle, the phallic cannon pointed straight for Vero's heart.

Sometimes Shane slides into Vero's dreams—real or imagined, she never knows—and she moans and writhes and comes, all without opening her eyes, and then she turns away to sleep again, Shane's heavy leg flung over her squashed thigh.

◊◊◊

Vero tries. Nobody can say that she does not try. One must try. She pulls herself from bed. *You need some movement*, Cheryl would say. *An object at rest stays at rest. Lethargy breeds lethargy.* With Cheryl's voice pushing her forward, Vero drags herself down to the Bikram studio, determined to sweat her way out of her funk. She will sweat until she is Vero again. She will sweat until her old life fits, until once again she is a pharmacist's wife who gets paid to fix engineers' grammar.

But there is no peace at the Bikram studio. Dreadlocks, placards, and ripped jeans fill the sidewalk, barring her way. "SWEAT!" screams one half of the crowd. "KILLS!" replies the other. Vero raises her hands to her face. Her skin feels real, smooth at the cheek, rough at the dry skin of her lips, three sharp hairs unplucked at her chin. She's awake?

A mother whose hair sticks flat to her head on one side and springs wildly from the other wears an infant strapped to her chest, its chubby red legs kicking. Across the baby's chest a sticker reads "My planet, my future!" A man sits in a wheelchair mounted with an oxygen tank, two tubes snaking into his nostrils. He holds a sign: "What's your footprint?" it asks, in angry red. Little blue words swim around the question. Vero tries to make them out: *sweat, laundry, towels, heat.* A woman in a pink sweat-suit rests a hand on his shoulder. Her other arm angrily jabs a sign at the sky: "Bikram yoga: destroying the environment one tree pose at a time!" In front of the wheelchair, a teenage boy with curly hair escaping a hand-knit toque stretches a long piece of paper across his chest: "I'm so angry I made a sign."

"Your sweat: killing our planet!" his girlfriend's sign screams.

Vero looks the other way. The crowd squishes around her.

"SWEAT!" A young man holds up Vero's arm as he yells, makes her one of them.

"KILLS!"

Who are these people?

"SWEAT!"

"KILLS!"

Vero is pulled with the crowd, one way then the next, forward and then back. She's lost all control over her own body. A "bottled water is bullshit" placard bangs her in the head. She takes a deep breath and with all her strength wiggles her way through the warm bodies. She must force the other warm bodies—the ones from Jamaica—from her mind. She curses her own body for responding to these around her now. Screaming and unaware of her, people bang and bump and rub up against her. *Sex is a metaphor*, she told Shane. Her body doesn't agree.

When she's nearly at the front of the crowd, she spots Roger tucked inside the glass door. She almost doesn't recognize him with his clothes on. In her mind, he's inseparable from his hot pink Lycra shorts. In street clothes, his posture is different. His neck hangs. He leans into the glass window as if he needs it to hold him up. The Bikram Yoga sign stencilled across the door cuts him in half.

The sight of him so unlike himself creates a surge of energy where she thought she had none. "Don't you have something better to protest?" she says to the picketer next to her, a university student waving a picture of a planet in flames. "Hot Enough For Ya Now, Bikram?" His white T-shirt is so thin she sees his nipples underneath. "Protest the oil sands, the war in Iraq, the cuts to public transit, for God's sakes." She hears her *for God's sakes*, the Mr and Mrs Schoeman in it.

"They're all the same thing," the young man replies with unexpected softness, meeting and holding her eyes. "Them and this. Same thing." She searches his face for anger, expects the muscles taut, strained at his temples and neck, but his features sit at rest, his eyes gentle. She'd like to invite him to her house for tea, ask him to elaborate, but how would she hide Ligaya? A domestic servant from the third world. It'd be "the same thing" too. This man would put his disapproval on a placard and run circles around Vero's house.

"Thank you," Vero says to him, putting a hand to his wrist, the one holding the placard. He doesn't flinch. She wonders what she means by it, *thank you*. "Thank you," she says again, letting go of his wrist and turning for home.

She's surprised when the crowd parts to let her exit. Escape is this easy only in a dream. Maybe she *is* sleeping, then.

◊◊◊

At home, Vero cleans. She will sweat like LiLi sweats, scrubbing away her lethargy. She slathers vinegar water on the bedroom windows, and scrubs until it seems there is no glass, just gaping holes cut into her bedroom walls. It is the smell of her childhood, this vinegar water. Cheryl poured buckets of it in the wake of every man who left. She'd tell them to leave, and then she'd scrub. With shirt soaked and arms aching, Vero carries her sloshing bucket of water into the en suite bathroom. She scrubs until the kids could eat off the floor. *Here*, she will say to Jamal and Eliot, *eat off it*.

The boys chatter downstairs, Jamal in his own nonsense language, but Vero cannot imagine what either child has to do with her. She dropped a thread in Jamaica, studies the bathroom floor as if she might find it there. She wonders if Danielle has re-adjusted to her home life, mended her situation with Henri. And then she wonders what these words could even mean: *adjusted, mended, situation*. In Jamaica, they admitted they were lying, playing at characters. Now, Vero wonders if there's any other way, anywhere. She pulls off her shirt, wet with sweat, and drops it with a splat into the bathtub, then sends her shorts after it. In her underwear, she scrubs again.

She's up on a stool in her wet bra and panties, reaching for the top shelf of the closet, when Shane comes upstairs.

"What are you doing?"

She follows his gaze into her own hands, sees the small pieces of cloth there. Red, black, pink. "I'm rolling my underwear in a ball and shoving it into the farthest corner I can reach in the top of the highest shelf in our bedroom." Her voice is loud and hollow, like she's reciting the words from a stage.

"Why?" Shane's eyes have not moved from her hands.

"Because I'm not comfortable with LiLi handling my dirty underwear, and if I don't hide them, she washes them."

"You don't think this—" He points at the stool, at the balled underwear clasped in her hands. "—is a little bit weird?"

"A lot is weird about our life right now, Shane."

He still stands in the doorway, and Vero waits on her stool for him to step forward to carry her down. She knows he will, but she also knows they won't talk about Jamaica. What happened there and what happens here will never touch each other. Shane can do that. Compartmentalize. Cheryl did it as well. The scrubbing helped. Vero will need to learn to do it too. She sees now that it's necessary. This disinfecting.

By the time that thought finishes passing through her mind, Vero realizes she's sitting on their bed, but doesn't remember Shane carrying her here, yet she is sure she didn't walk herself. "Thank you," she says, but she does not look at him. She stares out the windows so clean they seem to be without glass, perfectly shaped holes in her home. They could be exhibitionists here too. "Thank you, I mean, for helping me." Shane doesn't say anything, so she speaks again. "Aren't they clean? The windows. I scrubbed them."

"You need something."

I do, she thinks, *I need something to hold me down. I'm floating away.* She's surprised Shane can see it. She imagines her body lifting to the ceiling, her stomach and intestines left behind in a sloppy pile on the mattress, staining the comforter. LiLi will have to scrub.

"Some new work maybe. Something more challenging. More stimulating. To keep you busier. Engage your mind. Distract you."

Isn't that two different things, she thinks, *engagement and distraction?* And then she thinks, *distract me from what?* A bird flies into the window with a loud clunk. Vero thinks it must be dead, but then watches as it picks itself off the awning, shakes its feathers and flies off, quickly losing its stunned wobble.

"Or, I mean, maybe you need some medication. For a while. Just to right you."

"Is right a verb?" Vero hears her voice soft and high now. She's lost the performer's confidence she had up on the stool. If she heard a recording of this new soft voice, she wouldn't recognize it as her own.

"How about writing? You always wanted to be a writer." Shane has moved close to her on the mattress, but he hasn't yet touched her. "But not—" he puts a hand on her arm, its gentleness surprising. "—not *The Mommy's Alphabet*." She looks at his face and is relieved to see his smile. "Or how about yoga teacher training? You like yoga. The boys are getting bigger. We have LiLi. Do something for yourself." Shane moves his hand up and down Vero's arm, the way she rubs Eliot's back when he can't sleep.

"We don't…" Vero finally says, the weakness in her own voice an embarrassment to her. She takes a deep breath and tries again. Shane moves a hand onto her knee, but softly, as if he's scared to hurt her. Or scared that she'll start and run. "We don't know anything about her." Vero speaks without removing her eyes from the invisible pane of glass. She worries for the birds. She should stand and bang on the window, warn the poor birds away. "About LiLi. Nothing."

"Vero, that's not true."

"It is."

"LiLi lives with us. We're the only family she has here. She takes care of our children. Of course we know her." His voice sounds wrong too. It's too slow, the words too evenly spaced.

"We don't." Vero decides to stick to simple, truthful claims. They're safe. They're short. "She knows us more than we do her. And look how much she doesn't know." Vero lies back on the bed and rolls her face into the pillow.

"Look, we need to talk about something else…" Shane waits, as if Vero might fill in his blanks. She will never be one of those old married women who finishes her husband's sentences. She has no idea. He gives her a hint: "About Jamal…"

Still, she's quiet. She thinks about what Adele said to her before the adults sat down to dinner at Shane's birthday party: "You should get him checked. Something's wrong." *Nothing is wrong with my son.* Vero will not answer.

"He's still not speaking properly. We need to see someone. I've made him an appointment."

Make one for me too, Vero thinks, digging her head under the pillow. She will say nothing. She keeps her head there until she hears Shane leave, closing the bedroom door, not softly, behind him. Maybe Shane doesn't love her as much as Joss claimed. Maybe no woman should envy Vero anything.

Vero can't blame Shane. Even she has lost patience with herself.

◊◊◊

The silence in the waiting room is uncomfortable. Vero can hear her own breathing, an unhealthy click of phlegm deep in her throat. *Dr Wagner, Speech Therapist* reads the sign on the desk. Behind it, a red-headed secretary click-click-clicks on a keyboard. She meets their eyes when they come in, points her nose where they should sit, but she doesn't stop clicking.

Nobody's hair is really that colour of red, thinks Vero. And then: *Why are all my thoughts so hateful? What has happened to me?*

The room is full. Jamal must sit on her lap. Shane stands, leaning into a bookcase filled with stories and toys that nobody touches. Vero hadn't seen his fatigue until now; she's been too absorbed in her own. She wonders why none of the children speak, why they all look so scared. *What have we done to them?* The thought passes through her mind, and then she worries it has passed through her lips as well. She lifts a hand to her face, holds her mouth shut.

"I don't want to do this," she whispers to Shane through the hand. The phony-haired secretary raises her head, clicks on the keyboard, and pushes her lips upward. Shane puts his hand on Vero's shoulder but says nothing. This is not a place for speaking. That's what his hand says. She wants to point out the irony—a speech therapist's office being the place for no speech—but she's been silenced. Jamal curls into her shoulder like a baby, nibbles on the string in her hoodie.

Let's go, she wants to say, *he's fine.*

He'll learn in his own time, she wants to say.

I don't want my son measured and found lacking—this she pushes from her mind.

Jamal is so close she can feel the rise and fall of his breath, tries to synch her own, but hers is too fast, too shallow, too phlegmy.

Yesterday, Vero tried to engage LiLi in a discussion about Jamal's speech. "You spend more time with him than anyone," she said, the words scraping a raw bloody line up her throat. "What do you think? Should we be concerned? About his speech?"

"Oh, Vero," LiLi did not look up, busied herself scrubbing a spot of red tomato sauce stuck to the black granite countertops.

Stop bloody cleaning! Vero wanted to scream. *Please! Talk to me!*

"I cannot answer that," LiLi finally said, directing her words to the spot of tomato sauce. "My English not so good. I not from here. Of course." Vero would not let that be enough. She stared at LiLi's ear, holding her silence. If LiLi could not meet her eyes, Vero would win a staring contest with that ear. "I not a doctor," LiLi finally said. "Ma'am."

That single *ma'am* defeated Vero. Still? Vero cannot take what will not be given. Nobody can. Warm liquid tickled her eyelids. She blinked but made no effort to wipe the tears. Even when her cheeks were wet, she left them.

When LiLi finally had no choice but to look at Vero, she misunderstood, as Vero knew she would. Of course, LiLi thought the tears were for Jamal. Vero let her think so. LiLi would be embarrassed to know the tears were for her.

"Jamal, he a good boy," LiLi said, consoling. "A smart boy. He is okay, Vero."

Vero thought LiLi might reach out to hug her or rest one of her small hands against Vero's bare forearm. The momentum moved in that direction, a step, but then LiLi turned her back to Vero, all business. "I make you some tea. Maybe that help." She spoke loudly so Vero could hear her over the running water.

◊◊◊

Dr Wagner puts Shane and Vero at ease as he's been trained to do.

"Nice to meet you, Dr Wagner," Shane says in his medical professional voice. He pronounces the name the German way, *Vahg-ner*. "We appreciate you putting us on the cancellation list, getting us in on short notice." Shane sounds genuinely grateful, as if this is not the way it always works between medical professionals.

"I'm just Wagner with a wah," the doctor says, his eyes on Jamal. "Wag like a dog's tail." He smiles and sets a hand on Jamal's head. Vero wants to push it off. "And then Nurr," the doctor says, "like a Nerf ball."

There are posters of cats and monkeys taped to the ceiling, word bubbles above their heads. Vero expects the doctor to lay Jamal on the table so he can look at these ridiculous posters, as if he's sick and simple. She doesn't know how she will bear it. But then Dr Wagner sets Jamal in a regular chair and motions for Shane and Vero to stand by the wall. Vero does not like this either. He's made her unnecessary, redundant.

Dr Wagner pulls a picture of a tabby cat from a deck of cards and holds it before Jamal, who looks very small in the adult-sized chair. Dr Wagner says nothing, simply waits for him to speak.

"Pusa," Jamal says, "pusa."

"I think he means pussy, like cat," Vero says, her voice just as small as Jamal. Shane's hand curls around the back of her neck. *Shh*, that hand says, *shh*.

"Do you know any other words for this picture?" Dr Wagner prompts. He smiles while he waits.

"Pusa!" Jamal snarls, clearly annoyed now.

Dr Wagner puts the cat card face-down and holds up a picture of a car. "What's a good word for this picture, Jamal?"

Vero studies her shoes, winds the string from her hoodie around her forefinger, feels nausea clawing its way up her gut, bubbling in her chest, a slow burn behind her eyes.

"Kotse! Kotse! Kotse!" Jamal squeals, reaching for the picture of the car. Vero drops the string, goes to the chair, and pulls Jamal into her lap, wrapping both arms tight around her boy. *Leave him alone,* she wants to say. Shane stands passively at the wall as he's been instructed to do. Vero wants to scream. She hates the red-haired secretary, she hates Dr Wagner, she hates this room with talking animals taped to the ceiling, and she hates Shane.

"And this?" Dr Wagner holds up a picture of a green apple. Shane moves his body ever so slightly, just enough that he can look out the window rather than at Jamal.

"We eat red ones," Vero says. "He might not recognize that."

"Mahn-snahs," Jamal says, his tone languid. He's bored with Dr TailWag/NerfBall and this silly exercise.

Please make it stop, Vero thinks, and then, as if she's said it aloud, Dr Wagner puts his stack of cards aside and slaps his palms against his knees.

"Well, Mr and Mrs Schoeman—"

"Nanton," Vero says. "My name is Nanton." She wields her name because it's all she has, his small error.

"My apologies," Dr Wagner says with a polite smile. "Ms Nanton. Jamal is a very smart boy. I can assure you he has no problem with speech. No learning disabilities that you need to worry about at this point. I see no reason to pursue further testing."

He pauses. Shane and Vero wait. *Then what?* There must be more. Vero tries again to synch her breathing with her son's. She fails.

"Do you have a foreign nanny by chance?" The slightest hint of laughter presses against Dr Wagner's professional voice.

Vero and Shane nod mutely in unison.

"From the Philippines, perhaps?"

Vero knows what Dr Wagner will say before he says it. She would like to rise and silently walk out of the office before she has to hear it, but she stays sitting.

"Your son," Dr Wagner has the bright, upward look of a man on a barstool about to deliver his favourite punch line, "is speaking Tagalog."

◊◊◊

"Well," Shane says with one hand on the steering wheel and his eyes on the road. "Well." The word closes the conversation rather than opening it. Shane's *well* is a period, a drawn curtain, a final buzzer. An error of this magnitude will necessitate blame. Blunders like this don't simply happen. Someone commits them. Someone must accept responsibility. Vero knows the someone will be her. It's all there in that single word. *Well.*

Jamal falls asleep almost as soon as the car rolls. His parents' emotion too much for him, he escapes through sleep. His breath grates rhythmically over their red-hot silence.

"At least he snores in English." Shane doesn't look at Vero when he says this. A vein, the full length of his neck, pulses.

Vero says nothing. She can be mad too. She counts her reasons. She will forsake sleep—she does not deserve it—she will count injustices instead of sheep. That will keep her awake. Their anger grows into another person in the car, sitting between them, a foot kicking into Vero's face, a hand straight-arming Shane in the chest.

When it becomes clear the silence needs to break, Shane says, "He's a smart boy. Learning Tagalog." Shane licks his lips and looks out the side window before adding, almost quietly, "But any boy should, at the very least, speak the language of his mother." He narrowly beats Vero's own angry words. She chews on the inside of her cheek. She will win through silence.

For the rest of the ride, they listen to the sound of the tires circling against the wet pavement. When they most need to talk, Shane turns silent. There will be no "Shane Overshare" today.

In the driveway, Vero lifts Jamal out of the car. He's nearly too big to carry without waking, but he flings his arm around her and nestles his sweaty cheek into her neck. Shane sits, one hand on the steering wheel, eyes on the garage. When Vero closes the car door, he backs slowly down the drive, looking at neither of them.

CHAPTER SIXTEEN

Vero works through the night. First she washes underwear in her bathroom sink while LiLi sleeps. She moves furtively and keeps the room dimly lit. If she hangs the garments by midnight, they will be dry by eight in the morning, and she can put them away before LiLi starts work. Shane's voice rings in her head, *You don't think that's a little weird?* Vero feels the shame of it, a heavy wetness in her chest, her ribcage made of freshly poured concrete. She turns the water taps off and on slowly, hoping the rattle of pipes won't wake LiLi in the basement.

Their whole life is a little weird.

All lives are weird from the inside. Something Cheryl would say.

While the boys sleep, Vero silently cleans their closets. She must invent work. LiLi keeps the house show-suite clean. "I learned to clean—to *really* clean—in Hong Kong," LiLi told her. "My employer there, the Poons, they is very strict."

Are we strict? Vero wonders, but LiLi's cleaning never allows them space to exercise their authority, to explore the outer edges of their strictness on this matter. LiLi cleans things Vero did not even know needed to be cleaned. LiLi washes walls. She sterilizes telephone receivers. She takes a toothbrush to the crevices in the dishwasher door. She spreads the shower curtain flat on the back lawn, attacks it with the pot scrubber. LiLi's diligence has left nothing for Vero to clean in this wakeful night.

But only work will keep Vero awake, and she does not want Shane to catch her asleep, her head thrown back, mouth hanging slack. She wants to be ready for him and his accusations. Instead, she watches Jamal sleep, wondering that her dark-haired child should be the one to speak Tagalog. He could easily be mistaken for LiLi's own son. But, of course, his speech has nothing to do with the colour of his hair. Jamal is simply the youngest, the most susceptible, the one who did not yet speak English when LiLi arrived.

"You clever boy." Vero rests a finger at his hairline, always wet with sweat when he sleeps, and traces a soft line across his forehead, around his ear. "You will learn many languages."

As she hangs and folds his clothes, sorting the items he's outgrown into a bag to send to LiLi's village, Vero listens for the click of the front door. Maybe she and Shane will talk. Shane will put his hand on her knee, but not in that way that means *shh*. Instead, it will mean: *Don't worry, I will hold you together, we will help each other*. She will place her hand over his to show her gratitude.

Let's start over, she will say. That's what Eliot always says when he's in trouble, tears pooled in his mossy eyes. *Let's just start over.*

But there is no click, no soft pad of sock feet up the stairs to the bedroom.

Vero loses her battle against fatigue, the body's demands disregarding the mind's efforts. In the morning, she wakes curled on the floor of Jamal's closet, clutching his toddler T-shirts. The logos—a giraffe, a monkey, a bear—remind her of the posters taped to Dr Wagner's ceiling. As easily as that, the day before comes crashing down on her before she's fully pulled herself into this one.

A child should speak the language of his mother. At the very least.

That alone cannot account for Shane's anger, an anger so big it has kept him out through the night. Vero does not understand.

Jamal's bed is empty, the sheets pulled tightly across its surface. *You could bounce a quarter off that bed*, Vero thinks, and then wonders who would want to bounce a quarter off a bed anyway. None of it matters, these first-world standards.

She opens Eliot's bedroom door slowly, quietly against the creak, but Eliot is gone too, his bed made just as tightly. It's easy to imagine he never slept there at all. His stuffed animals, a St Bernard named Barnie and a Dalmatian named Spot, flop across the mattress, posed perfectly, the room photo-shoot ready. *I am the room of a happy normal boy in a happy normal family.* That's what the picture will say.

Vero used to sleep there in that slim bed with Eliot and Barnie and Spot, the exhaustion of early motherhood pulling her into dreams when she'd only meant to lie down for a moment, to comfort Eliot. It was her favourite part of parenting, sleeping with her babies. Her drifting. Their pliancy. The synching breath. The warm sighs on her bare skin. That sweetness feels like such a long time ago. Has she slept with Eliot since LiLi arrived? She must have. Surely. But she cannot recall. She closes the door, slowly, as if the creak might disturb Barnie and Spot.

She descends the stairs and enters the kitchen apologetically, like a late house guest. Even though she's been home for nearly two weeks, their house still feels too big after a week in the narrow space of a hotel room. Vero wants to pull the walls in so they fit more snugly around her shoulders. She's drowning in the loose bag of her own home. *Needs are not the same as wants*, she'd lectured Shane about his bikes. But nobody *needs* this much space. The stairs wear her out. She's desperate for a chair by the time she reaches the kitchen.

LiLi feeds the boys scrambled eggs and bacon, a meal she has learned to cook in North America. In the Philippines, they ate rice for breakfast. "Rice and salt fish. We eat rice breakfast, lunch, and dinner," she tells Eliot and Jamal, again and again, the flickering light of laughter in her voice. It's become an old joke between them.

◊◊◊

Ligaya squats at the children's table with Eliot and Jamal, encouraging each bite, but when she notices Vero standing behind them, she hands Eliot his spoon. "You eat by your own. You big boy now. You show your mama." She picks a spoon off the table and puts it in Jamal's hand, squeezing his fingers until he grips the utensil by himself. "You big too, JJ. Show your mother how big you are."

Something has changed.

Shane and Vero's holiday—their temporary absence—has allowed Ligaya to find her place in this house, to begin to get a foothold. Even when Shane and Vero return, Ligaya feels herself to be less of an interloper. She is thankful for this new confidence. Especially now. Shane and Vero act so peculiarly upon their return that the boys need Ligaya at her strongest.

"Yes, good, JJ. Show your mother."

JJ and Eliot sit still, each with a spoon in hand, lips pressed tight. Their quiet politeness in Vero's presence is new. Ligaya thinks Vero should be concerned, but in Vero's expression Ligaya sees only relief. She looks so tired—the kind of exhaustion that weighs down a face, the strain of gravity pulling on her features. Ligaya sees the heavy sag and imagines Vero's face made of an old dried apple, raisons for eyes, a peppercorn in the place of her nose. She knows Vero will accept the gift of these quiet, timid boys and be grateful for it.

Vero takes a seat at the dining room table, tall above the rest of her family. Ligaya must turn awkwardly in her seat to make conversation. "You working today? In house? I keep boys quiet. We go to park, maybe. How do you like that, boys?" She swings around to face Eliot and Jamal when she addresses them, resting a small hand between each set of shoulder blades.

Vero puts her own hands on the table in front of her, twists her fingers.

She should have work to do, shouldn't she? thinks Ligaya. *From the war tank plant? The instruction booklets she writes for their blasters? Or she could have the yoga or the running. Or the friend. Something to do.*

Vero's friend Joss telephoned yesterday afternoon, but when Ligaya said "Vero?" into the receiver, turning her eyes subtly in Vero's direction, Vero shook her head fast twice and dropped her eyes. "No, she not home now, Joss. I will tell her you call. When she come back home." Ligaya watched Vero, her blank eyes fixed out the front window. "Yes, I think she have a very nice vacation. She and Mister Shane. They both get darker skin, but seem happy." Ligaya added the "happy" as an afterthought. A lie. She sees the lie even more now—after Shane has stayed out all night and Vero—whom she found asleep on Eliot's closet floor—has come downstairs looking like she has not slept at all. None of this is Ligaya's business. Yet she lives here. In the middle of it.

Vero should have talked to Joss yesterday. She needs her friend. Neither of them will phone each other again for weeks now, Ligaya knows. Everybody is so busy. That is the favourite word in this place: bizz-ee. But Vero does not look busy now. She sits perfectly still.

Where is my husband? I've lost my husband.

That is the look on Vero's face.

Are you okay? What can I do?

Ligaya wants to ask, but cannot bring herself to voice these questions.

To offer this help. To intrude. This is not her place. The words burn in her chest like globules of undigested animal fat. *Not my place.*

"I wanted to be a writer," Vero says suddenly. "Once, that is what I wanted to be. When I was very young. Did I tell you that, LiLi? I started a project once, before you arrived, sort of, about caring for children." She moves her fingers back and forth across her lips as if she'd like to rub them right off. "*A is for Asylum*, I was going to call it. I thought Shane and I had made some progress since then, but maybe we're still there." Her hand falls from her lips to the table with a clunk, like it does not belong to her. "We were talking about you, LiLi, Shane and I. Shane says we know you. I say we don't. I say we know nothing about you."

There is anger in the last sentence. It's as if Vero hangs the words in the air one at a time. Ligaya pictures Nanay in a mood back home, pinning the clothes on the line, violently shaking out each piece before she attaches it. Ligaya will not take Vero's sullenness personally. Today Vero has a portion of blame for everyone. *She has slept on a closet floor. Her husband is gone. This is not my place.*

◊◊◊

If I wait, she will say something. Vero knows this to be true. She can see the words bubbling and forming behind LiLi's determined eyes. But LiLi will not speak until she gets the phrases just right.

And suddenly Vero does not want to hear LiLi's story. Not really. Fear surges through her body, hot at her throat.

Vero speaks quickly, forcing her words in front of LiLi's. "Or maybe we know each other as well as we need to. In the circumstances."

The bubble of LiLi's words fades to a simmer and then stops until her face is nothing but calm water.

"*The Mommy's Alphabet.*" Vero has not thought of this silliness since her night in the pantry, but it's all there now. "That was the subtitle of *A is for Asylum.*" She recites:

C is for the condoms
Your mommy shoulda thought to use.
They woulda saved her lotsa money
On her monthly bill for booze.

"Oh." LiLi wears the same expression that took hold of her face when she first saw snow. She's a goldfish in a bowl, face pressed to the cold glass of the window. *Oh, oh, oh.* Eventually, the silence is awkward, and LiLi drops her eyes to the floor, the skin from her neck to her hairline a deep red.

"I'm culture shocking you?" Vero bobs like a drowning swimmer. People talk of a fast descent into insanity as if the psyche only moves in one direction, but Vero dips and whirls; she has a grasp on the situation, and then she doesn't. She knows the appropriate thing to say, and then she loses it; there's enough air, and then there's none.

"Yes." LiLi's brow furrows. "I could never do such a thing—about the birth control—of my own children." She wipes a hand across her eyes, weary. "My brother and sister, I mean. Nene and Totoy." Her eyes glisten when she says their names, but her face stays hard. "We do not talk about—" She drops her voice as if speaking a dirty word against her will "—birth control, in my home."

"Maybe I'm not cut out to be a mother." Vero looks out the window addressing her confession to the forest, but she waits, breath held, for LiLi's response. She cannot imagine saying such a thing aloud to anyone else. LiLi is an empty container. Vero can put this thought there and leave it.

"Every woman feel that way sometimes, Vero. We do our best, when we can." The intensity in LiLi's voice surprises Vero. She's trying to tell Vero something, a thing of great importance to her, but again, Vero turns away from it. She has come so far, wanting a connection with this woman, this stranger in her home, but now she has doubts. What would a real connection mean? In this context?

"I will put you in my book too." Vero jerks the conversation back to safe ground. "In my *Mommy's Alphabet.*"

B is for the boredom
Of all that parenting work.
Thank goodness for the nanny
So mommy can her duties shirk.

Vero hears her own entreaty in the verse, a desperate plea lurking behind the strident rhyme, the offside joke. *Tell me I don't fall short. Tell me!*

"I don't know what this means. Shirk." LiLi is mad now. Vero knows it for certain. Her chair screeches around to face the children's table. She takes Jamal's spoon from him and shovels the last few bites of cold egg into his mouth. "We do five bites, JJ. You count with me." Eliot counts along—"one! two! three!"—but Jamal only chews. Vero thinks to tell LiLi that Jamal speaks Tagalog, but then she realizes that LiLi will, of course, know. LiLi knows many things about Vero's boys. Vero sits with this thought for a moment, her hands clenched as if in prayer, and then she lets it go. She decides it is okay, this life that exists beyond her. What else could it be?

◊◊◊

"Have you seen Mister Shane?" The words come up from Vero's throat like a cough, a gag.

Ligaya tries so hard to stay out of her employers' business, to live in their house but outside of their "personal affairs." Yet here is Vero *pulling* her in. Ligaya thinks *Vero* should read the nanny brochures. What good is it if only one of them knows the rules?

"*Mister Shane?* Good lord. Did you hear that? I need a coffee."

Vero is falling apart. That—a woman falling apart—looks the same in any country. Ligaya should try to help hold her together. But the holding together of the mother is not in Ligaya's job description.

Still, Ligaya likes Vero, a little bit. Better than she liked Madam Poon. Maybe Ligaya likes Vero for all of her trying. Madam Poon knew better than to try. Vero is not as smart as Madam Poon, or as practical.

Ligaya brews coffee and sets a cup—prepared just as Vero likes it— on the table in front of her. She hopes Vero will drink it and then go to her plant of army tanks, leaving the boys to their day. Caring about Vero is too much work. Ligaya has enough work.

"Oh, LiLi. Thank you. You're magic." She sips. "Coffee is magic." She takes the cup and stands at the window, her forehead pressed against the glass.

"I meant to say *Shane*. Just Shane. Have you seen him?"

This world is not made for women, thinks Ligaya. *Not in the Philippines. Not here. Maybe not anywhere.*

LiLi lifts her lips into a soft smile she rarely shares with adults here, the kind of smile she's especially careful not to share with Shane and Vero. The brochure has said to keep boundaries, to always maintain the privacy of the family. But today? This poor woman. How can Ligaya keep boundaries here with this sad mother whose husband is gone? Ligaya understand that sadness far better than she would like to.

"He will be at work now, yes? He be home for supper. I make his favourite."

Ligaya wonders if Vero knows what Shane's favourite dish is. Ligaya knows. She will make white fish with chili powder and canned tomatoes, served on white sticky rice. Shane always asks for seconds when she makes that meal. Pedro's favourite dish is chicken. He chews on the drumstick until his lips shine with grease, sucks every bit of marrow out of the bone, and then smiles at Ligaya with his chipped front tooth. She once asked him where it came from, that broken tooth. *You don't need to know everything about me, my Ligaya.* Now she wishes she knew nothing about him. She tells her mind to stay away from him, but her mind does not obey. There has been nobody else.

"Thank you, LiLi. Shane would like that. If you make his favourite. Thank you."

While LiLi washes the boys' hands and faces and marches them to the dishwasher with their empty plates, Vero watches as if she is at a movie theatre. Ligaya wonders if she searches her mind for a memory of putting Jamal and Eliot to bed last night. Brushing their teeth as the salt ran through the egg timer? Sitting between them as they stalled over the pages of their favourite book about a boy whose magic skates let him win at hockey? Putting her nose to their freshly washed hair as she kissed them goodnight? Vero will not find any such memories. Ligaya put them to bed, and Ligaya got up with them this morning.

"How long have you been working, LiLi?"

The question startles Ligaya, as if Vero has seen her naked thoughts. Ligaya waves her hand vaguely in the air. "No worries, Vero." It is a North American expression—*no worries!*—but sometimes seems to mean its opposite. "No worries at all." Ligaya smiles again.

Vero takes a long drink from her cup. It's already half empty, though she doesn't recall lifting it to her lips before now. The coffee is strong the way LiLi knows Vero likes it. Vero drinks deeply again, enjoying the burn of it against the back of her throat, the buzz of it through her veins.

But the caffeine heightens Vero's senses when she craves the opposite. She leaves her mug on the dining room table and goes in search of the blender. LiLi has gradually reorganized the entire kitchen until Vero can't find anything. By the time Vero locates the blender in the bottom corner of a cupboard near the stove, LiLi has already emptied Vero's cooling coffee down the drain, rinsed her cup, and placed it in the dishwasher. Everything about LiLi speaks of efficiency: her no-nonsense wardrobe, her brisk movements, her reluctance to smile for Vero or Shane—as if lifting her facial muscles would be a wasteful use of energy.

"You can ask me where is blender. I know." LiLi closes the dishwasher door in a huff of foul-smelling air. When she speaks again, she has faced away from Vero. LiLi's mood has shifted again. They're both unpredictable—irritable one moment, unexpectedly kind the next. There's a suffocating energy in the house, the air too close, too dense.

"You did not like the coffee," LiLi says before Vero can respond to the first accusation.

"I know a better breakfast drink." Vero stabs the blender's power jack into the wall. "I learned it in Jamaica."

Vero can make a milkshake as well as Mike the Jamaican bartender, and hers will come without the attitude: a Dirty Monkey with a smile rather than a snarl. She drops a banana into the blender.

"You and I can both have some. We'll celebrate." Vero swallows hard, trying to choke her own hysterical treble. "A homecoming party."

Vero counts to five as the brown syrup pours from the Kahlua bottle. *If you want something done right, you have to do it yourself.* Imena said this—in her black leather pants and bustier, a whip held firmly between her teeth as she stretched over the bar, breasts nearly spilling free, her thick, muscled arm reaching for the 151-proof rum that Mike kept hidden under the front counter. Imena free-poured into her own glass before tipping the bottle in Vero's direction. "Sometimes being a bit numb helps." She did not smile or invite Vero to respond. "Sometimes, but not always."

Vero measures the first shot of rum into the blender, but then, when she finds no other liqueurs in the cabinet, adds another splash of rum for character. And then another. "There's no such thing as too much character," she says aloud.

R is for the sweet, sweet rum
Most moms avoid til afternoon.
But mix it with bananas ... Voila!
A healthy drink! You can't have that too soon!

Vero sings under her breath, as much in Hedonism as she is in Sprucedale, her mouth watering in anticipation of this treat of booze-drenched ice cream, the cool sweet run down her throat, the weight in her belly, the warm lazy hum of it floating through her bloodstream.

"We play downstairs, Eliot. Bring your brother."

Eliot wails. He's been promised the park.

"Shh, Eliot, shh. We play our special game. In my basement. We do fun."

Vero presses *blend* to drown out the grating whine.

"We go to park later. We stay close by now. In case mommy needs us." LiLi speaks the last sentences with a forced loudness, so Vero will hear her over the blender, and then she hurries the boys downstairs.

LiLi will stay here. LiLi she can count on.

Shane keeps a beer mug in the freezer for that one post-ride beer. Nobody uses that mug except him. But Shane is not here. Vero takes his frosty mug and fills it to the rim with her Jamaican concoction.

LiLi, she thinks, *is always here, as reliable as my own shadow.*

Vero pays LiLi, of course, there is that, but who isn't paid? One way or another. Life: it's all a barter system. That's the lesson Vero learned in Hedonism.

"To LiLi," Vero lifts the heavy mug in the direction of the stairs. "To LiLi," she says again louder, hoping LiLi hears in the basement. Cold sweetness hits her throat first, but then the delicious burn of the rum chases away the numb ache. It's not bad, her concoction, not bad at all. "*To LiLi!*"

For her, Vero drinks again.

◊◊◊

Ligaya shoos Jamal and Eliot downstairs and puts them in front of the television. Usually she is good about limiting their screen time, but today, she needs space. Eliot happily watches the boy in the cape spelling English words to save the day. Jamal yammers away in Tagalog, running a string of trains up and down the wooden slide. "Mabilis tren! Tren fast!" He's oblivious to the television. *There is enough fun in this boy's head,* thinks Ligaya. *He does not need the television, this clever boy.*

No Tagalog, Ligaya thinks to say. *Only English. And no more Philippines*

Game. No more secret. She will say these words soon. Tomorrow. Or the next day. By September. Eliot starts junior kindergarten then. She and Jamal can work on English when Eliot goes to school.

"*Sakay na!* Choo choo!"

Ligaya has taken pleasure in Jamal's Tagalog this last year, the ease with which he took to the language. She knows Jamal is not hers, she has always known that, but he has been like hers.

When Nanay's face flickers onto Ligaya's computer screen, Ligaya does not try to smile for her. Not today.

Nanay has no patience for the sullenness on Ligaya's face. "Why is your brow furrowed?" Her voice cuts in and out. The static ages her voice, transforms her to an ancient croaking woman.

But with even this small glimpse of the Philippines, Ligaya finds Pedro on her mind, her head resting in the nook of his shoulder as she watched the thin white line marking an airplane's movement across the sky. She thinks of her cousin Corazon, too, and the two of them in the streets of Hong Kong, a red blanket across their laps, a box of steaming pansit noodles cupped in their hands. Ligaya likes Jamal—she likes him a lot, loves him even—but she would say goodbye to him right now for just one more hour in the company of either Pedro or Corazon. One more hour. The thought embarrasses her. *Pasensya na,* JJ, *so sorry.*

"Life is hard here, Nanay. I don't feel like smiling today. I get tired of pretending. My life here is not like I put on Facebook. All smiles and friends. I miss my home." Ligaya says the last part softly. She does not want Eliot and Jamal to hear. "You are at your sister's home now. Often. Maybe you don't understand my life."

"Yes," Nanay speaks curtly, "life is hard. I know that." She does not say it with kindness. She too is worn out today. "Nene and Totoy. They need school clothes. They need school textbooks." Ligaya tries to picture Totoy old enough for school, his black hair combed flat to his head, bleached white socks pulled high to his knees, nearly meeting his checkered school shorts. "Remember, Ligaya, it's all God's plan. This is necessary, not for your own fun."

Ligaya holds her breath and counts to three—*isa, dalawa, tatlo.* Only then does she allow herself to speak. "With that I agree, Nanay. I did not come here for fun. We can both say that is true."

"Not for fun."

Ligaya does not know why Nanay repeats her like this. The connection is poor today. Nanay's face flickers, and the sound of her words lags behind the sight of her moving lips. One moment the words are quiet under the static, the next they are loud and distorted.

"Show me the boys, Ligaya, take me on a walk around the basement."

But Ligaya does not want to show Nanay anything today. Somehow, it is today's distortion and flickering and static that allow Ligaya to ask the question—to say the name—that they have all been avoiding. "How is Pedro?" Ligaya says it slow and even, not letting herself drop her eyes, not letting anything that might be interpreted as weakness, or hope, sneak into her words.

"Ligaya, he is—" Ligaya is certain Nanay will lie, but then Nanay blinks hard twice and raises her small wrinkled hands to her face, rubs her eyes, which might be wet. It looks as though Nanay's hands spread the moisture to her cheeks. "It is best that you forget Pedro." Nanay says this with her eyes lowered, her voice choked. "Your father and I have forgotten him. The children will forget him soon enough." Nanay raises her eyes and waits for Ligaya to respond.

Ligaya will not. She can think of nothing to say. She watches her own impassive face in the computer. She already knew this anyway. Pedro's absence. She has no angry words for him now, no sorrow, no anguished tears. Where she expects to feel these emotions, she feels only the heavy weight of fatigue.

"I am sorry," Nanay finally says. "We are all sorry."

"Yes," Ligaya says. "I hear that word often. Everyone is sorry."

Only when Nanay has gone does LiLi hold her fingers to the blank computer screen. She speaks English into her mother's absence. "I love you, Mama."

She says it aloud just to hear how it sounds.

◊◊◊

Vero moves a rocking chair into the bay window in Shane's office and keeps lookout. She's almost forgotten about this view, a tiny corner of lake in the distance. *My room with a view*, she'd sighed with feigned rapture when they bought the house, before Shane claimed it as his office. Here, the two of them shared Argentinian Malbecs, toasting the house, toasting their own success, celebrating their ability to build themselves a perfect life. Here, she interviewed LiLi on that crackling line to Hong Kong. *I be your sister, ma'am, an auntie to your boys.* Here, LiLi trembled through Shane's weekly performance review meetings, Vero downstairs, left to guess what transpired between them.

Here, Vero will see Shane pull in. He must've spent the night in his office. He will be wrinkled, remorseful. This absence is unlike him. Funny that it has taken this, his son speaking Tagalog, for him to crack. But Vero knows it's not just that. Sometimes simply being alive is hard. Shane has saved up for a giant chasm, whereas Vero lets life take its toll gradually in miniature fissures sustained each and every day. "You feel too deeply," Cheryl said to her. "It will be your downfall." And then Cheryl retreated—choosing not to feel at all.

It's just words. That's what Vero will say when Shane returns with a hand cupped around the back of his neck, fingers tucked into his hair. *Jamal will learn other words.* But she realizes that Shane's anger has nothing to do with language. It has to do with Shane's realization of his own failure. What failure is felt more harshly than a failure in parenting? *A child should speak the language of its mother.* Vero knows that he thought *the language of his father* too. Only a personal failure could provoke such outrage. And to be outed in that way—by a peer, another medical professional in the same small city—before Shane could discover his shortcoming for himself. That was the worst of it.

He's ashamed. There's nothing a Schoeman hates worse than the shame of losing.

◊◊◊

Vero must work to focus on LiLi. Every time Vero sees LiLi today, it's as if she's looking for the first time: the perfectly round mole just above her lip, the gold cross hanging in the smooth dip at her neck, the hands small as a child's but always flying, busy with adult work.

"I am going crazy." Vero speaks the words loudly, straight into her wide mug, just to hear them echo back. She must fight her tongue to get it around each word. The loose enunciation that sounded natural in Jamaica is too clumsy here, too reckless, too dangerous. "I'm going crazy."

The boys laugh. They find Vero hysterical. Nothing is as funny as this crazy, silly mommy of theirs. But LiLi does not laugh.

"It's Shane, LiLi. He's gone." Arms hanging loose at her sides, Vero stares at LiLi: the mole, the cross, the hands. "It makes me sad. That he's gone. Sad and scared." She feels as though she's lifted a sheet and prostrated herself naked for judgment.

There's a quick twitch across LiLi's features. It moves like a shadow from her forehead to her eyes to her mouth and then it's gone. *It's fear,* thinks Vero, *LiLi does not want to know my real story any more than I want hers.*

"We all have bad days," LiLi says. "This pain…it get better and then you forget it."

Vero does not want LiLi to talk about pain. What she wants is for LiLi to say that Shane will come home. Of course he will. He must. But Vero wants to hear it, from some mouth other than her own. LiLi will not mention it, though. LiLi will speak neither of Shane's absence nor his return. Direct reference to the personal lives of her employers would be indelicate. LiLi has studied the nanny manuals well. LiLi is never indelicate.

In return, Vero will not mention LiLi's pain, the kind of pain that does not go away. The thought is out of Vero's mouth as quickly as she thinks it. "You make the rules here," she says. "Now you do."

This is drunkenness, this inability to distinguish between an outer and inner voice. This is why we drink: to give ourselves permission to confuse the two.

"I mean, you're doing a good job of running the household. That's what I meant to say. Any house needs rules." Her words are too loud and too wet. Her hand rests on Jamal's head, too heavy. He grins up at her. She's so funny, this crazy, silly mommy. Vero swallows and tries again. "Thank you. For everything." She puts her half-full mug on the counter, unable to drink another sip. A light Pinot Grigio is in order.

"Oh Vero." LiLi's smile reminds Vero of the spring day on the lawn, LiLi's face opening to the rare sun like a flower. "I do not make rules for you. For the boys, some rules." She busies herself clearing the dishes. "I glad you like my running of your house."

LiLi allows herself more words when Shane's gone. When it's just the two of them, Vero gets glimpses of the woman behind the veil of employee. The two of them—Vero and LiLi—could be more like a family without him. *Three adults is too many for one family.* Vero nearly says it aloud. *Indelicate,* she realizes, just in time.

CHAPTER SEVENTEEN

The day skips and jumps, Vero finds herself in conversations she doesn't remember starting, wonders how previous conversations ended, pours herself another glass of Pinot Grigio and forges on.

"Is a lion a predator or a prey?" Eliot's eyebrows push low down on his eyes. The answer is important.

"Predator," LiLi answers lightly, wiping milk from the corners of his mouth with her wet thumb.

"Is a seal a predator or a prey?"

"Mm, prey," LiLi says less confidently. "Though predator to fish." She scoops more green peas onto his plate. He spoons them into his mouth, his mind on the seal. LiLi nods at Vero over his head, pleased with this trick of taking advantage of his distraction. "He watch the animal show on television, Vero. You know Eliot. He like to understand everything."

The television runs in the background now too, but nobody watches it. Jamal's eyes stay stuck on Eliot. Vero reads comprehension in Jamal's features. He may not speak English, but he understands it.

But Vero and LiLi were talking about something else. Before this interruption of predators and prey. LiLi served them dinner: white fish with rice and tomatoes, a rub of cumin and curry and chili powder coating the fish. LiLi removed Vero's wine glass and wrapped her hands around a warm cup of black strong coffee. She took Vero's fingers and placed them just as she'd placed Jamal's fingers around his fork at breakfast.

Shane has not returned for dinner, but neither she nor LiLi acknowledges the space at his end of the table as they spoon his favourite meal into their mouths.

"What were we talking about? About Bernie?" The conversation has gotten away from Vero, caught in a gust of wind and whipped over the clouds. She can't reel it back in.

"Yes, Bernie is..." LiLi's sentence trails off, left for Vero to finish it, but Vero leaves it to hang, just like one of Shane's sentences. Why can't these people follow their own thoughts through to their own damn conclusions? Vero will wait.

"She is the other way. A tomboy, we say."

Still, Vero says nothing.

LiLi pushes fish and tomatoes around her plate, building small piles. Vero wonders when she will take a bite. She seems to do so only when Vero looks away. Rarely do they eat at the same table. "She has a girlfriend," LiLi finally says, resting her fork on the table. "Not boy."

Bernie is gay? Vero flushes with her own stupidity that she must be told this. By LiLi. How could Vero not have known? "Oh yes," she covers, "I thought so. We don't make such a big deal about those things here. Don't even differentiate one way or another, most of the time. Post-gay. That's the term we use." She cringes at the exclusion in her pronouns. *We versus you.* The implied superiority. We know, you don't. It is a trick Shane's parents would use. We, the white employer, you, the coloured servant. "There are gay people in the Philippines, then?"

It is a stupid question. Vero recognizes it as such immediately. She pours fast words over the stupidity to bury it. "I mean, it's so religious there. I thought homosexuals would be closeted." Vero does not know if LiLi will understand this expression. "I thought they might hide their sexual orientation, I mean."

"Yes, I know closeted, this way of saying." LiLi puts generous bowls of ice cream in front of Eliot and Jamal. "We have gays. In Philippines, they are more showy than here, men wearing makeup or the feminine clothes. Here, the gays, they are more—how you say?—subtle. It different in Philippines, though. So much about money. Business. Hard to know what's true and what's…for the necessity."

Vero tries to make sense of this, what it might mean for LiLi. Suddenly, Vero recognizes herself as the naïve one, the one who has lived a sheltered existence.

LiLi fills the silence. "But I only know about Bernie because she tell me herself."

Bernie told her?

"You two are good friends then?" Vero hears her own jealousy. A tight presence in her throat, the words have to squeeze by it to escape. "That's good." Vero forces air into her words. "I'm glad you have someone. Like that."

LiLi puts a large fork full of fish and rice into her mouth, chews with her hands across her lips. Nods.

"I suppose it can't be me," Vero says into her coffee mug. "That friend."

After dinner, Vero finds a nature show on television and puts Jamal and Eliot in front of it. She needs for them to be TV-comatose. For a while. *Telatose,* Shane calls it, when their eyes sink into their skulls and the muscles of their faces fall slack. Vero expects LiLi will go downstairs once her charges are occupied, but she busies herself with dishes and brooms and cloths. Vero doesn't stop her. She's learned that work is LiLi's way of staying upstairs. She's not comfortable with idleness, at least not in Vero's presence. She listens as she works, though, nods encouragement.

She boils strawberry tea, surprising Vero by taking a cup for herself and sitting on the couch next to Vero, legs curled under her. Amazing how this woman knows what Vero needs before Vero knows herself. "Mothering *me* is not exactly in your job description, is it?" Vero's face feels numb, but the hint of a headache creeps down her skull. She rests the warm cup at her temple, enjoys Jamal's hot lazy weight falling into her thigh. "Thank you, LiLi."

Vero is grateful for LiLi's company, but it's like sitting for a drink with a hummingbird. Any sharp movement will scare her off, and LiLi will be back flittering around the kitchen with a broom. Vero holds her breath, keeps both hands around her mug.

"In my country, when men want to socialize with the friends, they say '*Inuman na!*' It means, It's drinking time. The men like beer. Women, we only take alcohol on very special occasion," LiLi offers, setting her tea on the corner table and pulling Eliot into her lap. His eyes stay fixed on the television, but he melds to the spaces in LiLi's body. "And then only a little bit." LiLi fingers the gold cross at her throat. "Tomorrow, my mother birthday. I like to have a bit of wine. With you." She blushes like a teenager asking permission. "But maybe you have enough already."

Vero would like to pour them each a glass of cool wine, raise her rim to meet LiLi's. *To your mother! To Nanay!* But she's frightened that a large gesture will send LiLi flying downstairs. Vero simply sits. They both watch the boys watch television. LiLi leaves her lips against the warm mug even when she's not drinking, the other arm curled around Eliot's husky frame.

LiLi has dressed him in a green shirt that brings out the colour of his eyes. He starts school on Monday, only junior kindergarten, but Vero still finds it impossible to believe. The summer has left the tips of his hair golden. They curl at the nape of his neck. Vero tightens her own grip on Jamal. "God, they're beautiful," Vero says of her own boys, knowing it's indecorous to admire one's own offspring. She would never say it in public.

LiLi smiles her agreement. The smile softens her features. Vero sees pride in the smile, yet she does not feel threatened by it. She's grateful someone else can love her boys with such fullness.

"You're beautiful too." Vero watches the blush crawl up LiLi's neck in response. "You must have had many admirers at home. Here too, I imagine."

"Oh. Nobody say so anymore. Nobody say so for very long time." LiLi tucks a piece of hair behind her ear, exposing a stretch of neck. Danielle's neck with its suntan was the same colour. Vero had put her mouth right where the collarbone...

No.

Vero's gaze has made LiLi uncomfortable. Even the weight of a look will make this hummingbird fly. LiLi squirms and pushes herself up from the couch, takes Vero's empty mug from her hands. "I take the boys for a bath, now, Vero. You rest. It fine. I not mind."

◊◊◊

Vero listens to the faucets running above, the boys splashing in the water. Alone, she can think of nothing but Shane. By now, he's not simply at the office. She cannot be down here alone. Not with these thoughts. She pours herself a fresh cup of tea and follows the sounds of life. She brings LiLi a cup of tea too, but LiLi's hands are busy: she bends over the bathtub, bubbles up her forearms, her long hair dipping into the water. When she sees Vero, she wipes the steam from her face with the inside of her elbow, laughs at the wet mess the boys have made of the bathroom. "See, you crazy boys! Your mother fire me for this mess you make." She splashes water toward their faces to punctuate her joke.

Vero stays in the steamy doorway, socks dry, holding both cups. Eliot and Jamal smile at Vero over LiLi's head. The smile lets Vero feel the earth under her feet. Without it, she would be convinced she was no more than a ghost, hovering at the periphery of her own life. Not just redundant but insubstantial.

LiLi's shirt rides up, exposing the small of her back. So many North American women her age have decorated that spot with tattoos, but hers is blank. When she sees Vero staring, she tugs at her shirt, tucking it into the waistband of her sweatpants.

"LiLi, can you make sure you're using English? Always? With Jamal?" Vero keeps her voice soft. It is not LiLi's fault.

LiLi stops scrubbing Jamal's hair. She opens her mouth but then closes it again without making a sound. She nods once with her eyes lowered.

"Why am I so tired?" Vero puts the question to LiLi's back. "You're the one doing all the work." It's transparent, this praise used to soften the blow of weakly worded criticism. Vero doesn't try to hide that.

"My work gives me the energy." LiLi's hands move quickly against Jamal's scalp. "Too much time left to thinking—that tire anyone."

Vero does not respond. LiLi has matched her transparent praise with transparent criticism. Vero leaves LiLi to her work.

◊◊◊

After LiLi puts the boys to sleep, she joins Vero on the front porch.

"Let's have that glass of wine," Vero says, LiLi's reappearance cause for celebration. Normally, LiLi would slink downstairs to the basement after a cursory goodnight. They have made progress today, of a halting kind. "For your mother."

LiLi's willingness does not surprise Vero. Conversation on the front step must be a welcome alternative to the empty basement. Nobody should spend a beautiful early fall evening like this one underground. Although Vero and Shane rarely sit outside, they have placed comfortable chairs here that face out onto the range where Shane often bikes. The nights are cold in Sprucedale, and the trees have already started to turn, peppering the hillside with vibrant orange and golds. Vero feels no sadness at the impending end of summer, only a hint of hope offered by the fresh beginning of fall. She thinks of sending Eliot off to junior kindergarten and remembers Joss telling her, "Never make any major decisions about your relationship until both kids are in school. Until then: survive."

That freshness is in the air tonight, the smell of autumn. Vero brings blankets, places one over LiLi's legs as she hands her a glass of wine.

So much time passes before LiLi lifts her glass to her lips that Vero has started to suspect she will not drink the wine at all. LiLi swallows carefully and smiles her response. Her eyes have that familiar *oh, oh, oh* look, and Vero wonders if this is really the first time LiLi has tried wine.

"Shane bikes up there," Vero points to the steep slope. "On Cardiac Hill. Joss and I run the lower section. Used to." The moon rises above it even though the sun has not quite set yet. As soon as Vero hears her own words, she realizes she does not want to talk about Shane, about biking, about geography. She doesn't not even want to talk about Joss.

"Where are your friends tonight? We don't see them lately. The one who used to come here…Cheska?"

"She has a …" LiLi sways her head side to side like she has water in her ears. "… like a boyfriend."

"Where did she meet him?" Vero is surprised. These girls seem to stick to themselves. She hasn't imagined that kind of social opportunity for them. A boyfriend would be nice for LiLi. A happy ending. If she and Shane can do that for LiLi—can have brought her here where she could meet someone with financial means and start a good, easy life—that would be something, a kind of redemption.

"She meet him on the Internet, I think." LiLi raises the glass to her lips. Drinks deliberately. "Just because someone do something for money does not mean she do not like it. Too." LiLi pulls the blanket tighter, her eyes on the moon. They've left the front door open so they will hear the boys if they wake. As it gets darker, the light from the front hall casts a shadow across LiLi's face. Vero can only see half of her features.

Vero does not know what LiLi means about money. The boyfriend pays Cheska? Vero wonders if LiLi is cryptic on purpose, leaving these spaces for Vero to fill as she likes.

"I made a friend in Jamaica. She looks like you. The same dark eyes, especially." Vero fingers the edge of the blanket in her lap, picking at imagined lint, wonders why she's decided to tell LiLi this, now. "It's weird. I miss her. We became close in that short time. I guess I don't have many friends like that anymore. When the boys were little, I became … inward. This friend, she pulled me outward."

"Bernie … she became a friend like that to me when you and Shane is gone."

When LiLi finally drinks the last of her single serving of wine, Vero lifts the bottle to refill her glass, but LiLi covers it with her hand.

"No, this is enough for me. I go to my bed now. Goodnight, Vero. And thank you. For the wine. For the company."

"Thank you, LiLi. For today. For your help."

LiLi holds Vero's eyes for a moment and then she's gone.

"Goodnight," Vero says to the empty doorway.

◊◊◊

Vero does not fill her glass with LiLi gone. The taste of wine bores her. She moves into the living room, switches off the TV, and listens for sounds of life in the basement. The boys do not need her. They have both been quiet for hours. But Vero is not ready for sleep yet either. She listens for the hum of LiLi's television in the basement. She imagines padding down there in her pyjamas and bedroom slippers, bearing popcorn and tea, laughing with LiLi at all the canned punch lines. The basement is quiet, though. Nothing but the gentle hum of a bathroom fan.

Vero walks in circles—kitchen, living room, dining room, and back—she does not know what to do with herself. She's too aware of her own body: the prickle of air against her skin, the thrum of blood through her veins. She cannot sit. Her body insists that she move. She circles the kitchen again, running her fingers along the clean granite countertops, and then opens the liquor cabinet, pours herself a shot of rum, straight up like scotch, and takes a sip.

Maybe LiLi's bored. Maybe she'd appreciate a visit. Vero strains her head down the stairwell. It's not completely dark down there.

She circles again, fingers dragging on the shiny countertops, stops to listen at the upstairs hallway. There is no sound at all, as if her boys have evaporated. She circles again, this time stopping to look downstairs. There is only the slightest hint of light. What does LiLi do down there, every night alone?

Vero will go see. She will just say hi.

Hi, I wondered what you're up to.

Hi, we're both awake anyway, thought we could chat!

Hi, feel like some company?

Something like that. LiLi will appreciate the gesture. She will be kind in response to Vero initiating this development in their friendship.

The stairwell is dark, and Vero grips the railing, taking each step carefully, feeling the carpet with her toes before transferring her weight, imagining the embarrassment of a somersault to the bottom. *Well, hello!* Blood spurting from her nose. *Have a first-aid kit handy?*

Ligaya's bedroom door is closed, but a faint light shines through the crack at the floor. Vero flicks on the hallway light. She can't be fumbling around in the darkness like a criminal, in her own home. She rests her knuckles on the wood of LiLi's door, thinks to knock, but that feels absurd. It is her house. She needn't knock. She cups her hand around the doorknob. She simply wants to say hello, one lonely woman to another, what could be wrong with that?

CHAPTER EIGHTEEN

Ligaya puts on her nightgown with nothing underneath. Usually she wears at least her undergarments, sometimes wool socks and sweat pants too, so that Shane will not scold her for turning the temperature in the basement too high.

But tonight, she wears only the new nightgown, soft against her bare skin. As she sits on the edge of her mattress dressed for sleep, she does not feel tired. She even considers going back upstairs. She could visit more with Vero. To fill the time. To do something with this restless energy that has overtaken her. It has been an unusual day in their house, she and Vero hard and cruel with each other one minute, and then approaching friendship the next.

It is better Ligaya calls an end to this strange day and stays downstairs.

Now is the time of the month she misses Pedro most. That timing could also explain her restlessness, as well as her edginess with Vero. Ligaya is fertile. She learned to read the signs back home, after the birth of Totoy. She and Pedro could not have another baby. They knew that. When Ligaya wanted Pedro most, that was when she could not have him, so they found other ways. Thank God for that small bit of planning. Otherwise the two of them would bear the guilt of even more deserted children.

The box of pictures in Ligaya's bottom drawer pulls at her. She yearns to go to the drawer, spread the photographs in her lap, hold their smooth surfaces to her cheek. She fights the urge.

She can keep her mind hard against Pedro some of the time, but she has less control over her body. There has been nobody else. Pedro is still the only man she knows, and it is his body alone that she imagines on hers.

But Pedro has moved on. Nanay has told her so. Ligaya wonders if it is one of the younger women in the neighbourhood, a girl whose family has not yet sent her packing off to Hong Kong, who holds his attention now. Ligaya does not wish to think of his calloused hand spread across Analyn's curvy hips or his fingers open on Maria's slender waist. *I babysat Maria*, she thinks, *I babysat her, Pedro*. But Ligaya knows she will have no occasion to have this conversation with Pedro.

She falls back onto her pillow, stares at the ceiling, lets her hands rest on her own waist, no longer so slender. Not anymore. *It is not fair.* A child's thought, she knows. But still, it isn't. Ligaya is the one who has moved, but she cannot *move on*. With whom would she? The only men she knows are Lito and his friends from the coffee shop. They all have children back home. Children and wives.

Ligaya has not touched a man for a year here in Canada—a year next week. There was another full year before that in Hong Kong. And no man has touched her. How many times did she take Pedro's hands for granted back home? How many times did she shoo him away as he nuzzled her neck over the washing bin or tried to pull her into the trees when she was meant to be raking leaves. Now, alone in her room, Ligaya thinks of Pedro coming to her while she raked leaves, pulling on her hand, whispering warm promises close to her ear. Ligaya wishes someone would pull her into the trees now. Anyone.

She pulls up her nightgown and holds her fingers to her own warmth. Ligaya cannot satisfy herself the way Pedro once could, not quite, but she can come close. In her time away, she has learned, out of necessity.

◊◊◊

A single, dry finger rested across Ligaya's lips wakes her. Not a hand pressed hard into her mouth, holding. Just one finger, soft, tracing the outline of her mouth. "Shh," the sound so close to Ligaya's ear that she feels it more than she hears it. "Is this okay?" Ligaya thinks to pull her blanket around her body. But it's not her blanket. Not her bed. Nothing in this place belongs to Ligaya. She pulls her nightgown down over her naked hips and lets her arms remain loose at her sides, pliant. Warm skin slides in next to her, the blanket pulled tight until it cocoons both bodies. "Is this okay?"

Again.

A real question then.

No, that's the word Ligaya sees in angry red. *No, how could this be okay?* But her body tells a different story.

It has been so terribly long.

Teeth glance her bare shoulder, but there's no pain. *Harder*, Ligaya wants to say, but since leaving home, she's learned to swallow her words.

Go, that's what she should say. *Go away.* But this presence in her bed—it's warm and soft. Ligaya feels no fear—that particular flapping bird caged in her chest sleeps soundly. How could Ligaya be afraid of fingers in her hair, hot breath on the shallow dip in her throat, the promising hint of tongue at her earlobe? Ligaya's nipples rise to the warm skin above her.

Yes, says Ligaya's body, *more. Yes, it is okay. Please. God, yes.*

But Ligaya, she says nothing.

◊◊◊

Vero opens the door to Ligaya's room slowly, the same way she opened Eliot's door this morning, quiet against the creak. A candle flickers on the nightstand, Ligaya's body is visible only as a slight rise underneath her comforter. Ligaya does not turn to acknowledge Vero's entrance. The blanket remains still.

Vero steps close, weight on her toes, and rests a single, dry finger across Ligaya's lips to wake her. Not a hand pressed hard into her mouth, holding. Just one finger, soft, tracing the outline of her mouth. "Shh," she makes the sound close to Ligaya's ear so that Ligaya will feel it more than hear it. "Is this okay?" She doesn't want for Ligaya to be scared, to feel forced. Ligaya fiddles with the blanket at her chest, toys with her nightgown under the sheets, but then lets her arms fall loose at her sides, so that the blanket opens, making space for Vero.

The skin of their bare ankles and calves slides together, warm, and Vero pulls the blanket tight until it cocoons both bodies.

"Is this okay?" She says it again, needs to be sure.

Vero's voice doesn't sound loose anymore. Her tongue does not fight with the words. The world is clear around her, though dreams can be clear too. She has drunk herself sober. Ish. She likes that rush of sound past her tongue. *Isshhh.*

Post-drunk.

Post-gay.

Vero releases a giggle into Ligaya's hair, feels Ligaya's body quiver in response. A quiver of pleasure?

It must be.

Ligaya does not smell of coconuts like Danielle. Ligaya—Vero loves the roll of the name on her tongue—*Ligaya* smells like Dove soap and strawberry lip gloss. *She smells real*, Vero thinks. And then: *No, she smells like a teenager.*

In the dark, Vero can make out a hint of silver glitter across Ligaya's cheekbones. Ligaya and her friends have been spending their money at the Walmart again. She imagines Ligaya down here alone at night, playing with makeup in the bathroom mirror. "You don't need to live like a teenager," she says. "You are a woman." Still Ligaya says nothing.

Ligaya's nightgown sleeves are short. Vero pushes one up to bare a shoulder. She kisses it and then scrapes her teeth against the soft skin. She liked when Danielle's teeth pressed a line into her bare skin, the roughness of it, the way the teeth acknowledged a need and bit into it.

I am here.

Vero thinks she feels Ligaya pull on her clothes, tugging as if she wants Vero's teeth to press harder, into her skin. So Vero presses.

It's comfortable in this underground room. Cool and dark like a secret. *What happens in the basement, stays in the basement.* Vero snakes her hand under Ligaya's nightgown and strokes the length of body from Ligaya's underarm to her hip. Sometimes she forgets Ligaya's age—the way she cares for the whole family, she seems older than she is. But the softness of her skin reminds Vero that Ligaya is still young. She has her whole sexual life before her: a suitor, a husband, children. For now, her body and her life remain simple. She has packed everything into this one small room, like a college dorm.

The thought excites Vero. To imagine a life that could be so easily contained, so light.

Vero rolls on top of Ligaya and is met with no resistance. This melding of bodies seems inevitable, now. Someone was bound to come down here, one of them, Vero or Shane. It's only right that it should be Vero who has found herself in the basement, in the underground room of this lonely woman. Vero has tried the hardest. With LiLi. From the beginning.

"I care about you," she says, smelling the alcohol on her own breath where it hovers between her mouth and Ligaya's cheek. "Ligaya, I do." But then that doesn't seem enough. "I love you," she tries again, hears the drunk college girl in it, all those late-night *I-love-you-guys!* slurred in the pad above Shane's parents' garage. Vero wants Ligaya to know that it's not alcohol speaking. *I must show her.*

Still, Ligaya says nothing. She barely moves. But she does not object. She does not tell Vero to leave. It is consent of a kind. Vero will take it as such.

She winds her fingers into Ligaya's thick black hair, freshly brushed smooth for bed. She exhales hot boozy breath on the shallow dip in Ligaya's throat, flicks a hint of tongue at her earlobe. Her full weight bears down on Ligaya now, and she feels Ligaya's nipples harden, rising sharply to her own bare skin.

Vero is a guest here, in Ligaya's room, but she no longer feels apologetic. Ligaya's flesh invites her in, welcomes her, she knows it does.

This is how Vero would have liked to have been with Danielle—alone in a room with no audience. But with Ligaya, it is better. Their meeting has history behind it. History brings weight and meaning and depth. What is a sexual encounter without weight and meaning? No more than a back scratch. Danielle was a back scratch. Back scratch as performance art. Ligaya and Vero: they have built to this. It was inevitable. Vero tells herself so again.

Finally, Vero lets herself taste the plastic-strawberry flavour of Ligaya's plump lips and then—there it is—the flick of Ligaya's tongue meeting her own.

CHAPTER TWENTY

Vero does not know how late it is when Shane returns. She hears him on the stairs, his hesitant descent pounding through her post-wine headache. She holds her hand to her temples and pulls her body away from Ligaya's, keeping her eyes closed, squeezed tight. *No, not this. He's looking for me now. Now?*

Vero left the light on in the staircase. Shane has followed it to the bottom of the stairs, where Vero has left Ligaya's door a crack open, and the trail of her clothes wends its way from the doorway to the bed. Vero swallows, her mouth parched. She cannot open her eyes, does not want to see the outline of his body in Ligaya's doorway. His nylon jacket rustles between his arms and torso when he steps into the bedroom. Shane's jeans creak as he kneels at the foot of the bed. Vero braces herself for his attack, feels his words as a punch to the face before he speaks them.

Slut! Whore! Cheat!

She flinches, preparing for the sting of them.

But she gets nothing except silence.

When Shane finally does speak, his voice is low and chesty. His words hurt more than the ones she anticipated.

"I'm sorry," he says. "I should have known better."

Vero's whole body unclenches, her head relaxing into Ligaya's pillow. He *should* be sorry. It was his idea. *Have sex with a woman!* He'd practically begged her. *Girls gone wild. Everyone's doing it.* But just as quickly, Vero's relief is gone, the blame back in her own lap. Shane is not a puppeteer. Vero is not made of socks and buttons. The momentary reprieve of relief is swallowed by regret—What was *she* thinking? And then, as quickly as Vero feels regret, anger shoves it off: She is a grown woman. She can take responsibility for her own actions. How dare Shane try to take that from her?

Even her emotions are fickle and unstable.

"You have nothing to be sorry for." Vero throws on the lights, wishes them off again as soon as she sees Ligaya, her back pressed into the cold outside wall.

Ligaya's eyes are wide and unblinking, her body so still she could be dead but for the subtle move of the golden cross at the dip of her throat, rising and falling with each timid breath. Ligaya's vulnerability reminds Vero of her own nakedness. She wants to grab the blanket to cover herself, but that would leave Ligaya exposed.

Vero has to get out of here, can look at neither of them. She grabs her clothes from the floor and strides for the stairs, anger fuelling her movements. She dons this anger like a shield, taking the steps two at a time, and then three. She pulls her sweatshirt over her head as she runs.

Shane follows.

Neither of them says a thing to Ligaya as they leave, the bedroom door wide open behind them.

◊◊◊

Ligaya squeezes her eyes shut. If she does not open them—if she refuses—this day will never start. She cannot turn time back, but maybe, with an act of sheer will, she can stop it from moving forward. She cannot imagine what's on the other side of this chasm. Even in the Philippines, on the bus, a full-day plane ride in front of her, she could at least imagine the other side.

Finally, she slides her legs over the edge of her single bed. She is naked. Ligaya never sleeps naked. She pulls the sheet tightly around her body and holds her head in her hands.

Of course, the faces she sees are the ones she least wants to come to her now. Nanay. Tatay. Pedro. Uncle Andres.

Well, fuck them.

It is Vero's word. A word that is everywhere here in North America, no ruder than *shoot* or *darn*. But the word has never passed Ligaya's lips before. She forces it out now, needs to.

"Fuck them. Fuck them. Fuck them." The words mean nothing to her. They release none of her frustration and despair. She tries again in a harsher, louder voice, not caring who hears her. "*Putang ina!*"

She hears the hysteria in her voice. For the first time since her arrival, she is truly angry. Her family has sent her to this new place with its new rules. They are not here, and she will not let them judge her from that old place by the old rules. Rules they didn't follow anyway. Not in dark private rooms. *Putang ina.*

She says it again and pounds her hand into the wall. The room is too small, the ceiling too low. She wants to rip the screen from the window, force her head and shoulders out into the cool morning air.

There is a low hum in her body. Shame. She recognizes that.

But she recognizes something else too. Underneath the shame. Satisfaction. Satiation.

She was thirsty, and she drank.

A woman needs to drink.

She thinks this thought again—if she repeats it, says it over and over, maybe she can feel its calm, its inevitability. She can be resolute. *I was thirsty, I drank.*

But her breathing is too fast. The faster she breathes, the less air she has. She gets down on her knees. One hand against her chest, she feels its shallow rise and fall; her other hand pulls the box of pictures from her bottom drawer. She will summon her home, her former self, her other life. The palm trees out back, the tilapia swimming through the living room in the monsoon, the chickens fluttering up to the roof.

We survive, her father had said, the family table filled with chicken and rice. But that—the chicken, the fish, the children eating rice with their hands—that was life. *That was living.* This—this room in someone else's basement, these people she must face today in "the land of opportunity"—*this* is survival.

She fumbles through her box of memories, the faces a blur through her tears. She rips the picture of Pedro. Rips him in half and then in half again, and then in half again. Tears him until he is tiny bits, and then she does the same with her mother. Then her father. Tears them all. Lets the minuscule bits of them fall to the floor. Only Nene and Totoy she saves, taping them up carefully at the head of her bed.

She dresses with precision this morning. A long formal black skirt. A white flowing blouse. She has not yet worn these clothes in her new home. They are not practical, not for taking care of children, but today the children will not be her focus. She looks at herself in the square mirror propped at a slant on top of her dresser. With her buttons done up to her neck, she looks like she is ready for church in the Philippines or in Hong Kong. She undoes two of the buttons. Today, she will wear makeup—not like she and Cheska wear it on weekends, pasted on and deliberately playful, childlike. Today, Ligaya will apply the makeup with the subtle hand of a grown woman getting ready for work, for a business meeting in an office building. A high tower on a busy street that speaks of wealth and success and opportunity. A city in the movies. There is no such street here in Sprucedale.

◊◊◊

It is nearly lunch by the time Ligaya works up the courage to face Shane. He has been holed up in his gah-raj-mahal all morning. That is not the place Ligaya would choose to speak with him. But she has made herself sick with worrying about this conversation that needs to happen.

Ligaya opens the door and steps through. She pauses up in the mezzanine, remembering the first time she saw this space. She'd imagined it as a party hall in her home town, Pedro leaning over the railing from up here in the mezzanine, watching her dance in the space below. Ligaya barely recognizes herself in the woman who had that fantasy. She takes a deep breath and forces herself down the stairs.

Shane is surprised to see her. She sees it in the rise of his white eyebrows, so high they disappear beneath the fringe of his hair. It is not the good kind of surprise. He has the look Pedro wore when Ligaya first told him she was with child, with Nene.

I am not ready for this.

Shane has the face of a street cat about to be clutched around its tiny waist. The panic in his eyes is at odds with the calm in his voice. "Hello, LiLi. Come in."

Ligaya cannot tell what he has been doing out here. Working on his bikes, she supposes. The green one is upside down and he spins the tire, watches it go around and around. When he finally turns his eyes to her, they cannot find a place to rest. Eventually, he chooses a spot over her right shoulder. Maybe he catches a glimpse of her right ear. She supposes this is how she has looked at him over the past year. It is annoying, she can see that now. She forces herself to meet his eyes. To try to catch them with her own.

Be brave, my girl. For some reason, this is her father's voice that comes to her now. *Be brave.*

"Shane," Ligaya's heart pounds so forcefully against her breast bone she is sure Shane can see it—the fast punching from the inside. She wants to hold her hand over the spot, hide her fear from him. "I want to meet with you and Vero today. A family meeting. Today." Ligaya fears that she sounds too forceful, like Pedro in a bad temper, growling at Totoy for some misstep. "Please," she adds.

Shane does not seem surprised by her assertion. Ligaya wonders what she had expected, what she had feared. He simply looks back to his bike and spins the tire. The *click, click, click* of the free wheel fills the silence in the massive room. When the clicking slows, Shane speaks without turning to her. "Yes. We do need that. Good idea."

There's nothing for Ligaya to do now but turn and walk up the stairs to the mezzanine where she can go back into the house and leave Shane to his bicycles. But at the top of the stairs, she stops with a hand on the door knob. She speaks down over the mezzanine railing. "We will have this meeting at three o'clock then. In your office."

There.

Now Ligaya goes, holding her hand over the hard thudding beneath her breastbone.

◊◊◊

When Vero steps into the garage, she assumes Shane has gone away again. She's hoping to spend some time crouched amongst the bikes in this cool space where Ligaya never comes, but she realizes her mistake as soon as she steps down the stairs from the mezzanine into a cloud of heavy, sweet smoke. Shane's there. His elbows rest on his bike-maintenance stand, his posture stooped. His shoulders slouch forward like he hasn't the strength to hold them up. His chest collapses in on itself. Like FrenchMan.

Shane has removed the picture of Vero that he had taped above his bike bench after their trip. He'd scrawled *My Pin-Up Girl* under the photo of her dressed in her Jamaica clothes, standing confidently, hands on hips, shoulders thrust back. He has replaced Vero's photo with a picture of Lance Armstrong leaning into his handlebars, expression fierce. *Unity is strength, knowledge is power, and attitude is everything* is written in black block capitals against a lemon-yellow background.

"Family meeting," Shane says without turning around. He's holding his breath, keeping that marijuana in his lungs as long as he can. Vero waits for him to exhale loudly and watches his shoulders folding in further with the release of breath. "In my office in fifteen."

"Okay." It's all Vero can say.

"Vero." Shane does not turn around, does not unfold his shoulders. "I was going to say sorry. For disappearing. Before I came home and...Before everything. I get tired too."

"I know," she says softly, to the back of his head. It is not enough— this *I know*—it's nothing of what she feels, of what she needs to say, but she hasn't yet found a place to start.

When Vero goes up the stairs and opens the door to the house, Shane stops her again with his words. "It's not because of *you* I took your picture down. It's the rest of it. Hedonism. The clothes, the..."

Without waiting for him to finish, Vero closes the door gently behind her.

◊◊◊

Vero assumes Shane has called this meeting, but when she steps into the office, nobody sits behind his desk. His chair is pulled out in front of the desk and Ligaya perches there, stiff and awkward, freshly painted nails gripping the leather arms. She's not in the loose cotton clothes she wears to care for the children, but has dressed in a long skirt and a white, pressed blouse. She's lined her eyes and wears a hint of blusher. Vero looks away, tries to ignore the stirring in her own body, the tingling energy that could be desire or shame. Or both.

Shane perches on the windowsill in the nook, his arms across his chest. A reluctant child. Vero settles on the edge of the rocking chair next to him without meeting his eyes.

Post-married.

She must swallow her laughter. Vero has brought them all here, with her flirtation with madness. How could she not have known this would happen?

Or not this exactly. But something like it.

Someone needs to apologize today. Someone needs to forgive. Someone needs to express gratitude. *I am sorry. I forgive you. Please. Thank you. You're welcome.* These words all fall short. To utter any of them now would diminish the situation. Vero holds her breath and counts to ten. Shane and Ligaya watch her, matching expressions of alarm and impatience. It is a child's trick. She parts her lips, sipping at the air.

"Where are Eliot and Jamal?" She has to say something. It's all she can think of.

"Vince and Adele have them. Through the weekend. I figured we needed the time."

"Excellent. Drunkle Vinny can teach them how to bong beer."

"And you're in a position to judge? You want to talk about fit and unfit caregivers?" Anger distorts Shane's voice. He sounds like he has a wet dishcloth lodged in his throat. Vero attempts to work up some anger of her own, but Shane speaks again, too soon, his words clear. "I'm sorry."

Let's just start over. It's what Eliot would say. Vero wishes such a simple sentiment could work for her. For all of them.

"I can forget this." Ligaya interrupts them, her voice filled with calmness and patience, her features soft and stern at the same time, a combination Vero has seen her use on the children. "I forget very many things." Ligaya's smile is so sad that Vero must look away, again. "Forgetting is what I do. For now."

The silence that follows is palatable, the air heavy with it. Vero imagines scooping it into her mouth, eating it like ice cream. The three of them in this room have become a broken family, just like any other. They can't mend the fracture, but they will have to figure a way to duct-tape it together and hobble on. Vero feels the tickle of laughter at her lips, then it floods her body in a rushing tidal wave. Only the most inappropriate laughter can take hold of her like this. She puts a hand to her mouth. Tries to hold it in.

"What's so funny?"

Shane has the wet cloth in his throat again, and Vero fights to claw back the response that flies into her mind. She will not allow herself to drown in the tidal wave of her own hysteria. *Sex is just a metaphor, Shane.* That's what she wants to yell. But sex is not a metaphor. Vero chews on her lips. "Nothing. Sorry." She will be like LiLi. Vero will retreat into silence. What else is there for her to do?

She balls her hands into fists, sits on them, fingernails pressing into her palms.

This would never happen, thinks Vero, even as it's happening. Or, this is the kind of thing that only happens behind closed doors, the kind of thing that people never talk about. Shame and propriety have rendered this situation absurd, impossible.

Vero wants her mother. She cannot remember wanting her mother since childhood. Not like this. Perhaps she thought she wanted her mother during Jamal's birth—the excruciating pain, the impossibility of it. *I want my mom,* Vero thought then, but it wasn't Cheryl she wanted. God, no. Not Cheryl. It was some abstract concept of *mom* that Vero was after. Comfort. Solace. Love. But now, *Cheryl* is who Vero wants. Cheryl would have an idea. Something about the sisterhood, about first-world women building their careers on the backs of third-world women, about needing a revolution. But whether an idea birthed in Cheryl's world could stand up in Vero and Ligaya's world—that was another matter. Still, an idea would be something. An idea would be a start. Vero could work with an idea.

"Really." Vero puts energy into the words now, draws on Cheryl's strength. She wants to be sure she sounds like she truly means what she is about to say. "I am—so sorry." The apology floats high above them, attaching itself to no one.

"People from my country do worse. They sell sex to survive. And they survive that too." Again, Ligaya is patience and calm personified. This is the Ligaya of their first phone interview. She has practiced what she needs to say, and she will say it clearly, independent of Shane and Vero's words and actions. She looks right through them. Vero has never felt so irrelevant. "What happen here: it not as bad as that." Ligaya does not focus her gaze on them, but there is authority in her voice. "We make some house rules, please. Like the nanny manual say. We go on."

Vero's skin pulls tight with fear. She remembers their talk about the sex trade on the porch last night. Was it really only last night? What has happened between then and now has rendered them all barely recognizable. What had Ligaya said? *You can make money and enjoy it too.* With a punch to the gut, Vero knows that Ligaya has misunderstood—their conversation, their union, all of it. Ligaya is going to ask to be paid. For what happened. For what Vero did to Ligaya in Ligaya's bed. Hot shame grips Vero's intestines, claws its way up her neck. The prickle of sweat itches at her hairline.

But Ligaya presses her lips tight, eyes resting on the window behind Shane. She says nothing.

Shane clears his throat. Vero tries to measure how high he is. His eyes don't droop shut, but they are a subtle pink. "There's an issue with power imbalance that makes this especially awkward." He's trying hard to sound sober. He continues slowly, as if weighing each word on his tongue before adding it to the sentence. "A domestic worker from the developing world whose fate rests in an emp—"

"We cannot talk about all that," Ligaya interrupts, though her posture is meek. She speaks softly into her hands folded across her lap. "I am just me. You, just you."

Vero wants to applaud. Ligaya has staged a coup. *Us women—we won't let Shane take charge. You show him, Ligaya!*

But Ligaya continues talking without casting a glance in Vero's direction. She's not looking for an allegiance. "People in your country are good at remembering. Always they want talk, talk, talk." Ligaya's voice is so quiet that Vero must lean forward to hear her. She sounds tired, but her tone is firm. Ligaya wipes her forearm in the air in front of her face as if cleaning a window with her sleeve. "Sometimes, the best way is wipe clean. Begin again. Sometimes, the only way."

Let's start over. Her statement amounts to no more than that. Vero wants more. This much Eliot could give her. *Let's just start over.*

But then there's that energy in Ligaya's eyes. Ligaya has something important to say, but she will hold off speaking until she gets the words just perfect. This time Vero will wait. She watches Ligaya's fingers fidget at the dip in her throat, but the golden cross is gone. *People never change.* That is the common saying. But the opposite is true. People are ever-changing. Before Vero figures out who they are, before she can really focus in on their essence, they've already become someone else.

"I get my open-work visa in one more year. Less, maybe. I don't go back without it to my Philippines. I scared to lose job. I cannot go back to my family with the empty hands." Ligaya's fingers float away from her neck and land firmly on her lap again. She meets their eyes for just a moment. "To my children." Her gaze flits back to the window, her face so still that even her lips do not seem to move when she speaks again. "I cannot go back to my children with nothing. After all the sacrifice."

The word rushes through Vero, pure adrenaline. *Children.* She sits with it for a moment—*my children, Ligaya's children*—and realizes that she knew. Of course she knew. In Vero's body, where it counts, she has known since Ligaya first entered her basement bedroom and saw the framed photos of her own family. Those photos took the last bit of life out of Ligaya's face. Only a mother's remorse could explain the extent of the impact. That wasn't a sister missing her younger siblings. That was an amputee looking at a photo of her bleeding, severed limb.

Vero looks to Shane's face for confusion. There is none. They've both pretended to believe what was easiest. For them.

"Their father?" Shane clears his throat again. "The children. Their father..."

"Pedro." Ligaya has no patience for Shane's search for the right question. "He not wait for me. I am gone a long time. Too long for a man to wait." There's no wetness in her eyes, no tremble in her lip.

Who's the strong one? Who's the one who can cope in this world, as it is?

"Maybe Pedro take me back when I have put in my years to bring our whole family to North America. Then." Ligaya shrugs. "But maybe I not take him back. Then it will be my choice."

Vero tries to absorb the strength in that *my*, in that *choice*.

While Ligaya talks, Shane puts his hand on Vero's knee. It can't mean *shh* because she's been quiet. It's warm and heavy. She sneaks a look at his profile, wondering what she will see—apology, resignation, despair, goodbye—but he looks straight ahead, eyes not wavering from Ligaya's face. Vero cannot look there. Instead, she watches Shane's hand. After a while, she lets hers rest gently on top of it.

"We both need something." Ligaya's eyes do not plead. They're as hard as they are when she tells Eliot and Jamal: *It is the house rule. Mommy and Daddy's rule.* "Maybe we give what each need to one other."

"Because that's the way the world works." Shane lets out the words in a cynical huff of judgment.

"I not talk about the way world works. I talk about us. Here." Ligaya takes a deep breath and tries again. She's scared. Vero can see that now. "I think I come here and it be easy. I think a big house like this be mine. I think like child." She lifts her hand to her mouth, pinches her lower lip. When her hand falls, she looks straight to their faces and holds their eyes, though doing so is clearly an effort. "My family led me to this thinking. My government too. The advertisements. But I do it. *I.* The child's think. Now we all be adults. We must."

This outpouring of words brings Ligaya into focus. She's more than a mole, a golden cross, a pair of tiny hands. Vero can almost see the whole. Before now, Ligaya has let her words go grudgingly, each sentence a reluctant gift. Now, she thrusts them upon Shane and Vero.

"Ligaya—"

"No, Vero. Don't call me that. In the Philippines, we take many nicknames. Here, in your home, I am LiLi."

Vero studies the set of Ligaya's features for some resemblance to the timid girl she met at the Sprucedale airport only a year ago. Has Ligaya found this strength here? Perhaps it was there all along, but Vero saw only what she expected to see.

"This is not my home, and you, not my family. But I can make something for my family. Maybe."

I'm sorry, Vero thinks again. But this time she does not say it. It's not enough. She feels the remorse in Shane too—in his heavy hand on her knee, in his heavier silence—but Vero understands now that remorse will not suffice. They will have to build something of their remorse. It is Vero's turn to be silent, for a time. She will hold her words and make room for Ligaya—for LiLi. For whomever this woman decides to be here, in this new place.

Vero opens herself to LiLi's words and does not try to decode her. She does not try to make the words her own. *Maybe we give what each need to one other.* Vero simply breathes the words in and releases them.

You have to make yourself strong, Vero once told Shane, cupping his shoulders in her palms, squaring his body to her own. *Nobody can do it for you.* Vero must taste this advice for herself. She squeezes Shane's hands in her own. She does not reach for LiLi's hand. It is not hers to hold.

Vero turns to the window, pushing her knees against Shane, and lets her gaze follow LiLi's to that glimmering water in the distance. All three of them sit quietly, eyes resting on that far-off spot of lake.

CHAPTER TWENTY-ONE

Finally, Sprucedale is ready for LiLi to start her driving practice. She has waited all winter. Even Bernie insisted that the winter is no time to learn to drive. Not in Sprucedale. LiLi watched the snow fall for months. She remembered the feeling of Pedro's red bike, the strength in her legs as she pedalled her way from one village to the next. She would like to feel that strength and freedom here.

Over the winter, she imagined that driving a car would be like biking, but better. She imagined, and she watched the snow fall and fall, until city workers had to come and dig out the stop signs. Children threw themselves from second-storey windows into the deep white banks below.

LiLi takes off her sweater as she waits on the front steps for Bernie. She sighs into the heat on her skin, lifts her face to it. The change of seasons in this country still surprises LiLi. In the frozen days of February, when the very inside of her own nose turns to ice, it is impossible to imagine a day like today, a day with dry roads and the sun high in an azure sky.

The tulips filling the flower bed along LiLi's bedroom window have burst into bloom overnight, a wealth of colour after the winter of white. In the late fall, Cheryl—the grandmother whom LiLi heard about but never saw—finally came to visit, and she and Vero dug in bulbs, shoulder to shoulder, in the already-frozen ground. With her short hair, ball cap, and baggy overalls, Pedro would have called her a Man-Woman, contempt in his voice.

"These tulips," Cheryl smiled at LiLi. "Enjoy them at first bloom. The deer will have them all eaten by nightfall of day one."

LiLi enjoys them now. Already she is running out of time.

Bernie pulls up to the sidewalk in Shauna's compact Toyota Tercel. It is red like Pedro's bicycle. LiLi expected the big blue van, the one Bernie uses to shuttle all the Sprucedale nannies to English lessons at the office.

Bernie waves and jumps from the car, though she could have waited there in the front seat. LiLi has already risen from the stairs and pulled her sweater back over her bare shoulders.

She is funny, this Bernie. Her hair has grown over the winter and springs out of the sides of her head in two small but spirited pigtails. "Driving! Are we ready for this?" She stands on the car's door frame and pounds her flat palms against the red roof, shining in the spring sun. LiLi loves Bernie for these grand gestures.

Even though the sun is only warm enough to briefly tempt LiLi out of her heavy sweater, Bernie is already in a T-shirt and shorts. She will make the most out of this sunny occasion.

Bernie's driving instructions are minimal. She points at the gas and then at the brake. "You've studied. You know what to do. Just take her easy to start. Soft touch. If you lurch a bit, slow down, breathe, start over. It's easier than it seems at first. You'll get the hang of it."

In the heat of a Sprucedale summer, LiLi will stick to these black leather seats, but now they are comfortably warm against her back. She wishes Nene and Totoy could see this: their mama driving a car!

It's not her car. She's not in her country. She doesn't even have a true license. But she puts her foot on the gas, places her hands at ten and two, and then grips the wheel so tightly that her fingers ache as she eases her way into the deserted street.

Ligaya drives.

Acknowledgments

For enthusiastic support of the project, thank you to my agent Chris Bucci of Anne McDermid and Associates. For being a delight to work with, thank you to the Arsenal Pulp Press team. My initial impression of Brian Lam (publisher) and Susan Safyan (associate editor) was so positive that I figured I could only be disappointed. Nope. At each stage of the publishing process, my admiration and fondness for both of them have grown. Thank you also to Cynara Geissler (marketing) and Gerilee McBride (book design).

My gratitude also goes out to: Ruth Nina Pangan and her family; Robert Majzels for his work on women in the Philippines; Isabel Craig for translation/discussion of Majzel's work; Jaclyn Qua Hiansen for geographical/cultural insight; Susan McLelland for her March 2005 article about foreign nannies in *The Walrus*; Geraldine Sherman for "A Nanny's Life" (*Toronto Life*, September 2006); and the sharp-witted Jay Fraser for "Garage-Mahal."

For reading all the chapters long before they were ready, thanks to Andy Sinclair. For reading a full draft before I felt confident enough to send it anywhere else, thanks to Gyllian Phillips. For reading it when I dared let you, thanks to Marty Hafke. For reading it when

I'd given up hope and needed a cheering section, thanks to Robin Spano. For helping me out of various (metaphorical) pantries, thanks to Heather Kerr and Paul Michal. For taking care of children to allow me time to write, thanks to Johnna and Frank Abdou and Val and Georg Hafke. Thanks to Caroline Adderson for the great quotation about the importance of offending librarians (p. 11–12), which comes from her essay "Highlights for Children," originally published in *The New Quarterly*.

For influential discussions (whether or not you were aware of your influence), thanks to: Marina Endicott, Joie Alvaro Kent, Steven Heighton, Patricia Westerhoff, Douglas Brown, John Wooden, Susan Bandy, Ryan Knighton, Alison Calder, Warren Cariou, Amanda Racher, Timothy Taylor, Bonne Zabolotney, Antanas Sileika, Alison Pick, Andrea Nair, Deryn Collier, Jody Keon, Dave Bidini, Shelby Knudsen, and Maureen Brownlee.

The biggest thank you goes to my family. This was a hard one. I know that a simple "thanks" is glaringly insufficient. I love you guys (infinity times infinity).